THROUGH DAWN-GATE
OR DUSK-DOOR?

These were the entries to the evil-ridden caverns of Kraggen-Cor. And through one or the other King Durek's army must go to reclaim the ancient Dwarf realm from terror's sway.

Yet one entry lay sealed shut by a monster's wrath, and the other led straight to an uncrossable chasm that stretched to the very heart of the world. And these were but the first of the deadly barriers which Warrows, Dwarves, and humans must attempt to overcome on their desperate mission to conquer the vile Spawn of Kraggen-Cor!

BOOK ONE OF THE SILVER CALL DUOLOGY

TREK TO KRAGGEN–COR

DENNIS L. McKIERNAN

A SIGNET BOOK

NEW AMERICAN LIBRARY

A DIVISION OF PENGUIN BOOKS USA INC.

SIGNET TRADEMARK REG. U.S. PAT. OFF. AND FOREIGN COUNTRIES
REGISTERED TRADEMARK—MARCA REGISTRADA
HECHO EN DRESDEN, TN. U.S.A.

SIGNET, SIGNET CLASSIC, MENTOR, ONYX, PLUME, MERIDIAN
and NAL BOOKS are published by New American Library, a division of
Penguin Books USA Inc., 1633 Broadway, New York, New York 10019

First Signet Printing, April, 1987

5 6 7 8 9 10 11 12 13

PRINTED IN THE UNITED STATES OF AMERICA

"All dreams fetch with a silver call, and to some the belling of that treasured voice is irresistible."

Seventh Durek
December 13, 5E231

JOURNAL NOTES

Note 1: The source of this tale is a tattered copy of *The Fairhill Journal,* an incredibly fortunate find dating from the time before The Separation.

Note 2: The Great War of the Ban ended the Second Era (2E) of Mithgar. The Third Era (3E) began on the following Year's Start Day. The Third Era, too, eventually came to an end, and so started the Fourth Era (4E), and then the Fifth (5E). The tale recorded here began in October of 5E231. Although this adventure occurs some four millennia after the Ban War, and more than two centuries after the Winter War, the roots of the quest told herein lie directly in the events of those earlier times.

Note 3: There are many instances in this tale where, in the press of the moment, the Dwarves, Elves, Men, and Warrows speak in their own native tongues; yet, to avoid the awkwardness of burdensome translations, where necessary I have rendered their words in Pellarion, the Common Tongue of Mithgar. Some words, however, do not lend themselves to translation, and these I've left unchanged; yet other words may look to be in error, but are indeed correct—e.g., DelfLord is but a single word though a capital L nestles among its letters. Also note that waggon, traveller, and several other similar words are written in the Pendwyrian form of Pellarion and are not misspelled.

A WORD ABOUT WARROWS

Central to this tale are the Wee Ones, the Warrows. A brief description of this legendary Folk is given in the appendices at the end of Volume Two: *The Brega Path*.

FOREWORD

One Sunday afternoon (Memorial Day weekend of 1977) a car ran over me. I spent the next year or so either in traction, in casts, bedridden, in a wheelchair, on crutches . . . Lord! It's depressing just to think about it.

When I was put in a spica hip cast, to stay sane I began working on the tale you are about to read—a different version, to be sure, yet still the same basic tale. When I finished it—when I actually wrote **The End** on the final page of that first draft—a great sense of achievement and elation coursed through every fiber of my being. *Hey! I've done it!*

Then I began typing and revising it, and soon that second draft became the third or fourth. Ultimately I shipped the manuscript of *The Silver Call* to Doubleday. At that point I could have kicked back and waited for a response from them, but, flush with success, I was still itching to write. And the *History* outlined in *The Silver Call* was so intriguing that I just had to record it too.

So I began *The Iron Tower*, a tale set in time 231 years prior to *The Silver Call*.

I was well into this second novel when Pat LoBrutto, science fiction editor at Doubleday, called and made an offer on *The Silver Call*. Faith! I was pleased and flattered; but then to his utter surprise: Pat, I said, *Silver* is great (modesty is not one of my stronger attributes), but *Iron*, the novel that I am working on now, should be published first.

To make a long story short, Pat agreed to hold off until I finished *The Iron Tower* and he could look it over. Well, I finished, he looked, and it was published first.

Now we come to *The Silver Call*, written first but published second: Of quite a few authors, critics have been known to say that their second novel does not live up to the promise of their first. I wonder what they'll say about mine, since my first is actually my second . . . or, conversely, my second is my first. Almost no matter how you look at it, perhaps I already have, or will have, lived up to my promise.

Dennis L. McKiernan
Westerville, Ohio, 1983

CONTENTS

To my own Holly:
Martha Lee

TREK TO
KRAGGEN-COR

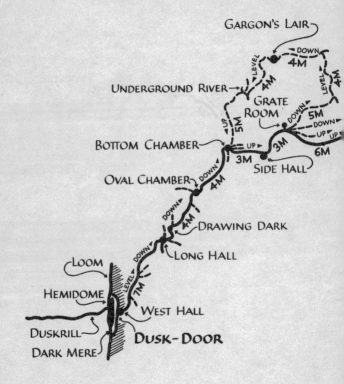

GARGON'S LAIR

DOWN
4M

LEVEL
4M
DOWN
4M

UNDERGROUND RIVER

LEVEL
4M

GRATE
ROOM

UP
5M

DOWN
5M

DOWN

BOTTOM CHAMBER

UP
3M

UP
UP

6M

3M
SIDE HALL

OVAL CHAMBER

DOWN
4M

DOWN
4M

DRAWING DARK

DOWN

LONG HALL

LOOM

LEVEL
7M

HEMIDOME

WEST HALL

DUSKRILL

DUSK-DOOR

DARK MERE

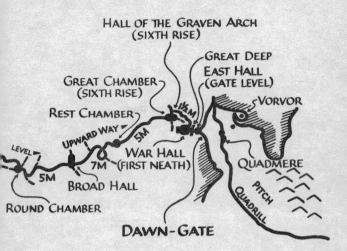

HALL OF THE GRAVEN ARCH
(SIXTH RISE)

GREAT DEEP
EAST HALL
(GATE LEVEL)

GREAT CHAMBER
(SIXTH RISE)

VORVOR

REST CHAMBER

1½M

UPWARD WAY

5M

LEVEL

5M

QUADMERE

7M

WAR HALL
(FIRST NEATH)

BROAD HALL

PITCH
QUADRILL

ROUND CHAMBER

DAWN-GATE

The Brega Path

PROLOGUE

Slowly the waggon trundled westward along the Crossland Road. Ahead, the three occupants could see a great, looming, dark mass reaching up toward the sky and standing across the way, extending far beyond seeing to the north and south. Spindlethorn it was, a great tangle of massive vines rearing fifty feet or more into the air, with razor-sharp spikes clawing outward—so thickly entwined that even birds found it difficult to penetrate the thorny mass. Through this mighty barricade the road went, and overhead the tangle interlaced, forming a shadowy tunnel of thorns leading down into the river valley from which sprang the fanged barrier.

Into the tunnel rolled the waggon, and the light fell blear along the path. And long did the trio ride in the thorny dimness.

At last, ahead the wayfarers could see an arch of light, and once more into the day they came as the route crossed a bridge over the Spindle River. Beyond the bridge on the far bank again the Barrier grew, and once more a dark tunnel bored through it. Two miles the travellers had come within the thorny way to reach the bridge, and nearly three more miles beyond would they go before escaping the Thornwall.

Onto the span they rolled, and the great timbers rumbled as the waggon crossed. And the three occupants stared in amazement at the massive dike of thorns rearing upward and clawing at the slash of blue sky jagging overhead. This great spiked rampart extended all the way around the Land the wayfarers were entering, growing in the river valleys along the borders. Soon they crossed the bridge and again entered the gloom.

17

In all, it took nearly two hours for the trio to pass completely through the Spindlethorn Barrier, but at last they emerged into the sunlight at the far side. The country-side they could see before them was one of rolling farm-land, and the road they followed ran on to the west, cresting a rise to disappear only to be seen again topping the crest beyond.

Along this way they went, and the warm Sun was pleasant. A mile or more they rode, and at last they saw workers in a nearby field harvesting grain. The driver stopped the waggon as it drew opposite the field hands.

"Hola!" hailed the waggoner. "Could you help us find our way?"

The swish of scythes fell silent as folk turned at the call to see who had hailed. But when their eyes fell upon the occupants of the waggon at roadside, the males who had been cutting stepped to the fore, while females and old-sters who had been bundling sheaves drifted to the rear, and the young ones who had been gleaning scurried to the back and peered around from behind skirts to look at the strangers. And they all stood in silence.

"We are here on the High King's business," called the driver, "and we seek the way to Sir Tuckerby's Warren."

"The King's business, you say?" piped a buccan in the fore, stepping to the side of the field and looking up in wonder at the strangers, while they in turn stared down at him in amazement. The wain riders saw before them one of the Wee Folk, a Warrow, for they had come into the Land of the Boskydells. Small he was, three and a half feet tall, yet those assembled behind him were no taller, though many were shorter, especially the wee young ones. His hair was black and cropped at the shoulder. His jerkin and breeks were the color of dusky leaves, and soft boots shod his feet. His ears were pointed like those of Elves, and there was also an Elven tilt to his bright, liquescent eyes—Utruni eyes, some would say, for the orbs of the Wee Folk resemble those of the Stone Giants. Yet, unlike the Giants, Warrow eyes are not true gems, but instead are astonishingly jewel-hued: sapphire blue; emerald green; and the third and last color, topaz gold.

"Sir Tuckerby's Warren is in Woody Hollow, some fifty miles to the west," said the Warrow, pointing down the Crossland Road. Then he turned his amber gaze back upon the strangers. "Could you use a drink of water on this warm day, or something to eat? For I know travellers build up a thirst from the dusty road . . . and get hungry, too."

"Thank you, but no, for we have food and drink with us, and our mission is urgent, else would we tarry awhile," answered the driver.

"Then fare thee well," responded the golden-eyed buccan in his piping voice, stepping back from the roadside.

With a chirk of his tongue and a flick of reins the driver urged the horses forward; and as they pulled away he waved to the Wee Folk in the field and they waved back, the tiny younglings running through the furrows amid trills of cascading laughter, keeping pace for a moment, only to turn back at sharp whistles from their sires.

"Hmph! So those are Waerans," growled one of the passengers, looking back. "I find it hard to think of such a small Folk as being legendary heroes."

"Yet heroes they are," said the driver, "and brave at that. I only hope that what we seek will be found in the journal we've come so very far to see."

"Aye, the diary of Sir Tuckerby Underbank, Hero of the Realm," grunted the other passenger. "Well do my kith honor his memory, even though his deeds lie more than two centuries in the past. Yet what my brother says is true: the iron of bravery seems to seek out this Folk; but I, too, would have deemed them too small to hold such mettle."

The driver turned to his seatmate. "Lore has it, though, that these Wee Ones—these Waerlinga—have played more than one key role in the fate of Mithgar, no matter their size—for stature alone does not measure the greatness of a heart."

Silence reigned in the waggon as legends of old tumbled through the occupants' minds, and the wain continued to roll westward on the King's business.

CHAPTER 1

THE UNEXPECTED PARTIES

"Hoy there, Mister Perry! Hoy there! Hoy there! They're coming to see you! Coming over from the Hall!"

Peregrin Fairhill sat in the October Sun on the stoop of his home, The Root of Woody Hollow. He looked up from the silver horn that he had been diligently polishing. *What in the Seven Dells is all this racket about?* he wondered. What he saw was a young buccan—that male Warrow period betwixt the end of the teens and the coming of age at thirty—rushing up the curved pathway to The Root. Onward came the buccan, running pell-mell, red-faced with effort, with two youngling Warrows capering and cartwheeling behind.

"Hold on there, Cotton! Slow down before you burst," called Perry, laughing. "And you two pinwheels stop your spinning."

The young buccan skidded to a halt in the path at the foot of the stoop; and the two tag-alongs, winded and panting, plopped down in the grass bordering the hedge and waited expectantly to see just exactly why it was that Cotton had been running. Pausing a moment to allow the young buccan to catch his breath, Perry finally asked, "All right now, Cotton, what's all this running about? Who wants me? Who's coming from the Hall?"

"Why, Sir, *they* want you," Cotton began, still huffing and puffing. "Hoy! Stop a minute. You two younglings" —he turned a baleful stare on the small Warrows—"this is not for your ears. Nip along now, so's I can tell my master what this is all about. Double-quick! On your way!" The two youngsters, being well-raised and Boskydell-mannered, as are all young Warrows of Woody Hollow—and realizing that nothing was going to be said as long as they were about—scampered down the rock-lined path and out of sight around the end of the hedge.

Satisfied, Cotton began again: "Sir, I never thought as I'd see the day. Folks like them have not been seen in the Dells since the old days before Tuckerby's time. And here they are! They just come marching right into the Hall, neat as may be, and asked for the Mayor. Yes sir, there I was, sweeping the floor like I do every midmonth and they just up and ask me—*me!*—for the Mayor.

"I couldn't believe my eyes was really seeing them, and I must've looked like the witless fool I am, standing there with my mouth hanging open in pure astonishment. I guess I'd've been there still, frozen to my broom, gaping, 'cept Mayor Whitlatch chose that very instant to come rushing in.

" 'Oh, Cotton,' says he, 'where's the—' Then he sees them, too, and is also struck dumb, but not for long. You can say what you want about Whitlatch's carryings-on, what with all his long-winded speechmaking and his love of ribbon-cutting ceremonies, but I'll give him this: after the first shock, he recovered as steady as you please and asked them if he could do something for them.

" 'We'd like to see the Mayor,' says the big one. 'I *am* the Mayor,' says Whitlatch. 'Mayor,' says the big one, 'is there some place where we can talk?' 'Follow me,' says the Mayor, and they all troop into his office.

"Well, I was just as full of curiosity as a new kitten, so I did all my sweeping right in front of the Mayor's door," Cotton continued, red-faced with embarrassment but with his jaw jutting out as if daring someone to call him an eavesdropper—though his gemlike emerald-green eyes did not meet the sapphire-blue ones of his master. "I couldn't hear nothing except voices murmuring so low as you can't recognize what's being said, them doors being as thick as they are. They all were in there talking low for about half an hour. Then I finally heard something more than just a mumble. It was Whitlatch. He said, 'Why you're right! Peregrin Fairhill is the one you want to see.' And with that he flings open the door shouting, 'Cotton! Cotton!' Then he sees I'm right next to him, so he lowers his voice and says, urgent-like, 'Cotton, run up to The Root and tell your master, Mister Perry, that I'm bringing these Boskydell visitors up from Hollow Hall to see him and Tuck's diary; they need him and his book. Now hop to it, and don't be a slowcoach about it.'

"Well, I dropped my broom and ran right here as quick as I could to bring you the news, Mister Perry, that they're coming here to The Root to see you and your *Raven Book* and all—though I'll be switched if I know why."

Perry stood and wrapped the small silver horn in its polishing cloth, gathering up the green and white baldric. He turned to go through the oaken door and into The Root, where he kept his copy of Tuck's chronicle. "But, Cotton," he turned back, perplexed, "you haven't told me the most important part: Just who are they that want to see me? Who or what are they that need me? Who are they that're coming to see the Account?"

"Ninnyhammer that I am!" Cotton smote his own forehead with a sharp slap. "Why you're perfectly right, Sir. I *have* left out the most important part."

Peering about to make sure that no one else could hear what he was going to say, Cotton completely missed the dancing, glittering eyes of the two small-fry Warrows lying on their stomachs and peering through from the other side of the hedge, where they'd got to when Cotton had commanded them to nip along. All the rest of their lives these two often would tell about the next words that Cotton would say. For as far as the Warrows of the Seven Dells in later days were concerned, this was the moment that the *real* adventure began: because what Cotton said was, "Sir, them as wants to see the *Raven Book?* Sir, well . . ." Once again he glanced around.

"Out with it, Cotton: who are they?"

"Why, Sir," he took a deep breath, then plunged on, "they're *Dwarves*, Sir! That's what they are: *Dwarves!*"

CHAPTER 2

WELCOME TO THE ROOT

"*Dwarves,* Cotton? Here in the Seven Dells? *Dwarves* to see *me?*"

"And a Man, Mister Perry, two Dwarves and a Man, too."

My goodness! thought a stunned Perry. *What a piece of news* this is! *A Man and Dwarves, too. And they've come to see me!* He spun on his heel and rushed into the burrow with Cotton right behind.

That was indeed a piece of news, for visits by Men or Dwarves are rare in the Boskydells—Men less so than Dwarves. Why, only at one time had there been many Men on this side of the Spindlethorn, and that was way back during the Winter War—after vile Modru had sent a great gang of Ghûls to overrun the Dells. And the Evil One's Reavers had nearly succeeded, too: looting, burning, slaying, whelming the Land, nearly ruining the Bosky with their rapacious grasp of the Seven Dells.

But then came Patrel Rushlock and Danner Bramblethorn, the greatest military heroes of all Warrowdom—greater even than Arbagon "Rückslayer" Fenner over in Weiunwood. Captains Patrel and Danner had returned to the Bosky during the Great Retreat. And they began to organize the Warrows to drive the blackguards out of the Land, scouring the Boskydells free of the invaders.

And the battles were mighty, and touch and go, until at last the Men came—Vidron's Legion—and then the Ghûls were routed . . . only to be replaced by one of Modru's Hordes. Yet still, allied with the Warrows, the Men fought until the Winter War came to an end.

And after the War, again Men came, to help rebuild the

23

Seven Dells—and rebuild they did. But rarely afterwards was a Man seen inside the Thornring, for King Galen in Pellar had declared the Boskydells a free Realm under the protection of his scepter. His edict was that no Man was to dwell in the Land of the Wee Folk. Hence, after the Winter War, those Men seen within the Barrier were usually just passing through along the Crossland Road, or the Upland Way, or down the Tineway. Oh, at rare times, Men would come to the Bosky as King's Messengers, bringing word of the King's doings; at other infrequent times, merchants would come to purchase Downdell leaf, melons, wicker works from Bigfen, or other Wee Folk trade goods. But, by Galen's edict, no Men came to stay. And when King Galen's son, Gareth, became Monarch, he reaffirmed the edict. And so it was and has been and is even unto this day that the Boskydell is a free Land in which no Men dwell, a Realm under the protection of the Kings in faraway Pellar.

But as scarce to the Dells as Men were, Dwarves were even rarer; though they were not forbidden entry into the Bosky, none had ever positively been seen by a Seven-Dells Warrow living in Perry's time. In fact, none had been sighted in such a span of time that they had become creatures of legend. Oh, an occasional Warrow travelling outside the Thornring, to Stonehill, would sometimes think that he had espied a Dwarf, but that was always a glimpse from afar so that afterwards the Warrow couldn't say absolutely that he'd actually laid eyes on one. Historically speaking, the last agreed-upon sighting of Dwarves within the Bosky itself was when several of them had passed through driving a waggon bearing weapons and armor, it was said to be used in their bitter clashes with the Rūcks. And that was way back, nearly two hundred twenty years before the Struggles, before the Winter War, before the Dragon Star—which meant that Dwarves had not been seen in the Boskydells for almost 450 years. Oh, they had been observed elsewhere, trading their Dwarf-crafted goods—just not in the Bosky. But now, if Cotton was right, both Man and Dwarf had returned.

Perry, with Cotton on his heels, rushed down the hall and into the study. The *study:* in this The Root was peculiar, for it was one of the few Warrow homes to have such a room.

Instead of books, Warrows in general much prefer their gardens and fields and fens and woods. Oh, not to say that most Warrows aren't educated to read and write and do their sums—oh no, not at all. Many of the Wee Folk can do these things well before their second-age-name change— much pride being taken by the winner of a spelldown, or by one who can recite from memory the names of all the local heroes, such as naming those of the Struggles. However, although many Warrows are educated, most would just rather be in their vegetable patch or down at the One-Eyed Crow or Blue Bull or Thirsty Horse or any of the other Bosky taverns, with a pipe and a mug of dark beer, than to be tucked away somewhere with a dusty tome. And even when they do read books, they prefer those filled with things they already know about—such as the familiar hearth tales containing numerous stories of Warrow cleverness at outwitting Giants, Dragons, Big Folk, and other *Outsiders*. In any case, books are to be found in the *proper* places—such as in the libraries at the Cliffs or at the Great Treehouse or at Eastpoint Hall—and *not* in a private dwelling.

Thus, the study at The Root was a curiosity among Warrow homes.

It was a large, spacious room, with burrow-windows opening to the west. The floor was made of oak, but the walls and ceiling were panelled with walnut. There were many comfortable seats inside, and there were two desks and a writing table against three of the walls. There was also a low table in the center of the room, with a lounge and different-sized chairs arranged around it. There were several floor-to-ceiling bookcases with manuscripts and pamphlets and tomes and scrolls jumbled haphazardly upon the shelves. But most striking of all, there were a number of large and small glass cases in which were displayed weapons and armor, flags and pennons, and other items of a like nature—all of a suitable size to fit Warrows.

It was in this study that Tuckerby's scriveners had transcribed most of *The Raven Book*, a journal started by Tuckerby Underbank on his way to join the Thornwalkers at Spindle Ford in the year the Winter War began. Tuck was the most famous Warrow in all history—even more renowned than Danner and Patrel—actually being the subject of Elven songs: it was Tuckerby who loosed the Red Quarrel and destroyed the Myrkenstone, and with it Modru's power and Gyphon's threat. And his journal, *The Raven Book*—or, as it is more formally known, *Sir Tuckerby Underbank's Unfinished Diary and His Accounting of the Winter War*—contained his story and the tale of the Dimmendark.

As the buccen swiftly entered this place of History, Perry hurriedly placed the baldric and the silver horn—still wrapped in its polishing cloth—into one of the glass cases. Then he turned to the other Warrow. "Cotton, while I unpack the *Raven Book,* find Holly and tell her that there'll likely be guests at The Root tonight: three—perhaps four if the Mayor stays—extra places at the table if you please . . . and beds as well. And, Cotton, have her set a place for you, too; for you've become versed in the tales of the '*Book,* and you've met these strangers . . . and, well, stick by me; I'd just feel better if I had you at my side."

Cotton, flustered and pleased that his master wanted him at hand when these *Outsiders* came to The Root, bolted away to find young Holly Northcolt, youngest dammsel of Jayar and Dot Northcolt.

Jayar, a former postmaster and now a country gentle-warrow, was well known for the cold spring on his land suitable for chilling buttermilk and melons. A no-nonsense buccan with definite opinions, Squire Northcolt had always greatly admired the Ravenbook Scholars; and he was deeply disturbed when he learned that the new curator of The Root—a Mister Peregrin Fairhill, as it were—was not only deeply involved in scholarly pursuits but also was struggling to keep up with the cleaning and dusting and ordering of foodstuff, and no doubt probably starving on his own cooking. And so Jayar overruled Dot's weeping objections and sent young Holly driving a two-wheeled pony-cart the fifty-one miles north from Thimble to Woody Hollow to "take charge of that Scholar's welfare."

Thus it was that one day Perry answered a knock at the door, and there before him stood pretty Holly, suitcase in hand, her dappled pony munching calmly upon the lawn. "I've come to manage this burrowhold," the golden-eyed damman announced matter-of-factly; and though Perry couldn't recall having advertised for a homekeeper—for in truth, he hadn't—he welcomed her in glad relief, for he *was* practically starving on his own cooking, at least he felt so.

And so Holly's timely appearance enlarged Perry's "family" to two; and, after she'd had a chance to size up the situation, through her insistence the household grew to three by the hiring of a handywarrow: Cotton. And things got mended and the lawn trimmed, and Cotton provided an eager ear for Mister Perry's scholarly thoughts and notions.

Hence, thanks to a determined Southdell Squire and his equally determined dammsel, The Root had acquired the gentle hand of a competent young damman to steer it past the shoals of starvation and beyond the reefs of untidyness and into a haven of domesticity.

And while Cotton dashed off in search of this young damman, Perry carefully slipped *The Raven Book* out of its rich-grained Eld-wood carrying case and placed it on the writing table. Looking around, he could see nothing else to do to get ready; so as soon as Cotton rejoined him, they returned to the stoop to wait for the visitors to arrive from Woody Hollow Hall.

Meanwhile, Holly was hurriedly bustling about inside, preparing for the unexpected guests while muttering to herself: "Gracious! Guests here at The Root! And Cotton said they were a Big Man and two Dwarves! And maybe Mayor Whitlatch, too! I wonder what it is that Dwarves eat? And where in the world can the Big Man sleep? Men being so tall as they are: twice as high as an ordinary Warrow, I hear. Now the Dwarves, though it is said that they are nearly of a proper size, I don't know what they eat. Perhaps they eat mushrooms, or rabbit stew, or . . ."

Perry and Cotton had just stepped back outside when Mayor Will Whitlatch, the Third, and the strangers arrived. Taking Perry by the arm, the Mayor turned to the visitors and said, "Master Peregrin Fairhill, may I present Lord Kian of Dael Township, and Mastercrafters Anval Ironfist and Borin Ironfist from the Undermountain Realm of Mineholt North."

And for the first time ever, Perry set his sapphire-blue Warrow eyes upon Man: *How tall they are . . . I wonder if the ceilings in The Root are high enough;* and Dwarf: *So broad and sturdy—as strong as the rock they delve.*

Lord Kian was a young Man, slender and straight and tall, almost twice the height of Perry. In his right hand he held an ash-wood stave, and he was dressed for an over-land walking journey: soft boots, sturdy breeks and jerkin, and a long cloak. His clothing was an elusive grey-green color that blended equally well with leaf, limb, or stone. On his head was a bowman's hat adorned with a single green feather. And belted over his shoulder was a plain quiver of green-fletched arrows and a curious bow—curious in that it was not a yew-wood longbow, but rather seemed to be made of strangely shaped bone, like long, curved, animal horns set into a silver handle. Kian's golden hair was cropped at his shoulders, and though his cheeks were clean-shaven, his fair countenance was graced with a well-trimmed yellow moustache which merged 'round the cor-ners of his mouth with an equally well-trimmed yellow beard. At his waist he wore a grey belt with a silver buckle that matched the silver brooch clasping the cloak around his shoulders. The color of this metal seemed somehow to live in the grey of his sharp, piercing eyes. *Is this the way all Men are? Silver and gold? Silver-grey eyes 'neath yellow-gold brow?*

In contrast to the tall, fair Lord Kian, Anval and Borin were only three hands or so taller than Perry, but were extraordinarily wide of shoulder, even for Dwarves, seem-ing at least half again as broad there as the young Man. They were outfitted in dark earthy browns for their jour-ney, but otherwise were dressed little different from Kian. However, instead of a rude stave, they each carried a carved ash-wood staff shod with a black-iron ferrule and topped with a cunningly shaped black-iron stave head: a bear for Anval and a ram for Borin. Strapped across their shoulders by carrying thongs were sturdy Dwarf War-axes: double-bitted, oak-hafted, rune-marked, steel-edged weap-ons. The Dwarves themselves, though not as fair-skinned as Lord Kian, had light complexions. But their look was dominated by black: Each had a black beard, long and forked as is the fashion of Dwarves. Not only were their beards and hair as black as the roots of a mountain, the color of their eyes was that of the blackest onyx. And

unlike Kian's smiling face, the look upon the Dwar
visages was somber, dark, wary. *Gracious, I can't tell th*
one from the other, why, they are as alike as two lumps of
forge coal!

Both Anval and Borin doffed the caps from their raven
locks and bowed stiffly, their black eyes never leaving
Perry's face. Lord Kian, too, bowed, and Perry returned
the courtesy to all with a sweeping bow of his own. Mayor
Whitlatch, not to be outdone and thoroughly caught up in
the ceremony, bowed to each and every one there in front
of The Root—except the two tagalongs, who were busily
bowing to one another on the far side of the hedge.

"And this is my friend and companion, Cotton Buckleburr," announced Perry, after which there ensued a second
round of bowing, including a repeat performance by the
Mayor. "I understand you want me—and my *Raven Book,*
too," continued Perry. "Let us all go inside, and I'll see
what I can do for you.

Much to Perry's surprise, Mayor Whitlatch declined:
"Oh no, Perry, I've got to get back to the Dingle. Lots to
do, you know. I have to be getting down to Budgens
tonight as well. A Mayor's work is never done."

Lord Kian turned to the Mayor. "Long have we journeyed to reach Sir Tuckerby's Warren. And you have
guided us on the final leg so that we may speak with
Master Perry . . . so that we may complete the King's
business. For that we thank you, Mayor. No longer will
we keep you from your pressing duties." Although Lord
Kian had not said it in so many words, it was clear that
Will Whitlatch was being dismissed.

Realizing that he was free to go, the Mayor, with visible
relief, said his farewells and left after again bowing to
them all. It is certain that Mayor Whitlatch was to a small
degree disappointed, because he knew that he was going to
miss one of Holly's guest meals at The Root; and since
Warrows love to eat—as many as five meals a day—and
since guest meals are by far the best meals, it was no small
sacrifice that the Mayor was making. But on the other side
of the balance scales, it *was*, after all, "King's business"
that was to be discussed, and that was very tricky indeed.
It was best that small Warrow Mayors of small Warrow
towns keep their noses where they belong, otherwise who

knows what might occur. Lawks! Look at what happened the last time Warrows got caught up with the King—why, there was all that business with the Myrkenstone. Oh no, that sort of thing was not going to happen to Will Whitlatch, the Third—even if he *did* have to miss a grand meal! Will hurried faster and faster down the pathway and was soon out of sight.

"Welcome to The Root," said Perry, and he turned and opened the oakpegged door.

CHAPTER 3

THE KING'S BUSINESS

Perry need not have worried about the ceilings at The Root, for Lord Kian could stand comfortably—though he did stoop a bit when going through the doorway.

But Perry hadn't been the only one who had wondered about the room heights, for as Lord Kian remarked, "I would have guessed that Waerling homes would be smaller, not large enough to permit a Man to roam about freely without knocking his head up against the beams."

"I thought you might be bumping up against the ceiling, too," laughed Perry as the visitors removed their hats and cloaks, "but *I* at least should have known better: you see, The Root is special."

"Special?" asked Lord Kian. "How so?"

"Well, it's not like most Warrow dwellings," answered Perry, "be they the burrow-holts of us Siven-Warrows, the tree flets of the Quiren-Warrows, the stilted fen-houses of the Othen, or the stone field-houses of the Paren."

"Your Folk live in four different kinds of dwellings? One for each strain?" grunted Anval, his dark scowl replaced by surprise.

"Ah," said Perry, "in the past that was true. But now many of us don't follow the old ways of the four Warrow-folk, and we live willy-nilly, skimble-skamble: burrow, flet, stilts, or stone, we lodge where we will, no matter what our lineage.

"Yet I stray . . . and, Lord Kian, you are right: The Root is extra large, as it were. Oh, it wasn't always this way." Perry gestured with a broad sweep of his hand. The visitors were being led down a wide central hallway, oak-panelled with rough-hewn beams overhead. There were

31

many doorways issuing off to either side into unseen rooms. The hall itself contained several high-backed chairs and two small, linen-covered tables set to either side against the walls. Each of the tables bore a vase of dried flowers placed there by Holly, and here and there hung pieces of tapestry and needlepoint. At the entrance end of the hallway an umbrella stand held two bumbershoots and a cane, with a many-pegged cloak-and-coat rack on the wall above it—which the visitors did not use. The other extent of the passageway terminated in a cross-hall, and the wings of that corridor disappeared around corners: on the westward side to the kitchen, scullery, and, further on, the storage rooms; and on the eastward side to the bedrooms.

"The original Root," Perry went on, "was an ordinary Warrow-sized home, scaled to fit Warrows—and, grown up, we range from three to four feet in height. I'm rather average at three and a half feet, with Cotton here a jot taller—by an inch or so. Anyway, as I was saying, the original Root was ordinary, but it was destroyed during the War: Modru's cruel reavers—Ghūls—finding no plunder, gutted and burned it along with many other dwellings in Hollow End. But after the War, Kingsmen came, as well as others, to help rebuild the homes—but especially to work on this burrow, Tuckerby's Warren, to make it better than new. And they did, as you can see—though it's not exactly 'new' anymore, those matters being some two hundred thirty years in the past. In any event, it was at that time Sir Tuckerby asked that the new Root be dug out large enough to house any future guest who might be a Man, Tuckerby having made many friends who were Men.

"So you see, Lord Kian, the ceilings are high enough for you, and there are many sturdy—and I hope comfortable—Man-sized chairs sprinkled throughout the rooms to accommodate one of your size." (And though Perry did not yet know of it, in one of the long-unused burrow-rooms Holly had rediscovered a Man-sized four-poster, much to her surprise and delight—for now she had a proper bedroom for each of the guests, including this "Man-giant," whom she had glimpsed simply *towering* over Perry and Cotton, the Man *soaring* up to an awesome height of six feet or so.)

"Do you mean that in any other Waerling home I would

have to get about on my hands and knees?'' asked Kian, reaching up and touching the oak panelling overhead.

''Not quite''—Perry smiled, warming to this tall young Lord—''though you would have to bend a bit.''

Halfway down the length of the hall, Perry ushered the group through a doorway to the left and into the walnut-walled study. As they laid their hats and cloaks aside, Perry gestured at the surrounding glass cases: ''The Root is special not only because of its scale; it's also special because it is a repository. You see, Warrows don't hold with memorials, the Monument at Budgens commemorating the Struggles being an exception. But this, my home, is an exception, too. Look about you; you see armor and weaponry, Elven cloaks, and many other things that are of the past. The Root is a home *and* a museum, a gallery dedicated to the Warrow heroes of the Winter War. It is a shrine, tended by the kindred of Sir Tuckerby: he who loosed the Red Quarrel; the Myrkenstone Slayer; and the last true owner of The Root. And I, Perry Fairhill, am the present curator of those glorious days.''

Perry turned to one corner of the room. ''Look, Anval, Borin, here's something that will surely catch your interest: a simple coat of chain mail.''

''Simple coat of mail!'' burst out Borin, his black eyes aglitter. He saw before him a small corselet of silver-shining armor. Amber gems were inset among the links, and a bejewelled belt—beryl and jade—was clasped about the waist. But the gemstones were not what caused Borin to cry out; he was amazed by the metal from which it was forged. ''This is starsilver! A thing like this has not been crafted in centuries. It is Châkka work, and is priceless.''

''Starsilver. Silveron,'' spoke Anval, his sturdy hand lightly brushing over the finely wrought links. ''Stronger than steel, lighter than down, soft as doeskin. This was forged in the smitheries of our ancestors—it is Kraggen-cor work.'' Suddenly Anval smacked a clenched fist into his open palm. ''Hah! I have it: this is the legendary coat given to Tuckerby by the Princess Laurelin, as the world stood on the brink of the Winter War.''

''Given to Tuckerby at War's beginning and worn by him to the very top of the Iron Tower.'' Perry nodded, surprised that the Dwarves knew of this armor—surprised, too, by the reverence that the silveron metal brought forth from the two of them. "But I ramble. Please be seated."

As they settled comfortably, Holly bustled into the room, her pretty face smiling, her eyes twinkling like great amber gems, and she carried a tray upon which rode an enormous pitcher of dark beer and several mugs. "I was thinking the travellers would have a thirst, Mister Perry, what with their walking and all." She set the tray down on the table in the center of the room and wiped her graceful hands on her solid blue apron. "Mind you now, Mister Perry, dinner will be ready in about two hours, so don't you go nattering on beyond that time; your guests look hungry." And with that she swept from the room as abruptly as she had entered it.

"Well"—Perry smiled, a bit discomfited at being shepherded in front of strangers by the slim three-foot-tall young damman—"as you can see, I have been given my marching orders by the Lady of The Root." He began pouring beer into the mugs and passing them around. "And we have but two hours before dinner. Yet that is perhaps time enough to satisfy my curiosity, which abounds. Imagine, two Dwarves and a Man in the Bosky, here on a mission to see the *Raven Book,* and from what you said to Mayor Whitlatch, it's the King's business that brought you." He set down the pitcher and turned to get the *'Book,* but Cotton had anticipated his move and was at Perry's elbow, holding forth the grey tome.

Taking the book from Cotton, who quickly retrieved his own mug of beer and took a satisfying gulp—Warrows do love beer—Perry turned back to his guests. "Well, here it is: *Sir Tuckerby Underbank's Unfinished Diary and His Accounting of the Winter War."* And he held it out to the visitors. Somewhat to his surprise, it was Borin and not Lord Kian who leaned forward to take the massive volume.

"So this is the famous book, eh?" Borin rumbled, turning it over and around and back again as if inspecting it for its crafting. Grunting his apparent acceptance of its outer cover and binding, the Dwarf opened the tome and, after another inspection, began avidly leafing through the pages.

"Well, not exactly," replied Perry, sipping his beer, "this is a duplicate of the original."

"What! Do you mean that we are not looking at the real thing?'' snapped Borin, slamming the book to, his Dwarf instincts against counterfeits and copies set ajangle by Perry's words.

"Kruk!" spat Anval. "What good will it do to look through a *copy* when it is genuine truth we seek?''

"Hoy now," protested Cotton, his temper rising, "wait up! It may not be the original *Raven Book* you're holding there, but you can bet your last copper that it's the 'genuine truth,' as you call it. I mean, well, Mister Perry made that duplicate himself, and so you know it's got to be accurate. Tell 'em, Mister Perry.''

"It's as accurate as you can get!'' exclaimed Perry, flustered, looking from Anval to Borin and back again. "It is an *exact* copy! It is one of several exact copies made through the years by the Scholars. It duplicates all of the original precisely, and I do mean *precisely:* even the spelling errors and the punctuation errors made in Tuck's original journal are copied faithfully. And as to the Account: places where words, phrases, sentences, even paragraphs, places where they were written in and then lined out by Tuck's scribes, even those are meticulously reproduced.

"Look, the real *Raven Book* used to be here at The Root, but no longer. Some years after the War, Tuckerby's dammsel, Raven Greylock, for whom the book is named —my great-grandam five generations removed—bore it west with her to the Cliffs, the Warrow strongholt that stood fast and did not fall during the Winter War. There, she and her husband, Willen, gathered some of Tuck's original scriveners, and others, and continued the great scribing of the History. Even now the work goes on, for history always has been and ever will be in the making. And it needs recording. But as to Tuck's original Account, the *'Book* remains at the Cliffs to this day, an heirloom of the Fairhills and Greylocks, the Underbanks and Fletchers, and others of Tuck's lineage. There at the Cliffs it is revered and tended by his kindred, occasionally being added to when some bit of lore or history bearing on the Winter War comes to light, appended therein by the family scholars—but only if after due deliberation it is unanimously accepted.

"But I digress It's from that original that the copies are made . . . and triple-, no, quadruple-checked. So, if it's truth you seek—the 'genuine truth'—then you hold it in your hands." Having given his pledge, Perry, though nettled, fell silent.

Regardless of the Warrow's passionately tendered personal guarantee of the book's accuracy, neither of the two Dwarves seemed willing to accept anything but the original. Disgruntled, they glanced at Lord Kian, and at the Man's curt nod, they reluctantly settled back and Borin resumed his search through the tome, leafing slowly through the pages. Soon his dark countenance took on a faintly baffled look. Then he stopped altogether. "Faugh! I go about this all wrong," he rumbled, at which statement Anval grunted his assent. "If what we seek is truly here, Waeran, then you must lead us to it."

"And what is that?" asked Perry, his vexation with the Dwarves yielding to a strange glow of excitement.

We've come to it now, thought Cotton, and he hardened himself as if for a blow.

"Kraggen-cor. Our ancient homeland. What you name Drimmen-deeve," answered Borin. "Durek the Deathbreaker is reborn, and we go to wrest stolen Kraggen-cor from the Foul Folk."

"Deathbreaker Durek?" asked Cotton, shivering. "Death-breaker? That sounds right unnatural, if you ask me. Just who is this Durek? And how did he get the name Deathbreaker?" Lord Kian smiled at the directness of this small Warrow.

"He is the First, the High Leader," replied Borin, "the Father of Durek's Folk, foremost among the five Châkka kindred. Think me no fool, Waeran, for not even Durek is Death's full master, for all mortal things perish. Yet, once in a great while an heir of Durek is born so like the First that he, too, is given the name Durek. When this happens —as it has happened again—we Châkka deem that indeed the true Durek has broken the bonds of Death and once more trods the Mountain roots anew.

"And now, being reborn, Durek desires to return to his home. He has gathered many of his kith—those descended in the Durek line—be they from the Mineholt North, the Red Caves, the Quartzen Hills, wherever Durek's Folk delve. And he has raised a great army. And we are to retake Kraggen-cor, to overthrow and slay the vile Squam, usurpers of that which is ours. We are to regain our homeland, the ancient Châkka Realm under the Grimwall.''

"Are there Spawn in Drimmen-deeve?" asked Perry. "The *Raven Book* tells that the mines were infested by those and other evil creatures during the War, but since then nothing has come concerning the Rūcks, Hlōks, and Ogrus that were there. Are they still in Drimmen-deeve?''

Lord Kian spoke; there was anger in his voice, and his countenance darkened. "They raid the countryside and wreak havoc with river traffic along the Great Argon.''

Alarmed by the Man's seething rage, both Perry and Cotton drew back in apprehension.

Seeing the effect of his ire upon the two Waerlinga, Lord Kian struggled to master his emotion. The young Man stood and walked to the open burrow-window and stared out into the gloaming, taking a moment to quell his wrath and to collect his thoughts. Through the portal could be heard the awakening hum of twilight insects. Cotton quietly got up and lighted several tapers; their flickering glow pressed back the early evening shadows.

"Let me tell it as it happened," said Lord Kian quietly, turning from the window to face his host:

"Though I am of North Riamon," he began, "I spent some years as a Realmsman serving the High King. I won the repute of knowing the Lands as few others do. Durek heard of this, and he knew of my friendship with the King; and Durek's emissaries sought me out and bade me to meet with him in the Dwarf halls of Mineholt North. At that meeting he told me of his plans to reclaim Drimmen-deeve and to re-enter it with his kindred and make it mighty as of old. He asked that I serve as guide and advisor to Anval and Borin and to take them to Pellar so that they might make Durek's plans known to High King Darion. We were not then aware that Spawn infested the Deeves, though we had heard rumors of some dark danger along that distant edge of Riamon.

"At the court, King Darion told us of the foul Yrm. The King explained that after the fall of Gron, Modru's minions either were destroyed, or were scattered, or they surrendered. Many discovered that they had been deceived

by the Evil One, and they swore fealty to the then High
King, Galen, and to his line, and were forgiven and allowed to return to their homelands. Others fled or fought
to the death. The Men of Hyree, the Rovers of Kistan,
some fought and died, some cast down their weapons,
some ran, some slew themselves in madness. But of the
Spawn—Ghol, Lōkh, Rukh, Troll, Vulg, Hèlsteed—those
all fought to the death, or died by the Ban, or fled into
darkness; none surrendered, for they had been too long in
bondage to the Evil One to yield.

"King Darion believes that many Rukha and Lōkha
and mayhap some Trolls escaped to Drimmen-deeve to
join those already there. They hid in the blackness for all
these many years, too sorely defeated to make themselves
known, too crushed by the fall of Gron to array themselves
in battle.

"In the Deeves, hatred and envy gnawed at their vitals,
and the worm of vengeance ate at their minds. But they
were leaderless, divided into many squabbling, petty
factions.

"Two years ago, belike through treachery and murder
and guile, a cruel tyrant seized the whip hand. He is Gnar,
one of the Lōkha, we think.

"It is he who is responsible for the renewed conflict
with the Free Folk. He lusts for total power, the dominion
of his will o'er all things. And to achieve that vile end, he
masters his minions through fear and terror, binding them
to his ruthless rule.

"Before Gnar arose, the Yrm made but limited forays
from Drimmen-deeve, and then only at night, driven by
their dread of the Sun and the doom of the Covenant to
return to the Deeves ere daybreak. They did not range far
enough to reach any homesteads, settlements, roads, or
trade routes—barely coming to the foot of the mountains,
reaching not beyond the eastern edge of the Pitch. But now
their fear of Gnar's cruelty is such that at his command
they issue forth from that mountain fastness to raid many
days' journey from Drimmen-deeve, besetting Valon—the
Land south of Larkenwald the Eldwood—and ranging as
far as the Great Argon River.

"The Yrm lie up in black holes, caves, splits in the
rock, and cracks in the hillsides when the Sun is in the

sky; thus, the Ban strikes them not. But at nightfall they gang together to waylay settlers and travellers alike—slaying them and despoiling their bodies—and to attack and loot and burn the steads and holts of Riamon and Valon, or to plunder river traffic, pirating the flatboats of the River Drummers. Gnar has decreed that there shall be no survivors from the raids, except when he orders a prisoner taken, upon whom he commits unspeakable abominations.

"All of this the King learned from a captured Rukh who boasted of it before he died when the dawn came and the Sun rose; for the Rukh was slain by High Adon's Covenant forever banning the evil Spawn to the night or to the lightless pits of the underearth when the Sun is on high.

"Upon hearing from the King that *Spaunen* held Drimmen-deeve, Anval and Borin were enraged, and pledged the Dwarf Host to the task of exterminating the Yrmish vermin from the Dwarves' ancestral home—a pledge since affirmed by Durek. This pledge was swiftly accepted by a grateful King Darion, for the Spawn present a grave problem to the Realm: the High King knows that all his cavalry and knights, his pikemen and archers, and his infantry and all other soldiery, though mighty upon any open field of battle, would be sorely pressed to fight the Yrm in the splits and cracks and other black holes under the mountains. Though he had planned to lay long siege to Drimmen-deeve, the problem of routing out the *Spaunen* still remained.

"Durek's pledge solved that problem, for there is no better underground warrior than a Dwarf—and they are always eager to avenge old wrongs upon their ancient adversary, the Yrm. Thus, the Dwarves are to issue into Drimmen-deeve and vanquish the enemy. They have asked King Darion to forego his planned siege that they might more readily take the Spawn by surprise; this the King has agreed to do. During the interim, Darion sends escort with traders and travellers to protect them, and he has gathered the farmers, woodcutters, woodsmen, and other settlers in to holdfasts til such time as the Dwarves smash the foe.

"Even now the Dwarf Host has mustered and, if things have gone as planned, is on the march from Mineholt North. Though Gnar's raids still go on, soon—we hope with your help, Perry—they shall be eliminated forever."

Lord Kian returned from the window and settled back in his chair and fixed Perry with a keen eye.

"But how can *I* help?" queried a puzzled Perry, wondering how the Dwarf mission could possibly bear upon *The Raven Book* and him.

Borin leaned forward and pushed the 'Book across the table to Perry. "Except for Braggi's doomed raid," Borin growled, "Châkka have not lived in Kraggen-cor for more than a thousand years—even though it is rightfully ours—for to our everlasting shame we were driven away long ago by a foe we could not withstand: the Ghath, now dead. And though our lore speaks of many things in Kraggen-cor, such as the Spiral Down or the Great Chamber, our knowledge of that eld Châkkaholt consists of legendary names and fragmentary descriptions. Our homeland is a mystery to us. We do not know how to get from one place to another. We do not know the paths and halls and rooms and caverns of mighty Kraggen-cor. If we must, we will fight the foul Grg enemy upon unknown ground and chance defeat—but only if we must.

"Yet, if our information is correct, it will not come to that end. We are told by King Darion that your *Raven Book*—at least the original—holds within it a description of a journey through stolen Kraggen-cor. If so, then from that description, that route, we can glean vital knowledge of the layout of at least a part of Kraggen-cor—knowledge needed to smash the Squam and retake the caverns."

"The High King knows about Mister Perry and his book?" asked Cotton in awe, momentarily overwhelmed by the idea that High King Darion could know of someone in the Boskydells.

"Aye, he does indeed know of your *Raven Book*," answered Anval, "for he, too, has a copy in Pellar—or did have. His book was out of the Kingdom when we were there—somewhere here in the Boskydells . . . or so he told us.

"Why, if it's not at the court it must be with my grand-uncle at the Cliffs," said Perry. "He's the Master of the Ravenbook Scholars—Uncle Gerontius Fairhill, I mean—and if he's got the King's copy, then they're adding to it the marginalia collected by the Scholars over the past fifty years or so. . . . Let me see: this would be only the third time it's been updated since its making long ago—''

"Be that as it may," interrupted Borin, "King Darion told us that Sir Tuckerby's diary and the original *Raven Book* were also here in the Boskydells—perhaps at Sir Tuckerby's Warren, being tended by the Fairhills, he thought. Hence we came, and your Mayor led us to you, Master Perry.

"Heed me: The account of the journey through Kraggen-cor is vital to us. We have travelled far to see the *Raven Book*. And if the tale is here in your *copy*, we would hear it for ourselves." Borin pushed the grey book across the table toward Perry.

Somewhat taken aback by the bruskness of the Dwarves, the two Warrows glanced at one another, and then at Lord Kian. Reassured by the smile upon the Man's face, Perry reached for the tome. "Oh, the tale is here all right," replied the buccan, turning the book around, preparing to open it; but then he paused. Only, I don't know exactly where to start. I think perhaps before I read to you of that trip through dreaded Drimmen-deeve, we should speak a bit about what went before, for mayhap it will have a bearing upon your quest."

"Say on," said Borin, "for we know not what may aid." And Anval, too, nodded his agreement while Lord Kian settled back in his chair.

"Who can say where an event begins?" mused Perry, "for surely all happenings have many threads reaching deep into the past, each strand winding its way through the fabric of time to weave in the great pattern. But let me start with the first battle of the Winter War, for two of the four comrades came together in its aftermath, and went on to meet the third, and they in turn came upon the fourth:

"As Modru's forces marched from the Wastes of Gron through the Shadowlight of Winternight and down upon the northern citadel of Challerain Keep, and as women and children and the old and infirm fell back toward the havens of Pellar and Wellen, of Valon and Jugo, and of other Lands to the south, some warriors hastened north, to answer the High King's call to arms. Among those mustered was a force of Warrows, skilled in archery; and one of these Vulg-fighting Warrows was Sir Tuckerby Underbank, known then simply as Tuck.

"The iron fist of War at last fell upon Challerain Keep, and you all know the outcome of that struggle, so I'll say nothing more of it, except that the order to retreat had been given and Tuck became separated from his companions. He had spent all of his arrows, and Rūcks, Hlōks, and Ghûls were closing in. To elude Modru's forces, Tuck took refuge in an old tomb; it was the barrow of Othran the Seer. There, too, by happenstance, came Galen, then Prince of Pellar, weaponless, for his sword had shattered in battle.

"Together the two waited until the enemy passed by, and then, riding double, they struck southward through the Dimmendark, their only arms being the Red Arrow, borne by Tuck, and a long-knife of Atala, carried by Galen— both weapons having been found in the tomb.

"They had ridden to the northern marches of the Battle Downs when they came upon a scene dire, one of butchery, for the entire escort as well as the helpless innocents of the last refugee waggon train had been slaughtered. Yet neither Galen's betrothed, Princess Laurelin of Riamon, nor his brother, Prince Igon, Captain of the escort, was among the slain."

"Modru Kinstealer," said Lord Kian softly, swirling the ale in his mug.

"Just so," answered Perry with a nod. "Princess Laurelin was taken captive. The track of a large force of mounted Ghûls bore eastward, deeper into the Dimmendark, toward the Grimwall. In pursuit along this track rode Galen and Tuck, pressing into Winternight.

"At last they came unto the Weiunwood, that shaggy forest, where they learned that here, too, a mighty battle had been fought; but here the Alliance had won, using Warrow woods-trickery and Elven lore and the strength of Men. Tuck and Galen met with Arbagon, Bockleman, and Inarion—leaders of the Warrows, Men, and Elves—and Galen was told that five days past a Hèlsteed-mounted Ghûlen force had hammered by, still bearing toward the Grimwall. And afterwards a lone rider had followed slowly in their wake.

"Again, Galen and Tuck bore east, and days later came to the Hidden Refuge, Arden. There they found Galen's brother, Igon, sorely wounded. It was he who had been the lone tracker of the Kinstealer force. But his wounds, taken in the attack upon the waggon train, had at last overcome him, and he would have died but that the Elves found him lying unconscious in the Winternight and saved him.

"Even as brother spoke to brother, to the Refuge came the Elf Lord Gildor bearing word that Galen's sire, King Aurion, had been slain and that Galen was now High King of all Mithgar.

"Galen was sore beset, for his heart told him to go north and somehow deliver Laurelin out of the enemy stronghold; yet his duty told him that as King he must turn south and come unto Pellar to gather the Host to face Modru's hordes.

"The next morning, with heavy hearts, Galen and Tuck bore southward, leaving Igon behind in Arden in the care of Elvenkind. With them rode Gildor, now Elven advisor to Galen as he had been to Aurion before. The three were making for Quadran Pass and beyond to the Larkenwald, Darda Galion. Gildor sought to warn his Elven kindred, the Lian, that it was almost certain that the Larkenwald, too, soon would be under attack. The companions planned to give warning and afterward to fare onward to Pellar and the Host.

"Through the Dimmendark the trio rode, ever bearing southward. They overtook a Swarm of Modru's forces also bearing south, marching toward Black Drimmen-deeve to make it into a vile fortress whence the Spawn would launch their attack upon Darda Galion.

"Silently passing by the Horde, southward rode the trio of Galen, Tuck, and Gildor, in haste now, to warn the Lian of the coming enemy. Far they rode, but at last came to a defile where they heard the sound of single combat, and happened upon a lone Dwarf and a solitary Hlōk, fighting amid a great slaughter of Dwarven and Rūcken dead—"

"Brega, Bekki's son!" burst out Anval, fiercely, raising a clenched fist; and Borin cried, "Warrior, hai!"

"Yes," confirmed Perry, "it was Brega, Bekki's son; and he slew the Hlōk. Then Brega alone stood, the last of a force of forty Dwarves from the Red Caves, marching north to join in the battle against Modru. Altogether, the forty had slain nearly two hundred maggot-folk; yet at the last all had fallen but Brega.''

Here Anval and Borin cast their hoods over their heads. *''Châkka shok (Dwarven axes),''* rumbled Borin; *''Châkka cor (Dwarven might),''* added Anval.

In respect, Perry paused a moment, and then continued: "Now the great southward-bound force of the *Spaunen* Horde was drawing nigh, and Brega stood ready to face them alone. Yet he was at last persuaded that to gain revenge for his slain brethren he must go south with Tuck and Galen and Gildor to join the Host to battle Modru. And so, somewhat reluctantly it seems, Brega mounted up behind Lord Gildor to ride to the Larkenwald and then beyond.

"Now, at last, you see, the Wheel of Fate had turned to bring the four together, and toward Quadran Pass they rode. Cross it they did, and had come partway down Quadran Run, down the flank of Stormhelm, heading for the Pitch and the Larkenwald beyond. But here they were thwarted, for a large force of mounted Ghûls—advance eyes for the Horde—was returning over the range, coming up the Run toward them.

"The four were forced back over the Gap, ahead of the Ghûls. Yet they planned to slip aside at first chance and hide until the Ghûls were beyond them and gone. But before they could do so, Vulgs from the Horde discovered them, and ahead of Modru's riders through the Dimmendark the companions fled.''

"Wouldn't you just know it!" blurted Cotton, frustrated by the turn of events even though they were more than two centuries in the past, and despite his having heard the tale many times before. Then, embarrassed by his outburst, the buccan took a sip from his mug and studiously peered at the alefroth, and avoided catching the eyes of the others.

"Southward they ran,'' continued Perry, ''til their horses were nearly foundered, for each was carrying double. And so, out of necessity, the four at last turned east into a valley, hoping to elude the Winternight pursuit. As they neared the head of the valley, Gildor recognized the land: it was Ragad Vale—the Valley of the Door—and they were coming toward the Dusk-Door, the abandoned western entrance into Black Drimmen-deeve. And the Door had been shut ages agone and had not been opened since.

"On they rode, forced ever eastward ahead of tracking Vulgs, finally to come to the great hemidome in the Loomwall of Grimspire; and a black lake was there. Along a causeway they went, til they reached a drawbridge, and it was up, raised high. While the others waited, Gildor swam across, and a great swirl in the water came nigh, for something lurked in the black depths.

"Yet the Elf safely gained the other side and began to lower the bridge; but the haul broke, and down the bascule came with a great crash. The sound boomed down the vale and brought the searching Ghûls riding at speed. The remaining comrades dashed across the bridge and joined the Elf, and all went past the sunken courtyard and to the great edifice of the Dusk-Door.

"Black water from the Dark Mere lapped at the steps rising up to the huge columns. Between these pillars the four ran, drawing the two horses behind, coming to the great portico.

"The Ghûls rode to the causeway, but then shied back, as if afraid to ride its length to get at the four.

"Brega, remembering the lore words, managed to open the Dusk-Door; yet the four were loath to enter Black Drimmen-deeve, for therein lived foul maggot-folk—but even more so, therein ruled the evil Gargon, Modru's Dread. Yet Fate offered them but two courses: to face the immediate threat of a great number of Ghûls standing athwart the path along the causeway, or to enter the Spawn-filled, Dread-ruled halls of Drimmen-deeve.

"But then all choice was snatched from them, for the lurker in the Dark Mere—the Krakenward—struck: hideous ropy arms writhed out of the black water and clutched the horses; and screaming in terror the steeds were drawn down the steps and under the dark surface. Gildor sprang forward to save Fleetfoot, but the Lian warrior was struck numb—for at that very moment, Vanidor, Gildor's twin, was slain at the Iron Tower, and Gildor felt his brother's death. A tentacle grasped Gildor as he fell, stunned, to his knees; but Galen, using the Atalar Blade, hacked at the arm, cleaving a great gash in it, and in the creature's pain it flung Gildor aside.

"Through the Dusk-Door the four fled, the enraged Monster clutching at them with slimy tentacles, lashing at them with a dead tree, pounding at the Door with a great stone, and wrenching at the gates.

"Into this nest of snakes Brega leapt and slapped his hand against one of the hinges and cried the Wizard-word to close the portal, leaping back to avoid the Monster's clutch. And slowly the doors ground shut, all the while the creature struggling to rend them open. And as the gates swung to, Brega's last sight was of the Krakenward wrenching at one of the great columns of the edifice, grinding it away from its base.

"The Door closed—*boom!*—and the four were shut inside Drimmendeeve, in the West Hall. Brega had a lantern in his pack, and as he unshuttered it, the four heard a loud crashing; they surmised it to be the great edifice collapsing, torn down by the maddened Hèlarms.

"Boom! Boom! Boom! The pounding of hurled stone shook the Dusk-Door, and though Brega tried, he could not get it to reopen even a crack so that they could see what was happening.

"Now they had no choice but to attempt to traverse the Deeves and escape out the Dawn-Gate. And as they left the West Hall on that fated journey through Black Drimmendeeve, the hammering of the enraged Monster echoed in their wake."

"Tchaaa!" hissed Borin, "I wonder if the foul Madûk yet lives."

"I cannot say," answered Perry, "but the *Raven Book* tells that the creature had been Dragon-borne in the black of night by the Cold-drake Skail and dropped into the old Gatemoat nearly five hundred years earlier. That was back before the Dragons began their thousand-year sleep. It is now believed that the Krakenward was a tool of Modru, placed there as part of his preparation for the coming of the Dragon Star."

"Living or no, tool or no, continue the tale," bade Anval, "for now we come to the nub of it, the part that may aid our quest."

"You are right, Anval," agreed Perry. "The time has come for me to read from the *Raven Book*." And at last Perry opened the great grey tome, turning past the part of the book that duplicated Tuck's *Unfinished Diary*—as the 'Stone Slayer had originally recorded it during his venture— and thumbing well into that part of the '*Book* Tuck later told to the scribes, recalled in full by him from his own terse journal. Finally Perry reached the proper page of the Account. "This is the tale of the four who fared Black Drimmen-deeve," he said, "the story of their flight through that dreadful place. Let me now read it to you."

And, pulling a candelabrum close, from the huge grey book he began to read of that fearful dash through Drimmen-deeve as the four sought to reach the eastern portal—Dawn-Gate—ere the Ghûls could cross back through Quadran Gap to bring word of the intruders to the dreaded Gargon and its *Spaunen* minions. Not all of Perry's words need be repeated here, for the tale is now famous and recounted elsewhere, and the full story of all the companions is long and takes many days to tell. But that evening in The Root, Perry read only that part of the story concerning the journey through Kraggen-cor, the journey of the four persons who became known as the Deevewalkers:

Perry began at the point where the four had fled from the Krakenward through the Dusk-Door and could not get back out. And from the West Hall, Gildor led them up the stairs and easterly; Gildor led, for in his youth he had gone on a trade mission through Drimmen-deeve while it was still a mighty Dwarvenholt—ere the Gargon broke free of the Lost Prison. Far they went, without encounter, for the western caverns were deserted of maggot-folk. Yet finally they had to stop to rest, the first they'd had in nearly two days.

Perry read of their pause in the Grate Room, where at last they felt a foreboding fear beating at them, and they knew then that the Ghûls had finally come to the Gargon with word of the four, and now that dreadful creature was bending its will to find them. And the halls became infested with *Spaunen* squads searching for them.

Onward they fled, deeper into fear, for they had to come nearer to the Dread in order to reach the Dawn-Gate. And as they went east, many times they eluded discovery.

Again they rested, for the way was arduous. At last they came to the Hall of the Gravenarch, and there they found the remains of Braggi's Raid, that ill-fated Dwarven mission to slay the evil Gargon.

Now the four Deevewalkers could feel the Dread approaching, for at last it could sense them—and it stalked them. Yet Brega thwarted it, for with a broken Warhammer he sundered the keystone of the Gravenarch, and the Hall collapsed, blocking the way. Through the fallen stone the Gargon's hatred beat upon them, and great waves of dread engulfed them, but the creature could not come at them. And onward they fled.

Perry read of them coming to the drawbridge over the Great Deep; and the bridge was lowered and unguarded. There, too, was oil and pitch, and they made ready to burn the wooden span and prevent pursuit. But ere they could fire it, the Gargon came upon them once more, and at last paralyzed them with its dire gaze.

And as the creature came to kill them, it made a fatal mistake, for it considered Tuck to be beneath its contempt, and the Warrow proved to be the key to the slaying of the Dread—for slay it they did.

Perry read of the fiery destruction of the bridge, and its collapse into the Deep, and the escape of the four out through the Dawn-Gate and onto the Pitch, coming at last to safe haven under the eaves of Darda Galion.

The candles were low and guttering when Perry finished reading. The room was silent as each reflected upon that which had just been recounted. Cotton got up to fetch some fresh candles to light, but at that moment Holly popped back in through the door. ''Dinner is served,'' she announced, and led them all off to the dining room.

CHAPTER 4

THE BREGA PATH

Dinner was superb; Holly had outdone herself. Mounds of steaming mushrooms were heaped upon large platters; and she had prepared her special recipe for rabbit stew: thick and creamy and filled with delicious morsels of tender coney and chunks of potatoes, parsnips, and other vegetables, all perfectly seasoned with her own blend of tangy spices and aromatic herbs. Dark ale in deep mugs sparkled in the warm, yellow lamplight, and the talk turned to things other than Rūcks and such.

"It must be a long way from Dael to Pellar to Woody Hollow," remarked Perry, popping another mushroom into his mouth. "Surely you didn't walk all the way."

"No," laughed Lord Kian. "That indeed would be a longsome stroll. Let me see, I deem we covered more than three thousand miles just going from Mineholt North to Pellar and back. Of course most of that journey was by boat on the Rissanin and Argon rivers. Then from the Mineholt to your Boskydells is nearly another thousand miles: we travelled the Landover Road to the Grimwall Mountains, where we crossed over Crestan Pass to come down near Arden, and then we followed the east-west Crossland Road to come to the Seven Dells."

"Goodness," breathed Perry, eyes aglitter. "Why, you've travelled four thousand miles in the past few months alone, and I've barely exceeded a hundred in my entire life—when I travelled from the Cliffs to here—and I am three years past my 'coming of age.' The wonderful sights you must have seen . . ." His voice trailed off in breathless speculation.

"Horses!" burst out Cotton, banging his mug of ale

49

down on the table, some foam sloshing out. "I'll bet you rode horses to the Bosky!"

"Ride horses?" snorted Anval. "A Châk ride a horse? Hmphh! A pony, mayhap, but not a full-grown horse. We have better sense than to climb aboard one of those great lumbering beasts. Aye, Cotton, we did use horses on the roads to the Boskydells—but we *drove* them, we didn't *ride* them. We travelled sensibly—by waggon."

"Well, if you rode in a waggon, where is it now?" asked Cotton, chagrined for not remembering the idle tavern talk that occasionally turned to the subject of Dwarves, and the hearsay that Dwarves, though brave at most things, for some reason seemed to fear being borne on the back of a horse. "You didn't arrive at Woody Hollow Hall ridin' in no waggon."

"You are right, Waeran," rumbled Anval, amused by Cotton's embarrassment, "we trod the final miles on foot. The waggon is in Budgens with a rock-broken wheel being mended by one of your Waeran wheelwrights. It will be ready ere our return journey to the Landover Road Ford."

"The Landover Road Ford?" asked Perry, vaguely remembering that the ford was somewhere on the River Argon beyond the Grimwall Mountains.

"Aye, Waeran," responded Anval, "a fortnight and a week hence, King Durek and the Army arrive at the ford; so it is there that we will await them."

"It is at the ford where Durek must decide how to enter Kraggen-cor," added Lord Kian, responding to Perry's puzzled expression. "Here, let me show you: If I line up these mushroom platters . . . there, now . . . then they can represent the Grimwall Mountains, as they run down from the Steppes of Jord and on toward Valon and Gûnar in the south ere curving away westerly. Along the eastern flank of the range runs the Argon River, flowing southward toward the Avagon Sea . . . and here where I put my spoon is the ford where the Landover Road crosses the river. The road goes on up the east flank and into the mountains where it then runs through Crestan Pass, crossing over the range to come back down at Arden on the west side. Now let this saltcellar represent Mineholt North, where Durek's army started their march. . . . Mineholt goes up here—nearly three hundred fifty miles of marching to the east and north of the ford. And finally we'll put this pepper mill down here, another two hundred miles south of the ford, where lies Drimmen-deeve, with its Dawn-Gate on the east side of the mountains and the Dusk-Door on the west.

"Now you can see it is at the ford where Durek, coming down from the north and east, must choose which way to invade the Deeves: he can cross over the mountains at Crestan Pass to Arden, march down the west flank of the range, and invade by Dusk-Door; or he can stay on the east side of the mountains, tramp south along the banks of the river Argon, then come over the wold . . . about here . . . and march up the Pitch to attack into Dawn-Gate. You can also see that his choice is crucial, for these two ways lie on opposite sides of a mighty wall of mountains, and he must decide at the ford, for there is the Crestan Pass—the Army's path across the range." Lord Kian lapsed into silence, taking a long pull from his mug.

"What about Quadran Pass?" asked Perry after a moment. "It is near Drimmen-deeve. The *Raven Book* says the western reach of the pass is less than a day's march north of the Dusk-Door, and the eastern end of the pass comes down onto the Pitch itself. I repeat: what about Quadran Pass? Couldn't Durek cross over there?"

"A good question, Perry," replied Kian, "and the answer is—perhaps. Durek might be able to cross there, but he is faced with two problems: First, the gap in the Quadran, at least on the Pitch side, may be guarded by *Spaunen,* and crossing there would alert Gnar and all his forces, and our edge of surprise would be lost. Second, early winter is nearly upon us, and by the time the Army can get to that pass, Quadran Gap in all likelihood will be snowed in and impassable. No, Durek must choose at Landover Road Ford, so that the Crestan Pass can be crossed if his choice is to attack by the western door, or so that he can turn south and follow the river if he chooses to invade through the eastern gate. And our mission now is to meet him at the ford with the information gleaned from your *Raven Book,* so that he can use that knowledge in making his decision." Again Lord Kian fell silent, and each stared at the problem laid out before him as the Man took another long pull from his mug.

"Wull, Dusk-Door or Dawn-Gate, it's a poser all right," said Cotton at last, eyeing the alignment of the mushroom platters. "But be that as it may, please pass me some of those Grimwall Mountains, and I'll have a bit of Mineholt saltcellar and Drimmen-deeve pepper mill, too, to make 'em more tasty." With a strangling cough, Lord Kian choked on his beer in laughter, and the others guffawed heartily as the Warrow piled mushrooms on his plate and salted and peppered them and began popping them into his widely grinning mouth, saying, "Mmmm, good mountains! Delicious peaks!"

The table talk continued in this fashion for two hours as the Warrows, the Dwarves, and the Man stuffed themselves with Holly's wonderful food. In time, all were satisfied, including Cotton, who had a reputation even among Warrows as an awesome trencher in spite of his slimness—slim for a Warrow, that is, for they tend to roundness. But Cotton had at last met his match, for at this table Anval had surpassed the hard-eating Cotton, having put away not one but two more pieces of apple pie than the doughty Warrow. It had been a superb guest meal, with rich and wholesome food, excellent ale, and much interesting talk.

Yet though he had consumed a vast quantity of food, Borin had not been drawn into the conversation, and there was a dark, brooding look upon his face. As they each lit up a clay pipe of Downdell leaf and settled back in comfort, with Cotton blowing an occasional smoke ring, Borin growled and at last revealed what it was that troubled him. "The *Raven Book* is of little or no help to us in the coming battle: it has not the detail to lead us through the caverns. True, the book has given us news—though bitter it is—for now we know that both of Durek's choices as to the way into Kraggen-cor are even more uncertain than we had thought: The east way across Baralan—the Pitch—and on into the delf may be all but impassable because the drawbridge has burned and fallen into the Great Dēop. To cross that gulf when it is defended on the far side by an army of foul Squam would be perilous enough even with a bridge— but without it, it may be impossible. And the west way in—the Dusken Door—that way is probably blocked and may be broken beyond repair.

"But even were we to get in unscathed by either portal, still would we be at great disadvantage to the Foul Folk, for we know not the pathways of our ancient home. Hence, the slobbering Grg are given great tactical advantage, able to issue at us from byways unknown, to ambush us from coverts beyond ken.

"Aye, Master Perry, your *Raven Book* has been of some aid, for it has shown us what Durek must choose between— though a hard choice it is. But what is needed most is detailed knowledge of the passageways of Kraggen-cor: step-by-step knowledge."

"Step-by-step! The Brega Path!" cried Perry, looking swiftly to Cotton and then back again. "Why, we may have the step-by-step knowledge you seek: Brega's record! It never occurred to me that his record might be of use to you . . . that is, until you said 'step-by-step.' Cotton, run and get the Scroll."

As Cotton bolted from the room, a look of skepticism passed between Anval and Borin; yet Perry ignored this exchange as he launched into an explanation: "Put in mind, one of those four who fled through Drimmen-deeve was the Dwarf Brega, who later became the DelfLord of the Red Hills. Years after the War, he and Tuckerby were reflecting on those dark days and fell to discussing their perilous journey through the Deeves. It was during that conversation that Brega claimed he knew every twist and turn, every up and down, every hall and cavern, every detail of that path of danger. Tuckerby begged him to set it all down in writing so that it could be appended to the *Raven Book,* and Brega did so to please his old companion."

Cotton rushed back into the room carrying a yellowed parchment scroll, rolled up and tied with a green ribbon; he gave it over to Perry. "This is Brega's record of that journey," continued Perry, fumbling at the knot, "a record which soon may be added to the *Raven Book.* I have to make a few more copies to send to the Scholars to study, so that all may agree that it is authentic and belongs in the History. I've already made . . . let me think . . . ah yes, eleven copies; and Cotton and I have thoroughly checked their accuracy against this original. If it proves to be of value to your quest, you may take as many copies as you need." Finally the ribbon came off, and Perry handed the scroll to Borin.

With reservation, the Dwarves spread out the scroll upon a hurriedly cleared section of the table, holding the parchment open by placing saltcellars and pepper mills at the corners, and all gathered around to view the document. "Hah!" burst out Anval, his dubious look replaced by one of exultation, "it is signed by Brega, Bekki's son; here is his Châkka rune. And look! Here are the secret marks! And see this! Now we know that this then is no counter-feit!" To each of Anval's exclamations Borin grunted his agreement; but what the secret marks were, or what the Dwarves had seen, neither Perry, Cotton, nor Lord Kian could discern, and not Anval nor Borin would say.

Borin began to read aloud from Brega's finely wrought script: " 'Here begins the journey at the Dusken Door: two hundred steps up the broad stair; one and twenty and seven hundred level paces in the main passage 'round right, left, right, and right turns passing three arches on the right and two crevices on the left; fifteen and eight hundred down paces in the main passage, a gentle slope . . .' "

Anval and Borin then read on silently; and as they read their elation grew, for here at last was the detail needed to invade their own ancestral homeland. Every now and again one or the other would exclaim aloud as some particular detail would confirm ancient lore: "The Long Hall . . . the Upward Way . . . Braggi's Stand . . . the Great Shelf . . ." and many more.

It was Anval who spoke first when they reached the end of the document, his look of triumph replaced by a brood-ing scowl. "There must be eight or nine hundred major twists and turns here, forks and splits—and twice that many minor ones," he growled, stroking his black beard.

"A good estimate, Anval," said Perry, returning to his chair, "but to be more exact, there are slightly more than a thousand major decisions—and, as you guessed, there are indeed about twice that many minor ones. That's many, many choices which must be made correctly to go from Dusk-Door to Dawn-Gate by this route. I know; I have committed it to memory. It adds up to nearly three thou-sand branchings and forks and splits in the trail—three thousand places to diverge from the course and lose the

way. And to think, this is but one path in Drimmen-deeve;
the total of your Kraggen-cor must be so vast as to defy
imagination!''

Overcome at the thought of the sheer magnitude of the
whole of Drimmen-deeve, Cotton plopped down in his
seat, a look of wonder upon his face.

For a few silent moments the Warrows settled back in
their comfortable chairs and puffed on their pipes in reflection; Cotton, with his feet up, again blew smoke rings at
the ceiling. Leaving the Dwarves studying the Brega Scroll,
Kian, too, returned to his seat.

After a while Perry asked a question that had been
puzzling him for three years—ever since he had become
Master of The Root and had discovered the Brega Scroll in
the far back of a cobweb-laden pigeonhole in a long-
unused desk in a dusty storeroom: ''It thrills me for you to
confirm that the scroll is authentic, but a thing I am
curious about, Borin: The *Raven Book* says that Gildor the
Elf, though he consulted Brega often, actually led the way
through Drimmen-deeve, for Brega's knowledge was of
little or no help. Yet here we are, ready to trust this
document written years later by him; though I must say
that found with the scroll was a note from that time written
for Tuck by Raven where she says that Brega swiftly and
easily recalled the route as if he had trod it only yesterday.
How can that be?''

''He was a Châk,'' replied Borin, glancing up from the
scroll, ''and once a Châk travels a path, it is with him
always, graven in his very being. But he must travel it
first, for he is no better nor worse than anyone else when it
comes to memorizing a route beforehand. But if a Châk
trods a passage, it comes alive within him. And though Elf
Gildor led that first time, had they ever travelled that way
again, it would have fallen to Brega to lead.

''Hence, Master Waeran, we too could memorize the
path described by this document, just as you have; yet we
would be but little different at it from you. Yet, let us step
it out but once, and no one except another Châk will ever
equal our mastery of it.'' The Dwarf paused in reflection.
''Without this gift, the Châkka could not dwell in the
labyrinths under the Mountains.''

As Borin had been speaking, a dark mood had stormed

across Anval's features. Glowering at the scroll, he slammed his fist to the table, causing the dishes to rattle, startling both Warrows, Cotton dropping his feet to the floor. *"Kruk!"* spat Anval. "Why did not Brega make such a record for the Châkka? We would have mastered it ere now! This is a long and complicated course—at least forty or more miles in length with many splits and twists." He paused a moment, again in dark thought, then once more struck the table in exasperation. "Pah! We cannot conduct a Squam-War where at every fork in the cavern we must consult a scroll!" He turned to Borin. "One or both of us must memorize this parchment and guide the Army, though mastering it will take weeks, perhaps months—time we can ill afford, for the Army is ready now. His black eyes filled with rage. "And the foul Grg raid, harass, maim, and slay each night."

Perry's heart was racing, and his face was flushed. His breathing was rapid and shallow. All during the evening a sense of destiny had been growing within him, as if a marvelous doom were about to fall. As a lad he had spent endless hours poring over his uncle's copy of *The Raven Book* and delving into other tomes of knowledge, filling his mind and heart and dreams with epic tales of grand heroism: of Egil One Eye and Arin and the Quest of the Green Stone; of Elyn and Thork and the Quest of Black Mountain; of Tuck and Danner and Patrel and the Winter War Quest; and many other eld tales of derring-do. And his daydreams had been filled with a whirl of Elves, Dwarves, Knights, Men, Wizards, Utruni, Dragons, and other peoples and creatures of legend. And in his childhood he had yearned to be a Warrow involved in another grand adventure. But quests—especially Warrow quests—never seem to happen to striplings, and so he dreamed and yearned. And his yearning had driven him to the study of the tales and records of Mithgar, and he had become a Historian, a Ravenbook Scholar.

And now Perry had heard the frustration in Borin's voice when the Dwarf had spoken of the time needed to memorize the Brega Scroll. Perry knew how to resolve the dilemma facing the Dwarves—but he was afraid. Yet even in his fear he realized that here was the chance for the adventure he'd always longed for, always dreamed of. But now the adventure was upon him and he found that he was not ready for it, not at all eager to reach out and grab it; he was unable to choose; it was too sudden.

Long moments fled, and no one said aught. And then Perry looked up into the faces of the visitors, and he saw the mixture of anguish and frustration and bitterness in Borin's and Anval's and Lord Kian's eyes as they thought upon the further *Spaunen* depredations that would occur. Perry was deeply moved, and in spite of his own trepidation, in spite of the risks involved, suddenly and without conscious thought he spoke: "What you need is a guide who already knows the Brega Path. You need me, Perry Fairhill. I will go with you."

CHAPTER 5

GOODBYE, HOLLY, WE'RE OFF
TO WAR

Cotton startled awake to find the late-morning Sun filling his bedroom with light. *Cotton Buckleburr*, he thought, *you slugabed, get up and serve your master*. The buccan rolled out of bed and splashed cold water from the pitcher into the basin on the washstand and quickly scrubbed his face. Throwing on his clothes, he rushed out of the room still stuffing his shirttail into his pants; and he nearly collided with Holly, who was at that moment passing by in the hallway, her arms laden with linen. *"Oomph!"* he grunted as he twisted aside to keep from running over her, bumping into the wall instead.

"Cotton Buckleburr," Holly laughed, her soft amber-jewelled eyes atwinkle, "you big oaf, you nearly scared me to death, jumping out of the doorway at me like that. Did you hurt yourself now, runnin' into the wall and all?"

"Oh no, Miss Holly, I'm all right, and I didn't mean to scare you. But I'm late getting up, and . . . say, where's Mister Perry? Is he awake? And the visitors, are they up and about?" asked Cotton, continuing to fumble with his shirttail.

"Why they were up and gone long ago, early this morning," replied Holly.

"Gone? Oh no!" wailed Cotton. "Mister Perry can't go away without me. He needs me! Much as I don't want to go, I've got to—for Mister Perry's sake."

"Wait, Cotton"—a puzzled frown settled upon Holly's gentle features—"only the strangers left this morning. Mister Perry is still here—here at The Root. He's in the study. But what's all this about his going away somewhere and you with him? Going where for what?"

58

"Why he's going off to Drimmen-deeve to fight Rūcks and such," answered Cotton. "And me, well I'm going with him." And a look of wonder fell upon Cotton as he realized what he had said. "That's right, Miss Holly, I'm going with him." Cotton turned and rushed away and did not see the frightened look that sprang up behind Holly's eyes.

Well I reckon he's put both of our feet into it now, right enough, and we're in a pretty pickle if you ask me, thought Cotton as he hurried toward the study. *I wonder where the visitors went off to this morning. And are Mister Perry and me really going away from the Bosky?*

Cotton slid to a stop in the doorway of the den, and his mouth dropped open in amazement: Peregrin Fairhill stood before him, armored in the silveron mail and grasping the long Elven-knife, Bane, in his right fist. "Cotton, look!" cried Perry, holding his arms straight out from his sides and pirouetting. "The starsilver fits me as if I were born to it. And Bane, well Bane is just the proper-sized sword for a Warrow hand." The buccan swished the blade through the air with an elaborate flourish.

"Oh, Cotton," continued Perry, his sapphirine gaze upon the upraised sword, "it seems I've dreamed of this all my scholarly years. It will be an adventure of a lifetime: swords and armor, phalanxes of marching warriors, pavilions and pennons, glittering helms, shields, hauberks, pikes. Oh, how *glorious* it will be!"

Cotton looked doubtful. "But Sir, it seems to me that War is just bloody slaughter. And this War won't be no different, except the fighting and killing will be done in a great, dark hole in the ground. Many a friend will perish. Shiny swords and pretty flags there'll be aplenty, but agony and Death will be there too.

"Of course, of course, Cotton"—Perry frowned—"everyone knows that killing the enemy is part of War. And you can't have a battle without taking a few wounds." Then Perry's jewel-like eyes seemed to focus upon a distant vision of splendor. "Glorious," he breathed.

"Pardon me, Mister Perry," Cotton interrupted Perry's woolgathering, "but just where have our visitors got off to? Holly says that they've gone away. How can we go off to Drimmen-deeve without them?"

"Oh, they'll be back. Lord Kian has just gone down to the marketplace to get supplies for our trip to the Landover Road Ford, and Anval and Borin are off to Budgens to get the waggon and team." Then Perry looked sharply at his friend. "What did you say, Cotton? Did you say that *we* were going to Drimmen-deeve? Do *you* mean to come too?" And when Cotton nodded dumbly, Perry shouted for joy and began capering about the room, slashing the air with Bane. "Take that and that and that, you Spawn!" He stabbed at imaginary foes. "Beware, maggot-folk, the Warrows are coming!" Then, slamming Bane home in the worn scabbard at his belt, Perry took Cotton by the arm. "We've got to get ourselves outfitted properly for this venture," he declared, and began rushing about the room selecting arms and armor for himself and Cotton.

His choices, though somewhat limited, were excellent: Cotton was fitted with an armored shirt of gilded chainmail; though it was light, it would turn aside all but the heaviest blades. This armor had a noble history, for during the Winter War this was the very chain corselet given over to Patrel by Laurelin from the royal armories to wear in the first great battle of the Dimmendark when one of Modru's hordes swept down upon Challerain Keep. Added to the armor was a rune-marked blade about the size and shape of Bane, but which had been forged years agone by the Men of the Lost Land—and a scabbard to hold it. Each of their belts also held a dagger, and both Warrows had chosen simple leather-and-iron helms. 'Round their shoulders they had fitted Elven cloaks which blended so well with any natural background that even the keenest eyes would be deceived if the wearer covered himself and remained still.

As the two buccen had sifted through the museum cases selecting Cotton's apparel, the small silver horn kept turning up in one or the other's hands. And as Perry started to set it aside once more, he paused, laughing, and suddenly changed his mind: "This horn seems bound and determined to go with us, Cotton. Here, let's hang it over your shoulder to rally friend around when faced with the foe."

It was thus that Lord Kian found them upon his return from Woody Hollow. "Ho! What's this? I go away leaving two meek Waerlinga and return to find two warriors abristle with weaponry." He smiled down at the small figures before him, accepting without speaking that Cotton, too, would accompany them to Drimmen-deeve.

Cotton squirmed under the young Man's gaze, uncomfortable in the unfamiliar golden gear, but Perry, in silver, stood proudly straighter and would have walked about except he feared—and rightly so—that he would end up strutting and preening.

"Well now, soldiers," said Lord Kian, "if I were you I'd doff that gear; it won't be required til we get to the Spawn—at least a thousand miles hence. Instead, you need to select travelling clothes: strong, sturdy, comfortable, warm travelling clothes. And good boots that will walk far and stay dry, and won't chafe your feet and will keep them warm. Remember: although it is just October now, early winter will be upon us ere we get there."

Somewhat abashed, the Warrows took off their armor and weaponry and, under Kian's critical eye, began selecting garments and other accoutrements necessary for the lengthy trip. They stopped only long enough to eat some of Holly's cold beef, cheese, fresh chewy bread, apples, and beer. After lunch they continued to choose their gear. The former Realmsman proved to be well experienced, for under his direction they selected only that which was essential for the journey. At last each Warrow had assembled the needed clothing and other travelling gear, all of it stowed in an easily manageable backpack topped off with a warm bedroll.

Late that afternoon, Borin and Anval returned, driving a small waggon drawn by a fine team of sturdy horses. The waggon had been crafted by Men of Dael, and had been chosen by Kian, Anval, and Borin as being more suitable for the journey than the available Dwarf wains, which were ponderous, made for hauling large loads of heavy cargo. The four-wheeler from Dael was made of ash wood, light but durable. There was room for two on the driver's seat, which was well padded and had a low back for support. The freight bed was short, with wooden sides and front, and had a hinged tailgate fastened with metal latches. The waggon was painted a deep red.

The Warrow wheelwright of Budgens, Ned Proudhand, had done a first-rate job on the wheel—replacing the iron rim and broken spoke, and regreasing not only the hub on the repaired wheel, but all the other hubs and the waggon-tongue pivot and the whiffletrees as well. He had painted the new spoke red to match the others. For this fine craftwork and conscientiousness, Anval grudgingly paid Ned with a tiny golden coin, the only one that Ned had ever seen, copper being his usual fare, with an occasional silver. But this coin was *gold!* Ned vowed to keep it all his life, on display, pledging never to spend it, claiming it as his Dwarf hoard, declaring that it would become an heirloom of the Proudhand clan.

Anval turned the rig over to Cotton, who drove it down to the common stables at the Pony Field on the southeastern edge of Hollow End. There he removed the harness and watered the two horses, whom he dubbed Brownie and Downy—one being all brown and the other a chestnut with an especially soft, fluffy, white mane. He rubbed them down and filled the feed bins in their stalls with an extra helping of oats. And after talking to them for a bit while combing their manes and tails, the buccan returned to The Root.

It was dusk when Cotton came up the walk toward the burrow. The autumn eve was mild, and from the open window of the study he could hear Perry's voice: ''. . . paces up the gentle rise from the First Neath to the East Hall at Gate Level; then it's two hundred forty level paces across the hall and out the Daūn Gate to freedom . . .''

Why, that's the Brega Path what Mister Perry's reciting, Cotton thought. *Why in the world . . .* Before his mind could carry on, he heard Borin grunt and Anval reply, but what was said he could not tell. *Hoy, hold on now! Why, them cheeky Dwarves are* testing *Mister Perry . . . as if they don't believe that us Warrows have good memories!* Cotton stormed toward the front entrance.

As the ired buccan stalked into the study, Borin looked up from the original Scroll; and Anval and Lord Kian glanced up from two of Perry's linen-paper copies. Empty-handed, Perry stood in room center.

''Well?'' asked Perry.

''Exact,'' grunted Borin, a growing look of approval in his eye.

"Your duplicate, too, is letter-perfect, Waeran," rumbled Anval, turning to Lord Kian, who also nodded.

Borin stood, his black eyes aglitter in the candlelight. "Master Perry, we have seen for ourselves the exactness of your copies of the Brega Scroll; hence, because that work has proved to be unerring, we no longer doubt the accuracy of your duplicate of the *Raven Book*. You are indeed a crafter of true worth."

Borin and then Anval bowed deeply to Perry, and the buccan smiled and bowed in return. Cotton, mollified by the Dwarves' respectful behavior, completely forgot the angry words he had come to heap upon them.

"Well then," said Perry, moving to the desk, "I'd better pack some of these copies to take to King Durek." He stood undecided a moment, then mumbled to himself, "I suppose I'll just take them all. . . ." As an afterthought, he opened a desk drawer and added a small chart to the stack. ". . . as well as this sketch of mine."

That evening, once more they feasted on Holly's fine cooking. This time the meal consisted of an overlarge kettle of well-spiced green beans slow-cooked for hours with a huge ham bone and gobbets of meat and large, peeled potatoes and parsnips. There was also freshly baked bread with honey, light golden beer, and cherry cobbler for dessert. Again Anval out-ate a straining Cotton. And the conversation touched upon hunting and gold, deer and gardens, delving and writing, weaponry and seeds, Wizards and Dragons, and many other things. This night Borin also joined in the talk 'round the table and proved to hold many tales of interest.

But all through the evening both Perry and Cotton would at times lapse into silence and gaze about them at their beloved Root, wondering when they would see it again.

The next morning ere dawn, Holly awakened them all, and they sat down to an enormous breakfast of scrambled eggs, hotcakes, honey, toast, and marmalade. "It is well we are leaving today," growled Anval. "Another week of this fare and I could not get into my armor."

At sunrise Lord Kian strode to the Pony Field stable and hitched up the team and drove the waggon down to the Market Square, where gaping Warrow merchants loaded the supplies the *Man* had purchased the day before. When he returned, the Dwarves and Warrows, dressed for the journey, were standing on the stoop—packs, bedrolls, armor, and weaponry ready. They placed all their goods in the waggon, and the Dwarves piled aboard with Kian. Perry and Cotton took one last long look around, reluctant to get aboard now that it had come to it. Cotton glanced at Perry and, at his nod, reached up to grasp the sideboard to climb into the wain. But before he could do so, Holly came rushing out of the door. She spun Cotton around and hugged him and whispered into his ear, "Goodbye, Cotton. Now you stay by Mister Perry, and take care of him, and keep him safe." Then she turned to Perry, and she hugged him and kissed him and then held him at arm's length and with brimming eyes looked at him as if to fill herself up with the sight of him for the long days to come. And Perry, stunned and dumbfounded, shuffled his feet and peered at the ground, unable to look again upon the anguish in Holly's face. She tried to say something, but could not and burst into tears, and with one last quick embrace she ran weeping back into The Root.

Perry stood a moment gaping at the pegged panels of the oaken door through which she had fled, and suddenly he realized how much he cared for her—in that quiet, Warrowish sort of way. Now his yen for adventure seemed somehow less important, but he glanced up into the wain where his companions were waiting; and in that instant— like countless others in all ages have found—he, too, learned the first lesson of quests: whether for good or ill, the needs of the quest overrule all else.

Curbing his confused feelings, Perry climbed into the waggon with Cotton and the others, and they drove away to the east.

CHAPTER 6

THE HORN OF THE REACH

Anval, Borin, Kian, Perry, and Cotton; they all rode away from The Root in silence, each deep in his own thoughts. In this fashion they passed down the canted road from Hollow End and on through Woody Hollow, past the mill and across the bridge over the Dingle-rill. And everywhere they passed, Warrows stood silent by the road or ran from their homes to watch the waggon roll by. This was, after all, an amazing sight, one not likely to be repeated in anyone's lifetime:

Imagine, two Dwarves and a Man, actually, right here in Woody Hollow! And Mister Perry and Cotton goin' away with them and all! Wonders never cease! It was to be the talk of the Boskydells for months, even years, to come.

A flock of chattering younglings, led by the two tag-alongs, ran ahead of, beside, and behind the wain all the way to the bridge over the Dingle-rill, where the children stopped and stood watching as the waggon slowly trundled across and went on. Some tykes silently waved, others gaily piped farewells, and some seemed instantly to lose interest, for they began playing tag or wrestling or simply went wandering off. Soon the horse-drawn vehicle was around the bend and over the hill and out of sight.

Nothing was said by anyone in the wain for a mile or so, and apart from an occasional bird or an insect coming awake with the warming of the Sun, the silence was broken only by the sounds of the waggon and team: the creak of harness, the jingle of singletrees, the clip-clop of hooves, an occasional whicker or blowing, the rattle of sideboards and tailgate, and above all else the unremitting grind of iron-rimmed wheels turning against the hard-packed earthen road. In this somber mood they rode without speaking til they came to the village of Budgens.

Upon sighting the small red waggon drawing nigh, the hundred or so citizens of that village, too, turned out to watch the wayfarers pass through, taking up a position on the Monument Knoll, with Ned Proudhand in the crowd forefront showing all who would look—and there were many—his Dwarf gold piece.

As the wayfarers rolled by the Monument, Cotton, driven by an inner urge, drew the silver horn from his pack and blew it. An electrifying note rang out, clear and bell-like, its pure tones carrying far across the countryside. A great cheer went up from the small crowd, and everyone there on the knoll stood straight and tall. The gloomy mood was lifted from the occupants of the waggon, and they waved to the gathering. A youngling Warrow broke from the ranks and ran down toward the wain; others saw this and also ran down the hillside and onto the road, joining him; soon all were thronging around and keeping pace with the van.

"Where you headin', Cotton?" cried a voice from the mob.

"Out east and south, Teddy," answered Cotton, his eye falling upon the one who had called forth.

What for? shouted several at once.

"The King says there's trouble in the mountains and we're fixin' to help set it right," replied Cotton, which brought forth a great cheer; for the folks living at Budgens, being near the Monument and all, thought that Warrows were the greatest resource that the King could draw upon. Why, it was only *natural*, only *right* and *proper*, that the King call upon a Warrow or two to help settle his troubles, whatever they might be.

Persons in the crowd continued in this fashion to shout out questions or give encouragement to the travellers as the wain slowly trundled through the village. And Cotton was aglow with it all: He introduced Lord Kian and Anval and Borin to the citizens, and much to their delight the Man actually stood up in the rolling waggon and gracefully bowed 'round to all, though the Dwarves merely grunted. Then Cotton reminded the Budgens folk as to just who

Mister Perry was; and the Ravenbook Scholar stood and bowed to the crowd, too. At each introduction, or reply to a question, or statement made by the wayfarers, the villagers cheered. And in this festive atmosphere the voyagers were escorted through Budgens. At the town limits they were given a *hip, hip, hurrah!* send-off, and soon were out of sight and hearing of the hamlet by the Rillmere.

"Well, now," said Lord Kian, white teeth smiling through yellow beard, as he turned upon the driver's seat to look back at his passengers in the van, "that was quite a lively band of citizens."

"Ever since the great battle, the folks of Budgens have had a reputation for being spirited," replied Perry. "Did you see that monument back there on the knoll? Well, that's a memorial not only to the nineteen Warrows actually killed in the Battle of Budgens in the Winter War, but also to the thirty wounded and the nearly three hundred others who took part in the fight to overthrow the reavers— evil Ghûls who were trying to usurp the Bosky, to steal our homeland during the days before the fall of Gron. And we were successful; we Warrows slew many of the corpse-foe, and later, with the help of the Men of Wellen, we drove them from the Bosky. But it was in Budgens where it really got started. Oh, the Warrows of that time had been in a lot of skirmishes with the Ghûls back when the reavers first invaded the Bosky, but it wasn't until Danner and Patrel came that the Warrows were organized properly. The first big battle of the Struggles took place in Budgens, a Warrow name of honor: *Brave as Budgens,* we say these days. The people of Budgens know that, and they see the Memorial every day, and carefully tend the garden there at the foot of the stone monument. The glory of those Warrows' bravery is with the folk of Budgens always, and they take pride for their part in history."

Borin looked at Perry. "So you Waerans have already dealt with usurpers, as we Châkka have yet to do," he rumbled, a new respect showing in his eye at the thought of these Wee Ones driving back a great gang of the reaving-foe, driving them out of Budgens—each Khôl twice Waeran size—and doing it while suffering a loss of only nineteen. "You are a small but mighty adversary."

Then Borin turned a curious eye to the other Warrow.

"Cotton, show me that silver horn upon which you blew the clarion call that stirred my spirit and made hope leap into my heart."

"It's the same horn, you know," said Cotton, rummaging in his pack. "It's the one Captain Patrel used to rally the Warrows in fight after fight with Modru's Reavers. That's why I blew it; it was back to Budgens again. Usually we blow it here once a year, on the battle anniversary; but it seemed like the thing to do today also, since we're setting off on a mission." Cotton passed the small bugle to Borin.

Perry spoke up: "It's called the Horn of the Reach, and it was given over to Patrel by Vidron himself, General of the Alliance, Whelmer of Modru's Horde. The *Raven Book* says the horn was found almost twenty-six hundred years ago in the hoard of Sleeth the Orm by Elgo, Sleeth's Doom; but of its history ere then, nothing is said."

"Elgo, Sleeth's Doom, you say? Thief Elgo, Foul Elgo, treasure stealer, *I* say," snapped Borin, angrily setting the horn aside, ire flashing in his eyes. "He slew the Dragon, true, but then he foully claimed the Châk treasure for his own. But it was not his! The Dragon hoard was ours! Sleeth came to Blackstone—the Châkka Halls of the Rigga Mountains—plundering, marauding, pillaging, slaying; we were driven out. Sleeth remained, sleeping for centuries upon a bed of stolen gold. Then Thief Elgo came and slew the great Cold-drake. By trick! When we heard that Sleeth was dead, we rejoiced, and asked for that which was rightfully ours. In sneering pride, Foul Elgo came to Kachar, to the throne of Brak, then DelfLord of those halls. And False Elgo laughed at and mocked us, flinging down a great pouch made of Dragon's hide at Brak's feet, scoffing. 'A purse such as this you must make ere you can fill your treasuries with *Dracongield;* yet beware, for only the brave may pluck this cloth from its loom.' " Borin chopped the edge of one hand into the palm of the other. "Such an affront could not be borne, and we were avenged against Jeering Elgo, who japed nevermore. But nought of Sleeth's stolen hoard was ever recovered by us, the Châkka, the true owners." Borin's eyes flashed darkly, and the muscles in his jaw clenched, and he breathed heavily.

Perry had listened with growing amazement to the anger

in Borin's voice, and saw that Anval, too, was grinding his teeth in suppressed rage. "But Borin, Anval," said the Warrow, baffled by the Dwarves' intense manner, "those events took place ages past, far from here, and concerned people long dead; yet it is you who seem ired, though it happened centuries and centuries before either of you were born."

"Elgo was a thief!" spat Borin. "And an insulter of my ancestors! He who seeks the wrath of the Châkka finds it! Forever!" Borin turned his face away from Perry, and his smoldering eyes stared without seeing over the passing countryside, and Anval sullenly fingered the edge of his axe.

Interminable moments passed, but at last Perry spoke: "Whether Elgo was a thief as you say, or a Dragon-slaying hero as some tell it, or both, I cannot say; but the silver horn at your side perhaps came from that disputed treasure."

And in the back of the rolling waggon, slowly and with visible effort, Borin at last mastered his Dwarvish passion; grudgingly, he began to examine the trumpet. "This was made by the Châkka," he muttered, and then he turned his attention to the engraved swift-running rider-mounted horses winding through carven runes twining 'round the flange of the horn-bell. Borin gave a start and sucked in air between his teeth, and looked hard at the clarion; and he hissed a Dwarf word—"*Narok!*"

Narok: Borin's taut utterance seemed to jerk Anval upright, and he stared sharply at his brother.

After a long while Borin passed the bugle to Anval, who studied it as intensely; and then, after another long while, Anval reluctantly gave the clarion back to Cotton, warning, "Beware, Waeran, this trump must be blown only in time of dire need." And about it neither Anval nor Borin would say more.

In wonder, Cotton took back the horn and looked at it with new eyes, studying it closely for the first time, driven by the Dwarves' curious behavior to seek what they had seen.

The companions had followed Woody Hollow Road to Byroad Lane, and then they had joined the Crossland

Road, which would carry them all the way to the Grimwall Mountains. And the wain continued to roll eastward during the day, through Willowdell, and Tillock, and beyond, one person driving while the others lounged in conversation on the packs and bedrolls in the cargo bed. Often they changed position when some bone or joint or muscle protested at being held in one place too long or at being jounced against a hard waggon-plank by an occasional rut or rock or washboarded section in the road—not that there were many; for the most part the road was smooth and the pace was swift. Nor did the travellers engage in continuous talk; at times they lapsed into long silences and simply watched the countryside roll by, the trees beginning to change hue in the quickening autumn—many reds and yellows and a few browns starting to show amid the predominant greens.

Frequently they would stop to rest the horses and water them, and to trade off driving, and to take care of other needs. At one of these stops they saw another sign of the changing seasons: two flocks of geese flew southward overhead, high in the sky, one wedge flying above and ahead of the other. Their lornful cries were faint with distance, and Perry, as always, felt a tugging at his heart. Lord Kian shaded his eyes and looked long: "Year after year, since time immemorial, they pass to and fro, their flight locked to the seasons. Little do they care that Kingdoms and tyrants rise and fall; it is as nothing to them in their unchanging journey through time. They fly so very high above our petty squabbles and fightings and Wars and slayings. How small we must seem to them."

At another stop they fed the horses some grain while they themselves lunched on the contents of a basket provided by Holly: cold beef sandwiches and crisp Bosky apples. Anval sighed when the food was gone. "I somehow feel that may be the last I eat of Holly's cookery," he said, rubbing his stomach. "You are a fortunate Waeran, Master Perry." Perry did not answer, though he gazed thoughtfully back to the west, his mind seeing amber damman eyes brimming with tears.

It was nearly sundown when the waggon drove through Raffin, where, as in each of the other hamlets the wayfarers had passed, the citizens gathered to gawp at this strange assortment of travellers. Yet though it was late in the day, the wain did not stop, for Lord Kian planned on reaching the Happy Otter, an inn located on the western edge of Greenfields, the next town, ten or so miles east of Raffin. He and Anval and Borin previously had noted the 'Otter when the trio had passed in the opposite direction on their journey to The Root to see *The Raven Book*. Upon hearing that they were heading for the inn, Cotton perked up, for he had heard of the 'Otter's beer, and, as he said, he had a mind to try it. Anval, too, smiled with anticipation and relish at the thought.

It was night when the waggon at last came to Greenfields; the inn was dark, for the hostelkeeper, Fennerly Cotter, had gone to bed. Borin leapt down from the wain and strode to the door and hammered upon it with the butt of his fist. After a long moment a lantern-light appeared in a second-storey front window, and the shutters banged open as Fennerly looked out, and then slammed shut again. Borin continued to pound the door in exasperation as the innkeeper's light slowly bobbed down the stairs and across the common room. Fennerly, in his nightcap, at last came grumbling to the door and opened it. Raising his lantern up to see just who in the Dell this door-banger was, the innkeeper swallowed half a yawn with a gulp and stumbled a step or two backwards as his now wide-awake eyes found a fierce Dwarf warrior, towering within his doorway, muttering something about Waeran innkeepers that went to bed with the chickens. But then scowling Borin was shouldered aside by smiling Anval with Cotton in tow; and he drew the Warrow to the taps, where he demanded they be served with the best ale in the house.

As Fennerly was to relate later to a rapt set of cronies, "Wull, at first I thought it were a Dwarf invasion. Gave me right a start, they did, and I was thinkin' about escapin' and soundin' the alarm bell at the Commons. Oh, I knowed that the strangers was in the Bosky, right enough, but I can't say as I was expectin' even one of them, much less all three, to come bargin' into my inn in the middle of the night—and draggin' two sleepy Warrows with 'em, no less. But in they came, the Big Man stoopin' a bit to miss the overhead beams while he and that Mister Perry was chuckling at some private joke of their own.

"Wull, let me tell you, them five drank up half my best

beer and ate all the kitchen leftovers, they did. And then them two Dwarves got to arm wrestling, and they grunted and strained and fairly turned the air blue, what with them strange, bloodcurdling Dwarf oaths they yelled. And each time one of 'em lost they'd take a swill of beer and change hands and go at it again. And the one was better with his right arm whilst t'other was better with his left. And the Big Man sat back and roared his laughter and puffed on his pipe. Then he arm wrestled with each, and though he finally lost, let me tell you it was a mighty struggle for them broad-shouldered Dwarves to finally put his knuckles to the wood. And all the while there was that Mister Perry sittin' there smilin' and yawnin' and blinkin' like a drowsy owl tryin' to stay awake, and Mister Cotton runnin' back and forth around the table, judgin' the contests and declarin' the victor when an arm was finally put down. But after a while the Big Man noticed that Mister Perry had fallen asleep, and so we all went to bed, and it was about time too.

"But it seemed I had no sooner got to sleep than that Dwarf, Mister Borin—the one as pounds doors—well, he were at it again, only this time it was my own bedroom door though. And he was glarin' and mutterin' something about Waeran innkeepers what *don't* get up with the chickens. I fed 'em breakfast, and they were off at the crack of dawn.

"Of course they paid me with good copper, they did, even though I hadn't got a bed large enough for the Big Man, who slept in the stable hayloft above the horses, slept right there even though they was callin' him 'Lord' —Lord Kian, that is. Don't that beat all if it's true? A Lord sleepin' in my stables! Him what is probably used to sleeping on silks and satins." Here Fennerly paused to fill the mugs and let the startling facts sink home, and sink home they did, for all the Warrows looked at each other in wonderment, and an excited buzz filled the taproom.

"Ahem," said Fennerly, clearing his throat, announcing that he was ready to resume his tale, and silence quickly fell upon the inn's common room. "Of course, by the time anyone else in the 'Fields was up, the strangers was long gone, miles east of this village. Didn't say what they was doin' or where they was goin' or nothin'. But I'll tell you

this: whatever it is they are doing, I'll bet a gold buckle
that it's somethin' big.'' And with that pronouncement,
Fennerly fell silent; and all of his cronies and listeners
sighed and mulled over their ale, for they had missed the
biggest event to happen in Greenfields since Tuckerby
Underbank himself had passed through on his return from
the Winter War. And no sooner would Fennerly finish his
tale than another 'Fieldite would come into the Happy
Otter, agog with the news, and the innkeeper would re-
count the events again, and all of the Warrows—each and
every one of them—would sit forward on the edges of
their seats so as not to miss a single one of Fennerly's
words—though some of the enthralled listeners were hearing the tale for the sixth or even the eighth time.

It was indeed the crack of dawn when the travellers left,
after breakfast, with Cotton's head pounding but Anval
seeming no less for the wear. Lord Kian was smiling and
Borin scowling and Perry rubbing sleep from his eyes. Yet
the road was smooth and the air crisp and fresh and soon
Cotton was his normal chipper self, and all the others were
wide awake and in cheerful good humor as the waggon
continued to roll on toward the Boskydell border some
fourteen miles to the east on the far side of the great
barricade.

In late morning they drove into the thorn tunnel through
the Spindlethorn Barrier, and then over the bridge above
the Spindle River, passing again into the spiked barricade
beyond. At last they emerged from the thorns on the far
side, coming once more into the day, leaving the Boskydells
behind. Looking backward, Cotton remarked to Perry:
''Well now, Sir, I really do believe that we are on our
way. Into what, I can't say, but on our way at last. I guess
I didn't believe it til just now; but somehow, lookin' back
at the Spindlethorn, well, Sir, it has smacked it home to
me that we have really and truly left the Boskydells and
are off to a Rūck War. And I don't know nothin' about
War and fighting, that's for sure. Why I'm along at all is a
mystery to me, except I somehow know I'll be needed
before we're through with this. And I don't mind telling
you, Mister Perry, I'm scared and that's the plain and
simple truth.''

"Oh piffle, Cotton!" snorted Perry, whose spirits had been on the rise all day. "That's not fear you're feeling, it's excitement! And as to why you're here, Cotton, well you've come along to help me, and I've come along to guide the Dwarves in the great adventure of our lifetime. But you are dead right about one thing: for our own safety we've got to learn to use the weapons we brought along. You'll see, Cotton, once we can protect urselves, nay, rather, once we can carry the fight to the Spawn, then all thoughts of fear will vanish forever. I'm sure that Lord Kian here will show us how to use our swords, and we have many days to practice before they'll become necessary."

"Well, my little friends," responded Kian, looking a bit askance at the two Waerlinga, "it isn't quite that simple. One doesn't become a master swordthane overnight. But I'll see what we can do between now and then to prepare you." Inwardly, the young Lord was relieved, for he had been about to broach the same subject to the Waerlinga. Ere now, those gentle Folk had had no need to learn the arts of War. But on this venture, like as not there would come a time when these two buccen would have to defend themselves, at least long enough for aid to reach them. The Waerlinga themselves had recognized their need to learn the rudiments of defense, thus he would not have to convince them of that; but they would have to train hard every day under deft guidance to be able to handle their long-knives by the time they reached Drimmen-deeve. Fortunately for the Warrows, Lord Kian possessed the needed skill to instruct them properly.

They drove til the westering Sun touched the rim of the Earth, and they pulled off the road to the eaves of the bordering forest, Edgewood, to camp for the night.

While Cotton and Perry made several trips to gather firewood, Lord Kian tended the horses, and Anval and Borin unloaded the evening supplies and found stones to set in a ring for the fire, which was soon crackling in the early autumn twilight. Kian refilled their leather bottles and the large waterskin from a clear freshette bubbling through the trees and running into the meadow.

As they were out gathering a final load of wood, Cotton took the opportunity to talk alone with Perry: "Mister

Perry, today I took another good hard look at that silver horn of ours. After the close way they both acted yesterday and what Anval said, any ninnyhammer could see there was a lot more left unsaid by the Dwarves than all we know. Well, lookin' at it, I saw something after a long time that, well, I don't rightly know what to make of it 'cause it only adds to the mystery. But anyway, what I mean to say is that them tiny little figures of the horsemen riding like the wind and curving all around the horn, well, Sir, them riders, if you study them up close, they ain't Men riders at all. They're *Dwarves!*''

"*What?*'' burst out Perry, astounded by this new information. ''That can't be! That horn has been known too long, seen by too many people for that to have been overlooked by all eyes til now.''

"I can't help it, Sir,'' responded Cotton stubbornly, ''but them eyes just didn't look close enough. They saw what they were expecting to see, if you catch my meaning. I'm saying that them people in Valon, well, they are a Folk what lives by the horse, and they purely saw those little figures as bein' riders just like they themselves are. And since Captain Patrel got the horn as a gift from the Valon people, well he saw Valon riders, too, just like everybody else has seen 'em since that time. Beggin' your pardon, Mister Perry, but after all, it *is* called the Horn of Valon—or the Horn of the Reach—and when people hear that name they don't really look hard at the riders to see whether or not they are Men, Dwarves, Elves, or even Warrows; they only see that there are riders on galloping horses, nothing more. And with that name, naturally the people think they're Valon riders. But it isn't so. Oh, they're Dwarves right enough, but you have to look real close to see it.''

"Cotton, I'm flabbergasted,'' said Perry, picking up another fallen branch. ''If what you say is true, then it is a detail that's been overlooked by us Warrows for more than two hundred years, and by the House of Valon for twenty-four hundred years before that—since the days of Elgo and of Elyn and Thork. Of course if the riders truly are Dwarves, it'd help explain the mysterious way that Borin and Anval acted.''

"Oh no, Sir, I beg to differ,'' said Cotton, breaking a

branch in two and tucking the pieces into his bundle, "I'd say it only deepens the mystery."

"No, no, Cotton, what I mean is that the horn must have some secret meaning to the Dwarves, and that's why Borin and Anval acted as they did," Perry said. "But what do you mean, Cotton, 'deepens the mystery'? How can it get more mysterious than it already is?"

"Well, Sir," replied Cotton, "you know the old tavern talk about Dwarves not riding horses. And you remember back at The Root how Anval told me that all of his Folk had better sense than to climb aboard real horses instead of just ponies—oh, they use the big horses right enough, so that shows they aren't afraid of 'em, but they just don't *ride* 'em. Well now, I ask you, if they don't ride horses, why in the world are there figures all around the silver horn of a bunch of *Dwarves* ridin' on the backs of galloping *horses?*"

Perry, of course, had no answer for Cotton's question. He knew that the animals on the horn were horses and not ponies, but he, too, had always thought that the riders, though small in relation to the horses, were Men. Perry was eager to examine the trumpet closely for himself at the first opportunity.

Gathering the rest of the firewood in silence, they each soon had a load. On the way back, Cotton, who had collected an enormous bundle of deadwood, stepped into a low spot and fell flat on his face, throwing the branches every which way as he flung out his arms to catch himself. *"Whuff!"* he grunted as he hit the earth and seemed to disappear in the deep grass.

"Cotton!" cried Perry. "Where did you go?"

"I'm down here, Sir," answered Cotton. "I stepped in a hole. It was just like taking that extra step at the top of the stairs only to find out there weren't one . . . or rather it was like not taking a step at the bottom of the stairs only to find out there were one. Lumme! I threw wood everywhere."

And Perry, seeing that Cotton was unhurt, began laughing and describing to Cotton the cascade of limbs launched through the air. Cotton, too, began laughing, and their serious mood over the Horn of Valon was dispelled. Happily, they collected the fallen wood, this time sharing the load evenly, and returned to the camp just in time for tea.

It had been a long day, and soon both Warrows were nodding drowsily. They spread their bedrolls and shortly were fast asleep in the open air. Anval and Borin bedded down also, leaving Lord Kian sitting on a log at the edge of the firelight, whittling with his sharp-bladed knife, for the travellers had decided that a watch would be kept, though they were hundreds of miles and many days away from peril.

Perry's turn came late in the night. He was unaccustomed to sentry duty and soon found his eyes drooping. To keep himself awake he slowly strolled around and around the camp, stopping now and again to add wood to the fire. While walking his post he began to softly hum the *Song of the Nightwatch,* for at last he truly understood it:

> *The flames, they flicker, the shadows dance,*
> *   Bright Stars pass overhead.*
> *Night flies the quicker, Dawn does advance,*
> *   For those snug in their bed.*
>
> *For one on guard who walks his round*
> *   And must remain awake,*
> *The Night goes hard, for he is bound*
> *   Another round to make.*

In this manner he passed his vigil as the stars wheeled through the vault above, and soon he awakened Anval, whose turn had come.

Shedding his Elven-cloak and folding it as a pillow, Perry crawled sleepily back into his bed, and as he slowly fell toward slumber his thoughts drifted across Cotton's revelation about the Horn of Valon. The rest of that night Perry's dreams were filled with thousands of horses endlessly thundering across open plains, making the earth shake with the pounding of their hooves. And upon the back of each rode a Dwarf.

CHAPTER 7
———

HICKORY SWORDS

Just before dawn, Cotton, standing the final guard, stirred
up the embers and added more wood to the fire. He fed the
horses some grain and made a pot of tea. When the brew
was ready he awakened the others, Lord Kian first and
Perry last. As daytide crept upon the land, Perry stumped
to the crystalline stream and splashed cold water on his
face and hands and the back of his neck, making great
whooshing sounds as the icy liquid startled him fully
awake. "Hoo, that's brisk!" he called to the camp. Then
he made his way back and took a bracing hot cup of tea.

Though there was not yet an autumn frost, the morning
was chill, and the fire was most welcome. The five huddled around the campblaze as they sipped hot drink and
breakfasted on dried venison and tough waybread, part of
the supplies obtained by Kian at Woody Hollow. In contrast to his overindulgence at The Root, Anval now ate
adequately but sparingly, as if to conserve the supplies.
Cotton, seeing the Dwarf's behavior and deeming it wise,
held rein on his own voracity, too. And Borin rumbled,
"Well done, Waeran Cotton, I see you learn travellers'
ways quickly. Fear not, though: our short-rations fast will
be broken tomorrow night when we reach Stonehill."

"With prime fare, too," reassured his fellow trencher,
Anval. "Yesterweek, as we came to the Boskydells, we
found that the White Unicorn sets a fine table—as good as
any in the Lands."

Lord Kian downed the last of his tea, then made his way
into the meadow to retrieve the hobbled horses. With
Cotton's help, he hitched Brownie and Downy to the
waggon, while Anval, Borin, and Perry broke camp—

dousing the fire, refilling the water bottles and skin, and loading the supplies. Packs were repacked and bedrolls rolled; all were tossed into the waggon. Soon the travellers were back on the road, the wain rolling for Stonehill, with Anval at the reins.

Though Perry had wanted to examine the figures engraved on the silver horn, he did not get the chance, for the moment they got under way, Cotton turned to Lord Kian and said, ''Well, Sir, seeing as how we're going off to fight Rūcks and such, it seems to me that Mister Perry and me are going to need to know something about what we'll be fighting—if you catch my drift, Sir.''

''Indeed I do 'catch your drift,' Cotton,'' said Kian, smiling, yet looking with respect at the canny Waerling, ''for to know more of your enemy than he knows of you gains vantage in battle.

''Withal, there are three of the enemy. First, the eld Rukha: foul creatures of ancient origin, of yore as numberless as worms in the earth, puff-adder-eyed, wide-gapped slit-mouthed, skinny-armed and bandy-legged, round-bellied, bat-wing-eared, small but tenacious, no taller than Dwarves, crude in the arts of battle but overwhelming in their very numbers. Second, the Lōkha: evil spawned by Gyphon, cruel masters of Rukha and Trolls, in appearance Rukh-like but tall as a Man, strong and skilled in battle, limited in number. Third and last, Trolls: enormous creatures—some say a giant Rukh—twice Man height, strong beyond belief, hard as a rock; they need have little or no skill with weaponry, depending instead upon their stone hide to turn aside blades or other arms, and upon their massive strength to crush foes; there are only rumors that any still exist.

''Rukha, Lōkha, and Trolls: all came from the Untargarda —from Neddra—and were stranded in Mithgar by the sundering of the way between the Middle and Lower planes. And they all suffer the Ban and must shun the sunlight, working instead their evil at night—though in Modru's time his malevolent will sustained them during day as well, for the Dimmendark was upon the land, and the Sun shone not.''

''What about Vulgs, Ghûls, and Hèlsteeds?'' asked Perry.
''Ah,'' responded Kian, ''as to them, we think that all

may have perished during the Winter War. The Wolf-like Vulgs, whose virulent fangs wreak death even though the victim is but scratched—''

"Vulg's black bite slays at night," interjected Cotton, reciting the old saw.

"Aye, Wee One," nodded Kian, " 'tis true. But neither Vulgs nor the cloven-hooved, rat-tailed, horse-like Hèlsteeds have been seen among any of the *Spaunen* raiding parties that issue out from Drimmen-deeve. Hence, they may no longer exist upon Mithgar.''

"And the Ghûls?" asked Perry.

"Ghola are not seen either," answered the Man. "And that is well, for they are a dreadful foe: nearly unkillable, taking dire wounds without hurt. Wood through the heart, dismemberment, fire: these are the ways to slay a Ghol.''

"But as I say, neither Vulg, Ghol, nor Hèlsteed has been seen since the Winter War, and I deem we need only concern ourselves with Rukh, Lōkh, and perhaps Troll— Spawn you name Rūck, Hlōk, and Ogru: these three you must be ready for. And so, my wee fledglings, to practice your swordplay to enable you to meet these enemies we need but follow a simple plan: To learn to fight the skilled, Man-sized Lōkha you shall instead fight me; I shall play that part. And to learn to engage the small, unskilled Rukha you shall do battle with each other.'' Here Kian smiled.

"What about the Trolls—the giant Ogrus?" interjected Cotton.

"Though I doubt if any still exist," said Kian, "if we come upon one, then you must flee, or you will be crushed like an ant under heel.''

"Flee? Flee?" protested Perry, taken aback. "Do you counsel us to flee in the midst of battle just because the foe is overlarge? Some would say that is cowardice and is unworthy advice.''

"Perry, Perry, green-Waerling Perry, you know not of what you speak,'' said Kian, shaking his head in rue. "Let me ask you this: If an avalanche were descending upon you, would you oppose it or would you flee? If a raging whirlwind were rending trees from the earth's bosom, would you slash at it with your sword or would you take shelter? Perry, Ogrus are like that: Trollish, nearly unstoppable, almost unkillable. Oh, they can be slain all right: by a great boulder dropped on them from a far height, or a fall from a mountainous precipice, to name two ways; but to slay them in battle is nigh impossible, requiring a fell weapon to be thrust just so: in the groin, or under the eyelid, or in the mouth, or in one or two other places of vulnerability. And even then the weapon may shatter against the Troll, no matter the blade's birthforge, for the Ogru is like a rock: hard and obdurate.''

"Bane! Bane will sorely wound *any* foe," averred Perry in a grim voice, setting his hand to the hilt of his sword. "It was made by the Elves, and it is said that Bane's blade-jewel shines with a blue light if Rūcks or other evil things come near." Swiftly, Perry drew the sword from its scabbard and flashed it to the sky, crying, "Bane! I trust my life to you!"

"Indeed, Bane is a fell weapon of Elvish origin," said Kian, reaching out a gentle hand to touch Perry on the shoulder as the Waerling lowered the glittering blade, "and it may penetrate even the Troll-hide of the Ogrus. But, Perry, Bane is just an Elven-knife, though a long one, and may not reach an Ogru's vitals. Bitterly wounded he may be, but crush you he still will. No, you must flee and let others more able try to vanquish this foe."

Borin, sitting beside Anval on the driver's seat, twisted about and growled, "Even Châkka, as skilled in fighting as we are, give Trolls wide berth, yielding back rather than doing battle. But if we must, we will attack in strength; great numbers of axes are needed to slay an Ogru. Even then, many warriors will perish."

Somewhat disconcerted by Kian's but especially by Borin's words, grim-lipped Perry slipped Bane back into the scabbard fastened to his pack. Cotton vowed, "Well you can be sure, right enough, that if ever I see a great Trollish Ogru he won't see me: I'm going to take to my heels and fly!"

Kian smiled at Cotton's words, then grew serious once more. "Heed me now," he said. "Time is short and much needs doing. We must take advantage of every moment to train you at swords. While travelling in the waggon we will speak on the art of swords and the strategy of fighting Rukha and Lōkha—for your tactics must vary according to the size of your opponent, the weapon he is wielding, and the armor he is wearing and bearing. And at each of our stops to rest the horses we will put that art and strategy into practice, drilling at swords.''

"But we've only been stopping a short while each hour," protested Cotton. "Is that enough time to learn? What I mean to ask, Sir, is, well, with such a little bit of practice, will we actually be able to fight Rūcks and Hlōks?''

Upon hearing Cotton's question, a surge of uncertainty washed through Perry, for now that it had come to the reality of beginning to learn swordplay, the buccan felt strangely reluctant to be schooled in the art of killing—as if some inner voice were saying, *Not for you, Warrow*.

Kian noted this hesitancy in Perry's eyes, and he knew that it was now or never: he had to start the training immediately, for it was vital that these gentle Waerlinga be able to defend themselves. "Let me show you, Cotton, Perry," he said, and turned to Anval, at the reins. "Anval, stop here. We must begin now."

Anval pulled off the road and into the eaves of the bordering woods. All jumped down from the waggon, Borin tending the horses. And then Kian revealed the product of his previous night's whittling: three swords made of hickory limb—two Warrow-sized and one Man-sized—blunt-tipped and dull-edged: the wood was green and supple and not apt to break. Unlike some who would have been chagrined at wielding wooden "toys," both Warrows seemed relieved at not having to practice with real weapons.

Kian allowed them each in turn to do unschooled "battle" with him, Cotton stepping back to allow Perry to "have the first go." The buccan started timidly, but the Man cried, "Ho, Waerling! Be not afraid of hurting me! Swing hard! Though I am not a real enemy, you must learn to strike with force as well as with finesse!"

With this encouragement, soon Perry was slashing and hacking at Lord Kian with abandon, yet the Man fended off the crude assaults with ease. Shortly, the Warrow began to see that swordplay was more than just wild swinging; furthermore, it came as no small surprise that no matter how cunningly he planned a cut, Lord Kian fended it, seemingly without effort.

When Cotton's turn came he attacked with a furious flurry, the clack of the wooden swords clitter-clattering among the trees of the verging forest, but he, too, could not pierce Lord Kian's defenses. Yet, on his part, the young Man was astonished at the native quickness of this small Folk. Each Warrow was breathless and panting in a matter of minutes; but their exuberance had grown, and each had collapsed upon the ground in laughter at the end of his turn at mock battle, whooping and guffawing at his own ineptness. Even so, they had passed the first hurdle; and now they were ready to begin their genuine schooling, with its slow, step-by-step, often tedious buildup of skill.

Much to the buccen's surprise, as breathless as they were, only a short while had passed; even so, it was time to get under way again. As the wain rolled back onto the road, Lord Kian began their formal instruction: "For your swords to be effective weapons in battle, the grip is critical: hold it too tightly and you cannot move the weapon quickly enough; hold it too loosely and you will forfeit your sword at first engagement. You must grasp the weapon as if it were a small live bird, firm enough so that it cannot escape your hand and fly away, yet gentle enough so as not to crush its life. . . ." And thus, in the bed of a rolling waggon, the young Lord began their first lesson, each Warrow repeatedly grasping his sword under Kian's critical eye while he spoke of defense against the *Spaunen*.

At their next stop, their drill followed the lesson of the wain: the grip. Lord Kian directed the buccen to deliberately grasp the sword too loosely, and showed that this would lead to their being disarmed immediately; then the opposite was purposely tried, where too hard a grip was used, so that the Warrows could experience the limited speed of response and the swift tiring of the wrist and forearm.

As the waggon got under way once more, Cotton exclaimed, "Well now, not only do I understand the right way to hold a sword, but the wrong way too! I like the way you teach, Lord Kian, and that's a fact!"

"It is the way I was taught, Cotton," replied the Man. "Not only did I learn the fit ways of fundamental swordsmanship, but the unfit ways as well, the differences between them, why some ways are superior to others, and, as it is in your case, how they all relate to fighting *Spaunen*. Yes, Cotton, my own swordmaster taught me by this means, and a good method it is.''

"Tried and true," rumbled Borin, then fell silent.

"Well, in any event," interjected Perry, "if what I've learned about the grip alone is any example of how well your approach works, then I just hope that you continue it throughout our journey.''

"Fear not, Wee One," responded Kian, "I plan on doing just that; in the days that follow, there'll be little or no time for aught else.

"Now, let us speak of balance: When facing a foe . . ." And again the Man took up the lessons of the sword, and the Warrows listened intently as the waggon rolled toward the next stop.

On that first day alone, by the time they reached their evening campsite on the southern slopes of the Battle Downs just after sunset, the Warrows not only knew how to grip a sword, but also the importance of balance, several stances, and how to fall and roll with a weapon in hand. And though they had not again crossed swords in mock battle, after but a single day's training, Perry and Cotton, though rank beginners, knew more about swordplay than nearly all other Warrows in the history of the Boskydells. And the two buccen were to become much more skilled in the long days ahead.

That night Cotton sat on a log near the campfire, polishing his Atalar sword with a soft red-flannel cloth. The golden runes inlaid along the silver blade glistened and sparkled in the firelight. For long moments Perry lay on his bedding and watched Cotton work, then reflected, "Your steel, Cotton, is but a long-knife to a Big Man, yet a full-sized sword to a Warrow. Recall, your blade was found north of here, in an ancient barrow, in the clutch of a long-dead seer of the Lost Land. Though nothing is known of its early years after forging, that weapon has a noble history after its finding—for it saved Gildor from the evil Krakenward.''

Cotton paused in his rubbing, and his voice took on the rhythm of a chant as he recited the runes that foretold that deed:

"Blade shall brave vile Warder
From the deep black slime."

"Just so," replied Perry, sleepily yawning. "That is the very same long-knife Galen used to hack at the Monster when it grasped Gildor, and the Elf was saved; Gildor, of course, later saved Tuck; and Tuck at last slew the 'Stone; and so it rightly can be said that because of that keen-edged sword you hold, Modru finally met his end."

"Lor," breathed Cotton upon hearing these words. And he returned to his task with renewed vigor, the cloth in his hand fairly dancing over the golden runes; and Perry fell aslumber among the sparkling shards of glistering light.

The third day of the journey was much like the second, with sword lessons in the waggon bed and practice drills with hickory swords whenever the horses were given rest periods. The Sun climbed upward through the morning and passed overhead to begin its long fall unto the night as slowly the travellers wended their way toward the hamlet of Stonehill.

Stonehill, with its hundred or so stone houses, was a hillside village on the western fringes of the sparsely settled Wilderland. But because the hamlet was situated at the junction where the east-west Crossland Road intersected the Post Road running north and south, strangers and out-of-towners were often seen—in fact, were welcomed. Stonehill's one inn, the White Unicorn, with its many rooms, usually had at least one or two wayfarers as well as a couple of nearby settlers staying overnight: travelling crafters and traders, merchants, or a Man and his wife from a faraway farmstead. . . . But occasionally there would be some *real* strangers, such as a company of journeying Dwarves, or King's soldiers from the south, or a Realmsman or two; in which case the local folk would be sure to drop in to the common room of the inn to have a mug and hear the news from far away.

On this night, as the waggon rolled onto the causeway over the dike and into the village through the west gate of the high guard wall, there was only one guest in the 'Unicorn: a distant farmer who had come to the hillside hamlet to buy his winter supplies, and who had gone to

bed with the setting of the Sun. Thus, when the two
Warrows, the Man, and the two Dwarves stepped in through
the front door, the proprietor, Mister Aylesworth Brewster, was pleased to see more guests for his inn; he bustled
to meet them, moving his large bulk past the long-table
where sat several locals who looked up from their pipes
and mugs at this strangely mixed set of wayfarers. They'd
seen Dwarves, of course, but not many. And Warrows
were not a strange people to them, since many of the Wee
Folk lived in the Weiunwood over the hill—though travelling Warrows were not very common. Men of course were
not at all uncommon. However, for the three Folk—Man,
Dwarf, and Warrow—to be travelling together, well, that
was an event never before seen.

*Lor, look there! Well that's a strange sight if ever I saw
one. I wonder if they're together or just came in the door
at the same time. Oh, they're together all right. See:
they're talking together. Dwarves, they don't talk to just
anyone, only other Dwarves, or those in their party, or
those they're doin' business with. Dwarves is close people,
right enough. The little uns are most likely from the Bosky,
by their accent; but the Man, well, he has the look of a
Realmsman, if you ask me.*

Ignoring the hum at the long-table, Aylesworth stepped
up to Lord Kian, his ruddy features brightening. "Well
now, Sir, welcome back to the White Unicorn. Will you
and your party be staying overnight?" At the young Lord's
nod, Aylesworth glanced out the front window at the team
and wain. "Ho, Bill!" he called. Responding to the innkeeper's cry, a slender young Man popped out from behind a door. "See to these folks' waggon and horses
whilst I fixes 'em up with rooms."

As Bill hurried to stable the team and house the wain,
Mister Brewster led the wayfarers out of the common
room and into one of the spacious wings that contained the
guest quarters. The White Unicorn was accustomed to
housing Men, Dwarves, and even an occasional Warrow;
thus its rooms were suitable for the various sizes of the
guests. Hence, Lord Kian was escorted to Man-sized quarters, and two more rooms with small-sized furnishings
were shown to the others: Anval and Borin in one, Perry
and Cotton in the other. As he was getting his guests

situated, Aylesworth suggested, "If you want to eat, there's a lamb on the spit that Molly will have ready in two quick shakes. In any case, you're welcome to join us in the common room for a bit of ale." And, wiping his hands on his white apron, he went bustling back down the hall.

Perry and Cotton quickly stepped into their quarters and removed their cloaks and began washing the dust off their hands and faces. "I don't mind telling you, Sir, I'm hungry as a spring bear, what with all this travelling and the exercise we've been getting with the swords," announced Cotton, splashing water on the back of his neck. "And I have a need for a mug or three of old Brewster's beer to wash down some of that dry Crossland Road grit."

"Me, too, Cotton," laughed Perry, wiping his wet face with a towel. "I've been anticipating the taste of the 'Unicorn's ale ever since we sighted Stonehill. By the way, I don't think we should advertise where we're going or why. Oh, not that it's a secret, but I just feel that if anyone asks, then Borin or Anval should decide what to say about our mission."

Having made themselves presentable, the buccen eagerly left their chamber and hastened down the hall to the common room. They threaded their way among the tables and chairs and past the curious locals to a board prepared by Aylesworth. The news had travelled like lightning, and the ranks of the Stonehill folk had swelled considerably, for many had come to see for themselves the oddly mixed group of wayfarers. In fact, every now and again another local would arrive and make his way to join a friend already there to find out what was afoot.

Gratefully accepting the two frothy mugs offered by a large, cheerful Woman—Molly Brewster, the innkeeper's wife—Cotton and Perry quickly discovered that the 'Unicorn's ale was just as tasty as the rumors back in the Boskydells made it out to be. Soon Borin, then Kian, and finally Anval joined the Warrows; and after a bit they all dug into a fine meal of roast lamb while listening to the songs being sung by the people gathered 'round the longtable. And they could hear Molly's robust soprano joining in from the kitchen as harried Bill popped in and out serving lamb to those who ordered it.

Surrounded by song, and partaking of good food and fine ale, the companions passed a pleasant hour.

The five had just finished their meal when one of the locals—a Warrow, as it were—began singing, and all at the long-table joined in chorus; though rustic, the song brought Perry to the edge of his seat:

> *From northern wastes came Dimmendark,*
> *It stalked down through the Land;*
> *Behind black wall was Winternight,*
> *Ruled by cruel Modru's hand.*
>
>> *Our Men and Elves and Warrows, all,*
>> *Stood fast in Brotherhood;*
>> *Left hearth and home and lofty hall*
>> *To band in Weiunwood.*
>
> *The Rūcks and Ghûls reaved through the Land,*
> *As Gron put forth its might;*
> *Before them not a one could stand*
> *In bitter Winternight.*
>
>> *But overhill in Weiunwood*
>> *The battle plans were laid,*
>> *To ply the strength of Brotherhood,*
>> *And arrow, pike, and blade.*
>
> *And nearer came the Rūckish Spawn,*
> *And closer came the Ghûl.*
> *The Dimmendark held back the dawn,*
> *The Land felt Modru's rule.*
>
>> *In Weiunwood—as Gron drew near—*
>> *The Allies' trap was laid,*
>> *With Warrow arrow, Man-borne pike,*
>> *And gleaming Elven-blade.*
>
> *Into the Weiunwood Gron came,*
> *Pursuing Elvenkind,*
> *Who ran before them in false fear*
> *And drew the Spawn behind.*
>
>> *In Weiunwood the trap was sprung*
>> *By Warrow, Elf, and Man;*
>> *They whelmed the Spawn, and it is sung*
>> *The Ghûlen rabble ran.*

Old Arbagon, he killed him eight,
And Bockleman got nine.
Though Uncle Bill, he got there late,
They say he did just fine.

> *The Men and Warrows and the Elves,*
> *In bravery they fought.*
> *Though many a good friend there was killed,*
> *They didn't die for nought.*

Modru, he raged and stormed and gnashed
When Spawn came running out;
They'd entered Weiunwood in pride,
But left it in a rout!

> *And all throughout the Winter War*
> *Vile Spawn again did try,*
> *But never took the Weiunwood;*
> *They had to pass it by.*

And so, my friend, drink to War's end,
It happened long ago.
But should it ever come again,
To Weiunwood we'll go.

> *And Arbagon, he'll kill him eight,*
> *While Bockleman gets nine.*
> *And Uncle Bill, oh he'll be late,*
> *But he will do just fine . . .*
> *And as for me . . . I won't be late . . .*
> *And I will do just fine—HEY!*

A glad shout and a great burst of laughter rang throughout the inn with the final *HEY!* at the end of the rustic
song. And all banged their mugs on the tables for more
ale; Brewster and his helper, Bill, rushed hither and thither
topping off tankards from large pitchers that Molly filled at
the tap as the rollicking gaiety continued, cheer echoing
throughout the rafters.

Amid the babble and happy chatter, Cotton burst out,
"What a corking good song! Why, it's all about the
Weiunwood and the Winter War and everything!"

"Weiunwood," mused Lord Kian, swirling his ale and
taking a sip. "The Wilderland holt that never fell: an island

of freedom deep within the clasp of Modru's Winternight—
hurling back his assaults or melting away before his force
only to strike unexpectedly into a weakness. And Modru's
iron grip could not close on those 'puny' forest fighters,
for it was like trying to clutch the wind.''

"Just so, Lord Kian," responded Perry. "And even
though the Stonehill song only narrowly reflects the heroic
deeds done in that place, still I must record it for the
Raven Book, for it has spirit and it is a song I've never
heard before. The Scholars will want it.''

Perry stood and stepped to the long-table and sat down
with the buccan who had started the song.

Later that night, as he and Cotton were climbing into
their beds, Perry remarked, "Isn't it strange, Cotton? Though
those folks knew and enjoyed the song, they didn't know
its origin or the full part that Stonehill played in the War.''

"Well, Sir, it took the Boskydells to set 'em right, sure
enough, what with you tellin' them the story in the *Raven
Book* and all,'' replied Cotton, recalling with pride how
Perry had enthralled the Stonehillers with a tale of Tuck
and the Myrkenstone. Perry had explained how the verses
in the song related to what had happened. The folks in the
'Unicorn were delighted to discover that the roles that
Stonehill and Weiunwood had played in the War were
actually recorded in a book. But happiest of all was
Aylesworth Brewster, for Perry affirmed that the Bockleman
of the song was Aylesworth's ancestor, Bockleman Brewster, owner of the inn during the War. "Mister Perry,''
continued Cotton, yawning sleepily, "in the song there
was a part about the Rūcks and such runnin' away. Do you
reckon they all ran to the Deeves?''

"Oh no, Cotton, the Spawn didn't all run straight to
Drimmen-deeve, for the War went on long after—though
we now know that many finally made their way there. I
suppose that most of the maggot-folk perished in the War.''
He paused a moment; then: "Oh, that reminds me: I
overheard Lord Kian talking to one of the Stonehill folk,
and when he found out that we were going to Landover
Road Ford, he warned Lord Kian that there were 'Yrm'
south on the Great Argon River—'heard it from a trader,'
he said.'' Perry's face took on a worried frown. "Things
must be bad down there, Cotton, for people way up north

here in Stonehill to hear about it. Cotton, do you think we've bitten off more than we can chew? Maybe we're just fooling ourselves by thinking we can become Rūck fighters.''

Cotton did not respond to Perry's question; in fact, he had not even heard it, for he was already fast asleep. Perry sighed, blew out the lamp, and crawled under the covers of his bed. But though he was weary, slumber escaped him.

Something had been nibbling at the edge of Perry's thoughts all evening, but he couldn't bring it forth. He lay for a time watching the flickering shadows cast by the dying fire on the hearth, unable to go to sleep immediately.

Finally, after a long while, just as he was drifting away, it came to him, and he bolted upright in bed. *The horn! That's it! I must look at the horn!*

Igniting a taper from the embers in the fireplace, he relighted the lamp and turned it up full. Fetching the silver horn from Cotton's pack, he held it next to the lantern and peered closely at the riders. The clarion was ancient, and the engraving was dearly worn by the many hands that had held it through the ages. But faintly, and only faintly, upon the faces of the riders could be discerned the dim traces of forked beards—a feature throughout all history borne only by Dwarves.

CHAPTER 8

SHOOTING STARS AND TALK
OF WAR

"Hammers and nails!" shouted Cotton, waking Perry from his sound sleep in time to hear the sharp rapping on the door. "Don't beat the door down! Come in, come in!" Perry opened his eyes just as the door flew open and Aylesworth Brewster, bearing a lantern, bustled across the room and threw back the drapes. Faint grey light showed that it was foredawn; the Sun had not yet crept over the horizon.

"Wake up, little masters," said Aylesworth as he lit the room lamp, "the day is adawning and the others tell me it's time you were afoot. Your bath awaits you in the bathing room, and breakfast is on Molly's griddle, so don't tarry." And with that he rushed from the room leaving the two Warrows sitting up in their beds rubbing sleep from their eyes.

"*Oooahhum,*" yawned Perry, stretching to his fullest. "Well, Cotton, it certainly isn't like living at The Root, this getting up before the Sun. But I suppose if we must, then we must." He slipped out of bed, and in his nightshirt, made for the door. Reluctantly, Cotton followed him, yawning all the way. They went down the hall to the bathing room, where they found Bill pouring hot water into a pair of large wooden tubs bound 'round with copper hoops. Soon the two Warrows were splashing and wallowing and sloshing in water and suds, occasionally splashing some over the rim and onto the stone floor. They were in a hurry and so did not loll or sing—though they chattered as gaily as ever.

"You were correct, Cotton," Perry said as they were towelling off, "the riders on the Horn of Valon are Dwarves all right, which helps to explain why no one has been able to read the runes. I think they must be written in the secret Dwarf tongue—Châkur. I wonder what they say.''

"Well, whatever they say, Sir, we'll not find it out from Anval or Borin, you can bet your last penny on that,'' said Cotton. "When it comes to that horn, they're as close-mouthed a pair as we'll ever see. Why, we'd get more out of a couple of rocks as we're likely to get out of them two.''

Quickly the two buccen returned to their chamber and dressed, then snatched up their packs, blew out the lamp, and hurried to the common room. There Anval, Borin, and Lord Kian were waiting. As the Warrows entered the room Aylesworth called, "Oh ho, little sirs, you're just in time for hot sausage and eggs.'' And with that he began serving them Molly's fare.

Across the room sat the farmer, Aylesworth's other guest. Throughout the meal he stared curiously at the mixed group, wondering what he'd missed the evening before by going to bed at his usual time of sundown. He was later to be told by Bill that "them five knew everything there was to know about Stonehill,'' and that "everything in all the old songs is true,'' and finally that "Aylesworth's ancestor, Bockleman Brewster, and nearly everyone else that lived in Stonehill at the time, fought and practically won the Winter War single-handedly.'' In his later years the farmer would often tell of the time that he and the Drimmen-deeve Rūck-fighters all stayed at the White Unicorn together. But for now he merely sat at breakfast watching the others eat and prepare for the road.

Bill had hitched up Brownie and Downy, and he loaded two full burlap sacks into the waggon—grain to feed the horses on the way to Landover Road Ford. Then he drove the wain 'round front just as Cotton stepped through the door. Cotton rummaged among the waggon supplies and came up with two carrots, one for each horse, which they eagerly accepted, then nuzzled him for more—for ever since leaving The Root the buccan had been giving the horses a carrot or an apple apiece each day; and he spoke gently to them. Cotton scratched each steed between the eyes, then helped load up to be off. By this time the Sun had climbed over the rim of the world and was casting its glancing light across the countryside. Clambering into the waggon, the travellers bade goodbye to Aylesworth and Bill, and to Molly, who popped out just long enough to say farewell before popping back inside.

Mister Brewster stood at the door of the inn wiping his hands on his white apron and watched the clattering wain til it went around the turn and out of sight. "Come on, Bill, there's work to be done," he finally said, and the two of them went back into the White Unicorn.

As the waggon rolled through the gate in the east wall, leaving the cobblestones of Stonehill behind, returning to the hard-packed earth of the Crossland Road, Lord Kian began instructing the Warrows on the forehand, backhand, and overhand sword strokes—how to deliver them and how to parry them—as he resumed their education in warfare. These lessons were to dominate every waking hour of the journey for the next fortnight or so. Oh, that is not to say that the travellers didn't speak of or do other things, or occasionally break out in song, for they did that and much else too—but only when each lesson was over: not before, not during, but after.

At the fourth or fifth stop of the day—after Perry and Cotton had absorbed in their earlier lessons some of the fundamentals of strokes, thrusts, and parries—Lord Kian again allowed them to do mock battle against him. This time, though he fended without being touched, he had a much more difficult engagement with each, for Warrows learn rapidly; and though they are not fleet, they are incredibly quick, and at times they pressed even Kian's skill to defend against their swift thrusts. Though he could have dispatched either buccan at will, the Man was well satisfied with their rapid progress. Again the Warrows whooped and laughed at the end of their engagement. Each was pleased with his own skill agrowing, and could see that the other was progressing as well. But what delighted them most was that each had not quite but almost touched Lord Kian.

"All right, my little cock-a-whoops," promised the Man above their gay braggadocio, tying his yellow hair back with a green headband, "at the next stop I will press you a bit to begin to sharpen up your defensive skills.

"Now listen, when an opponent comes at you with an overhand stroke, you can step to the side and let the blow slide away on your own blade by . . ." And in the back of the rolling waggon the lessons went on, and on, and on, for the ten or so hours each day that they were on the road; and for about ten minutes in each of these hours, Cotton and Perry drilled, ingraining through practice the art of swords. And though some would say that there were not enough days left for the Warrows to become sufficiently skilled at battle, as in other times and other places the press of War left no choice.

The first evening out of Stonehill the wayfarers camped in the woods north of the Bogland Bottoms; yet the plaguey gnats of these fens were not a problem, for the nights were now too chill.

The next day the five pressed on, and the evening of the sixth day of the journey from Woody Hollow found them encamped on the western slopes of Beacontor, a weathered mount at the southern end of the chain of the ancient Signal Mountains, a range so timeworn by wind and water that it was but a set of lofty hills. Beacontor had been the site of the First Watchtower, now but a remnant of a bygone era; the ruins still could be seen on the crest of the hill; the jagged ring of tumbled stonework yet stood guard in the Wilderland between Stonehill and Arden. Neither Perry nor Cotton nor anyone else in the party climbed up the tor to see the remains. Instead, the Warrows made the most of their last short practice session, and then they helped pitch camp; by this time it was dark, so they would have seen little of the ruins anyway. As before, during the night they each took a turn at ward.

It was midwatch when Borin wakened Perry for the buccan's stand at guard. The night was brilliant with stars, the air so crisp and clear that the Bright Veil seemed close enough to grasp, spreading its shimmering band from east to west across the star-studded sky. Perry noted that Borin seemed reluctant to turn in, preferring instead to gaze in wonder at the countless glints scintillating above in the spangled vault. "You seem spellbound by the heavens, Borin," remarked Perry.

"It is not often we Châkka come out from under the

Mountains and see the stars, friend Perry," replied Borin. "They are special to us: more brilliant than the brightest diamonds we delve, more precious than all we have ever or will ever unearth. They are celestial gems coursing through the night above—changeless, eternal, except for the five known wanderers that slowly shift across the wheeling pattern of the others; but even these nomads, in time, cycle through the same long journeys. Aye, the stars *are* special, for they give us their light to steer by—that one yon is forever fixed in the north—and they tell us the time of season or the depth of the night or the nearness of dawn. Never can we craft anything to rival their beauty or purpose, though we have striven to do so through the ages. We believe that each star has some special meaning—though we known not what it is—and that destiny and omens are sometimes written in the glittering patterns."

Perry was filled with a sense of discovery at hearing Borin speak thus of the stars. The Warrow had seen them all his life, and til this moment he had not considered the impact that the heavenly display would have upon those who lived most of their lives under the mountains. Perry gazed with new eyes at the celestial blaze, entranced as if he had never before seen its glory. And as he watched a streak flashed across the sky, flaring and coruscating, leaving behind a trail of golden fire that slowly faded. "Borin!" he cried, pointing. "Did you see that shooting star?" His voice was full of excitement, thrilled at the display. But Borin had cast his hood over his head and was looking somberly down at the earth. "What's the matter, Borin?" asked Perry, disturbed by this dark change in his companion and wanting to help.

"When a star falls it foretells that a friend, too, will soon fall and die," replied Borin. And without uttering another word the Dwarf went to his bedroll and lay down and did not look at the sky again that night.

The next morning, as the wayfarers broke camp, Perry looked up at the ruins on the crest of Beacontor and remarked, "If ever we come this way again I'd like to see the remains of the old Watchtower; they mark an age of greatness." Anval glanced sharply at Perry and seemed troubled, but said nothing.

That day and the following were much the same as those that had gone before, and the waggon slowly rolled eastward, finally coming to the western edge of the Wilderness Hills.

Dawn of the ninth day of the journey found the skies overcast, and as the five got under way beneath the dismal glower, Lord Kian predicted rain by nightfall.

The instruction went on as always, and Anval and Borin continued to take turns driving the waggon. Though progress with the sword training was rapid, the mood of the travellers was as glum as the brooding skies. Except for Lord Kian's instructions and an occasional question from either Perry or Cotton, little was said, and no songs were sung. Even the landscape seemed unredeeming, consisting of monotonous, relatively barren, uniform hills.

To dispel this gloomy mood and restore their former high spirits, Lord Kian decided to advance one stage of the training. Looking somberly at Perry and Cotton, he announced, "It is time you each fought your first Rukh."

"Wha . . . what? Rūck?" Perry's heart leapt to his mouth, and he looked quickly all around.

Cotton, also, scrambled to his knees and held on to a waggon sideboard, searching the empty countryside for an enemy. "Hey, now, just a moment here, it's daylight," protested Cotton, plopping back down. "Rūcks won't be about in the daytime."

Kian broke out in laughter, and the two Dwarves smiled. Perry, realizing that Cotton was right, slumped back into the waggon in relief. "No, no," said Kian, "not real Rukha. What I meant is that at our next stop you shall cross wooden swords with one another. But wear your armor; henceforth you shall train in battle dress."

By the time they rolled to a stop in a sparse roadside glade with a thin stream running along the eastern tree line, both Warrows were armored and wore their empty scabbards—leaving their true swords in the waggon.

At first when they faced one another, neither seemed eager to strike, and they began a timid tap-tapping engagement. Lord Kian, seeing the reluctance of two friends to confront one another, stopped them momentarily. Using blue clay from the banks of the stream, he daubed their faces, giving each a hollow-eyed, sunken-cheeked appearance, and made their mouths look broader and thinner and their eyebrows long and slanted. He turned each of their helms backwards on their heads and then had them face one another again. "There now," he said in a deep, sepulchral voice, "before you stands a Rukh." All broke out in raucous laughter, in the midst of which Cotton leapt forward with Rūck-like treachery and took a broad overhand cut at Perry; and the battle was on:

Though Cotton was stronger, Perry was more agile, and the duel between the two was an even match. During one engagement Perry maneuvered Cotton into falling backwards over a log; but on the other hand Perry was forced by Cotton into the stream bed and spent that contest splashing around in ankle-deep water trying to fight his way back onto the bank held by Cotton. They shouted battle cries and whooped and laughed, or fought long moments in grim silence. It went like this for the full practice: the buccen hacked and stabbed and parried and slashed all around the glen, each "killing" the other at least a half-dozen times. And when Kian called, "Enough!" Cotton and Perry collapsed together in laughter.

They washed away their blue-clay Rūck faces in the stream and climbed back aboard the waggon, chattering happily with Kian and the Dwarves and laughing over the pratfalls of one another. Even the usually taciturn Anval smiled at their antics, and Borin chuckled, too, as he drove the wain back onto the Crossland Road. Kian's tactic had worked: the somber mood had been broken.

The lessons went on in high spirits as Kian, using examples from the battle to illustrate his points, spoke on many things, such as the importance of holding the high ground and of knowing the obstacles behind as well as the enemy before. Every now and again the buccen broke out in broad laughter at mention of some blunder occasioned in their battle, but Kian drove home the lesson.

That evening the travellers pulled off the road next to a wooded draw. They could feel rain approaching on the wind across the Dellin Downs and over the valley of the Wilder River. The coming storm promised to be a heavy one, for as Cotton remarked, "This is sure to be a real frog strangler; why, the leaves on the trees have been turned right 'round backwards all day.'' All looked to the south and west and could see a dark wall of rain stalking the land and marching toward their campsite.

Among the trees, Anval and Borin skillfully used their axes to hastily construct a large, crude lean-to out of saplings as proof against the rain, with two smaller slant-roofs to either side. The Warrows scurried thither and yon to gather a supply of dry firewood and place it under shelter. And Kian unhitched the team, leading the horses beneath the eaves of the wood and tethering them in the protection of the trees. The companions had but barely finished pre-paring their camp when the first drops began to fall, followed by an onslaught of water cascading from the black skies.

It rained all that night, and though the watch was kept, the guard's main duty was to tend the fire under the large lean-to, for nought could be seen or heard beyond the curtain of hard-driven rain. Kian spent his watch shaping some new wooden swords, for the old ones were badly tattered from the beatings they had received; each of the other guardians simply kept up the fire in his own turn and huddled close to the blaze to ward away the wetness.

Toward morning the rain slackened as the storm moved away to the east, and by dawn it was gone and only the leaves dripped water to the ground. The Sun rose to a freshly washed land, and the day was to be crisp and bright with a high blue October sky.

In spite of the storm-troubled sleep, spirits in the wag-gon were as bright and cheerful as the day itself, and after each lesson there was much singing and laughter. In the early afternoon the travellers emerged from the low foot-hills and saw the road falling before them, down and across a short flat to the River Caire, the waterway curving out of the north and disappearing to the south and spar-kling in the midday Sun. Perry, filled with the clarity of the day, burst out in song:

> *The Road winds on before us—*
> *A Path to be unwound,*
> *A surprise around each Corner*
> *Just waiting to be found.*

> *And we, the happy travellers*
> *Who trek upon this way,*
> *Look forward in our eagerness*
> *And glance aback to say:*
>
> *The Road turns there behind us—*
> *A Path that we've unwound.*
> *Yet sights around the Corners*
> *Remain there to be found*
>
> *By those who come behind us*
> *And see what we have seen;*
> *The wonders will be as fresh*
> *As if we'd never been*
>
> *Along this way before them*
> *And gazing on this Land*
> *With beauty spread before us all . . .*
> *I say, oh isn't it Grand!*
>
> *I say, oh isn't it Grand!*

Both Perry and Cotton—who had joined in the singing—burst out in laughter. The hearts of the Man and the Dwarves were uplifted by the simple song the Warrows sang in celebration of the passing countryside. In the words of the song Lord Kian beheld two more facets of the nature of Waerlinga: *Not only do they take pleasure in seeing things of beauty, but they also take pleasure in knowing that others will share these things, too. And this gift of sharing is just one of the things that makes these small Folk special.* The Man was so moved by this knowledge that in the back of the rolling waggon he gruffly hugged Cotton to him with one arm while smiling and tousling Perry's fair hair with his free hand. Yet neither Warrow knew why.

"Ah, my wee Waerlinga," said Kian, "I think that every Kingdom, every court in every Land, needs a few of you little ones to keep up the good spirits and the cheer of the people—oh, not as court jesters, for I deem you too tenderhearted to fulfill that task. Instead, as a small, rustic Folk, close to the earth, of indomitable will and gentle good sense, you would set an example for all to see and hear of living life in the spirit in which it should be lived. You are an openhearted, cheerful, gentle, sturdy Folk, and this old world is leagues ahead of where it would be without you.''

Somewhat embarrassed by the praise, both Cotton and Perry said nought; yet each was pleased by the young Lord's words.

The waggon trundled across the Stone-arches Bridge over the river and came into Rhone, the share-shaped region of land known as the Plow, bounded on one side by the River Caire and on the other by the River Tumble, and extending north to the Rigga Mountains.

The road rose up again out of the river valley and wound into the middle regions of a dark-forested hill country known as Drearwood, in days of old a place of dire repute: Many were the tales of lone travellers or small bands who had ridden into the dim woods never to be seen again. From here, too, came accounts of larger, armored groups that had beaten off grim monsters half glimpsed in the night. And the Land had been shunned by all except those who had no choice but to cross it—or by those who sought fame. Yet no fell creatures had lived in the area for almost three hundred years, since the time of the Great Purging by the Lian Guardians. And the Crossland Road wound among the central regions of this hill country for eighty or so miles.

At sundown the waggon had just come into the beginning western edges of the slopes, and the travellers made camp.

That night was crystal clear, and a gibbous Moon, growing toward fullness, shed bright light over the landscape. When not on watch, each of the wayfarers slept extraordinarily well, partly because their sleep during the rain of the previous night had not been restful, but mainly because this day had gone so well.

The order of the watch remained the same, and at the end of Perry's duty he awakened Anval, this time with a cup of tea ready for the Dwarf. The two sat together in silence for a while, listening to the call of a far-off owl. Perry noted that Anval seemed more than just taciturn; the

Dwarf appeared instead to be brooding. "Does something bother you, Anval?" asked Perry, sipping his own tea and huddling in his cloak.

"Aye, Small One, and it is this: although your feet are set upon one course, your thoughts trace another path; and if you do not change, you will come to great harm," growled the Dwarf. He looked with his eyes of black at the buccan, whose mouth had dropped open in astonishment at Anval's reply. But before Perry could say aught, Anval went on, "You dwell too much in past glories and not enough in the reality of today, Waeran. Heed me: we are marching off to War—not to heroism and grandeur, but to slaying and horror—and I fear what the truth of War will do to you. War is not some Noble Game. Only in time does the vile stench of War become the sweet smell of victory. Whether in ballade or ode or book, History alone looks upon War as a grand achievement; all else look upon it as a dreadful last resort. And you, Perry, seem to see the world through events and eras of the past: past Kingdoms, past glories, past deeds, past trials, past victories. But time dims the horrors of those events and magnifies the good. We Châkka have a saying:

> "The Past, the Present, the Future,
> Time's Road winds through all three.
> Live for Today, but think of Tomorrow;
> Yesterday is just Memory."

Anval's black, forked beard shone darkly in the firelight. "You must forgo the past, Perry, and live for today, and tomorrow."

"But Anval," protested Perry, disturbed by the acuity of the Dwarf's insight, "we Warrows, too, have a saying:

> "Yesterday's Seeds are Tomorrow's Trees".

"The past points toward the future. By looking into history we can at times foretell events to come. Our quest could have been foretold: Dwarves were driven from Drimmen-deeve long ago and now seek to return, but Spawn were driven *into* Drimmen-deeve back when Gron fell, and War will result. So you see, Anval, yesterday's seeds *are* tomorrow's trees."

"Only if tended today do seeds grow into trees," gritted Anval. "Yesterday's deeds are but shadows of the past and are dead and gone, and tomorrow's are but visions of the future and are yet to come. The deeds of today are the images of import. Shun not the present and forfeit not the future in order to live on past glories, for that is the way of the Historian who dreams of glory and sees not horror. Your spirit will be crushed and you may even be slain if you follow the Historian's storybook way into the reality of War."

"But Anval," said Perry quietly, "I *am* a Historian."

"Oh no, little one, now you are a *warrior*." Anval turned and stared into the night, and in a low voice with driving urgency he declared, "You *must* become a warrior!" The Dwarf then strode to the perimeter and began his watch and said no more.

Perry lay down to sleep, but could not. He was disturbed by Anval's perception, and half denied, half accepted it, but thought, *How can Anval say such things? He tells me that I must forgo the past, as if he and Borin and all of Dwarfdom live that way. Yet, the mere mention of Elgo, Sleeth's Doom, drove both Anval and Borin into a frothing rage, even though Elgo won the Dragon's plunder nearly twenty-six hundred years ago. Forget the past? Hmmph! Do Dwarves? I should say not! I clearly recall Borin saying, "He who seeks the wrath of Dwarves, finds it! Forever!" That's certainly not forgoing the past.*

I think these Folk are full of contradiction: On the one hand they are suspicious; secretive; stiff-necked; proud, belllicose warriors, fierce in battle; and always ready, nay eager, to avenge old wrongs. But on the other hand they are crafters of great skill; steadfast, honorable companions; trusting enough to permit a virtual stranger to guide them in an undertaking of mortal peril; and they seem genuinely concerned over the welfare of newfound comrades. They are enthralled by the beauty of the stars, yet are afraid of their blazing omens. And, to cap it all, they appear to sincerely believe in sayings that fly directly in the face of the darker side of their own manifest nature

*. . . ah, but, in these things, are they different from any
other Folk?*

Yet, what Anval says is *true: I* must *become a warrior!*

And as Perry lay weighing Anval's words and pondering
the nature of Dwarves, he watched the bright Moon sinking behind a dark, western hill; and when the silver orb
was gone, the buccan was fast asleep.

CHAPTER 9

ARDEN FORD

The early morning of the thirteenth day of their journey found the travellers back in the waggon on the east-west Crossland Road, still wending their way toward the eastern margins of the Drearwood. Earlier, they had awakened to find the glades and hills covered with bright frost and the morning air cold and crisp; and they had huddled around the fire, warming themselves with flames and tea until the Sun's rays had spilled over the hillsides and down among the trees. Then they had broken camp and resumed the trek. And as they had ridden east, the frost faded under the Sun's warmth.

The slopes rising around them for the most part provided the only view: thick-coppiced hillsides mounting up, covered with green and bronze and scarlet and yellow-gold foliage. But now and again the waggon would overtop a crest, and to the east, down on the horizon, like a jagged bank of white-tipped low-lying dark clouds, the wayfarers could see the Grimwall. Their destination, the Landover Road Ford, lay on the other side of that somber range. Though the mountains were some distance away, the comrades expected to reach the lower margins by nightfall; they anticipated crossing the River Tumble at Arden Ford by midmorning, and passing Arden by midafternoon, leaving several hours to come among the foothills by sundown. They were aiming to cross the range through the Crestan Pass, the only direct route to Landover Road Ford. Assuming no delays, Kian reckoned that they should reach the banks of the Argon River in just six more days. There they planned to make camp and wait for Durek and the Army, due to arrive about ten days hence.

But for now, the land began falling steadily as the wain drew closer to the valley of the Tumble River. The sword training continued, and just after the fourth stop in the morning, the travellers followed the road through a dark pine forest and then into a grey-rock-walled pass cutting a lengthy slot through the saddle joining two hills.

The horses' hooves and waggon wheels echoed hollowly as they pulled through the long notch, but the echoes diminished and finally died as they emerged from the sheer-walled cleft. "Lor! Look at that!" cried Cotton, pointing ahead.

Before them the wayfarers saw the land fall steeply to a mile-wide flat running to the river where the shallow Arden Ford should have been, but was not. The valley was flooded! The river was raging: roiling water raced and plunged along the course, overspreading the banks and running far up onto the flatland. Both Anval and Borin vented bitter oaths.

"What has happened, Lord Kian?" asked Perry, looking upon the torrent. "The river looks as if it has gone quite mad, and the ford cannot be crossed."

"I do not know for certain," answered Kian, shading his eyes and gazing east and then pointing. Directly ahead in the near distance they could see the Grimwall Mountains; the jagged range marched out of the north and away to the south, a colossal barrier to cross should they ever breast the flood. "Mayhap the storm of four nights past was trapped upon the teeth of the mountains, and all its rain plunged onto the slopes and into the vales that issue into this valley, flooding it."

Cotton thought about the intensity and duration of the storm and tried to envision the enormous amount of water released on the walls of the mountains to flow down the watercourses to come to this place. He looked once more at the raging river below. "We couldn't even cross that in a boat, could we? Or a raft? No, I didn't think so. Well, Old Man Tumble has got us trapped here, right enough."

"And the problem is that there's not another way around, nor a bridge to cross, nor a ferry within hundreds of miles," said Kian, answering Borin's unspoken question. "We must cross here. Our only recourse is to wait for the waters to subside. Til then, we are blocked.

"Even so, in one way we are fortunate, for it was rain that fell everywhere and not snow, even in the high mountains; and though the ford is flooded, the Crestan Pass still seems to be open—not choked off by white. And this flood before us will eventually ebb. . . . When? I cannot say; yet ebb it will."

They camped high on the slope near the outlet of the rock-walled pass. Anval cut some stakes with his axe and walked the mile down to the edge of the rushing flood and there drove one of the wooden shafts into the earth as a marker. He then marched straight away from the water and every five paces planted another stake until there were five altogether. Cotton, who had gone with Anval, hefted a small round stone and eyed the far shore, then threw with all his might; with a splash, the stone fell short of the far bank by ten yards. He tried again with virtually identical results. Shaking his head in resignation, he trudged after Anval toward the camp.

"We will track the march of the water by using the stakes as a gauge," declared Anval to Cotton as they tramped back. "The place where I drove the markers had not yet been under flood. I deem the water is still rising." They looked back and could see that even now the first stake was being encroached upon. With a sigh from the buccan and an oath from the Dwarf, they turned and continued on toward the encampment.

Even a deluge, however, did not affect the sword instruction except to dampen somewhat the spirited play. And between lessons the five eyed the water's advance, trying to judge whether or not the river was beginning to crest. By sundown the Warrows had reached the stage where they were learning about shields and bucklers: their use, their strengths, and their weaknesses. And the water was still rising, having reached the third stake. Grumbling, Anval marched down in the twilight and drove five more markers.

That night, at each change of the watch, the guard being relieved went in the moonlight with a flaming brand to check the flood, passing the information on to the one remaining on ward. At the beginning of Perry's turn, Borin strode down to the river and looked, and the water had reached the fifth stake; at the end of Perry's watch, the buccan awakened Anval and then went to note the stage of the overflow, and it was still at the fifth marker. Perry returned to camp and reported to Anval and then fell asleep, dejected by this barrier.

It seemed that Perry had no sooner closed his eyes than he was jolted awake by Cotton whooping and laughing in the dawn: "It's goin' down! It's goin' down! It's between the fifth and fourth! Old Man Tumble is creeping back to his bed!"

Perry jumped up and ran with the others to the water's edge and saw that sometime in the night the crest had passed, and the river, though still raging and boiling, was at last receding.

All that day they watched the water's slow retreat back toward its original course. The sword training progressed at a faster pace than usual because questions or points could be illustrated instantly in false combat or in the practice drills without having to wait for a waggon-stop. This day Lord Kian showed the quick Warrows how to use a dagger in the left hand to ward an opponent's sword.

The next day an extraordinary thing occurred: Cotton "killed" Lord Kian. In mock battle the buccan actually got through Kian's defenses with a quick thrust that struck Kian above the heart. Kian was as surprised as everyone else, for he had thought that Perry, with his greater agility, would be the first to "slay" a "Lōkh." But it was Cotton who scored the first "kill." Perry looked on and was at the same time elated and frightened, for until now it had been an exciting game, but with this "kill" it suddenly became a deadly serious business. Anval tugged at his black beard and shook his head in regret, for he knew that these gentle Folk were not meant to be warriors, though necessity forced them so.

The following day the river continued to recede as the Warrows learned to combat opponents who wielded hammers, cudgels, maces, and axes. Here Anval and Borin shaped appropriate weapons out of wood and took over the teaching chores, with Borin saying, "Ükhs know not the way of these weapons, especially the axe, for they ply them as if they were hewing logs. But *this* is the true way—the Châkka way—of an axe.'' And, demonstrating, with two-handed grips the Dwarves grasped the oaken helves of their own runemarked axes, one hand high near the blade, the other near the haft butt. And they used the helves to parry imaginary sword blows, and stabbed forward with the cruel axe beaks, or shifted their grips to strike with power; and their axes danced and flashed in the sunlight and seemed to have a life of their own. And as for hammers, cudgels, and maces, the Dwarven way of their wielding was much the same.

The Warrows quickly learned that swords must be used differently against these massive weapons, and that agility becomes vital in waging against them, for a light sword would not halt and would but barely deflect the crushing blows. The strategy seemed to be ''Get out of the way and let the ponderous Grg-swing carry past, and before the Squam can recover, use your sword.'' In theory it was an excellent strategy, but not against Anval and Borin—and Dwarves in general—for with their massive shoulders they had extraordinary strength; and Dwarf power when coupled with Dwarf quickness allowed them to recover almost as if they were wielding a light wand instead of an axe, hammer, mace, or cudgel. And the Dwarf way of axe battle—helve, beak, and blade—was devastating. So Perry and Cotton received by far the worst drubbings in all of their training, as there by the swollen river they engaged Anval and Borin in mock combat. Yet, toward the end of the day the buccen had improved dramatically.

That evening, beneath a Hunter's Moon, Lord Kian announced to Warrow cheers that they would attempt a crossing on the morrow, for the river was back in its banks, though still raging. ''And though it will be risky,'' Kian added, ''we must cross over soon, for Durek and his Army should be at Landover Road Ford within five or six days, and we must be there to meet them.''

The seventeenth day of the journey dawned to clear skies. The travellers went together to the banks of the Arden Ford and looked upon the rushing water. It was still high and boiling, tumbling along in wild protest—a torrent. Cotton easily could throw a rock across, but it still was a good distance to have to ford, especially in these conditions. "I must set a safety line," declared Lord Kian as he shed his cloak and stripped to the waist. He tied a soft rope around his middle with the other end anchored to a tree. While Anval and Borin payed out the line, Lord Kian entered the chill rush and began wading across; and as he went he clung to great rocks thrusting up here and there through the plunging river. Kian had reached the halfway point and the water was up to his waist when he was upset by the driving current, losing his grip on one of the boulders, and was swept downstream to the end of the line, which then swung him back to the starting shore.

On the second attempt he was three quarters of the way across and nearly chest deep when again he was swept downstream, but this time his rope caught on a large up-jutting rock and he recovered near midstream.

"Third time pays for all," muttered Cotton as the Man struggled on through the race once more. This time Kian was almost to the other side when he fell, but he managed to catch hold of a low-set branch reaching out over the rapid flow, and he pulled himself to the far bank. The Warrows shouted cries of joyous relief, for they had feared for the young Lord's safety.

Kian tied his end of the rope to a tree on the far side so that the line hung low across the race, spanning from one bank to the other. Then, using the rope for a brace, he waded back to the near shore. "The water is cold and becomes deep near the far bank where the curve of the river has cut it so. It is nearly too deep for the horses pulling the waggon, for if they stumble the coursing rush may roll the wain. Yet the Waerlinga must ride." Kian turned to Perry and Cotton. "I fear your strength is not enough to cross by rope; you cannot touch the bottom for the greater part of the way, and if you tried the safety line you would have to hang on in the torrent and pull hand over hand to the other side. I would cross over by the rope twice, each time with one of you on my back, but I have fallen thrice ere now, and I think you'd each be swept away from me were I to fall again in such an attempt. I deem the waggon and sure-footed horses to be a safer way to pass over. Anval and Borin, you may use the rope if you wish—I fear not for your strength in that endeavor—but for the Waerlinga I choose the waggon.''

The Dwarves indicated that they, too, would trust to the horses, and the travellers returned to the fire; and as the others broke camp and hitched up Brownie and Downy, Kian warmed himself by the campblaze but did not change into dry clothes. ''We may fall in while crossing,'' he said as he instructed them all in what to do ''We shall drive the waggon to breast the flow upstream from the rope. If you then fall overboard you will be swept to the line; merely keep your head above water and catch the rope when you come to it. If you can't pull to shore, just hang on til I get there; I'll help you. Any questions?'' They all shook their heads *no* and prepared for the fording. Neither Perry nor Cotton felt it necessary to mention to Lord Kian that they could not swim a stroke—nor did the like thought occur to the Dwarves, either.

With Anval at the reins, Brownie and Downy pulled the waggon slowly into the stream while Perry and Cotton nervously peered over the sideboards at the flow. Borin and Kian sat in the far back in hopes that their weight over the rear axle would help anchor the waggon against the current. The horses seemed eager to test their strength after their nearly four-day rest, and they pulled steadily into the cold surge. The bottom was rocky, and the waggon jolted out to midstream, where the rushing water came just up to the waggon axles.

Slowly they pulled into deeper water, toward the far shore, the horses beginning to strain against the turbulent flow, and the waggon began to drift sideways, bumping and lurching on the rocky bottom. Perry started to say something when again the wain lurched sideways and passed over a deep hole and began to float, swiftly swinging in the current. With a sudden jolt the downstream rear wheel slapped laterally into a large underwater boulder, instantly halting the wain's sideways rush but pitching the waggon bed up with a lurch. And Perry was catapulted out into the boiling race. *''Mister Perry!''* cried Cotton, making a frantic grab and just missing. *''Mister Perry!''* he shouted again, and leapt in after his master.

Perry was swept away, churning and tumbling through the water with Cotton helplessly rolling and turning behind him. The icy force of the wild water was overwhelming, and neither Warrow knew up from down, being entirely at the mercy of the torrent. The mad current rolled each of them, cascading the buccen toward the safety rope. At times the raging river plunged first one then the other to the bottom; at other times it heaved them to the surface; but always it crushed their feeble efforts to breathe and to stay afloat, overturning them and smashing them under again. Perry saw the rope rushing at him and reached up, but the churning water forced him under, and he could not grasp the lifeline and was swept beyond it and away. Cotton never saw the safety line, but just as he, too, was about to pass beyond it he felt his wrist being gripped by a strong hand, and he was lifted up sputtering, and there was the rope. But he had breathed water and was coughing and had not the strength to hold on; and Kian, his rescuer, held the gasping, choking Warrow while allowing the current to press them both against the line.

Desperately, Lord Kian's sight swept downstream for some glimpse of Perry but saw no sign of the buccan among the roiling crests. Then Kian looked and there was Borin on the far shore running. Anval had managed to drive the waggon on across, and as soon as it had touched the bank Borin had leapt out and gone dashing downstream, with Anval following at a dead run, both Dwarves racing after Perry.

By this time Cotton had recovered enough to hold on to Lord Kian and ride pickaback, and the young Man used the rope and carried the Warrow toward safety. Far downstream they could see Anval and Borin splashing up to their waists in the water at a sharp bend in the river, struggling against the sweep to carry a limp burden to shore: it was Perry.

Kian scrambled up the far bank and Cotton swung down, and they sprinted to the curve, the long-legged Man far outstripping the flood-spent Warrow. When at last Cotton arrived he found the two Dwarves, their hoods cast over their bowed heads, standing above Perry's inert form, and Lord Kian on his knees beside him. "He is dead," stated Borin in a halting voice. "Drowned. The river swallowed him and killed him and swept him to shore. The star that fell was his."

Cotton burst into tears, but Lord Kian looked at Perry's pale white face and still form. "It is said among Realmsmen that the breath of the living can at times restore the breath of the drowned." And he sealed Perry's mouth with his own and breathed his breath into the Warrow. Twelve times he did this, while the Dwarves looked on in hooded silence and Cotton through his tears watched in quiet desperation. Twelve times Kian breathed into the buccan, and in between breaths he allowed Perry's chest to fall and the air to leave. Twelve times the Realmsman breathed, and the long moments seemed to stretch into forever, and Perry did not respond. But on the thirteenth breath Perry's chest suddenly heaved, and he began coughing and retching and gasping, and seemed on the verge of strangling—but at last he was breathing on his own.

"He lives!" cried Borin joyously, throwing back his hood, "He lives!" and he began leaping about and laughing and shouting in a strange tongue. Anval, too, threw back his own hood and could not contain his elation and grabbed Cotton up in a crushing embrace and swung him around and around til both were dizzy and fell to the ground.

Perry stopped retching and coughing in the midst of this gaiety and looked up at the capering Dwarves and the captive Cotton and at Lord Kian, who was on his knees and weeping into his hands, and said, "Well, hullo. What's all this fuss about?" And Lord Kian fell over on his side and began to roar with helpless laughter.

CHAPTER 10

THE CRESTAN PASS

As soon as Perry could manage it, the comrades made their way back to the waggon, stopping along the route while Lord Kian retrieved the rope, once more breasting the icy stream over and back to do so. Then they drove up out of the flood plain to the high ground where the wood was dry. There they stopped and built a large fire to warm themselves and change clothes, for they all had plunged into the icy tumult, and the October chill caused them to shiver uncontrollably and their teeth to chatter. They donned fresh garments drawn from the dry interiors of their packs, and they took time to make some hot tea and have a midmorning meal while warming by the fire.

"Let me tell you, Mister Perry," said Cotton, gingerly probing his own ribs and grimacing as he recounted his part in the venture, "the next time *I'll* be the one who recovers and *you* be the one that Anval grabs and squeezes and swings around. Why, Sir, he nearly mashed me silly!" They all laughed as Cotton looked askew at the Dwarf, with Anval roaring loudest of all.

"Well, friend Cotton, your skill had better improve ere you go splashing off on another rescue," growled Borin through his damp black beard, hefting a large rock, "for at the moment this stone floats better than you."

Again and again they burst out in laughter as each described his view of some aspect of the adventure, for the crossing had been perilous and they had but barely escaped; and as is the wont of close companions who walk on the edge of disaster and survive intact with all unharmed, their relief oft surfaces in rough jest, as if the retelling of the jeopardy in humorous account somehow lessens the past danger and reduces the future vulnerability of those involved.

Soon the five were warm and dry and had finished eating, and they could have comfortably camped for the rest of the day. But all felt an urgency to press on, for they had lost four days while waiting to cross, and the time of the rendezvous with Durek was nearly upon them. So they set out again—the waggon sideboards covered with river-drenched clothes wrung out and draped for drying—following the Crossland Road toward Arden Vale and to the Crestan Pass over the Grimwall Mountains.

It was early afternoon when they sighted the deep-cloven, concealed valley of Arden, site of the Hidden Stand, a secret Elven refuge in the north of the Land called Rell. It was here among the forested crags that many had paused during the Winter War, to rest and recover and gather strength to use against Modru. And it was said that though the Dimmendark had lain over this Land, it could not grasp the Elven Realm.

Through this narrow vale, seated between high sheer stone walls split out of the earth, ran the Tumble River, issuing out of the valley to turn west then south again. Supplied by the rains and the snows high upon the peaks of the Grimwall Mountains, this waterway fed the rich soil of Arden Gorge, and thick pine forests carpeted the valley floor. As the swift-running river emerged from the last walls of the cleft, it fell down a precipice in a wide cataract, and swirling vapors rose up and obscured the view into the canyon. It was the haze from this cascade that perpetually hid the valley from sight.

"I think I can dimly see what must be the Lone Eld Tree," said Perry, trying to pierce the mist with his gaze, "but I cannot tell if the leaves are dusky: the haze hides it. The *Raven Book* says that Eld Trees *gather* the twilight and *hold* it if Elves dwell nearby. And though it is said that the great Elven leader Talarin—Lian Guardian in Arden, Warder of the Northern Regions of Rell—no longer abides there, I thought that others did, and so I would hope to see the Eld Tree leaves be dusky." Perry turned to Lord Kian. "*Is* Arden deserted? *Are* the Elves gone? It would become a sad day indeed to find that the Elves are gone from Mithgar."

Kian answered, looking toward the hidden dale beyond the roiling mist of the engorged waterfall: "Elves do yet walk in Mithgar, though their numbers dwindle as more ride the Twilight Path. Some Elves—the Dylvana—still dwell in the Great Greenhall, Darda Erynian, or Blackwood as it was known of old. Dwarves from the Mineholt, Men of Dael, and the Baeron converse with them now and again: trading, bartering, or simply passing the time of day.

"As to the other Elves—the Lian—I think none live any longer in Darda Galion, the Larkenwald to the south above Valon and east of Drimmen-deeve, though travellers on the River Argon say they see movement therein at times.

"But as to Arden being deserted: that I do not know. It is said that after the Winter War, Talarin and Rael went south to dwell in the Eldwood yet a while; but at last they rode the Twilight Ride to Adonar in the company of the Coron of Darda Galion; it is also said that sons and daughters and others of the Elden stayed behind. But whether they and the Lian that lived here in Arden still do, I cannot say. It seems certain that their numbers have waned—though how many remain, if any, is unknown to me."

The waggon did not enter the gap into Arden, much to Cotton's disappointment, for he wanted to meet an Elf, having heard much of these tall, fair Folk. But instead the wain rolled on up the slope of the rising land, heading into the foothills along the road to the Crestan Pass through the Grimwall.

The travellers stopped late in the evening in a russet-leaved thicket in the hills on the low shoulders of the high mountains ahead. They pitched camp, and soon all but the watch retired, for the crossing of the swollen ford had been arduous, and they were weary.

That night Perry dreamed that he was again in the river. The rushing water was tumbling him about, and he could not shout for help, for if he opened his mouth to do so the torrent would gush in and drown him. Again he passed under the safety line, and he could not reach it and he could not breathe, for the crashing river was rolling him along the bottom, smashing him into the large rocks there. He was swept into a curve where the water was less overpowering though still turbulent, but he did not know how to swim and could not get to the surface, for a great tree root had grabbed him by the shoulder and was holding him under while the river shook him and shook him. He could not breathe, but he had to, and though he held out as long as he could, finally he gasped in a great lungful of . . . air, for he awakened at that instant to find Borin kneeling above him and shaking him by the shoulder. "You were moaning, friend Perry," said the Dwarf, "and I thought it best to awaken you. Your watch is upon us at any rate, and a stand at guard should dispel evil dreams."

"Hullo, Borin. I thought you were a tree root. Thanks for getting me out of that bad dream. Once a day is more than enough to have to fight a river, much less having to do it all over again in your sleep." Perry stood, throwing his cloak over his shoulders. "That's twice today you've gotten me out of that same river, and I thank you again for it—but I do hope it's the last time we ever have to do that."

The next day was a long hard period of uphill hauling for the horses, for they had finally come upon the full mountain slopes. All day the travellers wended upward, stopping frequently to rest Brownie and Downy, and late afternoon found them in the high country, nearing the timberline. Ahead they could see tier upon tier of barren stone rising out of the earth and marching up to the sky. The snow-covered peaks were massive, towering high above, and Perry felt diminished to the size of a tiny ant slowly crawling across their looming flanks. The setting Sun threw its dying rays into the crags and onto the massifs; and as the shadows mounted, the gaunt rock took on an aspect of blood—even the high snow shone with red: it was as if the great jagged peaks were reaching up and their sharpness was wounding the sky above. *Oh! What a dreadful omen,* thought Perry, and he cast his eyes downward and did not look up at the ruddy crags again.

In the dusk, the waggon stopped in a thick pine forest—the last of the timberline—and the comrades made camp on this eighteenth day of their long journey from Woody Hollow. "Tomorrow," explained Kian as they sat around the fire, "we cross through the Crestan Pass and come down the east side, to take the Landover Road toward the ford on the Argon. We should be there three evenings hence, mayhap but one day ahead of Durek.''

The next morning came, and the companions were awakened by Cotton to find it still dark; they were enwrapped in a dense, cold mist and could not see more than a few feet. ''I don't know whether it's a fog that's climbed up from the bottom or a cloud that's slid down from the top,'' said Cotton, ''but it's thick enough to cut doors and windows into, and maybe if we carved on it a bit we would let in some light. It's still dark, though I know it's time to be up and gone.''

''It's dark because the Sun is rising on the other side of the mountain and we are standing in its shadow,'' said Lord Kian. ''And this myrk makes it doubly dark. Let us hope it gets no thicker—the way is hard enough as it is without adding fog. There are many places ahead to go wrong—blind canyons, false trails, sudden precipices, blank walls, and such—and a cloaking mist we do not need. The way is before us, but I think I will not, cannot, find it til this shroud is gone.''

''You forget, Lord Kian, you are with Châkka,'' spoke Borin Ironfist in rough pride, running his fingers through his black locks, unevenly combing out the sleep tangles, ''and we trod this path on foot before—though backwards—on our way to fetch Perry. The fog is no obstacle. Were it pitch black, still could we go on, back the way we first came over this Mountain. Anval or I will lead this day til the way clears—by your leave.''

''Your pardon, friend Borin''—Kian smiled—''I did indeed forget the Dwarf talent. It is new to me and wondrous. Lead on, my fellow wayfinder; here it is I who shall follow.''

The road grew steep and narrow, with a sheer drop on one side and a towering wall on the other. The Warrows discovered that they and all of the party—except Anval, who drove the wain and worked the brakes—had to walk ahead of the waggon, leading the horses, for the way at times was so narrow that it was safer outside the waggon than in; further, by walking up the incline, thus lessening the load, they spared the steeds.

Slowly they made their way upward, stopping often to rest. Yet they moved surely through the fog, Borin leading, striding purposefully forward with his walking stave clicking against the stone path, confidently guiding the fellowship past hazards and false paths and up toward the notch of the Crestan Pass. The Warrows did not realize how sheer and far the drop-off beside the road fell until the midmorning Sun began to burn away the cold mist; shortly they could see, and soon the buccen were walking next to the wall as far away from the precipice as they could manage. And though the Sun had finally pierced the icy fog, the day had gotten colder, for now the comrades were up high on the mountain in the thin air; and they all donned extra wear.

It was in the midmorn that they stopped in a wide spot, and Kian instructed all the companions to take their backpacks and bedrolls from the waggon and strap them on. "We are coming to a dangerous part," explained the young Man, looking with keen grey eyes at the slopes above, "where the smallest sound of the wrong sort can start a rock slide or a snow avalanche. If that happens, the waggon may be swept away with all in it. If we survive, with our packs we can proceed onward to the Landover Road Ford with few problems; without them, the trip would be much harder; bear your burden with that thought in mind—though it won't make the knapsack lighter, it will ease the load." He turned to the Warrows. "From here you are to make as little sound as possible. Speak if you must only in a whisper. When we reach the other side and start down, most of the danger will be past. Til then, silence is the rule. Have you any questions? Speak now, it's your final chance."

"Do you mean to tell me that sounds can cause snow or rocks to fall?" asked Cotton, peering at the solid stone wall of the mountainside with some skepticism. "Begging your pardon, but that sounds like *Word from the Beyond,* if you want my opinion." Cotton, like most Boskydell Warrows, had always looked at news from outside the Seven Dells as being peculiar and suspect; thus, the saying *Word from the Beyond* indicated something which may or may not be true—something hard to accept until proven.

"Aye, Waeran," answered Anval before others could

speak. "But the rock or snow does not fall for just any sound. It must be the right sound. Did you ever see and hear a wineglass sing when someone nearby struck a note on a lute, or horn, or violin, or other musical instrument? Aye, I see you have. You can feel the glass ring in response to the note. Yet other notes do not seem to affect it. It must be the right sound, the right pitch, or nothing happens: the wineglass sits there without answering. And it is not only wineglasses that jing: some sounds cause windows to rattle, others make picture frames tilt, or dishes to clatter, pots and pans to clang, and hundreds of other things to tap and drum and jump around. We Châkka believe that each thing in this world will shake or rattle or fall or even shatter apart if just the right note is sounded on the right instrument. And here in the Mountains, where the snow hangs on high and the rocks poise on the slopes, at times, when the conditions are right, certain sounds seem to cause the stone or ice or snow to shiver just as does the wineglass, and the burden can break loose to cause ruin. It must be the right sound, though: a whipcrack or shrill voice or whistle or toot—any one may or may not start the avalanche. It may be something else, like a cough or whinny. The trouble is, we do not know what will start the fall, so we must be silent in all things."

Perry and Cotton listened with growing amazement, not only at what was being said but also at who was saying it; for since leaving the 'Thorn-ringed Boskydells, but for a few rare occasions, Anval had been given to speaking only in short, terse sentences. And the Warrows had begun to think that Dwarves were about as loquacious as lumps of iron; and for either Anval or Borin to talk prolongedly had come to be a strange and rare event. The buccen could only believe that Anval thought it was important enough to speak at length so that they would understand the danger. And understand it they now did; the Mastercrafter's discourse had clearly shown them the need for silence, for they had indeed seen wineglasses sing and windows rattle at the sound of a viol or the boom of a drum. Again Cotton eyed the slopes above, this time with respect. "Mum's the word," he whispered and then made a buttoning motion on his lip, and Perry smiled and nodded without speaking.

Shouldering their packs, Lord Kian, the Warrows, and

Borin went on ahead while Anval stayed back and drove the horses well to the rear. His place in line was by far the most dangerous, for the horses could not be instructed that "mum's the word."

Slowly they made their way toward the Crestan Pass, a notch through a saddle between two peaks of the Grimwall Mountains. They could see the cleft far above them silhouetted by the high morning Sun, whose light streamed through the col to glance off the rises overhead. The slopes were snow-covered, but here and there barren patches revealed a jumble of boulders, slabs, and jagged rocks balanced on the steep mountainsides. Quietly and cautiously they trudged toward the pass, making little or no sound. However, they could hear the horses' hooves calmly clip-clopping behind them and the waggon wheels grinding iron rims on flat stone. Cotton kept glancing up at the menace looming above them, thinking, *Please don't fall. Please don't fall on us or the waggon. I won't cough or sneeze, and you won't fall.*

Finally, when the Sun was standing at zenith, they at last reached the brow of the pass, and the rule of silence was over. They ate a meal and rested for a while; the path had been steep and the climb arduous in the thin air—and the pause was most welcomed. Shortly, though, they had to start down; they had to reach the lower slopes before nightfall, for they could not stay up in the peaks after duskingtide: at this time of year the dark at these heights was too cruel and bitter; the hard passage had to be made during the Sun of a single day.

They began their descent down the eastern flanks, continuing to wear their packs and lead the team and light waggon. They had gone but a mile or so when the horses began to shy and skit and pull back, and seemed reluctant to go farther. Kian stopped the party and carefully scanned the upward slopes. "I can see nothing awry," he said, "but steeds are oft wiser than Men. We shall go forth, but in caution."

Once more they started along the steep, narrow way, walking downward, again on a path caught between stone wall and sheer precipice. To the north and south they could see but little, for the flanks of the mountains on either side of the route blocked the far view; but straight

ahead to the east below they could see the Landover Road
wending through the foothills and out over a stretch of
plains to come at last to the Great Argon River, and run on
beyond into the vast Greenhall Forest—Darda Erynian—
now bedecked in bright fall foliage, whose far extent faded
away beyond the silver haze in the remote distance.

They had gone another mile and were beginning to think
that the skittish animals had perceived some false danger
when both Brownie and Downy reared up, whinnying
wildly, with nostrils flaring and blowing and eyes rolling
til the whites showed in terror; they would have bolted but
for Anval's strong arm. Lord Kian quickly stepped back
and caught the bit reins to stop the horses from plunging.
Cotton felt and heard a low rumbling from above and
glanced up and saw the mountain move, its side sliding
toward them. *"Look!"* he yelled and pointed, but the
others had already seen the danger.

"There ahead! To the wall!" shouted Borin, leaping
forward, racing toward a place where the looming mountainside partially overhung the path, providing shelter of a
sort. As thick slabs and huge boulders and rocks large and
small bounded and leapt and slid in a mighty avalanche
toward them, the comrades ran for the concavity, with
Anval driving and working the waggon brake and Kian, a
bit strap in each hand, desperately pulling the rearing,
plunging horses toward the cove. Even then all were being
pelted by the small, round stones forerunning the vast
slide, and at the last instant they lunged into shelter, Anval
grabbing up his axe and pack and wildly leaping from the
waggon and into the shallow depression just as a grey wall
of rock sheeted down over the edge.

The ground shook and rumbled as pebbles and boulders
alike cascaded down, so thick as to blot out the light, so
close as to reach out and touch, racing with a speed that
made them leap off the lip above and arch out over the
path, some stones not striking the roadway at all in their
rush to the depths below. But amid the thunder and roar,
one great, thick, flat slab slowly slid down and momentarily teetered on the rim above. "Look out!" cried Perry,
pointing at the giant mass, and they crowded back as far as
they could.

The immense slab slowly toppled over the edge above

and fell with a thunderous crash to crush the red waggon where it stood beyond the protection of the overhang; the great slab landed half on, half off the path, and slowly tilted on the edge of the precipice and began sliding over the brink, dragging the demolished waggon under it and hauling the steeds backward against their will, pulling them toward their doom. Borin leapt forward to add his strength to Anval's and Kian's to help the horses pull against the terrible weight slowly drawing them unto Death. The frightened animals at first lunged and lurched in terror at being dragged hindward, but then settled down to a hard, straining, steady pull when Cotton jumped forward and took the bit straps in hand. Perry, too, grabbed a hold and hauled with all his might along with the rest.

Tons of stone thundered past as the desperate struggle for life went on; but the giant weight gradually drew them all toward the rim; they were unable to check its ponderous drag. It seemed to pause, poised for a final plunge to carry the valiant steeds to their death below, when another great boulder slowly rolled over the edge above and dropped with an ear-splitting *crack!* onto the giant slab and then bounded on down the mountain. The waggon, though already crushed, was unable to stand more and burst asunder, releasing the slab and waggon bed to plunge over the precipice, while with a lurch the horses, Warrows, Dwarves, and Man stumbled forward into the hollow and to safety.

Cotton stroked the animals to calm them, and spoke to them even though he knew they could not hear him, for rock still thundered past. Finally the earth stopped shaking and shuddering as the slide slowly tailed off, trickling to an end with a few pebbles and an occasional rock rattling over the lip to fall below.

An immense silence beat upon their ears as they waited to see if the avalanche was truly ended. At last Borin stepped cautiously out, his boots scrutching loudly in the still. He eyed the mountain above. "It is now safe, I deem."

Slowly the others came out for a look. Perry walked through the talus to the edge of the path and carefully looked down to see where the vast quantity of stone had gone. Though he looked long, searching both down the precipice and mountain flanks below and up the slopes above, except for the rubble on the roadbed he could see no signs of the slide nor even of its passage; though to the companions the avalanche had been a momentous, desperate, life-or-death struggle, the great mountain had swallowed it up as if it were an unimportant event of minor consequence. Shaking his head in disbelief, Perry joined the others to help remove the waggon tongue from the horses' harness; it had been the only part of the wain to survive. They leaned the tongue against the mountain wall so that some passing waggoneer might salvage the beam and the whiffletrees, and then the comrades set forth once more.

"Where do slides come from?" quietly asked Perry as they continued on down. "I mean, well, the mountain has been here since the birth of Mithgar, ages and ages agone. It seems that all of the loose rock would have slid off by now."

Borin looked first at Anval then answered, his voice muted: "The Mountains were here when the Châkka came, and they will be here when we are gone, but even the Mountains themselves grow old and die. The water from rain and melting snows seeps into the clefts and crevices; and when it freezes and turns into ice it splits the stone, delving it as surely as if it were Châk pick shattering it asunder. Over the years great quantities of rock are broken loose, and ultimately some sound or earth shudder causes it to slide to the margins below, and the Mountain is diminished with each rockfall. Just as we Châkka delve the inner cores of Mountains, so do the actions of the world mine their outer slopes. And it may be that after uncountable ages, even the mightiest of Mountains will be humbled by this stone cracking to become but a lowly foothill— though neither Man, Waeran, nor Châk will exist on Mitheor long enough to see that come to pass."

Perry felt privileged to be trusted with this glimpse of Dwarf lore from the Mastercrafter. The buccan knew that what Borin had revealed was true, and he looked at the mountain and was stunned with the knowledge that such a great towering peak would someday become just a tall hill, like Beacontor—and he was awed by the thought that Beacontor itself might once have been a towering peak when the world was young. And the incredible scale of time involved overwhelmed him—why, all of recorded history was but a moment when compared to the span of a mountain.

The companions walked downward all that afternoon and were well below the timberline when it came time to make camp. It had gotten dark early, for the Sun was setting on the far side of the Grimwall, and they were in its shadow. Their last sight of the way below showed the Landover Road running eastward, waiting for them.

They set up camp in a thick pine grove, but had nothing to eat and no tea, for all their food had been carried over the edge by the avalanche.

CHAPTER 11

MARCH TO THE ARGON

"I don't mind telling you, Mister Perry," said Cotton, leading Downy along the Landover Road, "I sure hope that Lord Kian has some luck with that silver-handled bow of his. I'm so hungry I do believe I could have eaten some of the trees right out of the ground back there in the forest where we camped—or a pine cone or two at least." Anval grunted his agreement, for they all were ravenous—stomachs rumbling and complaining—having had nothing to eat since the noon meal up in the Crestan Pass; and now it was well into the midmorning of the day after.

They had arisen just before the Sun, appetites sharp-set, and Lord Kian had put forth a proposal: "I will take Brownie and ride on ahead. Down in the foothills below I'll stop at a likely spot and with my bow I'll try for some game. You follow on foot using Downy as a pack animal; rig the traces to carry our gear. Load everything on the horse except your weapons; we have come to the stage where it is better to become accustomed to going armed. If I leave now, with luck we should break our fast this forenoon."

In considering his plan, Lord Kian had known that the two Waerlinga had never ridden a full-grown horse, and that for some reason unknown to him the Dwarves would not ride even had they the skill. He had rejected the use of sledge or travois as essentially not being any faster than walking, and some time, though brief, would be lost in the construction. And by setting out now, the rendezvous with Durek could just be made if the pace was kept brisk and no more delays were encountered. He had considered riding on alone to meet Durek at Landover Road Ford to assure him that all was well, with the rest of the comrades arriving on foot later; but he rejected that plan, for he knew to make that march without food would be an ordeal for the Waerlinga and the Dwarves.

Thus the companions settled on the scheme Lord Kian proposed, and he rode off alone with his bow. The others set off down the lower flanks of the mountain at a sharp pace, for as Lord Kian had explained, they had but two days remaining before the assembly sixty miles to the east.

The Warrows had discovered upon awakening that their muscles protested mightily at being moved, for their taxing climb up the far side of the mountain followed by the equally strenuous trek down the near side had worked little-used muscles to their limits. As Cotton said, "I'm as sore as a boil about to pop." But as they marched, the ache gradually subsided as the pain worked its way out.

And now they had come down to the foothills and were striding along the Landover Road, and it was midmorning, and Cotton was commiserating with Anval over the lack of food. Amid torturous groans of longing, they had begun describing various meals to one another: succulent roast pig and chestnuts; woodland grouse in golden honey sauce; fresh trout on a bed of mushrooms. . . . Cotton had just come to the point where he had Anval agreeing that for their next meal they would split between the two of them an entire full-grown spitted cow, when Borin, slightly in the lead, held up his hand for silence as the four of them rounded a curve.

Ahead they could see a thin wraith of smoke rising above the treetops. Borin spoke: "It cannot be a Grg fire, for the Sun is up, and in any case we are too far north for Squam. It could be a traveller, trader, or hunter, or woods-man, though it is late in the day for a breakfast fire but early for a midday meal. It may not be a cook fire at all, but an encampment instead. Be wary and speak not of our mission, for even innocent tongues if captured can betray our plans." With that admonition they again started eastward.

Soon they came to the vicinity of the smoke and found what appeared to be a small unattended fire with four rabbits roasting above it on green-branch spits. They were looking on in wolfish hunger when Lord Kian stepped forth from behind a broad tree trunk. "What ho, boon companions!" he called with exaggerated formality as he made a low sweeping bow, "won't you partake with me this fine repast?" and then he burst out laughing as his messmates scrambled to join him.

After the meal, Cotton fetched both horses from the grassy glade where they had been tethered to graze and led them as the fellowship walked together along the Landover Road, caught up in conversation. They had gone east nearly eight more miles when they came to a stone cottage that served the Baeron as a toll station and Passwarden house.

In days of old, the Baeron, a sturdy clan of stalwart Men, had kept the Crestan Pass and the Landover Road Ford and the road in between clear of Rūcks and Hlōks and other Spawn, and safe for travellers and merchants; for this service, the Baeron charged tolls. But after the fall of Modru, the Foul Folk lived no longer in this region. The Baeron then took to keeping the road through the Crestan Pass clear of landslides and rockfalls, and to helping way-farers and their cargoes safely through the ford in the flood season; and they continued to charge tolls.

Each year a different family came from the Baeron Holds in Darda Erynian to tend the Crestan Pass, arriving on April the first—a few weeks before the spring melt opened the col for travel—and returning to the Great Greenhall Forest in autumn, when the high snows again closed the way for the winter. This year Baru was Passwarden, and he lived with his three tall sons in the small stone cote.

The four Baeron were pleased to see Lord Kian and the two Dwarves return over the pass, for Baru had wished them well when they had gone west through the gap toward the Boskydells on their "King's business" a month and a week and a day agone. Glad though they were to once more greet the Man and the Dwarves, the passkeepers were amazed to meet Perry and Cotton, for they had never before seen Waldana, and the small Folk were creatures of legend to the Baeron—harking back to the ancient time of the *Wanderjahre* when the Wee Folk had passed over the Argon on their journey west and south and west again, searching for a homeland.

Travel was halted, and traveller and roadkeeper alike paused to pass the news over a pot of tea. The Baeron also provided the wayfarers with some delicious dark bread covered with spring-cold butter that stuck to the ribs and filled up some hollow spots.

As they took this meal together, Lord Kian told Baru of the rock slide in the pass, mentioning that now there was scree on the roadway. Baru nodded and poured more tea and passed more bread to the wayfarers; and he cocked an eye at his sons and they nodded back, realizing that a job needed doing up in the col.

Even while Perry enjoyed the drink and tea-bread along with everyone else, he noted that Baru and his sons treated Lord Kian with a deep and abiding respect, almost as if Kian were their sovereign King. *Curious,* thought Perry.

The Baeron Men seemed to know about the maggot-folk in Drimmen-deeve and the Dwarves' pledge, for they spoke of the Spawn raids and wished Anval and Borin success in their venture. No fresh news had come to Baru from the south, which was not surprising, for most of his tidings came from travelling merchants faring to cross the Crestan Pass, and it was rare for anyone to attempt to go through this late in the year. Though Baru had no news from the south, he asked that a message be carried to the southern marches: "Sire, should you meet with our kinsman, Ursor, during your quest," said Baru to Lord Kian, "we ask that you tell him that all is well at home, and trust that his vengeance against the Wrg goes to his satisfaction." Perry reasoned that one of the Baeron was off fighting Drimmen-deeve Spawn, seeking revenge for some deed committed by the maggot-folk during one of the raids; but before more was said, it was time to leave—time to continue on to the east.

"Well now, m'Lord," observed Baru, "all your supplies went over the edge with your waggon. We've not much, yet you're welcome to take what food you need to stretch over the next two or three days—til your rendezvous with King Durek."

"My thanks, Passwarden," responded Kian, knowing that Baru and his sons would require most of their own meager provisions to see them through until they were home again in Darda Erynian. The young Man hefted his bow. "I can fell enough small game to keep us in meat, but perhaps some crue or hardtack would go well—"

"And some tea, please," interjected Cotton, slurping the dregs of his and setting the cup to the table, popping one last bit of bread into his mouth.

Swiftly, Grau, the eldest son, gathered up the rations and handed them over to Cotton, who had stepped forward to take them.

And so they all stood and filed out of the cottage and into the bright sunshine, Cotton packing the fare into his knapsack. And while the comrades made ready, Baru and his sons also prepared to go, to hike up into the pass to clear away the rubble from the slide.

As the travellers stepped out onto the road, Rolf, the middle son, approached Anval and respectfully said, "Sir Dwarf, you must advise Durek to hurry if he is to go over the mountain, for winter comes early in the high peaks; the frost is now with us down here, which means that the first snow will soon block the Crestan Pass." Anval nodded curtly, and then all the companions said farewell and set off again for the far rendezvous.

They started down the Road with Perry's thoughts still dwelling on these Men. Though the visit had been short, Perry had concluded that the Baeron would make good comrades in time of need. The buccan also reflected on the curious, deferential way the passkeepers had treated Kian, but before Perry could ask the young Lord as to the reason, the Daelsman had taken up his bow and remounted Brownie and galloped away to seek their supper.

The rest of the comrades marched swiftly throughout the day, and in the dusk an hour after sundown they once more came to where Lord Kian was encamped. Again he had been skillful with his bow, having downed a brace of grouse and three more rabbits.

Cotton tethered Brownie and Downy out in the rich grass of the wold and watched them as they began to eagerly crop their first substantial meal since noon of the previous day, for all of their grain had been swept away by the rockslide. Satisfied, the buccan returned to the camp-site, his stomach rumbling, for the aroma of game on the spit filled the air.

The companions had covered some thirty-one miles that

day, and had emerged from the foothills and were well out
upon the open plains—twenty-nine miles from the Argon
River ford crossing. The Warrows were bone-weary, unaccustomed as they were to climbing over a mountain on one
day and forcing march all the next; but though they were
tired, they fell to the meal with a voracity that would have
done a lion proud. Shortly they were sound asleep, and
Kian, Anval, and Borin let the buccen slumber the night
through without waking them to stand their turns at guard—
much to the vexation of the Warrows the next morning.

All day the comrades advanced across plains that gradually fell into the valley of the Argon. Perry and Cotton
and Anval and Borin tramped through a land of heather
and grasses, with only an occasional hill to break the
monotony of the flat, featureless country. Now and again
they would flush a pheasant or covey of birds from beside
the road, or surprise a fox trotting across their way, but for
the most part they marched without interruption on flat,
open prairie, silent except for the sigh of the chill wind
that swept from the mountains and rippled low through the
tall grass. Again, Kian on Brownie ranged ahead with his
bow, providing meat to go with the tea and hardtack given
to them by Baru. In this fashion they came to where they
could see on the horizon the four-mile-wide belt of trees
lining the Argon River; and they knew their journey would
soon come to an end.

As their march slowly drew them nearer, they saw that
there was little green left in the foliage of the river-border
woodland, the fall having worked its magic to transform
the leaves into yellow and gold, scarlet and russet, bronze
and brown. The only green was in the evergreens: spruce,
pine, cedar, yew, hemlock, and the like, clumped here and
there in the river-vale forest: like living jade and emeralds
among reaches of topaz and spinel and ruby 'mid bur-
nished bronze and old leather.

In late afternoon they walked under the eaves of the
river-vale forest, and then came at last to the banks of the
Great River Argon. It flowed past in a wide shallow
crossing—Landover Road Ford—and the companions stood
and watched the river's progress, and Cotton marveled at
its breadth.

Durek and the Army had not yet come, and so camp was pitched on the verge of a grassy clearing in the woods, just a stone's throw north of where the road met the river, where the wind from the plains did not reach, though it could be heard swirling through the overhead treetops. They had made the journey from the Boskydells to the ford in twenty-one days, a time that would have been somewhat less but for the flood at Arden Ford. It was now the last day of October, and Durek was due on the morrow, the first of November.

That night the Warrows again slept deeply, for they were weary; but they stood their turn at watch, having vociferously lectured their companions on the meanings of duty, honor, and the right to stand guard. It was quite a sight to see young Cotton, hands on hips in a defiant stance, his jaw outthrust, glaring up at the towering, smiling Lord Kian and telling the Man just "where to head in" when it comes to doing a turn at watch. And so it was that they spent the night, and finally Cotton awakened them all with the coming of the Sun.

In the early morning light Lord Kian took a length of twine from his pack and caught up his bow and quiver and went through the frost to the pools in the river shallows. Shortly he was back at the campsite bearing three large trout, having shot them with an arrow tied with a retrieval line.

After the breakfast of fresh fish, again the Man and two Warrows took up the sword lessons. The buccen had not practiced since the Arden Ford crossing, and this would perhaps be their last chance: "When Durek comes we begin the long march to Drimmen-deeve," said Kian. "There will be little or no time for practice, so when next you take up weapons it will be against the foe."

A thrill of fear shot through Perry at Kian's words, and his heart beat heavily, and his face became flushed, for he thought, *This is it. It is really going to happen. War with the maggot-folk. Me! Fighting Spawn!*

All that day the buccen practiced with their true swords. They had to learn the weight and balance of their own weapons, and so new wooden swords were not made to replace the old ones that had been lost when the waggon slid off the mountain. Except for the lesson of sword against quarterstaff, they did not engage in mock battle; Lord Kian did not want to risk an accidental wound to any of them. With staves, however, Kian demonstrated how a warrior with the extraordinary reach of a staff was indeed a formidable foe. *Spaunen* were not known to use light quarterstaffs, preferring instead heavy iron poles; and the strategy against those was similar to that used when fighting a hammer. But against a good staff, the sword wielder must depend doubly upon his agility and quickness and wait for an opening to get at close quarters with the foe in order to win.

At the end of the day the Warrows had developed an excellent feel for their weapons—which were much better balanced than the swords of wood and seemed lighter—and so the already quick Warrows became even swifter. Their skill level was extraordinarily high for such a short period of training, and Kian was well pleased.

But the revelation of the day was the sharpness of Perry's sword, Bane. Its edge was bitter indeed, and the point keen beyond reckoning. The rune-jewelled Elvenblade had sheared through or mutilated several quarterstaffs wielded by Kian, and a thrust of little effort would plunge it deeply into the heart of a nearby fallen tree. "Why, it's a wonder, Sir, that it doesn't cut itself right out of its own scabbard!" exclaimed Cotton.

Finally it was sundown, and still Durek had not arrived. The comrades supped again upon Argon trout, then settled down for the eventide. When Perry's turn at guard came, Borin awakened him and growled, "Keep a sharp watch with those Utruni eyes of yours, Waeran; the horses seem restless, though I have neither heard nor seen aught. Still, Wolves may be about, so stand ready." Borin then curled up in his cloak and blanket near the fire and soon was breathing slowly and deeply as sleep overtook him.

Perry stood in the shadows high on the bank and watched the river flow past, glittering silver in the pale light streaming from the waning Moon. The wind had died, and all was still except for the low murmuring of the water. *Quiet enough to hear a pinfeather fall,* thought the buccan. He stood and watched the Moon rise slowly toward the zenith, and the water glide by, and he was content: a small figure in silveron mail with belted sword and Elven cloak; he was a helmed warrior—untested, to be sure, but warrior still, or at least so he hoped, for he had thought long on Anval's words of warning and had tried to concentrate on survival rather than glory.

His watch was just drawing to a close and he was contemplating awakening Anval when he heard . . . something. It was faint and just at the edge of perception. He could sense rather than hear it: a slow, heavy movement nearby. *Where?* He searched with his eyes and ears, trying to quell the thudding of his heart. *There! On the other side of the river!* Something vast and dark was coming through the woods and moving slowly toward the ford. Perry slipped noiselessly to the encampment and roused Anval, finger to the Dwarf's lips. *"Shhh!* Listen! Something comes!" Perry whispered.

Dwarf and Warrow listened together: there came a faint jingle of metal from afar. *"Hist,"* breathed Anval, "that was the sound of armor. We are far north of Drimmen-deeve, yet it could be foul Grg raiders. We waken our comrades—silently."

Anval awakened Borin and Kian while Perry raised up Cotton, and the five slipped quietly into the shadows, armed and armored. Perry's heart was pounding so loudly he wondered why the others did not hear its beat. The horses stamped restlessly, and Cotton started to slip away to quieten them, to prevent a whinny; but Lord Kian grasped the Waerling's shoulder and whispered that their campfire had already shouted out their presence. So the comrades lay in the dark and stared hard through the gloom at the far bank—the source of subdued noise and hidden movement. Then in the wan moonlight they could make out dark shapes of figures coming slowly down the road to the river's edge, and they heard a strong voice call out twice, *"Châkka dök! Châkka dök!"*

At this sound, with a wild neigh, one of the horses belled a challenge, or pealed a welcome; but Anval and Borin leapt up and shouted for joy and rushed for the river. They had recognized the hidden language, for it was the command "Dwarves halt! Dwarves halt!" And they knew that Durek and the Army had come at last.

CHAPTER 12

THE COUNCIL OF DUREK

Lord Kian called after Anval and Borin, his words catching them at the river's edge. "Hold!" he counseled. "Go not into the current in darkness; wait for the dawn."

And so the Dwarves waited, impatiently, and neither side crossed the river that night. They hailed greetings to one another, for the sound carried well and voices across the water could be readily understood. Durek came down to the far bank, and he and Borin spoke back and forth, with Borin indicating that the Boskydells trip had met with success, and Durek saying that the Army would ford the river at dawn to camp and rest for a day or so while the Council of Captains met to hear what had been learned and to plan the campaign accordingly. After a time the comrades wisely returned to camp to catch what sleep remained, while the Army bedded down on the far side along the flanks of the road.

At dawn Cotton awakened Perry. "Mister Perry, hurry, Sir," Cotton urged, "they're starting across." Perry bolted up, and the two buccen scrambled to join Anval, Borin, and Lord Kian on the bank where Landover Road ran up out of the river. In the dim early light they could see a group of horsemen ride into the water and come splashing across at a rapid pace.

"Vanadurin!" cried Lord Kian, pleased. "Riders of Valon! Scouts for Durek's Army." And with but a swift glance at the five companions, the horsemen charged up and out of the river, and fanned wide as they rode into the woods beyond, their grim sharp eyes seeming to see everything and miss nothing.

"Lor!" breathed Cotton, watching the steel-helmed, spear-bearing, tall, fair Harlingar thunder past on their fleet steeds, "you can't tell where the horse leaves off and the Man begins. Why, they're all of one piece!"

"Ho! Brytta! *Hai roi!*" Kian called out to one of the riders, who sharply wheeled his great black horse around and checked it, seeming to stop and dismount at one and the same time.

"Lord Kian! Hail and well met!" cried the blond warrior, Brytta, a great smile beaming upon his broad features, his quick bright eyes dancing as he clasped the Daelsman by the forearm. The Man of Valon was in his early middle years, and, like his brethren, he held a spear in one hand, while a long-knife was at his belt; the fiery black steed bore Brytta's saber in a saddle scabbard on the left, while an unstrung bow and a quiver of arrows were affixed on the right. Brytta's helm flared darkly with raven's wings upon each side, and he was clothed in leathern breeks while soft brown boots shod his feet. A fleece vest covered his mail-clad torso, and a black-oxen horn depended at his side by a leather strap across his chest and one shoulder. Perry thought that he had never seen anyone look quite so magnificent, for here was a warrior bred.

"We saw your campfire early last night and knew you awaited the Army," Brytta said, "yet my Men did not call out to you, for they were on silent patrol—the advance scouts." Brytta paused; then, *"Waldfolc!"* he cried out in sharp wonderment as his eyes lighted upon Perry and Cotton. "Ai, Lord Kian, I knew you had gone to the Land of the Waldana, yet I did not think to see one here. My scouts thought yesternight that they were Dwarves, perhaps from far caverns, coming back with you to carry words to Durek. Ho! but we guessed not that *Waldfolc* came in your train. Yet wait!" He held up a hand, forestalling introductions. "I shall meet with each and every one later. But for now, we must first get this Army across the river." And as Lord Kian stepped back, Brytta sprang to his steed and with a cry of "Hai, Nightwind!" plunged after the other riders, leaving Cotton and Perry breathless in his thundering track.

Long moments fled, stretching out into endless minutes,

and the companions waited while the dawn sky lightened and morning crept silently upon the land. A quarter hour passed this way with nothing seeming to happen; but then they were startled to alertness by the flat *ta-roo* of a Valonian oxen horn pealing from the westerly direction the riders had gone: *Ta-roo! Ta-roo! Tan-tan, ta-roo! (All is clear! All is clear! Horsemen and allies, the way is clear!)*

A cold shiver ran up Perry's spine at this ancient call of safe passage, and he turned back toward the river and saw the first of the Dwarf Army just entering the wide ford four abreast, while stretching out in a line behind them to pass from view beyond the river-border woods was rank upon rank of tough, steadfast Dwarf warriors advancing upon the crossing. But in the forefront strode a Man, just now entering the water. The companions could not see his face in the shadowed daybreak, but Lord Kian sensed something familiar about the way the stranger carried himself. And then, as the vanguard reached midstream, Kian gave a great shout—"Rand! My Brother!"—and he ran splashing through the shallows to the center of the river and embraced the other. And arm in arm they laughed and waded their way back to the near shore where Kian presented his younger brother to the Waerlinga and Anval and Borin.

It did not take sharp eyes to see that Rand and Kian were close blood-kin: Rand, too, was slim and straight and tall, with the same grey eyes and golden hair as his elder brother; and they had much the same look about them— intense and alert, yet confident. While the younger Man was of the same height or perhaps a jot taller than Kian, Rand was the slimmer of the two, and he had a broad smile and seemed to be full of merriment just waiting to be released. But behind his quiet good humor Perry could sense a hidden strength, which was reflected in the somber manner of his dress: A grey cloak fell from his shoulders, and the gleam of light mail could be glimpsed under its cover; his breeks and boots were grey, and his hand rested casually upon the pommel of a black-handled sword. Yet 'round his head a colorful red-and-gold inlaid headband splashed gaudily across his brow, reflecting the cheer of his smiling eyes.

As Rand met the comrades he looked with intense interest at the Waerlinga, never having seen this Folk before; and to each buccan he gave a restrained bow. And as the young Man turned and greeted Anval and Borin, both Perry and Cotton detected a deep and abiding respect tendered to him by the Dwarves; the Warrows soon understood why, for the moment the formalities were over, Lord Kian spoke: "Rand, you rascal, why didn't you call across the water last night and tell me you were here? How came you to be with the Dwarves? I thought you north in Aven with the Realmsmen, but here you are at the Landover Road Ford. Did you come from Dael? Did you see Father? Mother?" Kian's words slid to a halt as Rand, laughing, held up his hands as if to ward off a blow.

"Please. One at a time, Brother," said Rand, "else I'll get lost. First, if I had called out to you in the night, then I would not have taken you unawares this morn—an opportunity too rare to forgo. Second, King Darion sent word releasing me from service in the northern provinces in order to guide King Durek's Legion to meet you—though I've since discovered that there are several Dwarves in this army who have travelled as far as Stonehill and who seem to know every tree, rock, twist, turn, and hole in the road on the way. Third, I came along because someone had to bring you your sword and mail shirt with which to fight this War, and I thought I might as well lug them about as anyone. Lastly, Father and Mother are both well, and Father sends word that he wants to step down and hand over the Crown, Scepter, and Throne to you as soon as this quest is ended, for he says he is old and deems the Kingdom needs your strong hand at the helm."

"Kingdom?" burst out Cotton, who had been listening with interest to Rand's words. "What Kingdom? What Throne?"

"Why, the Throne of North Riamon, of course," answered Rand, looking in amazement at the astonished young buccan. "Prince Kian, my brother, is to be its next King."

As rank after rank of Dwarves marched up out of the shallows and onward to the far edge of the border-forest to make camp for the day, the two Warrows looked with amazement at Lord Kian. It had not occurred to them to question why he was called "Lord," though they knew that it was a title of nobility; and now they discovered that he was not a "Lord" at all, but rather a Prince! Nay, not just a Prince, but a King-to-be! Perry at last understood why Passwarden Baru had treated Kian with such deference, for the Kingdom of North Riamon extended from the Grimwall Mountains in the west to the Land of Garia beyond the Ironwater River in the east, and from Aven over the Rimmen Mountains in the north to Larkenwald and the Greatwood in the south. The Holds of the Baeron lay near the center of this region, being in the middle-woods of Darda Erynian; and though these Baeron Men swore fealty to a Chieftain, he in turn pledged to the King of North Riamon. Thus, Baru and his sons had been speaking to their Liege Lord and future King when they had spoken to Kian. To think, all this time the Warrows had been travelling with, camping with, eating and drinking with, dueling with, and even scolding the next King of Riamon!

And in that long moment while the Warrows looked on in wonder, Kian seemed to take on a majesty: proud and tall, resolute and commanding. As Perry stood gaping, Cotton awkwardly—for Warrows know little of court manners—started to kneel before Lord Kian, but the Prince quickly stepped forward and raised him up. "Nay, Cotton, kneel not to me," enjoined the Man, "for the Waerlinga have knelt to no Sovereign for more than four thousand years—not since the Great War." Lord Kian then smiled and placed a hand on the shoulder of each buccan and said, "It changes nothing between us; just because one day I am to sit in a high seat, there shall be no bar between us. We are the same as we always have been, each of us growing and changing as circumstance and reason dictate, yet always around a central core of thoughts and ethics that makes you what you are and me what I am. Do not let a Kingship strip me of my friends."

Perry looked long at Kian and then took his hand and said, "A Kingship strip you of your friends? It cannot happen, for there is great strength in friendship, and it takes more than a mere change in station to put it aside or burst it asunder. Though you were the High King himself in Pellar, still would we be friends, for there is no more lasting a thing than the noble bond between boon companions; and this even a King must acknowledge.''

''Besides,'' chimed in Cotton, recovering from his shock, ''even a King—or for that matter a King-to-be—needs a couple of folks about who can keep him busy with something to do, like singing some rousing songs, or whacking away at each other with wooden swords; otherwise all he'd get to do is sign orders and issue edicts and inspect the army. Of course, every now and again we could jump into a flood and let you rescue us.'' They all laughed at Cotton's words, and smiling, turned to watch the crossing as the Dwarves continued to march by.

File after file of the forked-bearded Folk tramped past, each in a shirt of linked steel ringlets, each with an axe, each helmed with a steel cap; they made a formidable host. Dispersed along the train came trundling hued waggons bearing supplies. And occasionally, at this side of the column or that, another Valonian scout crossed; they were flank riders, drawn in for the crossing. Rand informed the companions that there were nearly four thousand one hundred warriors in the Dwarf army, and forty riders of the Valanreach—the scouts of Valon—as well as five hundred horse-drawn wains of supplies. And as they came up and out of the ford, every rider and Dwarf in the throng looked curiously at the Wee Folk, for only a few in that entire Legion had ever seen a Waeran—in the Weiunwood or Stonehill—but none had ever seen an armed or armored Waeran before, much less two of them.

''Where's this Deathbreaker Durek?'' asked Cotton, peering at the marching column.

''He shall come last,'' announced Borin with flat certainty, his statement confirmed by a grunt from Anval and a nod from Rand. ''In battle he shall be the first to the danger, but in travel he shall be the last to the comfort.''

It took almost two full hours for all the Dwarves and supply waggons to cross over, but at last the comrades saw the end of the column; and bringing up the very rear was Durek. He had gone down the line from head to tail as the march across the river began, speaking to his warriors, saying a word here and giving a nod there. And when he had reached the end of the long column he simply had turned about and brought up the rear. At last he crossed the river and came to the near shore; and he stopped and looked up on the bank at Anval and Borin, Kian and Rand, and lastly at Perry and Cotton. "Hah!" he barked in a rough, gravelly voice, "if only we had some Elves, Utruni Stone Giants, and a Wizard or two from Xian, we could resurrect the Grand Alliance of old."

As Anval and Borin stepped down to greet their King, Perry and Cotton saw before them a Dwarf slightly shorter than Anval or Borin, but one with an air of command and presence unmatched by the others. His hair and forked beard were black, but shot through with silver. His eyes were an arresting dark, dark grey. He was arrayed in black and grey and silver: grey cloak over black mail; the armor was embellished with five silver studs arranged in a circlet upon his chest; grey jerkin and breeks and black boots he wore, and a silver belt was fastened around his waist, and his cloak was clasped with a silver brooch; under one arm he held a black helm; and, as with the entire Dwarf army, he was armed with an axe scribed with blackmetal runes—yet his was an axe with a silveron-edged blade.

Borin presented the Warrows, and after greeting them and Lord Kian and acknowledging Rand's presence, Durek stated, "There is more here than meets the eye: I send you on a mission to gather knowledge of the ways in Kraggen-cor, and you return wth Waerans arrayed for battle." He scowled. "A tale lurks here for the telling, but first I must see that the Host is encamped for a day's rest; then we shall meet with my Captains and decide our course." And as the last of the Valonian riders—the rear scouts—rode across the river, Durek strode off to see to the Host-camp and to alert the Captains to the upcoming council, and Anval and Borin accompanied their King to speak of the mission to the Boskydells.

Rand led Kian and the Warrows to one of the cook-wains where food had been prepared, and along with many Dwarves they soon were digging into a hearty breakfast. While eating, Rand explained the Dwarf waggons to the others: "Most of them carry food. Some haul medicine and bandages. Certain ones carry hammers and tongs and forges and lanterns and other tools, and stores of firecoke and metal and wood. A few carry clothing and extra blankets, while others haul armor and extra axes—your

sword and mail are in one of these, Kian. Each waggon is
colored so that its hue tells what cargo is inside: green for
food, white for hospital supplies, red for armor and axes,
yellow for cook-waggons, blue for clothing, and black for
forges and tools. On the march each color is spaced evenly
among the main body of troops so that food or equipage or
medicine or any other cargo is at the head, and middle, as
well as at the rear of the column; thus, no type of provi-
sion is more than a few paces away from any warrior in
the force. And there are nearly five hundred waggons of
supplies, for this Army of four thousand must be self-
sufficient for many weeks; the goal is distant and the
march long. Durek has arranged with the Dwarves of the
Red Caverns to be restocked from that Dwarvenholt when
the waggon goods near exhaustion—but that should be
well after the issue of Drimmen-deeve is decided.''

After breakfast, Perry and Cotton returned to their campfire to laze around and catnap awhile, for their sleep had
been interrupted with the arrival of the Dwarves, and they
were yet tired from their trek over the mountains and
forced march to the river. But later that morning they
fashioned two swords from young alders, and Rand found
them engaged in a hard-fought duel when he came to fetch
them for the noon meal. He watched for a while, now and
again calling out encouragement during flèches and lunges,
or shouting approval at successful ripostes or when a touch
was scored.

"My brother said you were becoming good swordthanes,''
remarked Rand as they walked toward the nearest yellow
waggon, ''and I now see he was right.'' The Warrows
glowed with the praise.

The trio ate lunch, then strolled through the encampment. Everywhere, they found Dwarves sitting cross-legged
on the earth industriously oiling their chain-link shirts and
wiping down their double-bitted axes to prevent the forma-
tion of rust caused by the wetness of the river crossing.
The Dwarves at times stopped the Warrows to finger
Perry's silveron armor and to remark upon the fine crafting
of Cotton's gilded mail. Several spoke to Rand, but for the
most part they simply glanced up while continuing to treat
their armor. While the three were sauntering thus, they
were overtaken by a Dwarf runner: "King Durek sends his

greetings and bids that you now attend the Council of Captains in the camp of Anval and Borin where the road joins the river.''

Thus it was that when Perry and Cotton and Rand hurried back to camp, they found Durek and all his Captains sitting in a large circle, four deep, waiting for the two Warrows and the Realmsman to appear. Lord Kian and Anval and Borin were already there as well as Brytta, Captain of the Vanadurin. A spot to Durek's right was open for the trio. As soon as they had taken their place in the circle, Durek stood and spoke, his voice raspy yet clear:

"Captains, we are here to plan our attack upon the usurping Squam who defile our Kraggen-cor. It is now that I must decide whether we issue into our ancient Realm from the west, the Dusken Door, or from the east, Daūn Gate, or perhaps both, for we stand at a fork in the Unknown Cavern: we can march west over the Crestan Pass and south aflank the Mountains to the Dusken Door; or we can tramp along the Argon south and come to Kraggen-cor up the slope of Baralan. The choice is a hard one—hard as flint—for the two ways into our ancient home lie upon opposite sides of the Grimwall. If one way is wrong and the other way right, and if I err when I choose, then to correct the mistake we will have to march an extra eight hundred miles in all: four hundred miles south to Gūnarring Gap and four hundred miles back up the other side, for it will be winter and I deem the pass over the Mountains at Kraggen-cor will be blocked with snow when first we come to the Quadran.

"Upon the chosen route depends the course of the War— and the fates of us all. Hence, we must plan and plan well, and try to divine what may befall us by either approach.

"Here among us to help with this hard choice are three you already know: Prince Kian, who guided Anval and Borin Ironfist to Pellar and back, and then west to seek knowledge of the ways in Kraggen-cor; Prince Rand, who has guided us and advised us on our journey here, and who stands ready to continue on to the caverns; and Brytta of Valon, Marshal of the North Reach, and Captain of the Harlingar, who are the wide-ranging eyes of this army. There are also two here you do not know: Two Waerans—

Masters Peregrin Fairhill and Cotton Buckleburr of the Boskydells, western Land of legendary heroes, who stand ready to guide us through the passages of our ancient homeland.''

A low murmur broke out among the Captains at this last statement: *Waerans guide Dwarves? In Kraggen-cor?*

Durek held up his hand for silence, then continued: "It is a long tale that has brought us to this place, a tale rooted in the past yet growing through the present toward the future. Some of you have heard parts of this story, others have heard other parts; none of us has heard it all. But now, I propose we hear the whole of it ere I seek your counsel, for the decision I must make is one to be made in the fullest knowledge available.''

Durek called first upon Lord Kian, who spoke of the journey to Pellar and King Darion, telling in full about the outbreak of the *Spaunen* raids under the new Yrm leader, Gnar the Cruel. He recounted the pledge of Anval and Borin, in Durek's name, to eliminate the Spawn and reoccupy Drimmen-deeve. Then Kian told of the trip to the Boskydells to seek *The Raven Book* and to glean from it whatever detail of Drimmen-deeve it held. He related that the knowledge had been found, telling of Perry's offer to guide the Dwarves through the caverns. He then spoke briefly of the return journey, barely mentioning the sword training, the flood, and the avalanche—much to Cotton's disappointment, for the buccan would have made a very long, thrilling tale out of their two narrow escapes. Lord Kian was interrupted only twice during his narration: once when a Captain wanted to verify that King Darion had called off his planned siege of Kraggen-cor in order to give the Dwarves the element of surprise; and once more when Durek asked about the condition of the Crestan Pass. At the end of the tale Lord Kian resumed his seat.

Durek then asked Anval and Borin if there was aught they would add. After a long silence Anval stood and announced, "We Ironfists have named both Waerans *Châk-Sol (Dwarf-Friend)*." Then he sat down amid a hubbub of surprised conversation among the Dwarf Captains.

Durek held up his hand, and when silence fell he said to Perry and Cotton, "You have each been named *Châk-Sol* before the Council of Captains. So it was said; so shall it be.'' And Durek called a herald to the Council circle and proclaimed, "Let all the Host know that henceforth Peregrin Fairhill and Cotton Buckleburr, Waerans of the Boskydells, are each *Châk-Sol*. I, Durek, King of the Host, declare it so.''

Again the Council circle was filled with a low murmur, with the somber Dwarvish scowls of most Captains being replaced by brief smiles and curt nods to the Warrows. Though neither Perry nor Cotton knew it, to be named Dwarf-Friend was a signal honor shared by a rare few in past ages, and it was tantamount to being adopted as Dwarf-kith. It meant that the Warrows were privy to the secrets, councils, and counsels of all Dwarves of Durek's Kin.

Again Durek held up his hand for quiet; then he spoke to Perry: "Our campaign ahead is filled with many unknowns, but you can bring light into much of this darkness, for you have the knowledge of the last trek through lost Kraggen-cor. Only those of you who journeyed from the Boskydells have heard the full account of the Deevewalkers' flight through the caverns; none of the rest of us here know other than fragments of that tale. Tell us of the journey through the Châkkaholt of our ancestors, and then tell of the Brega Path.''

Perry had not known that he would be speaking before the assembly, but though he was taken by surprise, he was undaunted, for he had narrated that tale to Bosky folk many times and knew it well. Perry started at the point where the Four had failed in their attempt to cross the Quadran at Mount Coron, known as Rávenor by the Dwarves and Stormhelm by Men; and Perry's tale ended with the escape of the Deevewalkers onto the Pitch. Though he told it from memory, it was nearly as accurate as if he had been reading it from *The Raven Book* itself. The Dwarves sat enthralled, for Perry was a natural storyteller: they growled at mention of the Warder in the Dark Mere; and bitterly shook their heads at the blocking of Dusk-Door; they grunted at each mention of some legendary feature of Kraggen-cor; and cast hoods over their heads at the telling of the finding of Braggi's Stand; they groaned at the collapse of the Gravenarch; and scowled at the naming of the

Gargon; and muttered at the burning of the bridge over the Great Deep.

After telling of the flight of the survivors onto the Pitch, Perry spoke on the important meeting between Tuckerby and Brega, and the recording of the Brega Scroll. Cotton had fetched Perry's pack from the nearby campsite, and from it Perry took copies of the Scroll out of a waterproof pouch; they had been wrapped around a section of broomstick and tied with a ribbon; each copy was made on fine linen paper, and all of them together took up little space. Perry passed one copy to Durek, and the others to the Captains, and Borin assured the Council of the accuracy of the duplicates. They all studied the scrolls carefully, those in the back rows peering over the shoulders of those in front. The scrolls were passed from Captain to Captain til all had seen Brega's record.

Then Perry again addressed the Council: "The Brega Path is long and complex, being some six and forty miles from Dusk-Door to Dawn-Gate, with thousands of places to go wrong." Agreement muttered throughout the circle. "But I am prepared to guide you through, for I know the Brega Path by heart. It seems to me, however, that you will be able to plan the War more easily by seeing an overall picture of the Brega Path." And Perry again rummaged in his pack and then drew forth another paper. "This map is only my crude representation of that tortuous path and leaves out much, in fact most, of the detail of Brega's instructions, but it may be of aid in planning our strategy." And Perry passed the sketch to Durek.

Durek eagerly accepted the drawing and studied it long and hard, and then passed it to the Captains, who also scanned it carefully. A low swell of commentary rose up among the Dwarves as the map slowly made its way around the Council circle.

Neither Anval nor Borin nor Kian had seen this map til now. Perry had only remembered it the evening he had been tested by Anval and Borin, and the buccan had brought it along only as an afterthought. In truth he had not thought that the map was very useful, for it contained only the broadest detail of the Brega Scroll, and Perry had made it only to amuse himself some time after he had discovered the Scroll. But he could see that here, in the

Council of Captains, the map could be of some use in planning the broad strategy of the coming campaign; and so, what originally had been a scholar's diversion became an important tool in the planning of a War.

The Sun moved slowly down the sky while all in turn looked on this unique chart, studying it with care, seeing for the first time a plan showing some of the arrangement of the halls and chambers of mighty Kraggen-cor. After a long while the map came full circle back before Durek to lie alongside the copies of Brega's complex instructions. Durek held up his hand and gradually the babble died down.

"Now we have all heard the full tale and have seen the record of Brega, Bekki's son, and have looked upon the map of Friend Perry. Are there questions on these or upon the tale of the Four Who Strode Kraggen-cor, or upon Lord Kian's account? For on this evidence we must base our strategy."

To Durek's right, up stood a red-bearded Dwarf: Barak Hammerhand, doormaker and Gatemaster, Mastercrafter of the secret stone doorways and Dwarf portals into the mountain strongholds, one of Durek's Chief Captains. "Friend Perry, was the Dusken Door destroyed by the Monster of the Mere?" His question brought grunts of approval from the assembly, for it was a crucial point: if the Army was to invade by the western door, they must pass through the portal, and its condition would count heavily in any plan.

Perry answered: "The *Raven Book* says only that the creature had enormous strength and wrenched at the doors; Brega closed them and guessed from the sounds he heard that the Krakenward had torn down the great flanking pillars, and that the edifice collapsed, blocking the Door. They could all hear thunderous booming, as if the Monster were hurling great rocks against the Loom. In any event, the portal would not reopen, though when Brega attempted it, the doors seemed to tremble as if trying; on the other hand, the doors could have been trembling from the impact of stone being hurled by the Krakenward. Hence, the Door either may be blocked, or broken, or both. No one to my knowledge has actually seen the portal since that time, so I know not whether it can be reopened."

Barak was still standing at the end of Perry's answer, and again Durek nodded at the Gatemaster. "Friend Perry," Barak spoke up, "say again what your *Raven Book* tells us of the Great Dēop at the eastern gate." Once more Barak's question brought forth a low mutter of comment, for the state of that entrance would bear heavily in any invasion plan. Barak had put his finger on the two most critical points.

"The gulf is virtually bottomless," answered Perry, "and at least fifty feet across. The only span, the draw-bridge, was destroyed—burned—and fell into the depths, leaving no way to pass over."

Barak sat down and a white-bearded Dwarf across the circle stood. It was Turin Stonesplitter, Minemaster, delf shaper, chief of the tunnelmakers. "I also have two questions: Does the Krakenward still live? What know we of the foul Grg numbers now in stolen Kraggen-cor?"

Again Perry spoke: "As to your first question, I do not know if the Dusk-Door is still warded by the creature, for the *Raven Book* says nothing more of it. And since we are not certain of the Monster's origins, we have little to go on, little that might indicate its subsequent fate. Yet this we know: Gildor said that five hundred years before the Winter War, the Lian Guardians for weeks watched two mighty Trolls mine great stone slabs from the top of the Loom and cast them down into the vale below. And the Ogrus used these slabs to dam up the Duskrill, and slowly a black lake came into being.

"And when the Dark Mere had formed behind the Troll-dam, the Dragon Skail winged through the dark night, *bearing a writhing burden,* and dropped it in the old Gatemoat at the Dusk-Door. We now know that it was the Krakenward, a creature of power; but though the Krakenward had power, and the Dragon had power, just think of the hideously overwhelming force Modru need have wielded to cause such an evil thing to occur! Yet occur it did.

"The next day the Elves saw that the Dusk-Door had been sealed shut, by *Spaunen* hand, for now the Dark Mere with its Monster warded the west entrance.

"It was only after the Monster's attack upon the four Deevewalkers that Gildor pieced together all of the story, deducing that it was Modru's handiwork, preparing for the coming of the Winter War—*five hundred years in advance. . . .Nay! more than a thousand years, for the Evil One had previously used his art to have the Gargon set free long before!* For you see, Drimmen-deeve was to be the fortress from which would be launched Modru's conquest of Darda Galion.

"Yet I stray from your question: whence came the Monster of the Dark Mere, none can say, though Gildor did guess that it was a Hèlarms from the Great Maelstrom in the Boreal Sea."

Hèlarms? Maelstrom? A muttering again swelled up around the Council circle, but slowly subsided as Durek held up a hand for silence and Perry continued: "But as for now, the creature may still live and be in the lake, or may live elsewhere, or it may have perished with the lifting of the Dimmendark. I cannot say."

Lord Kan answered Turin's second question: "Little is known of the number of *Spaunen* dwelling in Drimmen-deeve, but there must be many, for the raids are frequent and in force. The captured Rukh questioned by King Darion said that his people were as numberless as the midges of the Great Swamp—the Gwasp—but that claim may have been spurred by false bravado to put fear into our hearts. The Rukh also spoke of Trolls in Drimmen-deeve, but that, too, may be a falsehood."

At the naming of Ogrus, fell looks came over the faces of the Captains, for they knew that the presence of these dire creatures would seriously affect the outcome of any battle. The Captains spoke in low, hushed voices at this revelation; many grimly fingered their axes. After a while Durek again held up his hand for silence. "War not with the Trolls until they stand before you, for to do otherwise is to battle with phantoms of rumor."

Brytta of Valon then spoke up: "I know not how to deal with Ogrus, but spies and ambushes along the way are my concern: what of the lands between here and the Black Hole; do enemies lurk therein?"

"As to that, I cannot say for certain," answered Lord Kian. "The Yrm raid east and south of the Pitch, along the rivers Rothro and Quadrill and Cellener to the banks of the Argon; they ravage my countrymen's holts in that southwest limit of Riamon, and raid beyond the River Nith and down the Great Escarpment into the camps and settlements of the North Reach in your Land of Valon, Brytta, as you well know, for it is your demesne they despoil.

"Yet I think the Spawn are not north of Darda Galion—the Larkenwald—for the land twixt here and there is nearly deserted, thus empty of plunder; and so, if we journey down this eastern side of the Grimwall Mountains, perhaps we will be unobserved and safe until we are nigh upon the Pitch, where we must at last encounter the Yrm raiders and patrols.

"As to the west side of the range, *Spaunen* may have crossed through Quadran Gap—yet we have no news of ravers in the Land of Rell, for that realm, too, is nearly abandoned, and Yrm would find little to carry back to Gnar's coffers. Hence, I think they come not down the western slopes; and should we march through the Crestan Pass and down that side of the mountains, we should reach unseen the very Doors of Dusk, the western gate.

"Even so, Brytta, by either route your scouts must ever be on the alert for signs of Spawn passage or spying eyes or ambush—even here in the north, especially in and near the mountains—for we know not for certain how far this *canker* has spread."

Again there was a mutter of agreement within the circle, and Durek let it run its course. Then he asked, "Are there other questions concerning the *Raven Book,* the Brega Path, or King Darion's information? No? Then let us consider our courses of action."

In the hours that followed much was said and many clever and not-so-clever courses were proposed, examined, and accepted or rejected. Often the map was referred to, and many actions were proffered based on distances between chambers and the sizes of halls. Nearly all was debated, and the Sun sank low and disappeared. A fire was kindled and still the deliberations continued. Many plans and counterplans were settled on, all depending upon the way the Host entered Kraggen-cor and the numbers and kinds of enemy encountered. Finally Durek rose to speak:

"We have before us two strike-plans which seem sound, but both abound with unknown risks, and by these risks may fail:

"First, we can invade by the eastern Daūn Gate and try to cross over the bottomless gulf. The thieving Grg must now have some sort of bridge over the chasm, for they issue in force from the Daūn Gate and withdraw through that same portal, and thus must have a way of passing over the Great Dēop. But it is certain that this bridge is constructed to foil invaders: perchance it is a drawbridge; for aught one knows it could be a span set to fall if the Squam vermin take certain actions. So we cannot count on capturing this overcrossing. Hence, to attack through this entrance we need construct invasion bridges of great span— mayhap building them in Blackwood—and haul them through the Daūn Gate and to the Dēop. This portal is certain to be heavily guarded, and Grg parties crawl all over the land betwixt Kraggen-cor and the Argon River—to launch an unexpected attack this way is unlikely. Aye, we can expect the entire Squam army to be waiting for us on the far side of the gulf; and to cross that rift in the teeth of a prepared enemy will be hard—perchance impossible— for no assailing force has ever won across the Great Dēop in a War, though many have tried.

"Our second course is to invade by the western Dusken Door. Here, mayhap there is a huge creature of great strength barring the way. And perchance the portal itself is buried under tons of rock. The very gates may be broken and no longer act—and Barak believes that such gates can be repaired only from the inside. Yet the chambers and passageways at that end are likely unguarded; and if we can gain entry through the western doors, we will take Gnar and all of his forces unaware. Our chances for success are much higher—if we can get in."

Durek stood in thought for a while, and silence reigned in the ring. All the Council waited. Cotton thought, *It's as plain as a pikestaff. The only sure way to get in is through the Dawn-Gate and over the gulf—but not if the Spawn army is there; and the only safe way to get in is past the Dark Mere and through Dusk-Door—but not if the Kraken-ward is there, and only if the door can be opened.*

At last Durek spoke: "This, then, I choose: we shall go by the Dusken Door." At these words, pent breaths were released; many in the Council relaxed: Durek had made his choice. The Dwarf King spoke on: "If we cannot get by the Warder, if it still lives and is there, or if we cannot open the doors, mayhap we can fare over the Quadran Gap and down the Quadran Run and invade by Daūn Gate—though I deem that snow will have barred that way across the Mountains. If the Gap is closed, then we must march south, through Gûnar Slot and the Gûnarring Gap, passing near the Red Hills, where we may winter. If so, then we launch our Daūn Gate invasion in the spring. Yet it is too soon to speak of failure, for we know not what awaits us at the Dusken Door.'' Durek then fell silent.

Anval had spoken little for most of the council, only grunting now and again his approval or disapproval as the plans had been put forth. He had listened to Durek's decision, and he knew as well as all the others that success hinged upon whether or not the portals at the Dusken Door could be opened. If they were damaged, then repairs could be made only from the inside. When Durek fell silent, Anval stood and was recognized. ''King Durek, that we can defeat a monster warding the Dusken Door, I do not doubt. And a Châkka army can clear tons of rubble with ease. But, as has been said here, if the doors do not open, then breaking them down or delving a new tunnel will cause enough sound to echo through the passages to alert the Grg forces, and they simply will pull the hidden linchpins—if the Squam have discovered that secret—and collapse the old tunnels, or at least delve and collapse them; and we will have to dig up an entire Mountain to get in: years of effort. Though we could then come at the eastern gate, all surprise would have been lost and the way well defended; and if we attack into an alerted enemy, it will be into their strength, and we will suffer high losses—perhaps too high. We could lay siege, but again that would take years of effort. Hence, what we need is a way to make certain that we can open the western doors; and for that I have a plan which, though it does not guarantee success, will give us a good chance at it:

''What I now propose is that a small sneak force slip through the Daūn Gate and follow the Brega Path backwards to the Dusken Door. A small force of no more than six or eight has a chance to reach the east entrance unseen and then pass undetected through the Mines and gain the western doors without alerting the Squam. Even if alerted, the foul usurpers would not connect the presence of such a small force to an impending invasion. But *if* undetected, we could put a crafter of Barak's skill at the Dusken Door, *on the inside*, to repair any damage and ensure that the doors will open to let the Army within. The gamble is great, but the stakes are high; yet he who dares, wins.'' And with these words, Anval sat back down.

A rising tide of agreement swelled throughout the circle of Captains: Brytta approved of this planned swift stroke, for it suited his bold spirit to cleave straight through the core of the enemy; Kian and Rand saw it as a brilliant yet dangerous strategy to tip Fortune's scales in their favor; the Châkka agreed, for it was an unexpected masterstroke to surprise and whelm an ancient, hated enemy; even the Warrows admired its Dwarvish nature: bold, clever, perilous, secret. But Durek cut through to the heart of the plan and found waiting there the sharp-pointed horns of yet another dilemma—and Perry was deeply shaken by Durek's next words: ''Well thought, Anval—but here is the rub of it: to succeed in this assay, Friend Perry would need guide you through the Mines along the Brega Path; and if he were delayed, captured, or slain, then there would be no guide for the Army if the Dusken Door is unbroken and we enter. Yet if the portal *is* broken, then you are right: to put Barak at the inside of the doors would all but assure victory.'' Durek then fell into deep thought, balancing the alternatives.

A dead silence fell over the Council as Durek considered the proposal. Only the crackle of the fire in the center of the circle broke the quiet. Perry felt a great foreboding, as if impending doom were about to strike; for to go into battle surrounded by an entire army is one thing, but to go among the teeming enemy with only six or seven allies is quite a different prospect. To penetrate Drimmen-deeve would mean passing through miles of lightless caverns infested with swarms of maggot-folk, avoiding detection in a place where a Rück squad could be lurking around every turn, passing through tunnels with no side passages to bolt into if trapped between groups of Spawn, and travelling along passageways with many side tunnels out of which Rücken forces could issue unexpectedly. Perry had visions of hiding furtively while maggot-folk marched past, and of

being lost in a black labyrinth, fleeing hordes of slavering
Spawn through an endless maze, and of being trapped
facing an evil army of advancing Rūcks and Hlōks. And
these visions made the buccan tremble in fear. But he
could also visualize the Dusk-Door swinging open and the
Dwarf Army marching through. The thought of passing
undetected through the center of the Rūcken forces terri-
fied Perry, but he understood the need only too well. The
risk was incalculable, but so, too, was the reward.

Shakily, Perry got to his feet and said in a small voice,
"King Durek, I will go with Anval and Barak if you
approve the plan."

In frustration, Durek slammed his clenched fist into his
palm. "*Kruk!* Had we known of the Brega Scroll but six
months ere now we could have trained another guide . .
nay, *many* other guides for this thrust! But as it is, we
have but one pathfinder where two are needed. Dare I send
our only wayleader on a mission of high risk? The reward
for success may be victory, but the penalty for failure may
be defeat. Oh, had I but another guide for my Army, then
we would take this gamble for victory."

Again the silence stretched out, drumming on the ears.
All were looking with downcast eyes at the ground, waiting for Durek to decide. Thus, few saw a small figure
stand, but all heard his words: "I know the way. I can
guide the Army along the Brega Path, even though it
means I'll be separated from my master." And Perry
looked up in astonishment, *for the speaker was Cotton!*

CHAPTER 13

THE STAVES OF NAROK

"Cotton!" exclaimed Perry, "Wha—Are you saying that *you* know the Brega Path?"

"Yes Sir," declared Cotton, "I memorized it when we were checking all those copies of the Brega Scroll you made for the Ravenbook Scholars. Riddle and reason, Mister Perry! After all, we did go over every one of them time after time til my eyes were falling out. Anybody would have learned the Brega Path if he had done what we did."

"Why, that's true, Cotton!" exclaimed Perry. "Oh, dunce that I am: I should have known that you, too, had learned the path by heart."

"Oh, Sir, you're not a dunce," asserted Cotton. "I would have told you earlier, but, you see, before the Council met, I just didn't think it was important. But after Anval told us his plan, well, I knew then that it was a matter of life and death; but there was my promise to your Miss Holly to think about: 'Goodbye, Cotton,' she said. 'Now you stay by Mister Perry, and take care of him, and keep him safe.' And I nodded *yes,* and that's a promise. I had to think of whether she'd ask me to keep it or not, knowing, as it were, how desperately these Folk need our help. And the only way we can give that help is for us to separate. I know Miss Holly would not hold me to a promise made in ignorance.

"Oh, Sir, I don't want to go away from you, but one of us must stay with Durek's Army—though that could be you as well as me. What I mean, Sir, is, well, you could guide the Army and let me go with them as is headed to the inside of the doors." Cotton hoped that Perry would accept the offer, for Cotton was thinking, *That will be a perilous trip, and I did promise Miss Holly to keep him safe.*

"Cotton, I thank you for the offer, but still I think it is mine to do. Besides, those who go through the caverns to the inside of the doors will travel the path backwards. That means the guide must be able to follow the Brega Scroll instructions in reverse: every 'up' will become a 'down,' every 'left' will then be a 'right,' every 'split' will become a 'join,' and so on. I've thought about it, and I am certain that still I can guide the penetrators—even though it is backwards on the Brega Path—for going backwards through the instructions with my mind is almost as easy as going forwards, even though I have to turn lefts into rights and make the other changes too." Perry looked searchingly at Cotton. "Knowing that everything will be all turned around in reverse, do you think you could guide the squad to the doors?"

Cotton appeared surprised. "I never thought of that, Mister Perry, but you are as right as rain: everything *will* be all backwards for them going through to the inside." Cotton then paused in inward concentration: he closed his emerald-green eyes, and a frown of intense effort crossed his countenance. After a short while, "Plague and pox!" he exclaimed, nettled, "this is worse even than trying to say the alphabet backwards after an ale night at the One-Eyed Crow! Seems like I have to start at the front most of the time and run to the place I want before I can back it up. Going forwards is easy. Going backwards is hard."

"Well, that settles it then," declared Perry. "If Durek chooses this course then I will go with the squad, and you will go with the Army."

Durek and the Council had heard all that Perry and Cotton had said, and a murmur rippled throughout the circle. Durek held up his hand for silence. "Friend Cotton, that you are certain the steps of the Brega Path are carved upon the tablets of your mind, I do not doubt, for you have been named *Châk-sol.* Even so, I cannot gamble the fate of mine Host upon skills untested—"

"Here begins the journey at the Dusken Door," interrupted Cotton, picking up one of the copies of the Brega Scroll and handing it to Durek. When the Dwarf King found the place, Cotton took a chin-up, chest-out, hands-behind-the-back, school-recitation stance and continued: "Two hundred steps up the broad stair; one and twenty and seven hundred level paces in the main passage 'round right . . ." And as Cotton recited from memory the words on the Scroll, Perry followed along in the mirror of his own mind while the Captains of the Council waited expectantly.

". . . then it's two hundred forty level paces across the hall and out the Daūn Gate to freedom." Cotton sat back down and for the first time looked at Mister Perry; and a great beaming smile was spread upon Perry's face.

Durek set the Brega Scroll aside and said simply, "We have our guide." And a rumble of approval rose up from the seated Captains as Cotton flushed in pleased embarrassment.

When silence fell, Durek turned to Anval Ironfist: "Yours is a perilous scheme for those who attempt it, but our need is dire and your plan worthy. The force must be kept small to avoid detection, yet large enough to include all the skills needed to reach the far doors and to repair the arcane hinges, if they are broken. This squad I must choose wisely, for success depends upon having the right skill at the right time." And Durek fell silent, thinking upon the problems likely to be faced.

"King Durek," said Kian, "first the force must reach Dawn-Gate. For that task a guide is needed who knows the way from here to the Pitch and thence to the east portal, a guide who is wise in the ways of woodcraftiness—to slip by Yrm parties—and one who is wise in the way of weaponry in the event of mischance and discovery. I am that guide." And Durek nodded his acceptance.

Borin stood. "In the caverns the squad will need speed and stealth, yet also strength and fury should the force be discovered: fighters to hold the way while others reach the doors and repairs are made; fighters to mislead the thieving Grg should the need arise. Warriors are wanted in this task, for which I propose myself and Anval." Durek again nodded his acceptance, for the Ironfists were the greatest of all his champions.

Red-bearded Barak spoke: "The doors of the west are known only in legend to me, yet I believe I can divine the way of their working. Two doorcrafters may be needed if repair is required, but in this I ask that three be sent, for one may be slain. For this task I propose myself and Delk and Tobin.'' Two other Dwarves stood in the Council circle: Delk Steelshank, brown-bearded and black-eyed, stern-visaged and strong-bodied; and Tobin Forgefire, fair beard and hair, smooth-faced, blue-eyed, slender for a Dwarf.

''And thus the Squad of Kraggen-cor is chosen,'' proclaimed Durek in his gravelly voice. ''Seven strong: Barak, Delk, Tobin, Anval, and Borin, and their guides and advisors: under the sky, Prince Kian, and in the caverns, Friend Perry. May success go with you.''

Then Durek took his axe by the haft at the blade and smote the earth with the butt of the handle and cried, *''Shok Châkka amonu! (The axes of the Dwarves are with you!)''* and all the Council of Captains took then their axes and together struck the haft butts hard to the ground and called out, *Shok Châkka amonu!* And the shout rang through the forest and across the river and beyond; and everywhere that Dwarf warriors of the encamped Army heard it, they knew that some of their comrades faced a grim mission.

Durek then spoke to his Captains: ''Gather your warriors on the morrow and tell them what has passed here in the Council tonight. Tomorrow, one hour after sunise, the Chief Captains are to return here for the detailed march planning.'' With that he dismissed the Council. The Dwarf King then summoned a scribe and gave over Perry's map with instructions to gather other scribes and make enough duplicates for the Chief Captains. And finally he turned to the Waerans and invited them to sup with him, and the three of them headed for the yellow waggon serving the Captains a late meal.

''Beggin' your pardon, King Durek,'' said Cotton as they sat on a log under the stars and ate by the light of the still-burning Council fire, ''but just how are we going to get to this Dusk-Door?''

''Prince Rand tells me that after we cross over the Crestan Pass we will follow the Old Rell Way down from Arden along the west side of the Grimwall Mountains; it will take us to the Quadran and the Door,'' answered

Durek, licking hot gravy from his fingers. "I am told that the Old Way is grown over and gone in many places, and all that remains are ancient pathways—sometimes wide, sometimes narrow. In places some of the old stonework even yet can be seen. The trek at times will be swift, and at other times slow, the wains holding us back. But in all, with no delays we could arrive at the western doors in a fortnight and four days, it being nearly sixty and one hundred leagues distant by that route. But we must start soon—tomorrow or the next day—for it is already the second of November, and the high snows are due to fly; we must be over the Crestan Pass ere that occurs."

"The second of November?" mused Perry. "Why, yes, it *is* already that date. I had forgotten. Today is the anniversary of when Tuck became a Thornwalker. And the ninth will be the anniversary of when Tuck and the others set out from Woody Hollow to join the Eastdell Fourth on Beyonder Guard and Wolf Patrol. The folks back home are probably angry at us, Cotton, for we have taken the Horn of the Reach with us, and they won't be able to sound it a week from now at dawn at the Commons to celebrate the beginning of what turned out to be Modru's downfall."

"Well, Sir, I'll just give it a toot right here and now, and that'll just have to do." And Cotton set his mess kit aside and jumped up and ran to his pack and pulled out the silver horn.

"Wait!" cried Perry. "Remember Anval's warning. He said to blow it only at dire need."

"Narok!" hissed Durek, and his face blenched at the sight of the trumpet. "Aie! The Ironfists told me that you had borne this token into our midst. And now I see that they spoke true. It *is* the harbinger of *Narok.*"

"That's what Borin said: '*Narok.*' Then he closed up tighter than a clam!" exclaimed Cotton, carrying the horn back to the log. "What in the world does *Narok* mean, anyhow?"

Durek looked long at Perry and Cotton and the bugle. Then he set his own mess kit down and spoke, for the Warrows had each been named Dwarf-Friend:

"Narok. I do not know what it apprehends, but it is terrible." Durek paused, and a chill ran down Perry's spine. The Dwarf continued: "The word '*Narok*' itself

means 'Death-War.' But the legend of *Narok* is an enigma
handed down from the time of First Durek. It was he who
brought the silver horn to the Châkka, having crafted it
himself, or mayhap he received it from some unknown
crafter—we know not the which of it. It bears the unmistak-
able stamp of being Châk-made, yet its creator we do not
know.

"Even in those elden days the horn was an object of
fear, and was sent north to be hidden away forever. And it
was shut away in a secret trove for thousands of years. But
it was lost to the Dwarves when Sleeth the Orm—great
Dragon of the Gronfang Mountains—came to the Châkkaholt
of Blackstone under the Rigga Mountains, slaying Châkka
and taking their home for his lair and their treasure for his
hoard.

"When Sleeth at last was slain and we heard not that the
horn was recovered, we thought mayhap it was gone forever, perchance having been unmade by the Dragon spew,
or even destroyed in the fire of Black Kalgalath's ruin.
And we rejoiced! But we knew not for certain; thus we
feared it still, for its Doom is dreadful, though we know
not its meaning."

"*Doom?* It has a *Doom* upon it?" asked Perry. "Why,
we have sounded it many, many times without harm.
Doom? I say nay! For oft times it rallied the Boskydells in
time of great need. It is not doomed; it is blessed. And
were you to hear its clarion call, you would know of its
power."

"That it has power, I have no doubt. And others may
sound it without hurt, for its Doom is not for them,"
answered Durek. "Châkka alone must face its destiny—
though when, I cannot foretell."

"We knew it had something to do with Dwarves,"
interjected Cotton, holding the horn in the firelight so that
Durek could see the riders and runes. "These riders are
Dwarves, yet Dwarves don't ride horses, if you catch my
meaning.

"I had not seen the horn til now, yet I have known
always the detail of its semblance. It is *because* of this
horn, and the legend, that Dwarves do not ride horses,"
answered Durek.

"But Brega, Bekki's son, rode horseback," said Perry.

"The *Raven Book* tells how he rode double with Gildor the Elf on the horse Fleetfoot, a steed of Arden—why, to the very doors of Drimmen-deeve, they rode. And later, Brega rode other horses, though he seemed to fear them: to Gûnarring Gap, to Gron, to Arden. So says *The Raven Book*."

"Brega was not afraid of horses," responded Durek. "He only feared the consequences of a Châk *riding* a horse, perhaps fulfilling a prophecy that would lead to the Death-War. Yet, in his time the need was great, for the world was coming to an end—impelled by the Enemy in Gron—and had Brega not been borne by steeds into battle the outcome may have been different, and that is why he rode.

"Even so, the Châkka on horses graven on this horn are known to all of Durek's Folk. And because of the legend we do not ride horses in hope that the Doom of Narok will not fall. Though we know not its meaning, we fear it."

"What is the legend? What do these runes of power mean?" asked Perry, shaken by the dread in Durek's look.

Durek paused, collecting his thoughts; then he spoke: "Translated, the runes say:

> "*Answer to*
> *The Silver Call.*

"That is but half of one couplet from the *Rime of Narok,* an ancient foretoken of the Doom from the age of First Durek. The complete rime is:

> "*Trump shall blow,*
> *Ground will pound*
> *As Dwarves on horses*
> *Riding 'round.*

> "*Stone shall rumble,*
> *Mountain tremble,*
> *In the battle*
> *Dwarves assemble.*

"Answer to
The Silver Call.
Death shall deem
The vault to fall.

"Many perish,
Death the Master.
Dwarves shall mourn
Forever after.

"These staves are known to all of Durek's Folk. They foretell a great sorrow to befall. Whence came these stanzas, none knows—perhaps from the crafter of the horn. And yet, the words of the staves do not rime in Châkur, only in Common. And its rhythm is strange to my ear; were this verse Châkka-written, it would have a different beat. Hence, we deem the crafter of this rime to be of a race other than my Folk. Horn and verse, they are a mystery. And though the stanza has been known and argued for ages, we are no closer to knowing the Doom than when the horn was first seen by Eld Durek. But we do know that the trump of the ode is the silver trumpet Friend Cotton holds. And we do not ride horses because of the rime and because of the graven images on the bugle. Aye, we believe that this small, silver horn will signal the Death-War—*Narok*—and I deem it bodes ill that it has come to us at this time."

Cotton looked at the bugle as if it were an alien thing. Always he had known that during the Winter War this trumpet had helped save the Bosky, and he believed that it was an instrument of good. Yet to the Dwarves it was a feared token of doom, foretelling of some great sorrow to come. They had rejoiced when it was lost with Sleeth, but now it was come among them again, to haunt them and to threaten their future.

Perry and Cotton and Durek sat in the flickering firelight and said nothing, each plunged deep in his own thoughts. Overhead the bright stars scintillated in black skies and wheeled through the heavens: remote, glittering, silent. At last Perry stood and took up the horn and spoke: "King Durek, we know not how to aid you against the ominous prophecy, for we know not its meaning either. But if possession of the horn will help you, then here, it is yours." And he held out the silver trumpet to Durek.

But Durek shook his head and said, "Nay. I do not want it. Though you offer me this thing in compassion for our unknown fate, I must refuse, for we are safer with it in hands other than our own."

And as he spoke Durek raised his hand to push the gift away. But at the very instant that his fingers touched the cold, silver metal, an awful portent befell! The skies aloft blazed with hundreds upon hundreds of incandescent, fiery shooting stars, streaking upon golden tails across the startled heavens. Their very numbers seemed uncountable as blaze after blaze sped to its doom. The coruscating barrage silently flared directly overhead and the land was illumed brightly as legions of burning points swept across the firmament to score the vault above.

Durek fell back in horror, his eyes wide and fixed upon the streaking fires aloft, the back of the hand that had touched the horn pressed against his mouth as air hissed in through his clenched teeth in a prolonged gasp. And a great moan of dismay rose up from the encamped Army.

And as the myriad incandescent trails faded and were gone and the land fell into darkness, Durek cast his hood over his head and walked away into the night.

CHAPTER 14

THE PARTING

It was an hour after sunrise, and the Chief Captains had gathered again at the Council fire. Spirits were subdued, for last night's awful portent, the shower of stars, had dismayed the Dwarves; they truly believed that each falling star signalled the death of a friend. But they had mastered their fear, if not their misgivings, and plans were being made for the march of the Army to the Dusk-Door and of the Squad to the Dawn-Gate:

Barak held the Council's attention: "The Dusken Door was crafted in the First Era by the greatest Gatemaster of all, Valki. He was aided in this one effort, though, by the Wizard Grevan, who cast the hidden theen signs on the portal. The lore words of vision cause the Wizard-metal runes and other markings to appear: pale in the daylight, brighter in the moonlight or starlight or on a darkling day, but brightest of all in the black of deep night. And when the markings become visible, then a wayfarer need only say the Wizard-word *Gaard,* meaning, we deem, *move,* and the doors will open—or rather, now, they may or may not open, depending upon the state of repair." Barak shook his head in regret. "Today we craft no Châk doors that open by word alone; their construction is a lost art. Yet I trust that the skill and loreknowledge that Tobin, Delk, and I hold will be equal to the challenge."

Barak paused, tugging on his red beard, and then spoke on: "But herein lies a problem: if the Army tries to open the doors from without ere the inside repairs are finished, it may create further damage. I know not for certain how long it will take Delk, Tobin, and me to set the doors aright, but time must be allowed for this task.

On the other hand, if the Squad tries to open the doors from within while still blocked without by broken stonework—as Brega tested—it could also worsen the damage. So time must be set aside to allow the Army to remove the blockage.

"It is my meaning that neither the Squad on the inside nor the Army on the outside should attempt to open the portal until both sides have completed their work. Yet how will each know that the other is ready? We must not signal through by tapping on the rock, for the rap may alert the Squam; the sound of hinge repair or rubble removal mayhap will do that in any event, but we must avoid hammer-signalling through the stone.

"As has been said, we must work to matched schedules, each side giving the other time to come to the doors and do the work, with some allowance for unknown mischance. I propose now that our separate march schedules be drawn up, and the work time allocated, and that we select the moment when King Durek speaks the words of power." Barak's counsel brought nods of approval from the Chief Captains. He continued, "King Durek, when you say the words of opening, if the portal does not swing wide, then it either will be because mischance has delayed us or because repairs are beyond our skill. If they do not open, say then *Gaard* once more, and the attempt to open will cease. In the event that perhaps we are delayed, I ask that you try again under the stars each mid of night for a sevenday. If after that time they still remain shut, then we will never come.

"I have but one more thing to say, and it is this: for our part at the Dusken Door, Delk, Tobin, and I will need no more than one day's time after we reach our goal; if we cannot repair it in a day, we cannot repair it at all."

Barak sat down and white-bearded Tunnelmaster Turin Stonesplitter stood and was recognized. "King Durek, I can only guess at the amount of rubble blocking the doors, but if necessary we have more than four thousand Châkka to remove it, whatever the quantity." Turin thought for a moment. "Give me four days—in four days we Châkka can move a small Mountain."

Prince Rand then spoke: "By the roads and paths that lie ahead of us it will take eighteen days to march to

Dusk-Door: two days and one half to reach the Grimwall Mountains, one day to cross through the Crestan Pass, one day to reach the Old Way below Arden, and the remainder to march to the western portal.''

"By my reckoning, then," calculated Durek, "by leaving here at noon today, the Army will be in position and ready to open the Dusken Door the evening of the twenty-fifth of November, two and twenty days hence. Will the Squad be ready by then?"

Lord Kian answered first: "If we use a raft by day to go down the River Argon to the wold above Darda Galion, and thence walk west across the land to the Pitch and on into the Dawn-Gate, then that will take twelve days in all: three days are needed to build the float, and at the rate the river flows, four more to raft to the point where we start overland; then, with four days of westward trek, we should reach the hills bordering the Pitch; finally, with but one more day of marching up the Pitch, we will come to the east portal."

Perry sat huddled with Anval, Borin, Barak, Delk, and Tobin. The six of them were closely studying one of the scribe-copies of Perry's map and muttering about distances and chambers and halls and stairs. At last Perry spoke up: "King Durek, the Brega Path is six and forty miles long, and two days should suffice for the passage. However, we cannot say how often we may have to hide from Spawn within the Deeves, or be delayed for other reasons yet unknown. Thus, we set aside one more day for delay. Hence, to reach the doors, we must allow three days to traverse Drimmen-deeve."

"And so," responded Durek, "twelve days to the Daūn Gate, three days to the Dusken Door, and one day for repairs: sixteen days in all for the Squad to complete the task. Since less time is needed for this venture than for the Army to be ready at the Door, you seven must delay along the way so that the completion of your task coincides with the completion of ours: start late, hold along the river, camp on the wold—do what must be done, but stay out of the danger of Kraggen-cor until it becomes necessary. The twenty-fifth of November is the appointed day that both sides must be ready.

"And now, Prince Kian, I have consulted with all of

your squadmates, and they are agreed: you are delegated as leader of the Squad of Kraggen-cor. In times of hard choice, yours shall be the final decision; I have but meager advice for you, and that is to draw upon your companions' knowledge and wisdom, listen closely to their counsel, and choose wisely.

"My Chief Captains and I have but to make final our plans for the march, and the Army shall embark at noon. You, too, must now gather the Squad together, and you must collect from the waggons the supplies you need to fulfill your task."

The seven penetrators withdrew twenty yards or so to the comrades' encampment and began discussing what was needed to carry out the mission. They spoke of food—such as crue—and water for their journey; tools to build the raft; heavy rope to bind the logs; light rope for other needs; hooded Dwarf-lanterns to light the way along dark paths; special tools—such as a small-forge and bellows and special firecoke, and augers and awls and hammers—to repair the hinges; clothing and armor and weaponry; and many other things. They did not take all they spoke of, but they considered well, and in the contemplation made firm some plans that required detailed thought.

Perry was surprised at how much yet needed to be decided and at how thorough the planning was, and he paid close heed to the deliberations. But every now and again he glanced up to see Cotton sitting in the other circle engaged in Army march planning. *Oh Cotton,* Perry thought, *you said you did not want to leave me, and in truth I, too, do not want to go away from you. But the need is great, and there is no other choice. It ever must be so in War: that best friends are separated by the circumstance of the moment. How often, I wonder, do they part never to meet again? Will we, Cotton, greet each other after today? Will either of us ever see the other, or the Boskydells, or The Root again?*

Soon the Squad completed its initial planning, and Perry went with the others to gather the needed supplies. Perry did not see the stricken look on Cotton's face as Cotton looked up and saw Perry leave; for Cotton, too, was dreading the impending separation, feeling as if he were about to be cast adrift, or abandoned, or as if he were somehow forsaking his "Mister Perry."

Anval and Borin, Barak and Delk and Tobin, Kian and Perry, all made repeated trips to the various, hued waggons, selecting supplies. At times they enlisted some local aid from Dwarves lounging in the vicinity of whatever waggon they were drawing from to help carry part of the provisions. The pile grew, and Perry wondered if all of this could actually be used by the seven of them between now and November twenty-fifth. *Oh well*, he thought, *what we don't use we can cache,* and the buccan continued collecting items under Kian's directions. Finally they were finished—and just in time, for the Army began the initial preparations necessary to start the long march.

The cook-waggons then served an early lunch, and the seven were joined by Durek, Cotton, and Rand for their last meal together before the parting. Their spirits were exceedingly glum, and for the greater part of the meal, no one said aught. Finally Durek broke the silence: "I know not what to advise, for I know not what you will meet on your mission—we are faced with too many imponderables. Still, stealth and secrecy seem called for, yet there may come times when dash and boldness will serve better. Only you can judge what will be necessary to pierce the caverns from Daūn Gate to the Dusken Door, and then only at the time you are doing it, for much of the journey cannot be foreplanned since it depends upon what the foul Grg adversary is doing. Yet this we know: You may travel under the Sun with impunity—though you must guard against Squam deadfalls and hidden traps—so make the most of daylight. At night, keep a good watch and burn not encampment fires once you are within the reach of Grg raiders. This too: enter Kraggen-cor in the morning Sun, for the east light of the dayrise will reach far into the portal, driving the Squam back, and it will be less well guarded; but the Sun will not protect you deep in the caverns, for there it does not penetrate except at the stone window-shafts; even in that light you are not safe since black-shafted poison Grg arrows can be loosed at you from the depths of the surrounding darkness. And so, take care."

And then Durek stood and said in his gravelly voice:

"Brega, Bekki's son, strode into legend along a steadfast course of honor. May the span of all our strides match his—for that is the true Brega path."

Durek then fell silent a moment, looking intently upon each member of the Squad as if to pierce the veil of the future and see their fate, but he could not; and at last he said, "May the eye of Adon watch over you, and His hand shield you from harm." And he bowed low to each of the seven. "And now we must part, for I have a far rendezvous to keep with seven trusted Friends at the mid of night on November the twenty-fifth." And the Dwarf King then turned and strode away.

At that moment Brytta rode to them on his black steed, Nightwind, and leaned down and clasped Lord Kian's forearm. "My Lord, fare you well. Eanor, King of all Valon, would bid you safe journey were he here, but he is not, so I speak for all of my countrymen: Good fortune to you all, each and every one!" And with a waving salute to the members of the Squad, the Man from Valon called out to his mount, and they thundered away.

Cotton went to Perry and they embraced. "Now, Sir, you are part of the Secret Seven, so don't go giving yourself away to no Rūcks. And stay out of trouble for your Miss Holly's sake."

"I don't envy you going back over the Crestan Pass again, Cotton, but say 'hullo' to Baru and his sons for us," responded Perry, attempting to be casual; but then: "Cotton, old friend, I'm going to miss you, but we shall meet again at the Dusk-Door."

Rand and Kian also embraced and looked long at one another. "The Kingdom needs your hand, Kian," said Rand. "Keep safe; wear that chain mail we hauled all the way from Dael."

"Rand, when this is over," pledged Kian, "you and I shall take the time to go on a long hunt as in days past: ahorse, with falcon, hawk, and dog. Til we meet at the west portal, fare thee well, my brother."

The Seven stood at the edge of the woods and watched as Brytta's mounted scouts of Valon—acting upon Rand's description of the lay of the land and the planned Dwarf Army march route—rode off in different directions out upon the grassy plains, while the Dwarf column formed up on the road: Dwarves four abreast in march order, waggons pulling into their assigned places in line, spare horses tethered to the tailgates of the black waggons. The Sun stood at the zenith when at last all was ready. Durek's voice rasped out, *"Châkka!"* There was a long pause while like a dying echo the order was repeated down the line by Captain after Captain. *"Hauk!"* And the Army began to move.

Like some vast multilegged creature, the Legion surged out onto the plains: Dwarf boots tramping on hard-packed road; hued waggons rolling slowly forward: the slap of sideboard, the creak of harness, the grind of iron rims rolling; the jingle of armor; the clop of hooves: all these sounds and more the four-mile-long column made as it undulated slowly out over the prairie. As Durek strode by at the head of the force, he and Rand saluted the Seven with an upraised right hand, and so did the Captains as each of them passed by. Rank after rank tramped past with tinted waggons spaced along the line: white, green, black, red, blue, and yellow. At last the Squad saw the end of the train approaching them, and at the very last came a yellow cook-waggon being drawn by Brownie and Downy, and beside the grey-bearded driver sat Cotton.

As this last waggon rolled by, Cotton, though distressed, smiled at his "Secret Seven" and waved. The wain slowly trundled past and moved out onto the prairie. Cotton stood and faced back toward the Seven and drew his sword and held it to the sky, the golden runes on silver blade burning in the sunlight, his gilded armor blazing as well. *"Shok Châkka amonu!"* he cried out, "and the swords of the Bosky, too!" And he quickly faced about and sat down, for he did not want them to see that he was weeping.

Perry stood by a birch tree and leaned his head against the smooth white bark as he watched the column march toward the Grimwall Mountains, dimly visible low on the horizon. The plains were flat, covered only by tall waving grass and heather, and so he watched for a long, long time as the Host moved out across the wold. The Sun had fallen past the zenith to midafternoon when the buccan at last turned away and trudged toward the campsite, unable to see the yellow waggon any longer.

CHAPTER 15

WAROO

"It ought not to be this way, Bomar," said Cotton to the grey-bearded Dwarf on the seat beside him, and then the buccan turned around again to look far back over the grassland toward the distant border-forest. "No sir, it just ought not to be this way. When you say goodbye to your best friend, you just ought to disappear with a flash and a bang and maybe a puff of smoke, and get the goodbye over with all at once. Instead, we said goodbye almost three hours ago, and here I can still see the silver glint of his armor in the Sun, and maybe he can still see the gold of mine. It just makes the parting last longer."

Cotton once more faced the mountains, but he could not remain that way for long, and again he turned to look back over the plains toward the river. "Oh," he said in a small, dismayed voice, for the argent glint was gone, and Cotton felt as if he had somehow betrayed Perry by not seeing the glimmer disappear. Glumly he faced forward along the direction of march.

Stretching out before him was the long Dwarf column, feet tramping and wheels rolling toward the mountains ahead. Except for the Army, and an occasional distant scout, Cotton could detect nothing else moving across the prairie, not even the wind. With little to distract him, the Warrow rode along in silence, feeling all alone amid an army of strangers, paying scant heed to anything except his own wretchedness.

"Put your sorrow behind you, Friend Cotton," advised Bomar after a while, flicking the reins lightly to edge Brownie and Downy a bit closer to the ranks ahead. "Though you have parted from a boon comrade, do not dwell upon the woe of separation; think instead upon the cheer of reunion, for you will have a tale to tell that he knows not and will hear from him an adventure new to you.

"But Bomar," protested Cotton, "if it's tales and adventures we're living, well then I'd rather be in the same story with my master than in a different one."

Bomar tugged on his grey beard and scowled. "Friend Cotton, you are not in a different venture from your 'Mister Perry.' Aye, you are now separated from him, yet the tale is the same—separate or together, we are all of us living in the same story: it is a tale that was started before the beginning, before the world was made; and it will go on after the end, when even the stars are unmade again. And in any tale such as this there are those whose accounts seem always to touch, and those who weave in and out of the tales of others, and many more whose narratives touch but once or never. Even twins, or brothers, or kindred, or just good companions will have times of separateness. We must savor the times we are together; and store up the times we are apart, like precious gems to show if ever we are united again. Let not the sadness of separation dull these jewels, but instead look with joy toward your reunion so that they will brightly sparkle."

"Why, you've hit the nail right square, Bomar!" exclaimed Cotton in surprise, seeing the separation in a different light. "We *are* still in the same story together. And I've got to start living my part of it, looking at things through happy eyes, not sad ones, so that when we get together again, well, I'll have some of them bright jewels to show him."

Had it been an overcast day, perhaps Cotton's somber mood would have clung longer, but the Sun was shining in a high blue sky, and the Warrow's spirits rose with every turn of the waggon wheel, until they were as bright as the day. "Bomar," added the Warrow after a long while, "I do hope that Mister Perry has someone as wise as you to set him right about being apart from a friend." A smile flickered over Bomar's face, but he said nought; and the waggon rolled on.

The column moved across the prairie all that afternoon, finally coming to a halt at dusk. They had covered some fourteen miles, and in the distance before them they could see the foothills rising up to meet the mountains—though where the column had stopped was still well out on the plains.

The cook-waggon rolled off the road and into the bordering grass and heather, parking beside a green food-waggon. Bomar and Cotton jumped down and were joined by eight bustling Dwarves, each of whom began to work at tasks under Bomar's directions: Nare made three fires using wood brought in the waggon from the river-border forest, for Bomar as well as the other cook-wain drivers had known the column would stop on the open treeless prairie, and each had cut, loaded, and hauled a supply of firewood from the margins of the Argon to use in preparing the evening meal. Caddor and Belor filled great teakettles with water from the barrels, while Naral set up hearth-arms to hang the kettles over the fires; and Oris, Crau, Funda, and Littor began preparing a vat of stew.

Cotton unhitched Brownie and Downy and led them a short way out into the lush prairie grass where he fed them some grain, then hobbled them to graze. He stood and talked to each horse awhile, stroking them, and then went back to the waggon.

When he arrived at the cook-site, the pots and kettles were bubbling and boiling merrily, and supper was on its way. Cotton pitched in and helped with the chores that remained. In about an hour the meal was ready, and the cook-crew served stew and honey-sweetened tea to one hundred or so hungry warriors, and to one lone scout who rode in after dark. Before sitting down to a meal of their own, Bomar's crew set a pair of large kettles of water to boil over two of the fires; they would be used by the warriors to wash and rinse their mess kits.

Cotton was just dishing up some stew for himself when Durek and Rand strode into the circle of firelight. "Well, Friend Cotton," rasped Durek, "though in your case it will not be critical til we reach the Dusken Door, the tail end of the train is a strange place for one of my pathfinders to be." Laughing, they sat down for a meal together.

When Cotton went to bed that night, after helping Bomar's crew clean up, he noted that the Dwarf Army had set up a picket of sentries; the buccan felt a twinge of regret that he wouldn't be standing his turn at ward; he had come to enjoy seeing the dawn sky slowly change from black to grey to purple to pink and orange, joyously heralding the arrival of the Sun.

The next morning Cotton was awakened by the sound of Bomar and his crew rattling pans and kettles, preparing the breakfast meal. Cotton jumped up and discovered that he had not missed dawn after all, for it was still dark; and as the buccan was to learn in the days to come, Bomar's day started early and ended late. The Warrow helped Bomar with the work, and watched the sky celebrate the coming of the golden orb; and the buccan served warriors as the Sun tipped over the rim of the world.

Following breakfast, Cotton went to Brownie and Downy. After greeting them with an apple treat, he removed their hobbles and led them back to the waggon and fed and watered them. Then he hitched them to the yellow wain while Bomar's crew loaded the utensils aboard. Soon the command to march came echoing down the line, and the cook-waggon pulled back onto the road.

In midmorning the Army entered the foothills and began slowly climbing higher as they moved up the shallow slopes of the lower flanks of the mountains. Cotton noted that in these uplands the leaves for the most part had lost their bright colors and had become a uniform rich brown, with just a few reds and yellows stubbornly remaining. And many of the leaves had fallen, to crackle and crunch and swirl 'neath tramping feet.

The march continued on through this umber woodland for the rest of the day, stopping a few moments each hour for a brief rest. During these stops Cotton would finger his sword and think of other days. It was early dusk when the Legion came to their final stop; they had marched some twenty-nine miles since dawn.

That evening Cotton again took a meal with Durek and Rand, but the Man and Dwarf brought with them three surprise guests—Grau, Rolf, and Wrall: Baru's sons; the head of the column had stopped at the Passwarden's stone cottage. As they ate, their conversation turned to the Crestan Pass. "Father says you have come just in time," said Rolf, "for he feels snow deep in his bones—has felt it these past five days, ever since we were up in the pass clearing away the scree from the slide our Lord Kian told us of. And Father says each day the feeling grows stronger: the weather must soon break."

Durek squinted through the dark in the direction of the pass. "In days agone we did not concern ourselves with the snows; the Mountain tops could be covered with ten fathoms or a hundred of snow, but that affected us not— for then we knew the way under."

"Under?" asked Grau. "Do you speak of the mythical pass beneath the mountain? Why, that's just a tale to amuse children."

"Nay," replied Durek, "the way is there. Though it is lost, it remains there still, hidden behind secret Châkka doors. These Mountains have many hidden entrances and exits which lead to the tunnels below. And here as in Kraggen-cor the caverns reach from one side of the range to the other."

"Hey!" exclaimed Cotton, "speaking of secret doors, I just remembered: Bosky legends warn about Rūck-doors under the Grimwall. They say Modru's Mines are down there, behind hidden Rūck-gates. I wonder if any of those Spawn-doors are nearabout."

"The Rutch-doors onto these slopes were destroyed by my forefathers," responded Grau. "We are told that the Baeron fought the Rutcha and Drōkha and Ogru-Trolls in the hills and mountains above Arden and Delon for many years. At last all of the Wrg-doors into the passes also were found and destroyed; that I have always believed to be true; but never did I deem the tale of the way under the mountain to be true til now."

"Even if we knew where it was, it'd be trouble, wouldn't it?" asked Cotton. "I mean, well, what about the maggot-folk? Aren't they still down there waiting?"

"No," replied Wrall. "The last of the Spawn were driven away by my forebearers in the time of the Winter War."

"Then why don't we just hunt up the Dwarf-doors to the way under and go that way, instead of worrying about snow?" asked Cotton.

"I am told that the secret doors of the Dwarven Folk are hidden too cunningly," answered Rand. "Unless you know exactly where they are, you'll never find them; they look just like unbroken rock walls, or large boulders, or even great slabs lying on the slopes. So, Cotton, it isn't just a matter of simply hunting up the doors, for we don't even know where these portals are or what they look like; and we can't pry up every rock and boulder on the mountain-side, or tap with hammers on every rock wall for hollow sounds. We'd be here til the mountains were gone before we'd find even one door.''

''Aye. Prince Rand has the right of it,'' growled Durek. ''Once the way is lost, it is usually lost forever. Without guidance, the entrances remain hidden. Even with instruc-tions, sometimes the way cannot be found. Even so, were we to stumble accidentally onto a door, still we would not pass under the Mountain, for we have no 'Brega Scroll' here to guide the way through.''

''Say!'' exclaimed Cotton, ''I just thought of some-thing: are we going to have trouble finding the Dusk-Door? Oh, I know the *Raven Book* says the Door had steps and columns and such, but, if Dwarf-doors are impossible to find, what about the door we're going to?''

''Worry not, Friend Cotton,'' replied Durek, ''the Dusken Door was meant to be found. It was made as part of an old trade route, and the way to it is well marked. It is not hidden, except perhaps now by stonework rubble.''

''Well that's good,'' said Cotton, '' 'cause I'd hate knock-ing on stone walls with hammers and prying up slabs with crowbars for the rest of my life.'' They all enjoyed a hearty laugh at Cotton's words, especially Durek, who found the image of a Waeran scrambling over stone with hammers and pry bars hilarious.

Though the talk was lively and the company pleasant, at last Durek and Rand had to leave to see to the roadside encampment and to plan the morrow's march. Reluctantly, Grau, Rolf, and Wrall also left, for they knew that it had been a long day's journey for their friends, and rest was needed for the upcoming trek. After the visitors were gone, Cotton pitched in to help Bomar and the rest of the crew clean up the utensils, and he bedded down about an hour later.

*   *   *

The Army got under way again shortly after sunrise. Soon Cotton's waggon rolled past the stone cottage, and he waved goodbye to Baru, Grau, Rolf, and Wrall, who called, ''Good fortune!'' And the Baeron watched as the column disappeared from sight in the wooded hills.

The march twined through the uplands, winding higher and higher upslope. The mountains now towered above the Host, the stone ramparts impervious to the many-legged creature crawling up the flanks. The Sun, too, climbed up the mountain, warming the escarpment above. The Army tramped upward along the road, which wove back and forth through the mountain forests. As the column climbed higher, the woods slowly changed from the lowland trees, such as oak and maple, to upland wood, such as aspen and other poplars, and at last to the evergreens of the high country.

It was midafternoon when the Army came to the last thick stand below the timberline, and the Legion was called to a halt. They had covered eighteen miles of upward march, and though there was daylight still, the trek was halted, for from here it was twenty miles of open mountain before timber would be reached again; and the nights of November were too bitter upon the open crests to permit travel after dark, and so camp was made early.

With a cry of horns, all of Brytta's scouts, too—point, flank, and rear—were called in to join the column at camp; all, that is, except for the Army's advance eyes: four Vanadurin outriders: a lead scout named Hogon—who had journeyed this way a year or so earlier—and three others, all of whom had ridden ahead and were even now crossing the range.

Cotton tethered the horses in the pines and returned to help build the fires. The Sun had passed behind the peaks, and a chill shadow lay over the land; but the encampment was much colder than the shadow would account for: a frigid iciness seeped down from the heights; borne on a raw drift of air that spilled from the summits and slid to the borders below. As evening approached, the drift became a breeze blowing downward. Cotton and others donned warmer clothes from their packs, but still the chill bit through, and the fires were built higher to provide more warmth.

An hour after sundown, the warriors had been fed and the supper cleanup was finished, though kettles of hot tea still remained over the cookfires as proof against the frigid cold. Cotton was just filling his cup when a Dwarf picket rang out a call—"Someone comes!"—and Cotton heard footsteps trotting up the road. As they sounded closer, Cotton could see in the firelight that it was a Man—it was Rolf!

"Rolf!" Cotton called. "Over here!" And the youth came winded to the fire.

Without speaking further, Cotton offered the panting young Man a cup of tea, but Rolf waved it away and croaked, "Water!" Far from being cold like those huddled around the campblaze, the youth was drenched with sweat from his run. Swiftly, Cotton dipped a cup into a water barrel and passed it to Rolf. The Man gulped the drink, gasping for air between draughts. After another cup and a few moments to catch his breath, he asked, "Where's Durek? A blizzard is coming, and he must be warned."

"Why, he's up front somewhere," answered Cotton, waving a hand up the road toward the mountain, and he watched as Rolf trotted away.

It was not quite an hour later that a Dwarf herald came through the night to each fire, finally arriving at Cotton's. "King Durek summons all Chief Captains and all who have travelled through the pass on other journeys to counsel him at midtrain," he announced to the group. And so Cotton, who had been through the Crestan Pass, stood to go—as did Bomar and Littor, both of whom had been over the mountains to Stonehill. Together the three walked toward the front of the long encampment, going nearly two miles to the midpoint of the column. There Durek had formed a Council circle.

Durek spoke to the gathering: "Rolf brings word from Baru. You must all hear, and prepare for what comes." And he indicated to Rolf—now wrapped in a blanket—that he was to speak.

"My father, Baru, says that a blizzard will be in the peaks ere noon tomorrow, announced the youth in a clear voice. He wetted a finger and held it up in the chill breeze. "That wind you feel is known as the breath of Waroo. To the Baeron children the story of Waroo is a hearthtale of a great white bear from the north with very cold breath who claws over the tops of the mountains to bring hard winters down onto the land. But upon growing older we find that Waroo the Blizzard is much more deadly than any white bear—for when a bear stalks it can be fled from, or, at last resort, it can be slain, but a blizzard at best can only be endured, never killed. And when Waroo approaches, his breath flows coldly adown the Grimwall, and it signals the first blizzard. When Father felt Waroo blowing down below, we knew we had to warn you, and I came, for I am the swiftest.

"If you are to pass over the mountain, you, too, must move swiftly, for you have twenty miles of barren high rock to cross before the shelter of timber is reached. You cannot go in the night, for it is too cold, yet you cannot delay overlong, for the storm will strike sometime tomorrow.

"Father advises that you do not go at all, for he is afraid you will perish in any attempt; yet he realizes that you feel you must. His next advice then is that you prepare tonight, dress in your warmest winter clothes, and start just before dawn. Still, it will be bitter that early, but leaving then at a quick step may get you across ere the snow flies—though he doubts it.

"I offered to guide you, but Father laughed and said, 'The only time you may guide a Dwarf is when he's not been there before. Durek needs not our guidance across the mountain, for he has Dwarves in his company who have crossed over ere now.' Father did say that he has felt this storm coming for a week or more, and he expects it to be an ill one." Rolf hitched his blanket around himself and sat down.

"How many here have walked the Crestan Pass?" asked Durek, pausing while he counted upraised hands. "I tally three and twenty Châkka. This then is what I propose: Gaynor, you shall head the column at Prince Rand's side; Berez, you shall walk with me along the train; Bomar, you shall hold your position at the last; let the rest count off and evenly space along the line—ten with the ten red waggons, the other ten with the black. If the storm strikes while we are yet upon the open stone and our sight is limited by the snow, let each guide lead a segment of the train to come down into the thick pines above Arden.

Stragglers are to follow the red and black wains; Bomar, you sweep up any who fall all the way to the rear. Marshal Brytta, hold your scouts with the column, spaced along the train with the white waggons. All in the Host shall wear their down-filled clothing on the march tomorrow, or tonight if needs dictate. We will leave one hour before sunrise, which will give us six hours to go the twenty miles if the snow does not come til midday. With a quick-march we may yet succeed in outstepping the storm. Any additions to the plan? Questions? No? Then, Captains, instruct your warriors; guides, count off and find your waggons.''

Durek turned to Rolf: "Baru's son, your warning may save our quest, for without it we surely would have started on our march tomorrow at a later hour, and we would have gone at a slower pace. Though your sire would have us turn back from this danger, we cannot, for delay of our mission means the evil in Kraggen-cor will live longer and more innocents will die. And though Baru holds us in concern, he knows we must go on.

"We welcome you to rest this eve with us, for you are weary from your gallant run. Stay the night, and bid us farewell in the morning, and carry the word to your father; he will see that it is borne to those who should hear tidings of the Host.''

Durek stood. "And now we must rest, for tomorrow promises to be a hard task. Oh, Waeran''—he looked across at Cotton—"if you have no goose-down winter suit in your pack, draw one from a blue waggon." Without further word, the Dwarf King turned and walked off toward the front of the column.

Accompanied by Brytta, Cotton and Bomar made their way back toward the rear of the train. There was a dark brooding upon the face of the Man from Valon. "You look like a storm about to burst, Brytta," said Cotton. "What's gnawing at you?"

"My far outriders, the advance scouts," Brytta replied grimly. "Hogon, Eddra, Arl, and Wylf, they are some leagues ahead of us, beyond the Crestan Pass. If there is a blizzard, it will strike them first. I would that they were among us rather than . . ." His voice trailed off, but Cotton and Bomar knew his feelings.

They soon came to the scouts' fires, and Brytta turned aside to join the Harlingar. Cotton and Bomar strode on, stopping only long enough at a blue wain to draw warm winter Dwarf-clothing; Cotton was given the smallest goose-down-filled quilted coat and quilted pants that the driver could find; they were still overlarge on the Warrow, but would have to serve.

It was yet black night when Cotton was awakened. The raw wind was blowing harder, but the down-filled clothes kept the Warrow warm. Bomar had shown him how to fasten the hood so that his face was protected, and the Warrow could peer out at the world through a fur-rimmed tunnel; Bomar had also given him some mittens, fastened together by a long cord that ran up one sleeve and down the other to prevent loss.

Cotton hitched the horses to the waggon, and after a cup of tea and a crue biscuit, he was ready to start. Upon command, warriors quenched the fires, and Dwarf-lanterns were unhooded along the column to bathe the train with their lambent soft blue-green light while all waited. Finally the order came, and the Dwarf column moved out at a quick-step pace. Shortly Cotton's waggon passed Rolf standing huddled in a cloak next to the only remaining camp-fire. Cotton's hood was back, and by the firelight Rolf recognized him and waved. Cotton called, "Goodbye, Rolf. And oh, by the by, say 'hullo' to Baru, and Grau and Wrall, too. Say 'hullo' for Mister Perry, also. Or maybe instead of saying 'hullo' you ought to say 'good-bye' for us. . . . Whatever."

And Rolf called back, "I'll untangle the greetings from the farewells, Cotton. Good fortune. Take care. And beware of Waroo, the White Bear." And the young Man watched as the last of the train moved away in the cold darkness, a long line of blue-green lanterns swinging and bobbing up the windy slopes.

The Legion marched swiftly, and after a while Cotton could tell by the sound of the waggon wheels and see by the glow of the lanterns that they were no longer in the woods. The strength of the wind increased, and it groaned and wailed through the crags and moaned down the side of the mountain, and the higher they went the more bodeful it sounded.

When daylight finally came it was dim, and fell through an overcast; and they could see an ominous blowing whiteness streaming from the crests, like enormous ragged clinging grey pennons slowly whipping and flowing in the wind that howled over the range from the far side. Cotton could see that the white streamings came from the old high snow as part of it was blown from the peaks and whipped about and carried up and far, far out to disappear—perhaps to sift down onto the foothills or plains far below, he could not tell which. The Host was about six miles from the Crestan Pass, and the cold was oppressive; and with the overcast the Sun would not warm the journey at all.

The nearer the Army came to the pass, the stronger grew the wind, for on the far slope whence the gale blew, the mountain flanks on either side of the route acted as a huge funnel, and the wide wind was channeled to blow through and over the constricted slot in the saddle. The shrieking gale frightened many of the teams on the narrow way, and they had to be led by those on foot, or even blindfolded and pulled against the screaming blast. Thus it was that as the column entered the pass, a howling gale-force tramontane pummeled and buffeted the Dwarves, and slammed at them, and tried to blow them and their horses and waggons away. The blast was so strong that Dwarves on foot had to lean and struggle to get through the gap, and most of the teams and waggons had to be pulled and pushed by warriors just to make it up the last slope. The wind took Cotton's breath away, and he had to struggle and gasp just to get air. Finally the column was through, past the neck of the funnel, though the wind tore and howled at them still, and voices could not be heard. With his elbow, Bomar jostled Cotton, getting the Warrow's attention and pointing ahead. With wind-watered eyes Cotton squinted out through his hood to see a roiling wall of white advancing up the reaches on the wind: the blizzard, Waroo, the White Bear, had come, and they were still ten miles from safety.

Driven by the yawling blast, the snow hurtled over the train, enveloping it in white obscurity. Signing Cotton to work the brake, Bomar climbed down and made his way to the horses; he took one of the bit reins in hand and began leading the team and waggon through the howling wind and slinging snow. The wind-whipped whiteness whistled up the precipice and along the wall, through crags and canyons, around bends and corners, and lashed into Cotton's face. He drew his hood tighter to fend the blast; still, he had to duck his head to keep the snow from driving through the fur tunnel and into his eyes. Now and again the Warrow glanced up to get a quick look at where they were going, but all that Cotton could see clearly were the Dwarves on foot directly in front, and the next waggon ahead; he could make out the vague shape of the waggon beyond, but could see no farther. He noted that at every side canyon and false trail, Bomar would move across to scan for stragglers, but so far had found none—though if they were more than twenty or thirty yards distant, an entire army could have been lost.

Slowly, for what seemed like days, the buffeted Legion moved down the raging mountainside. And the snow grew thicker until Cotton could but barely make out Bomar leading the horses. At first the driving wind did not allow the snow to collect on the path, whipping it off as fast as it tried to accumulate. But then at corners and crevices it began to gather in drifts. The train came to a complete halt at times; Cotton believed that the head of the column had come to a drift that had to be cleared before they could go on. In these places the braking was slippery, and often the waggon lurched perilously close to the edge of the precipice, with Cotton's heart hammering wildly.

The white wind howled and screamed and pummeled horse, Dwarf, Man, and Warrow alike, and it seemed to suck the heat right out of the body and dash it against the looming stone walls to be consumed without effect on those frigid surfaces. Sitting up high on the waggon seat, Cotton was chilled to the marrow, but as cold as he was, he worried more about Brownie and Downy: even though they were toiling, active with the labor of working the wain downward, moving against the storm, there was no doubt that if they did not reach shelter soon the horses would perish in the freezing shriek.

Bomar not only realized the plight of the horses, but he knew Cotton's condition, too, and the Dwarf arranged for one of the walking warriors to spell the buccan, who then helped lead the team. And even though the white wind raged and blasted him with snow, Cotton warmed a bit in the effort of walking, though he was still miserably cold.

They continued down the treacherous slopes, trapped on a howling trail, caught between a sheer wall and a steep precipice, passing by yawning canyons in the wall, trudging beyond forks in the path. At one false trail Bomar found a squad of lost Dwarves who had somehow become separated from the column in the obscuring whiteness. They had struggled down a wrong split but had realized that they were alone and had just fought their way back to the main route when the waggon rolled by. A long rope was tied to the tailgate, and the Dwarves gripped it and trailed along behind as the party pushed on for the unseen pines somewhere below.

Cotton had lost all sense of time and place and direction, stumbling along through the white blindness and into the teeth of the screaming blizzard. He was wretchedly cold—freezing—and wanted nothing more than to be in front of a blazing fire at The Root, or no, not even that, just to be warm *anywhere* would be enough. Numbly Cotton looked at the whistling whiteness flinging past and was thankful he was with Bomar, for without the sturdy Dwarf, Cotton knew that he and the others would not know the way and would die among the frozen crags.

They had collected another squad of stragglers, this time with a green waggon, and were pressing on into the icy blast. Cotton and several of the Dwarves took turns driving the two waggons, working the brakes while others led. And Cotton was on the seat of the yellow waggon when he discovered that they had just come among a few sparse trees. "Hurrah!" he hoarsely shouted. "We've made it!" But the wind whipped away his words and shredded them asunder, the fragments to be lost in the vast whiteness, and no one heard him.

Grimly, Bomar pressed on, for they had two miles to go to reach the thick pines, and in the blasting white gale it took another hour. But at last they came to the sheltering forest: Bomar leading and Cotton up on the yellow wain with nineteen lost Dwarves holding onto a rope trailing behind followed by a green waggon.

As Bomar and Cotton and the tagtails emerged from the swirling snow, Durek, who had been standing in the eaves of the wood, stepped forward and directed them into one of the shielded glens where lean-tos were being constructed and many fires blazed. And as the stragglers passed, Durek smiled, for they were the last.

There among the trees the wind was not as fierce, for the thick pine boughs held it aloft and warded the Host. Still the snow swirled and flew within the glens and collected heavily on the branches; and so the fires were kindled out from under the limbs—otherwise, the heat would melt the snow to come crashing down.

Cotton drove the waggon to the place indicated and numbly crawled down to accept a hot cup of tea from Rand, who was waiting; and the shivering Warrow diddered, "W . . . well, we m . . . m . . . made it. The w . . . worst is over."

"Not yet, Cotton," replied Rand grimly, gauging the snowfall. "We must move on again as soon as possible, for to stay here will trap us in deep drifts."

Night was falling, but the need to press on was urgent. Durek called his Chief Captains together, and their tallies showed that thanks to Bomar and the other guides, miraculously no one had been lost, though three waggons had slid over the edge, pulling the doomed horses with them—yet the drivers had each managed to leap to safety. Thus, all were accounted for except Brytta's four advance scouts, of which there was no sign. It was hoped that the quartet of Valonian riders had forged ahead to the low country ere the blizzard struck; yet Brytta fretted, though nothing could be done to aid his missing Men.

The Host was exhausted, chilled to the bone, and so Durek decided that the Army would rest in the pines until the snowfall became deep enough to be worrisome—judged by Rand to be about four or five hours hence. The Chief Captains made plans for a risky lantern-lit trek through the blizzard, should the need to move onward become imperative.

But they had reckoned not upon the course of the storm, for it doubled its fury within the next half hour; and the driven snow thickened, and the blizzard could not be endured out of the shelter of the pines; and so the planned night march was abandoned.

Later that night a drained Cotton wearily leaned his head against a pine tree trunk as he sat on a carpet of fallen needles and stared through the low, sheltering boughs at the fluttering fire under the nearby lean-to. The wind moaned aloft, and the snow thickly eddied and swirled down. Tired though he was, anxiety gnawed at Cotton's vitals, for all he could think of was, *What if we're trapped here? What if we don't get to Dusk-Door on time? The twenty-fifth will come and go, and Mister Perry and the others will be trapped down in the Rūck pits.*

Overhead, Waroo, the White Bear, raged and groaned and moaned and growled, and stalked about and clawed at the mountains and doubled his fury again.

CHAPTER 16

RIVER RIDE

Perry walked back into the campsite where the other members of the Squad were gathered. "Well, they've gone," he announced. "I stood and watched and could see them for three hours before the last waggon passed beyond my view on the flat prairie. Oh—I shall miss Cotton dearly, but we will meet again at the far door."

"Three hours?" questioned young Tobin Forgefire. "You watched them go away for all that time? Hmph! That was a long goodbye. In the caverns of Mineholt North—or in any Châkka cavern for that matter—goodbyes can last but a moment, for that is all it takes before the one who is leaving turns a corner or passes through a door and is lost to sight. On the other hand, hellos can last a goodly while, since those who are meeting can stand together and talk for as long as they wish. Hah! That is the way it should be: short goodbyes and long hellos."

Lord Kian looked up from the smooth bare ground in front of him. "Dwarves have the right idea when it comes to partings and meetings," he agreed. "You and I, Perry, can learn much from these Folk." Then Kian began scratching marks in the smooth earth with a short stick.

Perry watched for a while, puzzled, but just as he started to ask about it, Lord Kian called the Squad together. "When I was a lad in Dael," he began, smoothing over the loam, "often Rand and I would construct a raft out of tall, straight trees and float down the River Ironwater to the Inner Sea and visit the city of Rhondor." A faraway look came into Kian's eyes. "There we would sell the raft for a silver penny or two, for Rhondor is a city of fire-clay tile built on the coastal plain along the shores of the great

187

bay, and wood is always in short supply and welcomed by
the townspeople. And Rand and I would take our coins
and tour that city of merchants, where the market-stalls
had items of wonder from Pellar and Hurn and even
faraway Hyree. Ah, but it was glorious, running from
place to place, agonizing over what things of marvel to
buy: pastries and strange fruit; trinkets and bangles and
turtle-shell combs for Mother; curved knives and exotically
feathered falcon hoods for Father; horns made of seashells;
mysterious boxes—it was a place of endless fascination.
After spending our money on the singled-out items,
winnowed from the bedazzle, we would trek home to
bestow the largess upon Mother and Father, and to think
upon another raft.''

Kian smiled in fond remembrance, but then sobered and
drew with his stick in the smoothed earth. ''This is the
way of their construction,'' he said, and began outlining
the procedure for building a raft, indicating that they would
use white oak from the thick stand below the ford, where
the trees grew tall and straight and had no limbs for more
than half their length. The Dwarves listened intently, for
though they were crafters all, they never before had constructed a raft.

The next morning, just after breakfast, using woodcutters' axes they had taken from one of the black waggons,
Anval and Borin began felling the trees marked by Kian
the day previous. The rest of the Squad trimmed and
topped the fallen trees, then dragged the logs to a work site
at the edge of the river. It took a full day of hard labor by
each of the Seven to accomplish the task, and as dusk
approached, Lord Kian called a halt to the work.

Wearily they returned to camp and ate a supper meal,
then all bedded down except the guard. When Perry's turn
at watch came, he made slow rounds and wondered if
Cotton, too, was standing ward.

The following dawn, Perry groaned awake with sore
arms, neck, back, and legs; hewing and hauling is hard
labor, and once again the Warrow had called into play
little-used muscles. The others smiled sympathetically at
him and shook their heads in commiseration as he groaningly

stumped toward the fire. Aching, he hunkered down next to the warmth and moved as little as possible to avoid additional twinges while he took his breakfast.

Over the course of the day, however, Perry worked out the soreness as under Kian's directions the Seven toiled to construct the bed of the raft from the felled trees: Perry was sent to fetch rope while the other six comrades hoisted up the long straight timbers and laid them side by side upon two, shorter, crossways logs. And as the wee buccan struggled to drag each of the large coils of thick line to the work site, Anval and Borin notched the logs so that a long, sturdy, young tree—trimmed of branches and cut to length by the other three—could be laid completely across the raft in a groove that went from log to log; three times they did this: at each end of the raft and across the center. At each end, Barak and Delk bound the logs to one another with the heavy rope; and as the two went they lashed each of the three cross-members to each long raft log in turn. In the meantime, Kian, Anval, and Borin used augers to drill holes through the cross-members and through the raft logs below, while Perry helped fashion wooden pegs that he and Tobin then drove with mallets into the auger-holes to pin the structure together. This work took all of the second day to complete, and again the Squad wearily retired to the campsite.

The next morning dawned dull and overcast, and there was a chill wind blowing from the mountains. A rain of leaves whirled down, covering the woodland floor with a brown, crackling carpet. Glumly the Seven huddled around the campfire and breakfasted, each keeping an eye to the bleak sky for sign of cold rain.

That day began with the Squad constructing a platform in the center of the raft as a place to stow the supplies away from the water plashing upward, and they fashioned a simple lean-to as part of the platform in case of rain. To pole the raft, they cut and trimmed long saplings. Then they made two sculling sweeps, and crafted oarlocks, placing them at each end of the raft, fore and aft; the sweeps would be used to position the craft in the river current. Kian took time to instruct the others in the plying of these oars, as well as the poles.

Lord Kian and Perry went searching for boughs for the roof of the lean-to. Spying the color of evergreen through partially barren branches of the fall woodland, they climbed up a slope and emerged at last from the shelter of the trees to find themselves upon a clear knoll near a small stand of red pine. On the exposed hillock the chill wind from the mountains blew stronger, cutting sharply through their clothes. Lord Kian drew his cloak closely around himself and stared long over the forest and beyond the open grassland at the faraway peaks, the crests of which were shrouded by roiling white clouds under the higher overcast. "The White Bear stalks the mountains" he observed.

"Bear?" asked Perry, who had been half listening. "Did you just say something about a bear?"

"It is just an old tale told to children in Riamon," answered Kian, "about a white bear that brings cold wind and snow to the mountains."

"We have a legend like that in the Bosky," responded Perry, "except it isn't a bear, but a great white Wolf instead. The Wolf only comes with dire storms though, for that is the only time you can hear him howling outside the homes. The story may have come from the time of the Winter War, two hundred thirty-odd years ago—though as for me, I believe the tale is older than that. During the War, however, white Wolves came down from the north and pushed through the Spindlethorn Barrier and into the Boskydells. It was touch and go for many families, but the Gammer and others organized Wolf patrols—they went with bows and arrows and hunted the creatures, and finally the Wolves came to fear the sight of Warrows.

"But what about the bear? Does he, too, signal fierce weather? In the mountains? Oh, I hope the Army is down out of the high country." And thereafter Perry took to glancing often toward the mountains far to the west; he looked in that direction even after he and Kian returned to the raft site and the forest trees blocked the view.

The Squad laid log rollers down the bank from the raft to the river to launch the float, and they tied ropes to the craft to pull it over the rollers. By the time they had completed this work, night was drawing upon the land, but at last the raft was finished. "Tomorrow will be soon enough to load the supplies and launch our 'ship,' " announced Kian. "We've done enough for today. Let's bed down." And so the Seven returned to camp.

That evening there began a cold, thin drizzle, and though they stayed under the campsite lean-tos, the night became miserable for the comrades, and they got little rest.

The icy rain continued, and the next morning, as the Seven huddled under the shelters, Kian surveyed the group: "How many here can swim? None? None other than myself?"

"That should not surprise you, Prince Kian," grunted Barak, "for though there is water aplenty under the Mountains—pools and streams, and even lakes and rivers— we Châkka have no desire to plunge into the black depths merely for pleasure. Swimming is a sport of clear water and warm sunshine and open air, or it is a necessity for those who ply boats, but it is not an activity of stone delvers."

Borin nodded in agreement with Barak's words, then added, "Among the Châkka in this company, I deem that only Anval and I have ever spent much time on water, using the skills you taught us, Prince Kian, as you well know, to ply a boat on our journey to Pellar and back. Even so, we did not learn to swim."

Tobin lifted an eyebrow at Perry, and the Buccan responded: "As to Warrows, of the four strains, only the fen-dwelling Othen know much of boating and swimming— although some of the Siven strain, notably those living in Eastpoint, occasionally take up the sport. I was not one who did—as Lord Kian already knows."

"So be it," said the Man. "I was going to instruct you to leave off your mail, not only to take away its tiring burden, but also so that it would not weigh you down in the event you fall in. I think now not only will we forgo our armor, but also we will attach a safety line between each of us and the raft to haul us back aboard if we fall off.

"And now, since you have not ridden a raft before, remember, it is best if we do not all crowd together at times on one side or the other of the float, for it will tip; and although rafts seldom overturn—and do not sink as sometimes boats with heavy ballast or cargoes do—still it

will be better if we keep the craft floating on the level."
Kian stood. "Are there any questions?" he asked. "Then
let us stow the cargo and armor and launch our raft, and be
on our way."

They made several trips from the campsite to the float,
loading their supplies and packs and armor onto the platform in the center of the craft, covering it all around with a
waterproof canvas and lashing it in place. Finally, all was
ready for the launching. Anval and Borin knocked the
wedges from beneath the logs the raft was resting on, and
with the other five pulling on the launching ropes, the
massive craft slowly began rolling onto and over the hewed
trunks laid down the bank; and the raft ponderously trundled down with gathering speed to enter the river with a
great splash. It floated out, but was snubbed short by a
mooring line cinched to a tree, and cumbrously it swung in
the current back to the shore.

Lord Kian and Anval carried the two sweeps to the craft
and set them in the oarlocks while the others took the raft
poles aboard. Soon the Dwarves and Warrow had secured
safety lines around their waists and were pronounced ready.
With a last look around, Lord Kian untied the mooring line
from the tree and ran down the bank and jumped aboard.
Borin and Tobin and Delk poled away from shore, then
Kian and Anval used the sweeps to pull the float into the
swift current in midriver. Perry watched the shore slide by
and knew that they were on their way at last.

The icy rain continued, and the raft riders sat on the
supply tarpaulin, huddling under the on-board shelter, as
the craft floated through the drizzle. Occasionally, two
would use the sweeps to correct the raft's position in the
current, but for the most part the oars were shipped aboard
out of the water. The Squad travelled thusly all day, with
little change except occasionally one or another would
stand and stretch his legs.

The river continued to flow between bordering woods.
In places, the trees were thickset but slender; at other
places, old huge trees, set far apart, marched away to
either side for as far as the eye could see; still elsewhere,
the margins seemed to be nothing but dense thicketry.
Most of the foliage had turned brown, and at times sudden

gusts of wind caused the forest to shower down swirling, wet leaves; here and there all that was left behind were stark, barren branches clawing up toward the leaden skies. The Squad saw little animal life on the land, and only a few birds, mostly ravens.

That first day, the Seven floated for just over eight hours and covered nearly fifty miles, coming south from the ford to a point five miles above Great Isle. There they used the sweeps and poles to land on the west bank, where they tied up for the night.

Early the next day, ere dawn, the drizzle stopped and the wind died, and by midmorning the overcast was riven by great swaths of blue sky slashing overhead, and later on there were towering white clouds aloft, serenely moving to the east.

That day the raft drifted past Great Isle with its steep rocky banks and large gnarled trees of ancient age. The island was nearly twelve miles long, and it took two hours for the craft to float its length. At its northern end in ancient days there had been a fortress where guardians of the river dwelled. But they had been corrupted by the Evil One, and had begun marauding and harassing river trade, plundering merchants and pirating cargoes. Finally, the woodsmen of the Argon vales banded together to destroy the looters and lay the fortress to such great waste that nothing remains of it to this day—not even its name is remembered. Past this island the float drifted down the western side to come at last to the southern end, where the cloven river came together again.

Although the craft was large, still it was confining, and there was little to do. Even so, now that the raft was once more in midstream of the wide river and needed only minor corrections, Perry replaced Anval at the aft sweep. The Dwarves gathered in the center of the float just forward of the cargo, and fell to talking about the ways the Dusk-Door might be constructed; the red-bearded Gatemaster Barak did most of the talking while the others, including Anval and Borin, listened closely. The Dwarves sat up away from the lapping plash, each on a short section of log split in twain lengthwise and placed on the craft with the flat side up while the round side was down, trapped from rolling, lodged in the long clefts between raft logs. Thus the Châkka sat and debated while the craft was borne south by the River Argon.

Slowly the land changed, and the farther south they drifted, the sparser became the woods that lined the shores, until late in the afternoon they were floating between open plains with only an occasional thicket or a willow or two to break the view. They had come to the far northern reaches of the Dalgor March, and they camped that evening in a thicket at the edge of that land.

The next day the raft floated down past the point where the Dalgor River issued into the Great Argon River. The open Dalgor March had become more and more fenlike as they neared the tributary, and a breeze blew rattling through the tall, waving reeds, now brown with winter approaching. The sky was bright and the day clear, and Perry looked on this area with interest. It was here in this region that the Othen strain of the Wee Folk had settled and later fled, for here it was that savage battles were fought in the Great War with Gyphon, and heroes were slain, and the Dawn Sword vanished. It was an area steeped in the epic happenings of History, though now it was deserted of all but the wild things.

The float continued on past the southern reaches of the Dalgor March, and the land became less marshy and began to rise around them. Thickets began to reappear, and isolated large trees too; and by evening the Seven were again drifting between river-valley woodlands.

All during the morning of the next day, the land gently rose until it was well above the level of the river. The raft swept downstream at an ever-increasing pace, for as the land had risen, the watercourse had narrowed.

In the early afternoon the float approached a long, strait, high-walled canyon known as the Race; and the closer the raft drew to the gorge, the louder came the roar of crashing water within. The Race was the narrowest point on the Argon below Landover Road Ford, and the current was swift and strong; here river traffic going north had to travel overland along the portage-way on top of the eastern bluffs; but river traffic going south needed only to stay in the rushing center of the river, away from the jagged rocks at each side.

Lord Kian and Anval used the sweeps to position the rude craft as close to dead center as they could judge, and then shipped the oars on board. Kian shouted the command to "Hold fast!" and the raft plunged into the bellowing gap.

The uproar in the ravine shook Perry's small frame, for the river thundered between the high stone palisades, the deafening sound trapped betwixt the high walls to reverberate and roar and shout and rend the air with the thunder of water plunging apace along the ramparts, cresting and rolling and breaking over hidden barriers, smashing around great rocks to leap and fall crashing back only to drive into the next barrier and the next and the next. And amid the crests and troughs and rolling swells came the raft: out in midstream and turning slowly, beyond the control of the two sweeps.

Perry and the others tightly clung to the cargo frame as the craft pumped and smashed over roiling, roaring billows; and the cold river water crashed again and again up through the gaps between the logs to spray and drench them all with the icy splash.

Again and again the raft leapt up, to pause, and then to plummet back to the water; and Perry caught his breath each time the craft fell; he and the others were jolted and jarred each time the timbers smacked down; and once Perry was knocked to his knees, but he held on tightly with both hands and lifted himself up again before the next plummet. The turning, pitching float bucked and plunged downriver, racing toward a place where the canyon walls drew inward. As Perry saw the notch rapidly loom closer, he fleetingly pictured the cliffs pinching together to crush these insignificant intruders; but then they passed up a swell and through the constriction and slid down a long ramp into a deep trough, to spin and plummet onward.

Suddenly the walls began to diminish and recede as the land sloped downward and the watercourse grew wide. The thundering roar became a rumble, and the plunging crests smoothed to long, undulating rolls; and then they were back on the broad, smooth river curving between quiet, brown, riverborder woodlands, with the din just a faint, dying echo behind.

"Whew!" exclaimed Perry, his voice seeming unnaturally loud on the rewon stillness, "that was quite a wild ride. I could not hear my own thoughts back there, it was so deafening."

"Aye, Friend Perry," agreed Delk, "mayhap it is the loudest spot in the known Kingdoms." And he dug a little finger into one ear and yawned and swallowed to try to regain his full hearing.

"One would think so," said Kian, untying the canvas so that all could change into dry clothes, "but the river itself has a place of even more roar: it is Bellon, the great cataract to the south. Its voice shouts endlessly as it plunges down the Great Escarpment and into the Cauldron. It is a sound that not only assaults the ears but also thunders into your entire being to shake and rattle your very essence. Ah yes, the Race is thunderous—but Bellon is whelming."

Anval and Borin grunted their agreement, for twice within Ctor's shout they had walked the Over Stair, an ancient portage-way across the Great Escarpment to pass around Bellon. There, too—five miles to the west—could be seen the silvery Falls of Vanil, where the River Nith plummets down the Escarpment and into the Cauldron to join the mighty Argon.

Late in the afternoon Barak and Delk used the sweeps to bring the craft to the western shore, and the Squad made their final landing, for it was the sunset of the fourth day of travel, and they had come to the wold above Darda Galion. The Pitch, Dawn-Gate, Drimmen-deeve, all lay directly to the west: a march of five days would bring the Seven to the eastern entrance of Kraggen-cor.

196   DENNIS L. MCKIERNAN

quiet, brown, overcoated woodland, with the din just a
faint, dying echo behind.

CHAPTER 17

WARRIORS ON THE WOLD

That same evening, as the Squad sat around the campfire
and took supper together, Kian announced, "Now comes
the long wait: here we must tarry for six full days, and
start west on the seventh, for we must pace our arrival to fit
with Durek's plan. Once we start overland we will burn no
more fires; but here in this uninhabited realm we are far
north of the raiders' range; for as I have said before, the
Yrm harass the people in the regions south of Darda
Galion, down the Great Escarpment and beyond into the
North Reach of Valon, and they strike southeastward at the
river traffic along the Argon above and below Bellon
Falls. Hence they come not into this empty region, and
here we will wait.

"While we wait, we will lay our final plans, and study
Perry's map, and think closely upon what we must do to
aid our chances at success. For one thing, Perry, we must
do something about that bright silver armor of yours—
mayhap blacken it—so it will not shine like a lost gem in
the *Spaunen* torchlight within the caverns of Drimmen-
deeve."

Perry held up a silver-clad arm and turned it slowly and
saw that it glittered in the firelight. "I simply could wear a
long-sleeved jerkin over it," he suggested, seeing that
something indeed had to be done to hide its glint. The
Warrow stepped toward his belongings. "What about our
faces? We should blacken them, too, else they'll show in
the torchlight. Perhaps we should use charred wood—or
mud, as Cotton and I did in the Wilderness Hills when we
were 'Rücks.' " Perry began rummaging through his pack.

"Châkka armor is already black iron," grunted Delk.

"And we have with us the Châkka blackener for hands and face, and so our Squad need not use ashes or dirt. As to how to spend the next six days, I deem we need to discuss further the way the Dusken Door is perhaps made, for I have had some new thoughts concerning it."

"There," interrupted Perry, "how's this?" He had slipped a dark green shirt over his starsilver armor; it brought nods of approval from all the company, for no longer did he gleam like a minor beacon: the shimmering corselet was completely hidden.

"We must also select which of these things we mean to carry to the Dusken Door," said Tobin, waving a hand toward the pile of supplies. "What I would wish is that we carry only our axes to caress Squam necks. But, alas, we must eat, and drink, and work on the Door as well." Tobin's remark brought grim smiles of agreement from the other Dwarves.

The discussion continued as each proposed ways of using the six-day waiting period. They spoke of maps, and of making alternate plans for crossing the Great Deep should there be no Spawnish bridge for them to sneak over, and of the need to deal with sentries and patrols; those and many other topics were debated far into the night. Finally they all felt the need for sleep and so bedded down, except for the one on watch. They maintained the same order of guard duty that they had been using since the ford—Kian, Anval, Tobin, Perry, Barak, Borin, Delk— each in turn patrolling the perimeter, heeding Lord Kian's reminder to keep their eyes off the fire, the better to see into the dark.

That night, after Perry had awakened Barak for his turn, as was their custom they talked while the Warrow stoked the campblaze and the Dwarf stood looking into the night and sipped upon a cup of tea. Perry looked forward to these nighttime conversations with Barak, for the red-bearded Dwarf spoke intensely of many things not heretofore known to the Warrow. "Barak," asked Perry, "what do you plan to do after this is all over?"

"When it is over? Pah! Waeran, you know not these Squam. War with the Grg will never be over—not until the last of them are slain or are driven from this world, from Mitheor," growled Barak. The Dwarf held up a hand to forestall Perry's interruption. "Yet, Friend Perry, I *do* understand your question. As to what I plan when we have driven the Squam from our homeland: I shall search out all the other doorways of Kraggen-cor and discover each of their ways of working, and put them in order."

"Other doorways?" asked Perry, puzzled. "What other doorways?"

"Hah! Kraggen-cor has many other doors, some hidden, some plain. But it is the secret doors I would discover: there are those within the caverns to hidden rooms; and those that issue out, to the east, west, north, south, and points in between. There are high doors and low doors, many openings onto the slopes of the Quadran, onto the four great Mountains: Uchan, Ghatan, Aggarath, and Rávenor. Heed: the Dusken Door and Daün Gate are not the only ways in and out, they are just the only *known* ways; the others are lost. But once inside the caverns, the doors can be found again: at what looks to be dead ends of passageways; under arches against blank walls; behind uncommon slabs in chambers; and near special, secret marks.

"When found again, I aspire to divine their means of opening: Some doors open by keys, some by secret levers hidden behind intricate carvings or simple blocks; other doors are opened by pressing special places on the stone. Some Châkka portals are fashioned after the way of the Lian, an ancient Elf race of Mastercrafters from whom we learned much; these doors usually are opened by Elven-made things, such as carven jewels that fit in special crevices, or a glamoured key, a spellbound blade, or an ensorcelled ring; or they are opened by speaking the correct word or phrase, such as is the fashion of the Dusken Door.

"As to why I seek these hidden doors . . . Hai! It is to discover what they conceal! Some doors lead to secret treasure rooms, or secret weapons rooms, or secret hideaways. My heart hammers to think of these doors, for they will open into chambers that contain things hidden away for hundreds, even thousands of years. Yet such rooms must be entered with caution, for once inside, the door may close and vanish, trapping the unwary in a sealed vault—it is a defence against looters and other evil beings.

Yet all delved chambers have ways in and ways out, if you can find the secrets of the doors and have the keys. The trick is first to find where each portal might be and then to divine the means required to open it. Without the key, even a Wizard or an evil Vûlk cannot pass through some hidden doors.

"Aye, Perry, I shall search out the lost portals of Kraggen-cor. And when I locate them and deduce the ways of their opening, I shall pass through those doors and tread where no Châk has trod for centuries . . . and I shall *discover*." Barak paused, staring out into the darkness beyond the campblaze, lost in thought. After a moment he roused himself as Perry threw another log on the dying fire. "That is my dream. What is yours?"

"Mine? My dream? Well now, I haven't thought of what I'll do. Go back to my studies at The Root, I suppose. Or maybe write this adventure up as another chapter to be added to the *Raven Book,* since our tale does have its roots in the War and all." Perry sighed. "Of course, it seems to me that all we've done is wait, and then we rush to some other place just to wait again. I mean, well, it isn't much of an adventure that has its principal characters just sitting around waiting for something to happen."

Barak momentarily turned away from his vigil of the dark beyond the limits of the firelight and looked hard into Perry's jewel-like, sapphirine eyes. "I would that this were all the action any of us *ever* sees," he said sharply. "That Kraggen-cor were totally deserted would be best for us all. But we know that is not so. Let us next hope that the Squam are few and the fighting short."

Perry was taken aback by the sudden intensity of Barak's manner, but he did not know what caused it or what to say. After a while he said good night and went to his bedroll. He lay and watched the stars, and just before he drifted off he saw one fall, and then another, and then two more. *How can such a wondrous thing be the awful portent to the Dwarves that it is?* he mused drowsily. *Falling stars always seem to come this time of year. And besides, when two or more strangers far, far apart see the same falling star, for which is it meant? And what about when a star falls which no one sees? I must ask Borin about this;*

it seems that . . . But Perry fell asleep before he could complete his thought.

Morning came, and Perry awakened late. But he was not alone in his slugabed manners: the only ones up and about were Delk and Lord Kian, who had decided that there was no need to disturb the others since no journey or immediate project was at hand. Perry arose and took breakfast and watched as one by one the others awakened and joined the circle around the fire.

That day they considered several of the courses of action they had spoken of last night: The Dwarves continued to debate the manner of the Dusk-Door. Ways of crossing the Great Deep were discussed. Methods of dealing with sentries and patrols were explored. The map was studied by all. That night again they slept and stood guard in turn.

Resting and discussing: that was the pattern the Seven followed for two days. On the third full day at the campsite a wind blew up from the south, and it rained; little was done that day. The next two days were spent as before. And as the plans materialized, the comrades began to select from among the supplies those things that they would need: The only food they would take was crue, a waybread prepared by bakers throughout Mithgar, though that which the Seven took was oven-made in Mineholt North; each of the tough, easy-to-carry, nutritious biscuits would sustain a traveller over many hours, the single disadvantage being that the waybread was relatively tasteless. In addition to the crue, each of the Squad members would carry a leather water bottle, to be filled from streams along the way. Barak selected tools for the Dusk-Door. And the Squad chose miscellaneous all-purpose items, such as rope, to add to the packs. Each of the comrades took up one of the small, hooded Dwarf-lanterns; these were finely wrought of metal and crystal, and glowed with a soft blue-green light; the hood could be adjusted to allow no light, or a tiny gleam, or a widespread lambent glow, or any level in between; Perry could not divine the way of their working, for no fire needed to be kindled and no fuel seemed consumed. Slowly the Squad came to decide upon their final plans, to lay out alternative courses of action, and to select needed items. Thus passed five days in the campsite on the edge of the wold.

The night of the fifth day came with a chill cold; it was the eventide of the fifteenth of November, and winter was at hand. The Squad would start for Dawn-Gate on the morning of the seventeenth, but for now they slept around a fire built higher to press back the bite; they would lose this luxury when they started for Drimmen-deeve.

Tobin had awakened Perry to stand his turn at guard. They spoke briefly, and then the Dwarf went to his bedroll as the Warrow cast two more logs on the fire. It blazed up and cracked and popped a few times and then settled back. Perry stood and began to pace his rounds out on the perimeter.

He had walked slowly around the camp several times when he heard another *pop!* and thought, *The fire . . . but no! Wait! That sound came from the darkness!* And he stared into the deep blackness in the direction of the noise. *Snap!* Perry's head jerked toward the point of the crack. *There! Another sound!* He unsheathed Bane, *and a blue fire was streaming from the blade-jewel and running along the sword's bitter edges!*

Perry stared dumbly at the cobalt flame a moment, his wit having fled him, and then he shouted with all the force he could muster, "Spawn! Awake! The Spawn foe is—" But at the same moment, with a great cry of snarls and grating shouts, a howling, Hlōk-led force of Rūcks crashed into the camp, iron cudgels flailing, curved scimitars swinging.

Perry was overborne in the charge, knocked sprawling backwards into the campsite, Bane flying from his grip to land in the dirt near the fire. The Dwarves started up at Perry's cry, hands instinctively grasping for axes. Lord Kian leapt forward with sword in hand to slash at the forefront and blunt the hoarse charge just enough for the Dwarves to orient themselves to the rush.

Perry was stepped on and kicked by scuffling feet. He crawled and scuttled for Bane, but was smashed to the ground by a falling dead Rūck. He could not reach his blade, and several of the enemy swooped toward him. At the last moment, red-bearded Barak leapt to his defense and swung his bloody axe, mortally cleaving two of the Squam.

Lord Kian slashed his sword in a wide, two-handed arc and gutted another of the foe. Tobin and Delk stood back to back, both bleeding from wounds, but their deadly axes lashed out as they swung at and chopped and slew the archenemy. And Anval and Borin, those mighty warriors, venting oaths and howling War cries, smashed aside cudgels and scimitars alike and sundered Grg with every swing. But the Rück numbers were many and the Squad but seven strong, and it would be only a matter of moments til the comrades would be overwhelmed.

Perry was still on the ground amid dead Spawn, grasping in the dirt for Bane; and Barak, above him, fought for both of their lives.

The Hlōk leader jumped forward with his curved scimitar slashing, and Barak engaged the larger foe. There was a clanging of axe on blade, and Perry was kicked aside. The Warrow glanced up and saw that Barak was pressing the Hlōk back; yet a Rück from behind smashed a long iron cudgel into the Dwarf's skull, and Barak fell. The Hlōk leapt over Barak's still form and grabbed Perry by the front of his tunic, jerking him up off the ground, feet flailing and kicking. And with a slobbering, leering laugh, the huge Hlōk drew back his scimitar, preparing to backhandedly lop off the Warrow's head.

Just then a loud, venomous oath barked from the dimness beyond the firelight: *"Hai, Rûpt!"* At this cry the Hlōk's head snapped up, and with fear in his eyes he looked frantically into the gloom for the source of the challenge, the Warrow dangling from his grip momentarily forgotten.

At the moment the Rücken leader jerked up to see—*Sss-thok!*—an arrow hissed out of the blackness and struck the creature between the eyes, the shaft seeming to spring full-grown from his forehead as it crashed into his brain. Black blood splattered Perry full in the face, and the Hlōk pitched over backwards, dead before he hit the earth, his hairy fist still locked onto Perry's jerkin. With a *whoof!* Perry smashed into the Hlōk's chest as they struck the ground, and his face was pressed against the foul, scratchy jaw of the dead Rück leader. Hammered by panic, Perry

jerked and twisted, lunging backwards, wrenching sideways, frantic to be free of this dead thing that held him
clenched in its final grip. Tearing loose at last, he rolled
away and sprang to his feet, his breath whistling in and out
of his constricted throat; and he stared in horror at the dead
Hlōk, for its feet were spasmodically drumming the ground.

"*Down, Waerling!*" came a cry from the night. "*Down,
fool! You block my arrow shot!*"

Perry did not even hear the warning cry, for he was
frozen in horror, his eyes locked upon the dead but jerking
Hlōk, and he was unable to tear his gaze away. He did not
see the Rūck behind racing toward his unprotected back,
spiked iron cudgel upraised to crash through Perry's skull.
But then in that instant a huge, bearlike Man silently
hurtled out of the writhing shadows beyond the guttering
firelight, and a massive forearm smashed Perry aside,
while at the same time the Man swung a great, black mace
overhand and with a looping blow crushed the Rūck like a
bloated spider under heel.

Perry again had been knocked to the ground, but this
time his hand fell near the hilt of Bane, cobalt flames
blazing forth from the blade-jewel and down the fiery
edge. He grasped the weapon and looked up. Straight
ahead, Tobin and a Rūck with an iron War-hammer were
locked in furious battle. Tobin stumbled backward over the
corpse of a fallen foe, and the Rūck swung at the off-
balance Dwarf. Though falling, Tobin warded with his axe,
and the great hammer struck the blade with a *clang!* But
the sledge was only deflected, and it cracked into the
Dwarf's leg, and Tobin fell with a cry. The Rūck drew
back his mallet for the final blow, but instead screamed in
agony, blood bursting forth from his throat as he tumbled
forward—for Perry had leapt up and plunged Bane into the
Rūck's back.

" 'Ware, Waldan!" the huge Man shouted, and Perry
turned in time to see another Rūck leaping on bandy legs
at him; and without thinking, Perry lunged full-length
under the other's guard to pierce him through. As the dead
Rūck fell, another took his place. Perry stared across
Bane's blue flame into the swart, snarling face and glaring, viperous, yellow eyes of the enemy; and the Warrow
attacked with a running flèche. Perry's backhanded slash

hewed the foe across his free hand, shearing off the knobby thumb and first two fingers. The Rūck screamed, and threw his scimitar at Perry, and ran off shrieking, only to be hewn down in passing by Anval.

Arrows flew from the darkness, hissing into the camp-site to fell Rūck after Rūck, and the huge stranger crushed the foe with his great black mace. Kian, Anval, Borin, and Delk still stood and clove Squam with sword and axes, and now at last Perry, too, with blue-flamed Bane slashed and felled the enemy. Even so, the battle would have gone to the Rūcks, for there were too many of them; but at that moment, with cries of *Hai, Rucha!* a new force of green-clad warriors with bright long-knives and glimmering swords charged out of the night to beset the maggot-folk. There ensued a fierce, short skirmish, and with wails of dismay the Rūcks were routed, their new assailants and the huge Man with the black mace in deadly pursuit.

As the din and cry of battle receded, Perry ran to Tobin's side and dragged the dead Rūck from the Dwarf's chest. Tobin was barely conscious and covered with gore, most of it foe's blood. He was in agony, and his leg was twisted at an odd angle: the hammer had broken it above the knee. Perry was joined over Tobin's form by a bow-carrying, green-clad warrior who directed, "Move him not until I can splint the leg." And before Perry could say aught, the warrior vanished into the dark, returning shortly with cut saplings.

Lord Kian and Delk joined them, and under the stranger's guidance they examined Tobin's leg to see if the bone had pierced through to cause bleeding; it had not, and so the leg was pulled straight and bound in splints. "We must get him across the river to my people in Darda Erynian," said the newcomer, "for his own thews will soon twist the bone out of line again unless it is given constant pull using rope and weight."

Tobin looked up at the stranger and gritted through his pain, "You and your companions saved our lives, and now you treat my injury. For that I am grateful, and I thank you for us all. I am called Tobin Forgefire. May I have your name, good Elf?"

Elf? Perry looked at this warrior in amazement. He saw before him what looked to be a lean-limbed youth with

golden hair cropped at the shoulder and tied back with a
simple leather headband. He had a fair face with grey eyes
atilt, and his ears were pointed like those of Warrows. His
hands were long and slender and deft. He carried a longbow and an empty quiver, having spent all his arrows
killing *Spaunen*. He was clad in green and wore a golden
belt which held a long-knife. His feet were shod in soft
leather. His slim height fell short of Lord Kian's by a
hand.

"I am called Shannon by the Dylvana, and Silverleaf by
Men, though my Elden-name is Vanidar," replied the Elf
softly. "Now rest, Drimm Tobin. Your strength is needed,
for you have ahead of you a journey of several days to
reach a place of peace and healing." And he placed his
hand on the Dwarf's forehead, and *lo!* Tobin closed his
eyes and fell into a deep sleep.

"Barak!" cried Perry, suddenly remembering, and he
turned toward where the red-bearded Gatemaster had fallen.
But he saw a sight that filled him with dread: Anval and
Borin were standing above the Dwarf's still form with
their hoods cast over their heads. Barak was dead, his
skull crushed by the Rück cudgel while he fought, defend-
ing the fallen Warrow.

That night Kian, Anval, Borin, Delk, and Perry washed
the blood from themselves and treated their wounds, taking extra care that the cuts they had taken, though slight,
were clean—for Spawn often poison their blades, and
death could befall a warrior days after taking but a minor
hurt from one of these evil edges. Afterward, Kian and
Shannon spoke together softly, while Perry sat alone and
stared numbly into the darkness.

As the next day was dawning, the force of green-clad
Elves and the bearlike Man returned and quietly spoke
with Shannon. Then, while the Elven company dragged
the dead foe out into the sunlight where Adon's Ban turned
the corpses into dust, Shannon came forward with the big
Man, and the two sat down with the Dwarves and Kian
and Perry. "This is Ursor, the Baeran," said Silverleaf.
"He has deep grievance against the *Rûpt*."

Ursor was a giant of a Man, almost two hands taller

than Lord Kian. He had brown hair with a reddish cast, but it was lighter colored on the tips, giving it a silvery, grizzled appearance; his full, close-cropped beard was the same grizzled brown; and his eyes were a dark amber. He was dressed in deep umber with a dark brown boiled-leather breastplate. At his side depended the great black mace. "There were no survivors among the Wrg raiders," Ursor grunted fiercely, striking a fist into an open palm.

Shannon looked into the drawn faces of each member of the Squad. Then the Elf spoke: "We had been tracking, pursuing, that band for four nights from the glens below the River Nith in Darda Galion. Without knowing, we drove them toward your party, and that I regret, for I grieve with you in your loss. An hour before the battle, we had lost them, and they would have escaped, except they unwisely chose to assault your seemingly defenseless group. We were spread wide, searching, when we each heard the clamor of combat and came. I was nearest and arrived first, with Ursor coming shortly after. Then the rest of my force arrived."

"In the nick of time for most of us," said Kian softly, "but too late for Barak." And they regarded the Dwarf's still form, now enfolded in a blanket.

"You must tend to him, for he fought bravely and deserves a hero's burial," said Shannon.

"Stone or fire," came Anval's gruff voice from within his hood. "He must be laid to rest in stone, or be placed on a fitting pyre. Nought else will serve. It is the way of the Châkka."

And so Anval carried Barak Hammerhand to the raft, while Borin and Delk followed. And they laid the slain warrior to rest on the central platform on a soft bed of pine boughs. And they washed the blood from him, and combed his hair and beard, and placed his helm upon his head. At his side they placed his axe, and they crossed his hands upon his breast. The weapons of the fallen Squam were laid at his feet, and more pine boughs were heaped all around him. And then Anval and Borin and Delk stood near him and spoke in the hidden tongue, while the company of Elves stood upon the shore and looked on in sorrow. Ursor and Kian had borne wounded Tobin on a litter to the shore, and he, too, spoke the words in unison

with his brethren. And Perry took Barak's hand in his own
and bowed his head and wept. "Oh, Barak," he cried,
"you fought to save me, and now you will never get to
pursue your dream and search out the hidden doors of
Kraggen-cor."

Then Lord Kian stripped to his breeks and stepped on
board with a flaming brand in hand. Perry was led weeping from the craft by Delk and Anval and Borin, and
Shannon cast loose the mooring line. Kian poled a short
way to the edge of the swift current, and set the pine
boughs ablaze; and he dived into the river and swam back
to shore, where he was wrapped in a blanket.

The flaming craft was caught in the wide current and
slowly borne away as all the company and Squad watched,
and many wept. Shannon Silverleaf stepped to the water's
edge and sang, his clear voice rising unto the sky:

> "From mountain snows of its birth
>   The River runs down toward the Deep,
> Now added to by clear cold rain
>   That flows by stream from lush green land,
> To rush at last into the Sea,
>   Great Mother of the rains that fall
> And snows upon the mountains high,
>   Take our Brother into your arms
>   And cradle him in final sleep."

The flames blazed up furiously as the burning raft swept
somberly around a bend, the pyre gradually disappearing
from view. But still the smoke rising above the bordering
trees marked its passage, until at last that, too, was gone.

Later that morning, as planned by Lord Kian and Shannon Silverleaf ere dawn, the company of Elves set off to
the south, bearing Tobin's litter. As they were leaving,
Tobin rose up on his elbows and gritted through his pain to
Kian: "Go on. Complete the mission. King Durek needs
you." And he fell back in a swoon and was borne away.
The Elves were just a short march from a hidden cache of
Elven-boats; they would ply them down the river and to
the other side, taking Tobin with them to a place of refuge
in Darda Erynian, near the ruins of Caer Lindor. But

Shannon and giant Ursor remained behind: Kian had asked that they sit in council with the Squad.

The small assembly gathered around the fire, and Kian told the Elf and the Baeran of the mission to Kraggen-cor. Durek's Army, the Brega Path, the Dusk-Door, the Squad's mission: Kian spoke of it all; and the Sun rose high during his words. And when he was finished with the telling, he spoke of that which now troubled him: "This is our dilemma," Kian declared. "We have lost two of our Gatemasters to the ill fortunes of War; only one, Delk, remains, where we started with three. Yet, at the Council of Durek, it was said that two were needed to work on the Door; and though two are needed, we have but one. I now seek counsel on how to proceed."

Delk responded, his voice a low growl: "Tobin spoke my mind: we must go on with our mission, for King Durek needs our aid. Grievous is the loss of Barak . . . and Tobin too; yet still we must try to succeed. Heed me: Anval and Borin have both taken part in the debates of how the Dusken Door may be repaired. They are both Mastercrafters, and though their skill has not heretofore been used on gates, still their aptness when joined with mine will be considerable. We *must* try to repair the Door! We *must* go on!"

"But then," growled Borin, "who will defend the way? Who will mislead the Squam if we are discovered? That was the charge Anval and I accepted from Durek when we joined the Squad."

"Regardless as to what your duty was then," responded Delk, "our larger responsibility is to get to the Door and repair it so that Durek can lead the Army through."

"I can mislead the Yrm," interjected Kian. "Once we reach the Deeves, my task as guide is ended and Perry's begins. I had always planned on becoming a decoy, or holding the way with Anval and Borin as it became necessary; but now if we are discovered, I will mislead the *Spaunen* alone."

Shannon glanced up at Ursor, who nodded in unspoken agreement. "What of us?" asked the Elf. "We are indirectly responsible for your predicament. Had we not driven the *Rûpt* north, they would not have fallen upon your band. King Durek's plan is sound, yet it is a plan weakened by your unexpected losses here on the banks of the Argon. Hence, let the two of us—a Baeran and an Elf—go with you to act as warrior escort, to hold the way in time of need, for in this we have a debt and an obligation and a duty.''

Ursor looked at Lord Kian. "Durek's mission, Sire, must succeed," rumbled the giant, and his hand went to his mace, "for with this one blow the Wrg will be crushed from the Black Hole forever."

Lord Kian nodded and glanced around the circle, receiving nods of assent from each of the others. "So be it!" he declared. "Once we were seven strong, and so we are again. And though we cannot replace Barak or Tobin, still we can complete our mission."

He stood and bade them all, "Let us now break our fast, and then speak of that which we have planned, for tomorrow we start for Kraggen-cor, and our new companions must be prepared."

Perry spoke little that day. He had said nothing at council, and later responded only to questions put directly to him. And he did not seem to want to be with the others, preferring instead to sit alone on a log down by the river near the point where Barak's funeral barge had been cast free. At the campsite Shannon glanced away toward the water's edge and the Warrow, and Lord Kian quietly said, "It is his first brush with War. He is numb with the realization of what killing and slaughter and battle are truly like. But there is a sturdy spirit inside of him. I think that he and his gentle people are capable of withstanding much and contributing greatly in times of terror and distress. He will soon come to grips with his pain, and will emerge whole and sound from this shell he is in."

Later the Elf went to the riverside to cleanse the smũt from the arrows retrieved from the dead Rũck bodies. He squatted at the shore a step or two away from the Warrow and laved the shafts.

"It was so confused," said Perry without preamble. "Nothing was as the tales and songs would have you believe. There were no long duels of sword-play or axe wielding. There were no glorious stands where one lone hero held an army of villains at bay with his flashing weaponry to emerge victorious over all. There were only sudden rushes and quick, grim slaughter, only slashing and hacking and friends being maimed; hurtling bodies, shoving, grunting, wild swinging and stumbling, and people falling down and being trampled . . . and Death.'' Perry buried his face in his hands only to see Hlōk heels drumming against the ground.

Shannon Silverleaf gazed with softness upon the weeping Waerling. "War is never glorious," quietly said the Elf. "Nay, glory has no part in it. Instead, it is a tedious, chaotic, repugnant chore: It is tedious because most of the time warriors are waiting for something to happen, or are days on the march, or are encamped and unengaged. It is chaotic, for during combat there is only slaying and struggle and confusion. And it is repugnant because the killing even of *Spaunen* and other fell creatures in time of battle is still the slaughter of living beings. Yes, War against the *Rûpt* is abhorrent, but think how much more hideous it would be if it were Waerling against Waerling, or Man against Man. In this be grateful you are fighting a real and present evil that must be destroyed—for there have been times when the only evil was in the minds of the opposing leaders of innocent, trusting followers." Shannon, his task completed, stood and turned to the buccan. "Master Perry, all War is terrible—even those that are Just—but though terrible and horrifying, this War must be fought and the foul wickedness in Black Drimmen-deeve eliminated, for to do anything less will allow the vileness to fester and grow and wreak more death upon the defenseless." Shannon touched his hand to that of the Waerling, and then turned and walked away; and with brimming eyes, Perry watched him go.

That night Perry sat on sentry duty, staring without seeing into the darkness beyond the campsite; Bane had been drawn and was at hand, embedded in a log, sticking upright: a silent sentinel whose blue flame would blaze if Rūcks or other Spawn came near, now shining with nought but reflected firelight.

Huge Ursor came and eased his bulk down to sit beside the Warrow. In silence they watched the night flow by. Finally Perry spoke: "All the time I was making my copy of *The Raven Book,* my mind was filled with the sweep of glorious battles and visions of heroic deeds against dark forces. I thought, 'Oh, wouldn't it be wonderful if I, too, could be caught up in such an adventure.' Well now I am in a like venture, and the reality of it is nearly more than I can bear.

"I did not stop to think that a great battle is nothing more than large-scale butchery. But even in battle what it really boils down to is that someone with a weapon is trying to slash, hack, smash, or pierce someone else while at the same time trying to keep from being maimed or killed in return. And the incredible thing is that though the battle involves entire armies, each fight is just one against one, one against one a thousand or ten thousand times over: thousands of desperate pairs locked in combat. And in each pair one will fall and the other one will go on to find another and do it all over again until it is ended.

"I never thought of it being that way. I never thought that someone I could see and hear and smell and touch would be trying to kill me, striving to snuff out my life, while I would be struggling to kill him in return." Perry's eyes widened in remembered horror and filled with tears, and he stared down unseeing at a point within the earth as remote as the stars, and his voice rose and trembled in distress. "But that's the way it really is: the enemy right there in front of you, face to face, grunting, sweating, straining, gasping for breath, trying to break your guard, and trying to keep from being hurt. It doesn't really matter whether you're in a battle, or in a skirmish, or are all alone when you meet your foe, it's all the same: just one against one. Even if you are outnumbered, still each is fleetingly met one at a time.

"And none of my visions included staring across a sword blade directly into the eyes of an enemy. I always dreamed that battle would be clean and heroic and remote; but I've found that it is anything but heroic: the first Rūck I slew, I stabbed him in the back—that's how noble it is. It isn't pure and gallant and distant at all; instead, it is dirty and desperate and suffocatingly close.

"And I'm frightened. I know nothing of weaponry. This company needs warriors, not dreamers and scholars. I don't belong here: I belong back at The Root or at the

Cliffs locked away someplace among books, tediously copying ancient tomes. My Scholar's dream was to go awarring—to be a hero—but in reality I am only a frightened Scribe.

"I am a terrible, worthless liability to this company. Barak died because of me. He tried to save me, and instead he is dead." Perry began to weep silently, his mind filled with chaotic visions of the desperate stand that red-bearded Barak had made above him while he scuffled ineffectually in the dirt below, and how Barak had finally fallen, crushed from behind by a Rūck cudgel."

Giant Ursor shifted his weight on the log where he sat. "You are right, Waldan," he rumbled, "and you are wrong. You are right in your assessment of the reality of battle. You are wrong in the valuation of your worth. You are a warrior, for you slew a foe who was about to slay a companion. And though overwhelmed, you engaged the enemy when you gained your feet, with weapon in hand, until the enemy was routed. In your fear and revulsion, you are no different from any other warrior. Yet I believe if you think on it, you will find you suffered no fear during each engagement, only afterward; for while locked in a duel there is only time to act and to react and no time to quail.

"As to your worth to the company: the mission cannot go on without you; if others fall, it will go on, but not if you fall. Only you can guide this group through the caverns; only you can deliver a Crafter to the Dusk-Door. Barak knew this. Of all those beset, he chose to fight by your side, for not only were you his friend, you are also the hope of this mission.

"And this mission *must* succeed, for the growing evil in the Black Hole must be *crushed*"— Ursor's great hands made grasping, strangling motions, and his voice gritted out between clenched teeth—"for they slay the innocent and unprotected. My bride of two summers, Grael, and my newborn . . ." but Ursor could say no more, and he stood and stalked to the edge of the darkness.

Wiping his eyes on his sleeve, Perry watched the big Man walk to the distant limit of the light and halt. At last the buccan knew why the giant was at war with the Spawn; and Perry was crushed with the knowledge of the other's

pain, the Warrow's own anguish diminished in the light of
the Baeran's grief. "Ursor," he called, "I'm so sorry. I
didn't know . . ." Perry fell silent, his thoughts awhirl.
How long he sat thus, he did not know.

Finally the buccan rose and took up Bane—for he was
still on guard—and walked to the side of his newfound
friend, not knowing what to say, his heart reaching out to
Ursor. Long the Warrow stood in silence beside the Man,
peering out into the darkness at the vague black shapes of
barren trees sleeping in the early-winter night. Then at last
Perry spoke, his voice falling softly in the quiet: "Ursor, I
feel your pain, and I grieve with you. But I do not know . . ."
Again Perry lapsed into silence.

After a moment Ursor placed a huge hand on Perry's
small shoulder. "It is enough, Wee One. It is enough."

Again they stood quietly and looked out upon the night.
Then once more Perry spoke, and firm resolve filled his
voice: "You are right, Ursor, you are right about everything. The evil in Drimmen-deeve must be crushed—and
our mission will see to that." The Warrow looked grimly
to the west, as if willing his sight to fly far overland and
pierce the darkness and see deep into the heart of the Black
Deeves. "Tomorrow we start the final leg to Kraggen-cor,
and beginnings are often times of oath-takings and predic-
tions. Yet I'll not make a prediction, though I do have
something to say. I said it once before when I knew
nothing, but now I say it again: Beware, maggot-folk."

CHAPTER 18

SNOWBOUND

Cotton thrust his head from beneath the squat, snow-covered shelter and out into the howling grey morning. Still the blizzard moaned up the mountain slopes and toward the Crestan Pass, and the driven snow hid all but the nearby view. The Warrow peered but could see no movement of anyone, and there was little sign of the Host; only three other shelters were visible to him—small mounds in the snow.

Last night, when the storm had worsened and the cold had become cruelly bitter, Durek had issued the order for warriors to pair up and spread out and gather pine boughs to make shelters. The entire Army of four thousand had then moved into the forest in couplets to collect the branches, to return and construct the tiny bowers—a form of snow refuge known to those who dwell on and within the mountains. Bomar had selected Cotton as his shelter-mate simply by grunting, "Come with me"; and they had taken up a lantern and some rope and had moved out through the drifts and into the woods.

When Cotton had glimpsed through the flying snow that the Army was spreading out and separating during a blizzard, the buccan had protested: "Bomar, this is madness!" he had cried above the shrieking wind. "We'll all be lost in the storm; the Army will be destroyed, split apart. We'll never find the others again—and they won't ever find us, neither."

"Remember, Friend Cotton," Bomar had shouted back, "you are with Châkka, and although we often do not know where we are going, we always know exactly where we have been—even in a blizzard at night." And Cotton and

Bomar had waded onward through the swirling, moaning wind and knee-deep snow.

They had cut boughs, and lashed them together using the rope; they had dragged the bundle like a sledge back to the glen; and Bomar had made their shelter: First he had fashioned a frame of bent branches, and had pegged it to the ground with iron spikes he called ''rock-nails.'' Then he had lashed boughs thickly to the frame, so close that when he and Cotton had piled snow on, none sifted through the matting.

Then the two had crawled inside, and there was just enough room for both of them. They had thus spent the night in snug warmth.

And now it was morning, and still the blizzard enveloped them. ''What's going to happen now, Bomar?'' asked Cotton as he pulled his head back into the bower.

Bomar reached for the lantern filling the refuge with a blue-green radiance, and dropped the hood so that the glow was extinguished; and grey morning light filtered down through the flying snow and into the shelter opening. ''Nothing,'' he rumbled. ''We do nothing til the storm abates.''

''I wonder when that will be,'' fretted Cotton in the dimness. ''I mean, well, I don't know much about blizzards—especially mountain blizzards. In the Bosky we seldom get real mean snowstorms. Why, let me see, there's only been one bad storm that I can remember; only once has the White Wolf howled around Hollow End and The Root since I've been there. And it lasted for two days, and it put almost two foot of snow on the ground. But I hear mountain blizzards can last for weeks. . . .

''Oh, Bomar, I don't know why I'm nattering on about that. What I'm really afraid of is that we're going to get caught here, and we won't reach the Dusk-Door in time for Mister Perry, and they'll be trapped in that black puzzle with all the Rūcks and Hlōks and Ogru-Trolls after them—''

''Hush, Waeran,'' growled Bomar. ''It does no good to a warrior's heart to think of his comrades in need of aid when that aid cannot be given. We have no choice but to wait for the blizzard to slacken. We cannot go on, for I have seen this kind of storm before: here in the protection of the thick forest it is not too severe; but out in the open the snow fills the air with whiteness—nothing can be seen more than a yard or two distant. And the cold wind is a terrible enemy: it sucks the heat away with its icy blast, and an animal will fall in midstride, to freeze in moments. We cannot go forth into that. We must wait.''

"Animals? Freeze? What about Brownie and Downy?'' asked Cotton anxiously. "For that matter, what about *all* the horses? Are they going to drop in their tracks and freeze? We can't let that happen! We've got to do something!'' And Cotton started to crawl out, but was stopped by Bomar.

"Hold, Cotton!'' demanded the Dwarf, gripping the Warrow by the shoulder "The horses are all right. Aye, they are chilled, but they are not freezing. Only in the open blast would they be in danger; but here in the pines they are well protected from the wind.''

"Well let's go see anyway,'' insisted Cotton. "My legs need the stretch.''

Bomar saw how concerned the buccan was; and with a shrug of his shoulders he pulled his hood up snug, motioning the Waeran to do likewise. They crawled from the shelter and struck out for the pen where Brownie and Downy were held, Bomar leading the way.

The snow came to Cotton's midthigh, though in places the drifts were deeper, but the sturdy Dwarf broke the path, and the smaller Warrow followed in his wake. They struggled through the swirling white, stopping frequently to rest, while the wind moaned aloft in the treetops. A blinding sheet of whiteness raced by overhead on its flight to the mountain crests, and only a portion of the howling fling fell swirling through the boughs to coldly blanket the forest below. But even the small part that came down was enough to curb vision and pile snow deeply, to be driven into larger drifts.

At last Cotton and Bomar reached a thick grove of low pines; a large group of horses stood huddled within its protection where the snow was less deep and the wind did not cut. The animals seemed glad to see the two; and eagerly they pressed forward for a smell and a look, for they had seen no person since the previous night, when each had been fed a small portion of grain and then had

been driven with the others to cluster in the simple rope
pens among the thick, low, sheltering pines near the encampment glens.

Cotton and Bomar spent a good while walking among
the animals, patting their flanks and rubbing their necks
and muzzles. Though they spoke to the horses, the wind
drowned out their words; but their very presence seemed to
reassure the steeds that all was well. Cotton finally located
Downy and later Brownie, and they each nuzzled him; and
thus Cotton, too, felt assured that the horses were faring
well.

The Warrow and Dwarf had worked their way through
the herd when Cotton leaned over and called above the
wind moan, ''What we need is a hot cup of tea, but we'll
never get one in this storm.''

Bomar snorted and declared, ''Come with me; we will
go make some.''

Breasting the snow, they toiled back to the glen, where
they located a black waggon; from it they took a small-
forge and a supply of black firecoke, and carried it to the
lean-to beside their yellow waggon. Shortly they had a hot
blaze going in the forge, and they melted snow in the large
kettle to brew the tea. Leaving Cotton to tend the pot and
make the drink, Bomar trudged out into the swirl and
located other shelters and invited those within to join
them. Soon Dwarves straggled to the fire, and Cotton
served hot tea to go with their crue biscuits.

Thus the Warrow and Bomar passed the day—tending
the kettle on the forge in the lean-to, brewing hot tea, and
serving grateful Dwarves—while all around the snow spun
and the wind groaned. Busy as he was, Cotton still fretted
and worried, vexed by the storm but helpless to do anything about it. *Stranded!* he thought. *Stranded here on the
mountainside. Rolf said, ''Beware of Waroo,'' and he was
right: the White Bear has us trapped like bugs on a board.
Oh, Mister Perry, what's to become of you?*

The next morning, before dawn, Cotton bolted upright
in the shelter thinking, *What's that?* but he struck his head
against a thick branch in the shelter roof and flinched back
down, rubbing his crown through his hood. *What did I
hear that made me bump my noggin?* he wondered, and he

listened intently, but heard only Bomar's quiet breathing in the still night. Excitedly, he grabbed Bomar's shoulder and shook him. "Bomar! Bomar, listen! What do you hear?" he cried. Bomar came groggily awake and cracked open the lantern hood, and blinked and rolled his eyes in the phosphorescent light. "Listen, Bomar, what do you hear?" repeated Cotton.

Bomar listened quietly and then exclaimed with fierce exultation, "Nothing! I hear nothing!"

"That's just it!" chortled Cotton. "Nothing! No sound at all! No wind! No howl! The storm is over!" And he grabbed the lantern and scrambled from the shelter with Bomar right behind. And the buccan was correct: the wind that had howled and moaned and groaned and shrieked for two days was gone; the blizzard had blown itself out; all that remained was a light snow falling gently through the pines. And the Warrow laughed and danced and capered in the deep snow by the blue-green radiance of the lantern, while the usually somber Dwarf looked on with a great grin upon his face.

As dawn broke, Bomar and his crew again had prepared a hot breakfast, and had served storm-weary but grimly smiling warriors. The light fall had stopped, and the skies had begun to clear. Now the meal was over and the utensils cleaned and stored, and still the command to prepare for the march did not come. Two more hours passed and yet no orders came and nothing was heard. Finally a Chief Captain arrived and called the warriors of the glen together. "The way is blocked by great drifts," he announced—and Cotton's high spirits plummeted into despair—"but three miles downslope they diminish, and the snow on the road beyond is not deep, and it can be travelled. Hence, we must dig a path to freedom.

"There are four thousand Châkka to open the way, yet we have but a limited number of shovels. Heed: use any scoop to move the snow—spare pots and pans and kettles from the cook-waggons, the beds from the smallforges, and aught else that works.

"Our first task is to clear a route from here to the road; let lie any snow that is less than knee deep, for the horses can broach that. When we reach the road we are to work in shifts with other companies.

"We are already delayed, and the Seven depend upon us to be at the Dusken Door and ready to enter on the twenty-fifth''—and the Chief Captain raised his voice in a shout—''so let us work as only Durek's Folk can!'' And the squadron gave a great yell, and Dwarves rushed out to be at the task, while Cotton, Bomar, and the cook-waggon crew remained behind to prepare hot food and drink for the road workers.

The snowbound Army inched a clear path down the mountain as the bright Sun climbed up in the sky to shine down on the white slopes. Each Dwarf pulled his hood tight and peered out through the resulting fur tunnel, using it to screen out the intense glare and ward off snowblindness. And they scooped snow with shovels, pots, pans, forge-beds, boards, helms—anything that could be used. And slowly they crept downward.

Company relieved company, and the toil continued. Weary Dwarves trudged back to their campsites to grab a hot bite to eat and drink, and then to cast themselves down in their shelters for a short rest—which ended all too quickly, for in due time they were called upon to relieve yet another company. The cycle went on and on. And at one of the busy yellow waggons—Bomar's—Cotton helped with the work. And it seemed to the Waeran that no sooner did he finish feeding one crew than another would line up for a meal.

Progress down the mountain was measured in tens of feet. Cotton spoke to the returning crews and got reports on the headway: a giant wide drift at the quarter-mile mark slowed progress to a creep. The Dwarves finally broke through just before noon, and the advance went more swiftly.

It was not long after when there came the flat *Tan-ta-ra* of a Valonian black-oxen horn faintly bugling up over the snow from the slopes far below. Instantly, it was answered from a nearby glen by Brytta's great ebon horn. Again and again they called to one another, at times in short bursts of but a few notes, at other times with long flourishes . . . and finally they fell still.

Cotton wondered at the signals, and when Brytta eventually came, searching for the Warrow to speak with him and to take a meal, there was a huge grin upon the face of the Marshal of the Valanreach. "It is Hogon!" he exulted. "And Eddra and Arl and Wylf! My advance scouts. They are safe! They spent the blizzard with their horses, out of the blast—in a cave five or six miles downslope. Aye, I should have known that Wylf would have one eye out for comfort. Arl claims that at first flake-fall Wylf declared 'twas time for snug shelter, and led them on a line no bee could have flown straighter nor swifter direct to the hole; Eddra and Hogon checked it for the bears that were not there, and in they went, horses and all, two steps ahead of the white wind. And this morning they kicked and clawed and dug their way out through the snow that had drifted over the cave mouth. Ah, but they are safe! And they wait below for us to break through."

"You learned all that just from tootling horns across a snowfield at one another?" Cotton asked, and at Brytta's pleased nod the Warrow marveled at this, to him, heretofore unrealized potential of horn calls. And though Cotton had not met the advance scouts, he felt eased that they had come to no harm. Yet his relief was tempered by the realization that time was slipping away from the Army, and Mister Perry and the Squad depended upon them to be ready on schedule at the Dusk-Door; and here they were—drift-trapped.

In the early afternoon the army of digging Dwarves passed the half-mile point, but then the snow deepened, slowing the forward way. At sundown the road had been cleared for a mile, and work went on by lantern-glow and by the light of the stars. At midnight, the mile-and-a-half point was reached.

Bomar urged Cotton to take to his shelter for a rest. The buccan had been working nonstop all day, and was bone weary. Yet he was frustrated, for he had the irrational feeling that if only he were *out there shoveling rather than back here cooking, well, the road would just get cleared a whole lot faster. What can be taking so long? I mean, a whole army ought to be able to do this job in just an hour or two.* Not only was Cotton frustrated by the snail's pace of the progress, he was angry with himself for being frustrated in the first place, for he knew that the Dwarves were advancing downslope as quickly as possible, and he could make his best contribution to the effort by working with the cook-crew and *not* with the road crew.

After only five hours of sleep, the Warrow awakened and trudged back to the cook-waggon. He took a bite to eat and drank a cup of hot tea, and then relieved Bomar. It was false dawn, and the sky was pale grey. A thin crescent of a waning Moon rode low over the mountaintops. Cotton and three of the cook-crew were on duty, and soon another shift came to be fed. Cotton discovered that the road crews had just passed the two-mile point.

Dawn came, followed by another bright morning. The exhausting, backbreaking job went on, and again the Sun marched up the sky. Word came that the road gangs had encountered another giant drift, and the advance was stalled just a half mile from the end. Cotton felt both helpless rage and unremitting despair at the news, and he threw himself more than ever into his work.

Before noon, Bomar and the other five Dwarves rejoined the cook-crew, and the discouraged Warrow took a mug of hot tea and wandered to the edge of the glen where it was quiet and he could rest a moment. The Sun was just reaching the zenith when from far off something rumbled low and long, like distant thunder among the crests. Cotton stared in the direction from which the roll had come, but the trees obscured his vision, and he could see nothing to indicate the source of this unknown, far-off roar. A few moments later the buccan returned to the cook-waggon and asked Bomar, "What would make a great rumble up in the high peaks?"

"Snow avalanche," replied Bomar. "That was a distant avalanche. Something caused a Mountainside of snow to give way and cascade down; it comes as a giant wall and carries all things before it, snapping off trees both large and small and rolling great boulders along under it, causing other snow to cataract down too. Sometimes it slides for miles, a great wave growing wider and higher as it thunders down to wreak its destruction and bury is victims."

"Lawks!" responded Cotton. "I thought the rock slide was bad, but this sounds worse. I hope no snow avalanche decides to slip this way."

About two hours before sundown a ragged distant cheer

echoed up over the quiet snow to those in the glen; the road crews had broken through the last drift, and the way before them held only diminishing snow. The word came to harness up the teams and prepare to move out; no more time was to be spent in the high country; the Army was to trek down to the foothills, marching part of the night.

And so, even though they were weary, the Host gladly shouldered their packs or hitched up the horses or otherwise prepared to travel. Just as the Sun disappeared, the trek began, and lanterns were carried to illuminate the way.

The Host moved slowly out of the glens and onto the road. Cotton and Bomar in the yellow waggon again brought up the rear, and often they would come to a complete halt, to stand and wait for long minutes while the leading teams and wains struggled through places still deep in snow, with Dwarves pushing and pulling and straining to roll the stuck vehicles forward by grasping and turning the wooden-spoked wheels. Then the column would move ahead once more until the next deep place was encountered and the horses again needed help.

And thus the train moved down the mountain, sometimes easily, sometimes struggling. It proceeded like a great undulating caterpillar, bunching up behind barriers and lengthening out beyond them. At the rear of the column, the only trouble Cotton and Bomar encountered was that of the waggon oft' sliding where the snow had been packed unto ice by the four thousand warriors and nearly five hundred waggons ahead of them: here, Brownie and Downy found the footing treacherous, and the wain brake was of little help. Even so, still they managed to work the waggon past these slick stretches to come to safer purchase.

In places the wain went between high, close walls cloven through the long, deep drifts. At times the snow ramparts were well over the heads of the Warrow and Dwarf sitting up high on the waggon seat; and at last Cotton could envision the massive effort required to clear the road, and he was humbled.

The long line of swaying, bobbing lanterns wended slowly along the carven track set within the snow. In harness again, the horses seemed eager to press forward,

and their breath blew white from flaring nostrils in the cold
night air as they worked the waggons downward through
the drifts, following after the leaders as repeatedly they
emerged from one long, narrow, deep channel and into the
open, only to enter another long notch.

Thus they passed the three miles from the glens and
down through the deep snow to come at last to the shallow
fall. It had taken the Army a day and a night and yet
another day of incredible labor to dig the three-mile path,
and now Cotton and Bomar had driven its length in less
than two hours.

The Host continued the march for six hours, and came
down out of the high country and into the foothills above
Arden, covering some fifteen miles in all. The lower they
came, the less snow there was, until it but barely covered
the rim of a waggon wheel where it touched the ground.
At last Durek called a halt to the march; the Captains
posted a picket of warders as Dwarves made campfires;
and weary warriors fell asleep wherever they found
themselves.

Just as Cotton was preparing to lie down, Durek and
Rand came walking to his fire. The buccan had not seen
either for three days, but they said little to one another, for
all were spent; this night neither King nor Prince returned
to the head of the column; this night they bedded down by
the last fire instead of the first.

And as Cotton was drifting off he heard another long,
low rumble of distant thunder, and he knew that somewhere a white avalanche had cascaded down the mountainside. He wondered if their old, high-country camps and
glens had been buried, and if the backbreaking work of
days had been covered in mere moments by masses of
slipping snow; but before he could speculate more, he fell
fast asleep.

CHAPTER 19

WRATH AT THE DOOR

The next morning, Durek, Rand, and Cotton broke fast together. Each felt the pressing need to get under way, for the snowstorm had trapped the Host for three days, and their rendezvous with the Seven was now in serious jeopardy.

"We are late and the Legion is weary," rasped Durek, "and the goal is far south down a ruined road through rough, inhospitable land. Yet we must somehow recapture the days lost to the storm but not expend the whole of the strength of the Host in a race for the Dusken Door; we must not be exhausted when we enter Kraggen-cor, for there we must be strong to meet the foe. I have thought long as to how we might gain back the time without losing our strength, but no good plan comes to mind except a forced march, where our brawn will wane with each day of the pace. We cannot ride the waggons, for there are too many of us—and the wains may be too slow in any case. Prince Rand, a question: Can we float down the River Tumble on rafts? Dwarves know not the skill of swimming nor the art of these craft; yet we would go that way if it would regain the lost time and husband our strength."

"Nay, not the Tumble," answered Rand, shaking his head. "Oh, as to the rafts, though I could teach you the way of their making—and the manner of poling and steering them is simple—still we could not use them down the Tumble, for the river is truly named: there are many rapids and falls between Arden and the place south where the watercourse turns west to join the Caire, where we would strike for Drimmen-deeve overland . . . . Nay, the Tumble is no river for a raft.

"And since the Army can ride neither water nor wain, I,

too, believe we have no choice but to force march down Rell Way. There is no other means, and we cannot be late to the rendezvous with my brother and the others."

"On that we agree," gritted the Dwarf, vexed, "yet such a course will but weary our Legion more. We do not want to arrive too spent to swing Châkka axes at Grg necks." Frustration loomed in his eyes.

"King Durek, if we can force march but a week or so, we can draw almost even with our first plan," said Rand, "and that will leave us five days at normal pace to regain strength before reaching the Dusk-Door. And at the Door, only those removing the rubble will be working; all others will rest until it is their turn at that task."

"Again our thoughts agree," growled Durek, "but for an army going into battle, a long rapid march is a heavy burden to bear."

"Speaking of heavy burdens," piped up Cotton, "why don't we give the armor a ride? What I mean is, well, we can't very well give every warrior a ride, but armor is a different thing. Most of the food waggons are now only partly full and so there's room; and the horses can pull the extra weight. Chain mail is a burden, right enough, and warriors would march lighter and faster without that load of iron."

Durek and Rand turned to one another in surprise. That simple suggestion was completely obvious to one unaccustomed to wearing mail—such as the Warrow—but Dwarves made light of heavy burdens, and a Dwarf going to War *always* wore his mail shirt; neither Durek nor Rand had ever considered it being any other way. This mail had in fact been worn all the way from Mineholt North, and thus the idea simply had not occurred to either. Durek roared with laughter and clapped his hands together, for Cotton, of course, was right.

Thus it was that when the Army began its march, nearly all the armor rode in the green waggons, and the Dwarves marched "lighter and faster without that load of iron," though each Dwarf still bore his pack and his beloved axe.

The Riders of the Valanreach swiftly ranged far to the fore and aft and out on the flanks of the Host as down out of the last of the snow they came at a forced pace, down from the high foothills; and ere they came nigh the southern reach of the cloven vale of Arden, southward they turned onto an eld abandoned roadbed: the long-disused Old Rell Way, grown over with weeds now dead in the winter cold.

The land the Legion entered was rough, and the trees sparse, there being only barren thickets or lone giants with empty branches clutching at the sky. In the folds of the land grew brush and brambles, but for the most part the region was one of open high moors and heather. Into these uplands they forced march south on the ancient way—and though they did not know it, they were paralleling the path taken by Tuck, Galen, and Gildor more than two hundred and thirty years past; those three, however, had gone secretly in the Dimmendark and had not taken to the Old Way until they were nearly fifty leagues south of the Hidden Vale, for in those days the Way near Arden was patrolled by Ghûls—Modru's Reavers.

At times the ancient road was blocked by thicket growth or fallen stones, or by a washout that cut the track; but the waggons were guided around the blockage, or many Dwarves gathered and removed the barrier. Twice the roadbed completely disappeared, but Rand led the train along pathways that soon rejoined the Old Way.

The day was bright and the pace was swift, and the Host stopped but once for a rest and a quick noon meal of crue and water. They marched all day at the same hard stride, always bearing southward with the Grimwall Mountains towering off to their left. And when they stopped that night they had covered twenty-nine miles, and Rand and Durek were well pleased.

They continued this swift pace for two more days, going some sixty miles more. But on the next day it rained, slowing progress, for the roadbed was ancient and did not drain well, and by the time the latter part of the train came, the pathway was a sea of mud, churned to muck by all the tramping Dwarf boots and turning waggon wheels and driving horse hooves that had gone before. At times the late wains became mired beyond the strength of the horses to pull them free, and Dwarves and spare horses would then help wrest the waggons out.

Being at the very last of the train, Cotton and Bomar's

yellow cook-waggon was often bogged down, and their usual good tempers suffered as a result. "You know, Bomar," complained Cotton, nettled, "the trouble with being at the tail end of things is not only do we get stuck a lot, but also we're the last ones to find out what's going on. I mean, here we are, just as important as anyone else in this army, but we never seem to know what's going on. It's either stand around and wait, or rush to get ready, and we never find out what's happening til we fall in a hole, or get stuck, or what have you. I don't much like it, Bomar, this not knowing, and I don't like all of this hurry up and wait either."

"Hah! Friend Cotton," laughed Bomar, "now I know that you are at last a true campaigner, for you have just voiced the warrior's eternal plaint. It has ever been so in armies since time began and shall be so for as long as they exist. It is the soldier's lot to 'never know' and to 'hurry up and wait.' " Dwarf and Warrow, they both laughed long, and thereafter their spirits were high, even though the waggon often mired and one or the other had then to jump down to help roll it free.

The column stretched out in length for nearly eight miles as the front of the train made good time while the last did not. Thus it was that when it came time to stop, although the front halted, the rear was far behind and had to keep travelling to close up the line; and Cotton and Bomar did not arrive until three more hours had elapsed.

That day the column moved only twenty-two miles.

The next day was clear, and as the Legion marched, the roadbed dried out, and so good progress was made. Far ahead they could see an arm of the mountains standing across the land to block their way, but as they drew nearer, the Old Rell Way swung out on a southwesterly course to go around this spur. They forced march this direction for three more days, and on the fourth day the Way again swung back to the south and east as they rounded the side-chain and at last headed on a line for the Quadran and Drimmen-deeve. It was the sixteenth day since they had left Landover Road Ford and the ninth day of march from the Crestan Pass; the Host was weary, yet on this day Rand dropped back the pace, for he reasoned that they had drawn nearly even with their original plan.

The way began rising up again through the foothills as the Army tramped toward the Quadran; and finally there hove into view the four great mountains under which Kraggen-cor was delved: Greytower, Loftcrag, Grimspire, and mighty Stormhelm. The Legion's goal, the Dusk-Door, was carved in the Loom of Grimspire, a hard day's trek south of Stormhelm's flanks. Yet now that the four soaring peaks were in sight, all of those striding south along Old Rell Way felt that they could nearly see their destination; their spirits lifted and new vigor coursed through their veins.

That night, Rand estimated that four more days on the march would bring them to the Door.

Two days later, just at sundown, the column pitched camp at an old fork in the road. Rand and Durek and Brytta looked at the ways before them. "The left-hand course—Quadran Road—goes up to Quadran Pass," said Rand, "to climb over the Grimwall and come down the Quadran Run to the Pitch below. We can no longer cross over; the entire saddle is white; the way is barred by snow. The right-hand course bears south to the Dusk-Door; it is the continuation of the old trade route between the Elves of Lianion—called Rell by Men—and your ancestors in Kraggen-cor, King Durek. By this route—the Old Rell Way—we will come to the Door in a half and one day."

"It is as I feared back at the ford," rasped Durek, his sight leaping up the stone ramparts to the snowbound gap above. "The way over the Mountain is blocked. The blizzard that nearly thwarted us at the Crestan Pass had wide wings, and here the slot is closed. Yet but had we the knowledge of the Elden, even now the col might still afford entry into Kraggen-cor: Châkka lore has it that a secret High Gate opens into the Quadran Gap. Yet in these latter days we know not where it lies—whether this side or that, or in between, in the clear or buried under snow, we know it not. But, though we here are ignorant, perhaps it has been discovered by the foul Squam since their occupation of Kraggen-cor; and even now hostile eyes may be upon us, spying out our every move." At these words

Brytta's hand strayed to his spear, and Durek grimly smiled at the warrior's reaction. "Yet I think not, Reachmarshal, for the High Gate was secret, and even Gatemaster Barak may find it hard to discover its location, much less the manner of its working."

Durek's words did not soothe Marshal Brytta, for his sharp eyes continued to search the upward slopes.

"And so," continued Durek, "with the pass closed, if we fail to open the Dusken Door, then we must go far south through Gûnar Slot to the Gûnarring Gap to come to the other side of the Mountains. But let us not speak of failure; instead, let us go to sit with Friend Cotton at the last fire." And they strode to the far yellow waggon, arriving in time to eat.

The waxing Moon had risen in the early afternoon and passed overhead two hours after supper. Speculatively, Cotton gazed up at the silver orb. "I wonder what Mister Perry and Lord Kian and Anval and Borin and the others are doing right now. Do you think they're looking up at the same Moon and wondering what we're doing?"

"Perhaps, Cotton, perhaps," answered Rand. "If I have reckoned correctly, this is the twentieth day of November, and they are drawing nigh to the Pitch. Tomorrow they should fare up the slope and arrive at Dawn-Gate. And the next day, they enter the Deeves."

At these words Cotton's heart gave a lurch, for with the Quadran at hand the dire mission of the Squad took on grim reality.

"If all has gone aright with them, they will be in the caverns and on the Brega Path when first we come to the Door," said Durek, and Cotton's heart sank even further. "It is we who are late—by one day," growled the Dwarf King, a dark look upon his face "Let us hope that there is enough time to uncover the portal, once we arrive."

"We are not a full day behind, King Durek," amended Rand, "but only one half a day instead. We should arrive by mid of day the day after tomorrow."

Still, even with these words, the Dwarf King's heart did not seem eased, and the conversation dwindled to a halt. At last, Brytta, Durek, and Rand bade good night to Cotton and returned to the front of the train to settle down for the eventide.

Yet, for much of the rest of that night, Brytta's thoughts dwelled upon the ancient, secret High Gate somewhere in Quadran Pass, a Gate lost by the Dwarves in eld times, but perhaps now known to the Wrg. And he could not banish the specter of skulking Rutcha slipping in and out of that hidden portal, of treacherous Drōken eyes spying out their every move, of sly Wrg mouths whispering to Cruel Gnar word of the Dwarves' mission. And by the light of the westering Moon and the wheeling stars overhead, Brytta's own gaze turned ever and again toward Quadran Col, searching up the high slopes for sign of the enemy but seeing none; and sleep was a long time coming.

Thus it was that at dawn, as the column came awake and plans were made for the day's march, the Reachmarshal called Eddra, Arl, and Wylf to him to confer with Prince Rand. Acting upon Brytta's wary suspicions, those three riders were to set watch upon the Gap. As Brytta explained, ''I would rather set a ward against a danger that never comes than to pay in blood for an unseen thrust.'' And so, Rand described the lay of the land between the col and Dusk-Door, and plans were made to light a balefire at the top of Redguard—one of the lesser mountains overlooking the road to the gap—as a warning beacon to the Legion should an army of Spawn issue from the secret High Gate to fall upon the Dwarves' back. Hence, as the column got under way, tramping to the south toward the Dusk-Door, three silent riders of the Valanreach detached themselves from the Host and cantered to the east toward Mount Redguard.

Cotton had looked forward to another day of swift march; but early in the morning the Legion came to a place where the old road had been washed away over the years by heavy rains and melting snows, and a narrow but deep ravine blocked the route. Brytta's mounted scouts rode east and west and soon a way was found around the channel; yet the detour took several hours to negotiate because of the roughness of the trail.

The next day, the Army finally came along the ancient Rell Way to the deep channel through which the Duskrill once flowed; but not even a thin trickle could be seen down among the stained rocks, though a few standing pools showed the glimmer of water. Here the way forked, and the Host took the leftward path—the Spur—following a route that wound along the edge of the empty stream bed for several miles.

As they marched now to the east, the land around them rose, and soon they were travelling in a deep valley—the Ragad—that shut off their view of all but the highest peaks of the mountains ahead. At last, as heralded by the black-oxen horns of the Valonian point scouts, the fore of the column wound to journey's end; the Old Way Spur rounded a foothill near the head of the valley to turn eastward again where the road cut upward along the face of a high stone cliff, a cliff down which the Duskrill had once tumbled in a graceful waterfall to drop into a wide basin in the deep ravine beside the Spur. Here the Host ground to a halt, facing the bluff.

Carved in the jut of the cliff was a steep stairway leading up beyond the rim, continuing on up to a sentinel stand atop a high spire overlooking the valley where in days of old Châkka warders had stood watch o'er the vale. And beyond the rampart and dwarfing it was a great massif of the Grimspire mountain rising into the sky.

Up the stairs Durek, Rand, and Turin Stonesplitter climbed. As they mounted upward they began to see before them a stonework dam across the width of a ravine above the lip of the linn and blocking the Duskrill. "The *Raven Book* may be right, for this dam is not Châkka-made," noted Turin, looking at the bulwark. "Nor does it look Ükkish. The stones are too great; powerful energy was needed for this: it is the vile work of Troll-folk, I deem."

On up the stairway they continued, and above them, hovering over, was the great natural hemidome of the Loomwall. Up beside the dam they mounted, til they came to the top of the bluff, and behind the dam and embraced by the cavernous Loom lay a long, narrow, black lakelet, running a half mile to the north and nearly two miles to the south. The massive stone flank of the hemidome sprang up along the distant shore to arch upward and overhead; and delved somewhere along this massif was the Dusk-Door, ancient trade entrance and way into Grimspire and the caverns of Kraggen-cor.

"Across this foul black lake and south of the old Sentinel Falls shall be the Dusken Door carven in the Loom," declared Durek, peering over the still, dark mere at the great flank.

"Look!" cried Turin. "There is the old bridge! And see, below!" And he pointed at a place a short distance southward along the base of the hemidome and beyond the ruins of an old drawbridge; and there rubble, boulders, and other debris were piled high against the Loom. "That must be it. If so, the *Raven Book* is right, and the way is blocked. I must cross over to see what needs be done to uncover the portal. It does not appear to be more than two days' labor, from here; but ere I say for certain, I must give it close scrutiny, for we are some distance away."

"I judge it to be slightly more than a quarter mile across this dark tarn," said Rand, gauging the distance by eye, "but we must walk around the north end to come to the pile, and that is a trek of more than a mile but less than two.

Durek called down to one of the Valonian scouts and bade him to ride back along the train and tell the Host that they had arrived at the long-sought goal and to make camp along the north flank of the valley. He also instructed the scout to herald the Chief Captains to the Sentinel Falls to see the Loom and await a Council. Finally, he bade the scout to ask Friend Cotton to gather his belongings and move to the head of the train and then to join the Council.

As the rider sped away, Durek, Rand, and Turin tramped northward along the barren shoreline. They crossed the place where the Spur wound on upward; here the road topped the bluff and started across the swale toward the Door, only to plunge under the ebon surface of the Dark Mere, blocked by the black lake in the desolate, water-filled valley. Neither bird nor beast nor small furry thing did they see in the tangles of the brush and stunted bushes and brown grass on the slopes; and no fish or frog or watersnake or creature of any sort was seen in the dismal water under the ocherous scum that lapped the shore, nor among the brown strands of dead waterplants reaching up from the unseen depths to clutch at the dull lake surface.

But it was winter, and much life elsewhere had gone to warmer climes, or had denned to sleep through the cold, and plants had browned and lost leaves and would not green again until spring; thus the lack of living things was not remarkable. Yet this lifeless vale was somehow . . . ominous.

Hundreds of feet overhead arched the Great Loom, and the two Dwarves and the Man strode below the black granite burden. Soon they reached the far north end of the Dark Mere, where they stepped through shallow, weed-infested, stagnant water that barred the way; the torpid swash of their passage sluggishly seeped through dead reeds, and the bottom sucked at their boots with slime-laden silt. The trio crossed over and walked south on the narrow strip of rocky land trapped between the water, dark and forbidding to their right, and the Loom, stern and towering to their left. They came to the Spur again, now a causeway, sundered by time; here the shattered roadway lay along the Loom and ran south to an ancient draw-bridge, ageworn and weatherbeaten. The bridge was lowered and could not be raised, for its haul was broken.

"This bridge was once a Kraggen-cor defence," stated Durek. "It was raised in time of trouble. It is said that once the span remained up for three years, never lowered. Ah, but it is down now, and ancient. Yet look! Still it will bear the weight of an army." Durek stamped his foot on the bed, proud of his ancestors' crafting. Then he peered over the side at the nearby black water. "Lore tells us that here should begin an arc of a moat, hemming in a courtyard—a *moat*, not this . . . this dark blot."

Across the bridge they strode and south, finally to come to the steps rising up from a drowned courtyard, and to the pile ramped high against the Loom face. Up close they saw that the rubble consisted of large broken stone columns, and the work of a great edifice, cracked and split in shards; and among the rock were huge uptorn trees with broken roots and splintered trunks.

"Aie!" moaned Turin. "The destruction of such a work." And he fell into silent, anguished study.

"Some of these stones are larger than I gauged from the far shore; moving them will be a chore, indeed," reflected Turin after a time, his manner now that of a Crafter with a task. "Yet I deem we can remove all of this in one half and two days."

"*Kala!*" replied Durek, pleased, "for it is now the afternoon of the twenty-second of November; you will finish on the twenty-fifth, exactly on time to meet the Seven." He turned and looked at Rand, who was studying the ramp with a brooding look. "Something disturbs you, Prince Rand?"

"These stones, King Durek, these broken columns," replied the Man, his manner intense. "Look at how huge they are, and at how they are split and cracked—as if flung by some awful power, to shatter in the smash of their impact. The strength of the Krakenward was greater than I imagined; to hurl stones this enormous, even in hatred, takes incredible power."

At mention of the monster's name, the two Dwarves uneasily eyed the dark expanse of motionless water just a few paces away.

When word came down the line that they had arrived, like a wave a cheer washed along the column. Thus, Cotton suspected the news even before the herald came to confirm it. But when the horseman also informed the Warrow of Durek's request that Cotton move to the head of the column, the buccan felt both eager to be there and reluctant to go: he was eager because he was anxious to get the Door open and see Perry again, and reluctant because he would be leaving his friend, Bomar. But Bomar put things in perspective for Cotton by clapping him on the shoulder and rumbling, "Aye, Friend Cotton, I would that you could stay with me and be at my side when we take on the thieving Grg; but your mission is up front, guiding the Host into the ancient homeland, whereas my duty is at the hind as part of the trailing rearguard. Set forth, Pathfinder, for King Durek needs you to point the way."

Cotton leapt down from the waggon and hurriedly donned his armor and buckled on his sword and dagger and gathered up his pack. "Well, Bomar," he said, "we've come a good long way together, and I expect to chat with you after this is all over. So, as you said to me that first day, store up the memories of the time we're apart, and I'll store up mine, and when we get together again we'll have some tales to tell.''

Then Cotton stepped to the horses and patted them; they nuzzled him, and he gave them each a carrot. The buccan called to Bomar, "Take good care of Brownie and Downy," then turned and started for the head of the column.

As Cotton walked up the line, horses were pulling waggons off the Spur, and warriors bustled to prepare campsites upon the slopes. Dwarves were retrieving their iron-mail corselets from their temporary storage in the green wains and armoring themselves again. Cotton nodded to many as he strode by, and they smiled or nodded back, some hailing this doughty golden warrior who was to lead them through the caverns.

Cotton reached the head of the column where were assembled the Chief Captains. They gazed up at the linn high above them, now just a stark rock precipice over which no stream tumbled. As they looked, Durek stepped into view on the edge and motioned for them to mount up the steps.

When Cotton arrived at the top with the others, he stared uneasily at the flat, still, dark waters and thought, *Well, now, there's something about this lake that isn't right. It's like the water itself is dead.* And then he saw that neither cloud nor sky nor the towering Loom was mirrored in its depths; not even light itself seemed to reflect back from the dull surface. And as if to underscore the unpleasantness generated by this dark pool, several large bubbles rose to the surface nearby to burst with soft plopping sounds and release a foul-smelling reek of rotted matter, while the dark rings of passage writhed and intertwined and spread outward and quickly died to leave the sullen surface without motion once more.

"Over there," Durek rasped, pointing, "lies the Dusken Door. That pile of rock against the Loom holds within it the shattered edifice and columns spoken of in the *Raven Book*. We can see the facings whence they were sundered, shallow with age but still sign of where it all once stood flanking and capping the portal—a massive work, now destroyed. There, too, are uptorn trees, rent from the drowned courtyard. Yet, even with all the stone and wood, Turin estimates that but one half and two days are needed to clear the way, which will put us at the Door on the twenty-fifth, as planned.''

There was a general murmur of approval, and Cotton's heart leapt for joy; he had been worried about being late, and now his anxiety fled with the news.

"Turin has a plan," continued King Durek, "of how to array the stone workers to make short shrift of this labor."

Durek stepped down from the large stone upon which he had stood to address the Council, and Turin Stonesplitter, Masterdelver, mounted up in the Dwarf King's stead. "First, we shall divide ourselves into the same shifts as were used against the snow," he began, and then went on to describe how the pile would be reduced and what tools were needed.

And though Cotton tried to pay attention, his eye was irresistibly drawn to the darkling mere, its ominous surface lying dead and dull. And Turin's voice faded from the Warrow's consciousness as he swept the length of the lake with his sight, to see . . . nothing.

The westering Sun was low and the Great Loom bloomed orange with its setting, yet the tarn showed only dismal gloom in its bodeful murk. And as the Council came to an end, the planning over, and the Captains made their way down the stairs in the dusk, Cotton took a last look at the lake as he brought up the rear; he heard a soft plopping and saw out in the center large rings rippling shoreward, and he wondered if they, too, were caused by bubbles.

Work began early the next morning as hundreds of delvers lined along the base of the Loom on either side of the ramped rubble while many more scrambled up the face of the heap. With picks and mattocks and sledges and spikes and levers and ropes, they began loosening and breaking up the pile, freeing stone and tumbling it down for the others to carry or drag away. As Rand had noted the day before, much of the rock was already split and shattered, and great shards were toppled to slither down to those waiting below. Yet there were large fragments requiring many Dwarves hauling upon strong ropes to nudge them, grinding, away from the ramp. Slowly the workers uncovered one of the great trees, and they brought into play axes and saws to hew the branches and sever the trunk, and Dwarves dragged and rolled the hacked and sawn timber aside.

Amid all this activity, directing the work forces, white-bearded Turin Stonesplitter climbed and pointed and gesticulated—in command. The laboring Dwarves set to with great energy: shoving, rolling, pulling, hauling, pushing, and dragging the great stones and timbers away, while others hammered and pried and tied and chopped and sawed, tumbling the wood and rock down. Shifts changed, but the toil ceased not.

Across the lakelet, Cotton sat atop the dam and watched the work proceed; he was far enough away so that he marveled at how much like an anthill the activity seemed. All day he looked on, only taking time away for a quick lunch, watching the pile slowly diminish, measuring its fall by its height on the Loom.

It was nearly sundown when Rand, Durek, and Brytta mounted up the carven steps. "Ho, Cotton!" hailed Rand, "we are going around to see the progress made on this day. Care to join us?"

Would he? Yes indeed! Cotton eagerly jumped to his feet. He had been itching to go take a look, yet had not wanted to be in the way; but now it was an altogether different prospect, for he had an excuse: he was going with the King to inspect the work.

As they trudged through the sere grass and brown weeds, and around the clots of thorny, woodlike, dried brambles tangling through the stunted, twisted, withered trees along the scum-laden shore of the dull pool, making their way toward the north end of the Dark Mere, Durek spoke: "This vale seems utterly dead, unlike the tales of old when it was said that lush grass and slender green trees and fruit-laden bushes carpeted the land and stood upon the slopes; and the dell was a verdant emerald set among the towering Mountains. But now it is Death-struck, as if this dark lake were a great strangling cesspool of choking black poison, and it seems as if the very earth of this once beautiful Ragad Vale has been slain by this evil."

Cotton looked around and shuddered at Durek's imagery; and Brytta added, "Aye, this vale indeed seems cursed, for Nightwind and the other steeds will not touch this foul pasturage. Yet there is not enough grain nor clear water to long support the herd, for there are more than a thousand of your horses, and forty-four of ours. We must move the steeds, and so I have sent a scout looking; shortly we will drive them south to the great winter grasslands of the western vales—that is, as soon as you succeed in uncovering the Door and enter the caverns.''

Durek nodded and sighed. ''Just so, Brytta, though I had hoped we would not have to take this step as you foresaw we might; for I have come to depend heavily upon the eyes of the Vanadurin, and the loss will be greatly felt—though we have little or no choice.''

''Even so,'' Brytta growled, ''it rowels me to know that we will not be with you at the Wrg-slaughter, avenging the victims of North Reach and elsewhere. But we Sons of Harl are better suited to deal with the horses, and to watch the Quadran Col should Spawn come that way—though the high snows blocking the gap would seem to bar that event.

''Yet, the Rutcha and Drōkha may have found the High Gate you spoke of, and may now have a way to march from that direction. But even though it is more likely that the Spawn will come at you through the dark passages of the Black Maze, I swear that they shall not strike at your back by coming down from the Quadran Pass and through this valley, for we shall keep sentinels posted at the gap, and they shall light a signal fire should the Wrg come; and we will abandon the herd and harass the Spawn to draw them aside and keep them from falling upon you from behind.

''And when you enter the caverns and the battle begins, should any flee your axes and escape through this west Door, ere they can debouch Ragad Vale, another of my guards posted here will strike a signal fire and summon the Harlingar from herd duty, and the craven Spawn will fall prey to our lances.''

Here, Brytta flourished his spear, thrusting it forward as if he were lancing from horseback. ''Perhaps we shall see some fighting yet—though it seems likely that it will not come to pass, and some of us will merely watch in vain for Rutcha and Drōkha, while the rest of us keep the drove.

''Nay, galling or not, we must tend the herd and guard the vale, for it is better we do these necessary things we know than to flounder about in a dark crack in the earth, more a hindrance than an aid, for the Black Hole is no warring place for a plainsman bred.''

"Hah!" cried Durek, clapping the Man of Valon upon the shoulder. "Plainsman bred you are and plainsmen bred we need: to be our eyes, and to guard our flanks, and to speed tidings of our fortunes along the margins of Valon where lies the mineholt of my kindred in the Red Hills, and thence to your King Eanor in Vanar; and to ride beyond Valon to Pellar and bear the news to High King Darion at Caer Pendwyr. And aye, we need you to ward horses, as Vanadurin have done throughout the centuries. And further, we need you to stand fast at our backs and guard against unseen assault. Yet think not that these are but small tasks, Brytta of the Valanreach, for without the Riders of Valon, much would go amiss.''

And Durek clasped the forearm of the Reachmarshal, and the blond warrior smiled down upon the Dwarf King; and Prince Rand and Cotton the Waerling witnessed the final healing of the ancient rift between the Men of Valon and the Line of Durek, and they were glad.

The four strode up to the north end of the black pool and crossed over the torpid water, there to turn south along the Loom. Cotton did not like wading through the skirt of the stagnated mere, his boots sliding and sucking through the muck; and the clinging slime and yellowed scum made his feet feel befouled even though they were shod, as if something evil and unclean had defiled him. He tried to shake off this impression but did not succeed, and still his jewel-like viridian eyes strayed over the menace of the dull black waters. He felt certain that the Krakenward was gone, for surely by now it would have attacked the workers; yet somehow the dark mere seemed to bode an ominous doom—a threat he felt growing with the coming of darkness.

The four of them crossed the bridge and came to the northern arm of the work force, and Durek nodded and smiled at the workers as he passed, saying words to a few. And then they came to the pile, and Turin jumped down to speak to his King. To Cotton and Brytta the remaining heap looked enormous at hand, but to Rand and Durek, who had seen it before, it was greatly diminished.

"We are doing better than I gauged," said Turin. "We may finish earlier than expected."

Durek smiled and said something in return, but Cotton did not hear it.

A great feeling of dread overwhelmed the buccan and he turned to look at the lake, the hair on the nape of his neck standing erect. He could see nothing, yet fear coursed through him and his heart pounded. The Sun was low and sinking, and work had been called to a halt. The Dwarves were retrieving their mail from the base of the Loom and donning it, slipping their broad-bladed axes back into their carrying thongs. Again voices around Cotton seemed to become muffled, and he felt an impending doom approaching.

The Sun sank lower, and now its rays crept up and away from the black mere until they struck only the Great Arch of the Loom. And at the moment that the last ray left the lake and its leaden surface fell into shadow, Cotton's searching eyes saw a huge ominous wave flowing out of the dim recesses of the southernmost end—as if something large and fast were speeding just below the surface . . . speeding toward the Door.

"Look!" Cotton shouted and pointed. "The Warder comes!"

Durek spun and saw the fast-flowing wake, a hurtling wedge of water, its point aimed at the Dwarves. *"Châkka shok!"* he barked, and all the Dwarves grimly drew their axes, and Cotton and Rand unsheathed their swords, while Brytta gripped his spear.

On came the great wave, a massive flowing heave in the ebon waters, a foaming black wake churning behind, hard-driven by some hidden leviathan menace. Onward rushed the dark billow, toward the grim-faced Warrow and Men and Dwarves, sword and axes at the ready. And Cotton trembled to see how swiftly it came. Onward the crest of the huge wedge sped, straight toward the Door, nearer and nearer, the wave at last surging and boiling over the strand.

And then a hideous creature was upon them:

Great ropy tentacles writhed out of the water to grasp at the intruders on the shore. Dwarves coiled back and cries of dismay rent the air. Brytta set his black-oxen horn to his lips, but ere he could sound it a huge tendril slapped him aside, and he was whelmed against the Great Loom and fell senseless to the ground at its base.

Then a Dwarf was snared, and another, and another, and drawn struggling in vain back across the strand and pulled beneath the water. Other Dwarves hewed at the slimy arms, but the axes did not cut through the thick, unyielding hide. And Durek was grasped about the waist, a great tendril wrapped about him several times, and he was thrown to his knees and his axe flew forward, lost to his grip; he was slowly dragged toward the foul black water, as if a malevolent evil intelligence was toying with a helpless small thing—torturing it, slowly drawing it toward a horrid death.

Rand sprang forward and drove his black-handled sword down onto the arm, but the blade merely bounced from the vile hide; again and again he struck, but to no avail, and Durek was drawn onward.

Rand flung his own useless sword aside and caught up Durek's silveron-edged axe; but ere the Man could use it, Cotton brought his weapon of the Men of the Lost Land to bear—this Atalar blade had been forged to battle against powers of evil, and its golden runes flashed bright in the dying sunlight. Cotton dropped to one knee and slashed the blade downward in a great overhead two-handed stroke which landed athwart the snaky arm and clove a deep gash in it. Instantly Rand hewed the glittering axe into the opening made by Cotton's weapon; the end of the tentacle was shorn off, to drop from Durek's waist and flop and writhe and coil and lash out with a life of its own. The main tentacle gushed forth black blood and was whipped back into the water as Durek stumbled hindward to the Loomwall.

And the creature went mad, for only once before had it ever felt pain, and that was when it had been dealt a wound *by the very same Atalar Blade*, a blade wielded long ago by yet another who sought to enter the Door; but that pain then was as nothing compared to now, for golden-runed sword and silveron-edged axe together had maimed it dearly.

The foul water roiled with the creature's anger, and a great stench filled the air as twenty or more tentacles boiled forth to lash out and grab Dwarves and fling them against the Loom, and to wrench others into the black lake, swiftly now in rage and no longer slowly in calculated cruelty. The creature grasped a huge boulder and pounded it like a great stone maul, smashing with dreadful effect into the helpless Dwarves. It snatched up several of the Châkka and rolled them in tentacles to squeeze them lifeless; the dead were flung down and others caught up; thus did Turin Stonesplitter die.

Durek looked on with horrified eyes at the havoc being wrought as tens and twenties of his kindred were destroyed. "Flee!" he cried. "Back!" And Rand, calling upon a reserve of hidden strength unexpected in one of his slim build, hoisted unconscious Brytta over his shoulder and carried the stunned warrior as they all scrambled and fled northward, trapped within the creature's reach on the narrow strand between the Loom and the water.

Cotton ran in terror, stumbling and scuttling over the rocks and slabs as the creature's great tentacles lashed and flailed all around him, grasping and smashing and slaying. A huge tendril whipped into the rocks just ahead of him, but the Warrow leapt over it and ran on as it snatched empty air inches behind him. A Dwarf was grabbed up from beside him and hurled into the Loom. A ropy arm cracked the great rock hammer to smash into the ground to miss Cotton again. Another tentacle shot out to bar the way, but the buccan slashed it with his sword of Atala, and again the bitter blade gashed the creature; the cut arm lashed back and forth, but Cotton fell flat and it swept overhead.

The frightened Warrow scrambled up and fled onward, across the bridge and along the sundered causeway. And all around him, before and after, others ran and fell and scuttled and fled and died as the Hèlarms pursued, still under the black surface, with only its huge tentacles worming and writhing and grasping and smashing fleeing victims, until the quarry came to the north end where the water was too shallow for the creature to follow. Even then its great bulk flanked the shore as the survivors made for the dam, but they stayed well up out of the Monster's reach as, weeping and defeated, they came stumbling down the hill to the Host.

* * *

An hour passed and the dusk deepened, and still Durek sat on a rock, unmoving, with his hood cast over his head. The gathered Legion waited in silence, even those who wept. Brytta had regained his senses, and he, too, sat grim and silent as Hogon bandaged the Reachmarshal's right hand, broken by the Krakenward's slap. Rand stood with his own hands tightly clasped behind his back, his face stern, staring at the fading violet sky to the west as dusk yielded to night and the vale gradually fell into darkness. Cotton sat nearby on the slopes in the twilight as slowly his horror and grief gave way to a dull red hate. And then from across the lake there sounded a great clatter of rock, and a sentry came down from the top of the hill and said to Durek, "Sire, the Madûk heaps more stone upon the Door."

Durek sat a moment without moving; then he cast back his hood, and there was a fell look upon his face. "This cannot be borne," his voice grated. "We shall slay that spawn of evil. Get Gaynor to me, and Berez, and Bomar. Bring Tror and his Hammerers and Felor with his Drillers. Before this night is over, it shall be done."

As Cotton watched, the message went forth, and Dwarves arrived, bearing with them tools from the black waggons. Lanterns were unhooded and carried up the stairs to the face of the dam. Gaynor, Berez, and Bomar were all accounted Masterdelvers and had been second only to dead Turin. With King Durek they crawled over the stone face of the dam, studying the fissures in the rock, judging its faults. Then Tror with twelve other Dwarves carrying sledge hammers, and Felor with as many carrying tongs and pointed iron rods and wedges, climbed up to the sites indicated by the Delvers; and they set the rods and irons in place and began hammering them and wedging them into the cracks and crevices. The Host and waggons and animals were gathered up out of the valley and moved to high ground. And by the blue-green light of the Dwarf-lanterns the pounding and delving went on.

They were going to break the dam.

They had hammered but a short time when suddenly a great tentacle looped over the top of the barrier and wrapped about the neck of a Driller, snapping it and then flinging the Dwarf aside. With cries of terror, the others fled downward as more arms writhed and slithered over, reaching and grasping, clutching two more ere the others escaped.

A moan of dismay rose up from the watching Legion as the creature slew their kin and then wrenched loose the drills to throw them aside. The arms lashed and whipped menacingly, then sinuously withdrew as the creature lurked on the far side of the dam. Many Dwarves tore at their beards in rage, but Durek's look became more resolute than ever, and he called the Chief Captains to him. "Fire," he ordered in a grim voice. "Build me a fire on the dam above the drilling site. Make it as fierce, as hot as the heart of a crucible, or an iron forge. Spread it along the top above the work point farther than the Madûk can reach."

Wood was gathered and brands lit; oil was spread on the tinder. It was quietly carried up to the stonework and placed on top and fired. More timber was added, and the flames shot high. When the heat became nearly unbearable the drilling work resumed under the blazing barrier. Drillers and Hammerers were spelled often, for it was like working in a furnace; sweat poured off even those watching from the vale sides, and cloaks and jerkins were removed.

When the pounding began again, the creature once more reached a tentacle out of the water, but the flames repelled it; and it moved to a place where the fire was not and groped over the dam but could not reach the workers. There was a great beating and lashing of the water as the frustrated Krakenward whipped the surface in its fury. Then it raced to the other end of the flames, but there, too, it was thwarted; and the water boiled and foamed in the Monster's rage; a malodorous reek rose up, and an ominous hissing could be heard, as if from some reptilian source. But the work went on.

The nearly full Moon slowly came over the mountains and added its silver radiance to the firelight and the lanternglow. And still the work continued.

Clang! Clang! Chink! Clank! The great sledges drove home the drills and wedges under the roar of the fire. Mighty thews swung the mallets with Dwarf-driven force, and each Driller held the rods with the tongs until they were wedged deeply; then they placed longer ones in the crevices when the shorter ones had been driven home. And the stone split slowly along the weakened fissures as many teams cracked the rock in two separate vertical lines some twenty feet apart.

Chank! Clank! Thunk! Chang! The crews nearest the top of the wall—nearest the fire—had to be relieved most often, but those at the bottom required spelling, too. And on the vale sides, Dwarves gathered wood and placed it at the disposal of the fire teams, who kept the blaze going. The entire Host now worked to slay the creature: many who had never drilled took shifts and handled the tongs and irons; others swung the sledges; still others placed wedges to be driven in; wood gatherers and fire teams rotated. Cotton, Rand, Brytta and his Men from Valon, and all the Dwarves were struggling to destroy a creature that alone could slay the entire Army.

And slowly the fissures were widened and deepened. Gaynor went up into the heat and examined the splits, and then he ordered everyone out except four teams—two on each breech—for the fissures now seeped water and would soon give way.

Bang! Clank! Dlang! Chunk! The pounding resumed. But then a great wave smashed into the dam, quenching part of the fire. The creature had found a weapon! Water! Another great dark surge slammed into the dam, and more of the flames were drowned.

Bang! Chank! Fire teams ran with dry wood to start new blazes in the gaps, but sinuous tentacles reached up to smash the Dwarves aside.

Chank! Clang! Blang! Now began a desperate race between stone delvers and a cunning evil monster. Once more the creature used its great bulk and raced toward the dam, pushing the water in a high crest ahead of it. With a great *whoosh*, a last large wave washed over the top and extinguished the remainder of the fire directly above the workers.

Bang! Clank! Chunk! By the luminous phosphorescence of the Dwarf-lanterns and the pale radiance of the bright Moon overhead, the Host saw slimy wet tendrils slowly snake over the top, to find the flames gone. Then the tentacles plunged toward the now-fleeing Dwarves, catching up one: Gaynor. It held the Dwarf high and reached up a second hideous arm to grasp him also, and then it exerted its terrible strength and tore him in two and flung the remains down.

Many Dwarves wept and gnashed their teeth and tore at their hair in helpless rage, for the Monster had won. And they watched as the great slimy tendrils groped for more of these small creatures to fling to their deaths, and to smash with rocks, and to squeeze to pulp, and to drown struggling, and to rend in twain. It reached down, but found only more rods to rip out and fling away. It had triumphed! It raised up its hideous tentacles, seeming to celebrate its victory. Cotton wept, while King Durek looked on grimly. Berez raged, and Brytta clenched even his broken fist, while Rand closed his eyes in silent grief. Bomar gazed at the failed delving in . . . but wait! He stared hard and saw . . . ''King Durek!'' he shouted. ''Look! Look at the fissures!''

Slowly the great long cracks were widening, and water was beginning to gush forth, faster and faster. Almost imperceptibly the ponderous slab began to tilt outward; a splitting and cracking rent the air, and a deep heavy grinding of massive stone upon stone sounded. Then, with a thunderous crash that shook the vale, the giant slab toppled over to smash into the stone of the Sentinel Falls precipice; and then it fell onward, tumbling down the linn to shatter at the bottom. Right behind came a great roar of water, freed at last from its centuries-old trap to blast outward in a great torrent and leap to freedom over the cliff, to plunge toward the Ragad Valley in a massive wall of water that carried giant boulders bouncing and smashing along the ravine and rent great trees from the earth to lash and tumble and splinter in the deluge.

When the slab toppled and the water thundered out, the Krakenward was caught directly in front of the gap. Impelled by a force it had never felt before, the evil creature was hurled toward the gaping space, borne outward by the massive surge. Yet as the Monster passed into the roaring slot, it flung out all of its malignant tentacles to grasp the walls of the dam and throw all of its evil power into a mighty pull to propel it back into the depths. But the

Madûk reckoned not with the whelming dint of the escaping flood, for the creature's bulk was inexorably drawn
through the gap. With a malevolent surge of power it
slowly drew back inward, yet all the malefic energy coiled
within the great ropy arms could draw it but partway back
through the slot. And for the first time within its evil
memory, the Madûk felt something more powerful than
itself.

Fear drove into its malignant core, and it frantically
redoubled its effort. But then the dam, unable to withstand
the force of the rush of the water, broke again—first on
one side of the gap and then on the other. And the
Krakenward was hurled down the falls still clutching the
great slabs that had been the flanks of the slot. The Monster smashed into the stone basin below; and the creature's
pain was great as it was flung into the walls and shoulders
of the ravine and boulders ground over it.

The Host had watched the mighty struggle by the light
of the waxing Moon, and when the Madûk was carried
over the brink to smash into the darkness below, a great
shout of victory rose up.

The dark waters of the black mere continued to pour
out. Great masses of foetid rot from the lake bottom were
borne forth by the roaring flood, and a putrid fetor swept
over the vale. The Army reeled back from this foul stink,
and many gagged and retched in the charnel rank. More of
the dam crumbled. Giant slabs of stone fell to the falls
precipice, and the torrent widened and blasted through the
huge rocks to rush over the lip and cascade down.

Hours passed. The Moon set. The water level in the lake
sank as it emptied, and the strength of the flood ebbed.
What had been a torrent became a rush and then a broad
outflow; slowly it continued to wane until it reduced to a
wide stream runneling between the huge chunks of
fragmented dam up on the precipice to fall in several
separate streams to the basin below.

It was now dawn, for the breaking of the dam and the
Krakenward's struggle and the emptying of the lake had
taken all night. The gloom in the vale of the Sentinel Falls
was slowly driven back as the day came; but the Sun rose
on the east side of the mountains and the vale was on the

west side, and thus it stood in the shadow of the range. Yet the dark retreated and the stars winked out as day broke on the land. As the sky lightened, still the Host watched, looking toward the dark ravine down which the water and rocks and creature and the tons of sludge and filth and rot had all disappeared.

Cotton sat leaning back against a rock, his eyes closed, drained of energy. Exhausted, he was drifting off to sleep when he heard a shouting of voices and a clamor of disbelief and fear. The Warrow snapped open his eyes to see what the commotion was about just as a warrior stepped to Durek's side and pointed to the face of the Sentinel Falls precipice. "Sire, the Madûk, it lives," he announced grimly.

Cotton looked and saw in the early morning light first one tentacle and then another groping upward through the falling water along the cliff face, straining to reach the top of the precipice but falling short.

Durek stood and stared, his eyes filled with rage. His teeth ground together and his hands clenched into fists. His face turned black as anger shook his frame, and his voice rose in a hoarse cry—"To me! To me! Châkka to me!" —and he sprang down the hill. Cotton and Rand, Brytta and Bomar, Berez, Tror, Felor, all leapt after him with Drillers and Hammerers and Delvers close behind.

Plunging down the slope, they charged onto the top of the linn, splashing through the flow to come to the head of the falls and look over the lip through the streams of cascading water and down into the basin below. There in the blackness Cotton could dimly see a huge mass in a bed of runny sludge and black filth and foetid rot; it flopped and writhed with sucking noises as it heaved and hitched its horrid bulk through the muck and churn at the base of the precipice. Though he could not see it clearly in the darkness, Cotton could discern that the Monster was bloated and blotched, slimy and foul, repulsive and horrifying. Long was its swollen body, and from one end a roiling nest of suckered tendrils writhed. Some of these tentacles had been crushed by rock, and one of the creature's eyes had been torn open; but the other baleful red eye glared malignantly up, and a wave of evil incarnate beat at them. The Madûk could see the people limned against the pale morning sky, and a dozen huge tentacles boiled up out of the blackness and lashed at the wall. A hissing was heard and a great stench rose up. But the Monster could not reach them, and the light of the day bore hurtfully through its one good eye and blazed into its brain. In an earlier age, before the Ban, ere it had been borne here, its own malevolence had driven it even unto the sunlight to wreak havoc upon ships plying the lanes near the Great Maelstrom. But now the coming of the Sun meant that it must hide away, and it was frantic to be back in its dark den at the bottom of the black water; and it clutched and grasped futilely at the linn-wall.

Durek glowered down in hatred at the malignant creature, then he turned and gritted, ''We shall slay it with stone.''

He called Dwarves to him, and with Cotton and Rand and broken-hand Brytta helping, they struggled and strained, pushing and pulling, as from the shattered dam they levered a massive granite block that ground and grated and slowly slid to the lip of the precipice. Gradually it edged out above the Monster, to tip and balance on the rim. Then with a final heave it was prized up to ponderously slide with a rush over the edge to fall silently, slowly turning, to come down upon the Monster and land with a great squashing *splat!*—smashing into and through the bulk. Many of the huge tentacles fell lifeless, and others plucked feebly at the massive stone.

A triumphant shout burst forth from the Host, and Durek looked down and grunted in grim satisfaction. Then he stepped back and raised up a clenched fist and hoarsely called out in a loud voice, ''Let all the Companies each in turn cast a block down upon this spawn of evil so that every Châk in the Legion can share in this revenge.'' And as one body the Dwarf Army wrathfully surged forward, silent and grim, each warrior chafing to extract personal retribution for his fallen brethren.

And Brytta of Valon stood fast and raised his great black-oxen horn to his lips and winded it, summoning the company of the Vanadurin to him to avenge their slain allies, as Durek, Cotton, Rand, and Bomar turned and walked back up the hill in the morning light of a new day.

''Bomar,'' rasped Durek, ''we must go see how much is

to be done—how much rubble is to be removed from over the Door—for the Madûk heaped more on. I fear we may now have more work to do than there is time to do it. Tomorrow is the day set for the rendezvous, and the Seven are now within the caverns and may already be at work on the hinges. We cannot fail them; we *must* succeed.''

And as the four walked around the foetid rotting black crater where once stood the lake, the Host of Dwarves of Kraggen-cor dragged great slabs of rock from the broken dam to the precipice and cast them down to crush the Monster. They had fought the Madûk with axe and sword and Atalar blade, and hammer and tong and wedge and drill, and fire and water, and at last they slew it with stone. They had finally won, but barely.

Here ends the first part of the tale of **The Silver Call.**
The second part is called The Brega Path. *It concludes the stories of Perry and Cotton and their allies in the quest of the Dwarves to wrest Kraggon-cor from the clutches of the evil Spawn.''*

"Brega, Bekki's son, strode into legend along a steadfast course of honor. May the span of our strides match his—for that is the true Brega path."

Seventh Durek
November 3, 5E231

ABOUT THE AUTHOR

DENNIS L. MCKIERNAN was born April 4, 1932, in Moberly, Missouri, where he lived until age eighteen when he joined the U.S. Air Force, serving four years spanning the Korean War. He received a B.S. in Electrical Engineering from the University of Missouri in 1958, and, similarly, an M.S. from Duke University in 1964. Employed by a leading research and development laboratory, he resides with his family in Westerville, Ohio. His debut novel was the critically acclaimed trilogy of **The Iron Tower.** His second novel, **The Silver Call** duology, continues the Mithgarian saga.